LITTLE MUSHROOM

SHISI

TRANSLATED BY
XIAO

PEACH FLOWER HOUSE

ISBN 978-1-7365009-8-9 (print)
ISBN 978-1-7365009-9-6 (ebook)

Translation by Xiao
Editing by Molly Rabbitt
Proofing by D. Gareau and Lori Parks
Cover Illustration by Carm
Cover Design by D. Gareau

This is a work of fiction. Names, characters, business, events and incidents are
the products of the author's imagination. Any resemblance to actual persons,
living or dead, or actual events is entirely coincidental.

Published originally under the title of <<小蘑菇>>
English edition rights under license granted by Beijing Jinjiang Original
Network Technology Co. Ltd through Wuhan Loretta Media Agency Co., Ltd.

Printed in China

Published by Peach Flower House LLC 2022
PO Box 1156
Monterey Park, CA 91754
Visit www.peachflowerhouse.com

Learn how to pronounce the character names here!

https://www.peachflowerhouse.com/
pronunciation-guide/little-mushroom

BOOK ONE: JUDGMENT DAY

1

"YOU'RE JUST A TINY LITTLE MUSHROOM"

THE CAVE WAS dark and damp, with only weak fluorescence from the plants providing illumination.

Tangled vines clung to the cliff face. Deep green, purple, and inky black, they resembled snakes tied into large knots.

A black insect with six stiff wings and three proboscises barged into the cave, its flight path erratic.

In the next second, a massive dark purple bulge suddenly appeared amidst the tangled vines and swiftly split open, mouth-like, before snapping shut around the flying insect.

The vines gradually began to wriggle, and the part that had bulged out retreated bit by bit until it returned to its original state.

Within the cave was a sound like that of flapping wings. A drop of mucus, translucent strands trailing in its wake, fell from the ceiling and plopped onto the sticky moss below. The moss began to subtly squirm, and the drop of sparkling mucus vanished into the ground as it was rapidly absorbed.

In a corner lit up by the fluorescence of green fungi, a tide of white poured forth from the crevices in the rocks and soil, blanketing a large area. It was a snow-white mycelium. It grew, spread out, and extended hundreds of millions of tendrils, then crept toward the center of the cave, gathered together, merged, and elongated to form a figure. A single foot stepped upon the thick and delicately soft moss and sank down into it, leaving only a snow-white ankle visible.

An Zhe looked at his ankle. Though his human body was sustained by a skeleton, muscles, blood vessels, and had mobile joints, it was not flexible due to the human skeleton's limitations.

Layers of keratin formed round and translucent fingernails; these were vestigial remnants originating from the sharp claws of beasts.

He lifted a leg and took a step forward. The damp, springy moss pressed down by his foot gathered together again after he left, looking like earthworms standing erect.

This time, he stepped on something different—a skeletal human arm.

In the darkness, An Zhe looked at the skeleton.

Fungi and vines had already taken root in the depths of its bones. Deep green vines wound around the hip and leg bones, while colorful small mushrooms resembling flowers in bloom grew upon the ribs.

Fluorescent mushrooms emerged from its empty eye sockets and sparse teeth. The green glow they gave off was like fine shifting sand, very blurry in the misty cave.

An Zhe looked at it for a long time. At last, he bent down and picked up a backpack made of animal skin that had been lying next to the skeleton. The contents of the backpack were unaffected by moisture. There were a few articles of clothing, human food and water, and a blue electronic chip half the size of a human palm that was engraved with a string of numbers: 3261170514.

Three days ago, this skeleton was still a live human.

"3261170514," the young human rasped brokenly as the weak green fluorescence illuminated the contours of his face.

"My ID number. This is my ID card, and only by having it can I go back to the human base."

An Zhe asked, "Can I help you go back there?"

The human smiled, and the fingers of his right hand dropped to rest at his side. The chip tumbled from his hand and disappeared in the uneven moss. As he leaned back against the crags, he lifted his head and pressed his left hand to his chest, where a huge wound had opened up. Pale splinters of bone pierced through his chest, exiting from his back, and the surrounding skin had already festered. Part of it was pale gray, with cottony flesh covering the surface of the bone splinters, while the rest exhibited a blackish-green hue and released a continuous drip of dark liquid in time with the rhythm of his breathing.

After taking a few breaths, he said softly, "I can't go back anymore, little mushroom."

His shirt was dyed through, his skin looked pallid, his lips were chapped, and his body trembled at irregular intervals.

An Zhe looked at him, unsure what to say. In the end, he only murmured this young human's name. "An Ze?"

"You've just about learned the human language now." The human looked down at his own body.

Apart from pus and blood, he was also covered with snow-white hyphae, which were part of An Zhe's body. The hyphae meandered along, adhering securely to the wounds on An Ze's limbs and torso. The mushroom's original intent was to stanch the dying human's bleeding, but the hyphae also instinctively absorbed and digested the fresh blood that flowed out at the same time.

"You learned so many things just by eating my genes, huh? The pollution index here is indeed very high," the human said.

Fragmented scraps of knowledge unfolded within An Zhe's mind. After a five-second-long conversion, he understood that the pollution index referred to the speed at which genes transformed. Now, human genes were flowing into his body along with An Ze's blood.

"Perhaps... once I'm dead and you've completely eaten my body... you'll obtain a lot more things." An Ze looked at the cave ceiling, a smile tugging at the corner of his lips. "Then it seems that I will have done something meaningful as well, although I don't know if it will be good or bad for you."

Without saying anything, An Zhe moved his entire body toward An Ze. He hugged An Ze's shoulders with his newly grown human arm, and many hyphae flowed forth and piled up next to An Ze to support his sagging body.

The only sounds in the quiet cavern came from the dying human's gasping breaths.

After a long time passed, An Ze finally spoke up again. "I'm someone whose life had no meaning."

"... I don't have any outstanding qualities whatsoever, so it's very normal that they abandoned me. In truth, I'm very happy to not go back to the human base. Just like the wilderness, they're both... places where only people with value can live on. I've wanted to die for a long time already. I just didn't think I'd encounter a gentle creature like you before I died, little mushroom."

An Zhe didn't really understand the meaning of those words such as "value" or "die." He only caught that phrase once more: human base.

As he leaned against An Ze's shoulder, he said, "I wish to go to the human base."

"Why?" An Ze asked.

An Zhe lifted his left arm slightly and made a gesture with his fingers, seeming as though he wanted to grab a bit of the air, but he grabbed nothing at all.

It was just like his body.

His body was empty.

A massive void had formed in the innermost depths of his

body, impossible to fill and impossible to heal, and in its wake was an infinite hollowness and panic that clung to him day in and day out.

Sorting out the words of the human language, he slowly said, "I lost... my spore."

"Spore?"

"My... seed." He didn't know how to explain.

Every mushroom would have spores in its lifetime. Some would have countless spores while others would have just one. A spore was a mushroom's seed. It would grow out of the lamella, be dispersed by the wind to any random place within the jungle, take root wherever it landed, and turn into a new mushroom. Then this mushroom would also grow up little by little and have its own spores. Raising its spores to maturity was a mushroom's sole lifelong mission, but he had lost his only spore when it was far from maturing.

An Ze slowly turned his head, and An Zhe could hear his bones click like an old piece of human machinery when he did so.

"Don't go there." The human's raspy words sped up. "You'll die."

An Zhe recited that word once again. "... Die?"

"Only humans can enter the human base. You won't be able to escape the Judges' eyes." An Ze coughed a few times, then drew a labored breath. "Don't go... little mushroom."

Confused, An Zhe said, "I..."

The human abruptly grabbed An Zhe's hyphae with great force, and his harsh breathing became more hurried.

"Listen to me." After violently trembling and gasping for breath, An Ze slowly closed his eyes. In a very soft voice, he said, "You don't have any attack power or means of defending yourself. You're just... a tiny little mushroom."

· · ·

Sometimes, An Zhe deeply regretted telling An Ze about wanting to go to the human base.

If he hadn't told An Ze, An Ze wouldn't have spent his final moments on deterring him. Perhaps he could have listened to An Ze tell a story, or perhaps he could have taken An Ze away from this dark cave for one last look at the fluctuating aurora in the sky. But An Ze's eyes would never open again.

The brief memory disappeared into the air, just like how An Ze's life suddenly disappeared from this world. In front of An Zhe, there remained only a snow-white skeleton.

But he had to go against An Ze's wishes regardless.

He slowly uncurled the fingers of one hand.

A brassy cylindrical bullet shell made of metal quietly lay upon the delicate skin and pale lines of his palm. It was very heavy, and there were some incomprehensible but definitely unusual grooves on its surface. He had found it at the place where he lost his spore, and ever since then, he hadn't let go of it.

Supposing there was still a one-in-ten-thousand chance that he could get his spore back, then this one-in-ten-thousand chance lay with the bullet shell, a human creation.

With a soft sigh, he put the bullet shell in the animal skin backpack An Ze left behind, then bent down and picked up the clothes that An Ze had once worn: a light gray long-sleeved shirt stained with blood, hardened black overalls, and black leather boots.

After doing all of those things, he walked toward the cave exit. As he walked, the slightly baggy clothes rubbed against his skin, and tiny electric currents traveled from the nerve endings hidden beneath the skin to his core. An Zhe, who had taken human form for the first time, was unused to it, and he frowned as he rolled up the loose shirt's sleeves.

The vines that had accumulated along the long and winding cave's walls jostled each other, but when An Zhe passed through, they receded like the tide and settled on the cave ceiling.

Three turns later, a moisture-laden wind blew in. The mushroom pushed aside the withered vines dangling in front of the cave mouth, and vast swaths of mushrooms, his kindred, stretched out as far as the eye could see. They seemed to extend up to the sky, and everything was quiet, with not a sound to be heard. Dim daylight shone in from between the cover of the mushroom caps, and the gray sky twinkled, a lustrous volatile green. An Zhe smelled rainwater, fog, snake slough, and decaying plants.

It was still evening. He sat down beneath the cap of the light gray mushroom nearest to the cave entrance and took out a yellowed map from his backpack. The map was covered with blocks of color that varied in shade, which indicated the degree of danger in the different areas. An Ze had once pointed out to An Zhe the approximate location of the cave they were in. It was the darkest part of the entire map, which meant that it was a region that boasted six-star danger and pollution levels, and it was named "Abyss." On the map, the area containing the Abyss had also been marked with many strange symbols, so An Zhe checked them one by one against the legend in the lower right corner. The marks meant that within the Abyss were scattered dense growths of mushrooms, cannibal vines, cannibal shrubs, simple mammalian monsters, hybrid mammalian monsters, common reptilian monsters, poisonous reptilian monsters, winged monsters, amphibious monsters, hybrid polymorphic monsters, humanoid monsters... and so on. At the same time, within the Abyss, there were also geographic features such as canyons, hills, mountains, abandoned human cities, and the remnants of roads.

The top of the map corresponded to north, and his gaze traveled all the way up. On the upper right of this colorful map, there was a pure white area marked with a bright red star, and the area's name was written to the right of the star: Northern Base.

The green lights in the sky intensified, and the color behind it darkened little by little into pitch blackness. At midnight, An Zhe managed with difficulty to recognize the stars in the sky. He knew the brightest one was called Polaris and could be used to navigate by.

So he pointed the upward-facing arrow on the map's upper left corner toward Polaris and walked out over decaying wood, fallen leaves, hyphae, and soil, one step at a time.

Although it was nighttime, it wasn't dark. In the sky, those shifting green lights—humans called them the aurora—illuminated everything up ahead, and all An Zhe could see was mushrooms.

Yellow ones, red ones, brown ones, all with massive caps. Small ones that clumped thickly together on the mountain rocks. Round puffballs that lay scattered on the ground and would, after maturing, release fog-like clouds of spores.

Upon landing, these spores would split open upon the damp fallen leaves and soil and grow into spherical puffballs just like their mother.

There were also mushrooms with no caps, consisting of only white or yellow stems that were either grouped together or radially separated. These swayed in the wind like seaweed.

But this was not a world of only mushrooms. Vines, mosses, shrubs, cannibal flowers, and twisted trees quietly concealed themselves in the night. In the jungle of plants, dark shadows and strange shapes—either animals or fusions of humans and animals—ran, howled, and fought. Animals fought against animals, animals fought against plants, and plants fought against plants. High- and low-pitched howls beat against An Zhe's eardrums, and the rocks and soil were mixed with fresh bloodstains of various colors. He witnessed a pine tree bend down its trunk to devour a long snake with jet-black scales and two tails.

He also saw a massive toad extend and curl its bright red tongue around a flying bat that had human arms growing out of its back. Five minutes after swallowing the bat, a pair of black wings grew out of the toad's bumpy and slimy back, soft and furled. This was only one out of ten thousand sights the mushroom had seen, and he had long ago become used to them.

Right at that moment, a gray animal with four eyes and a body covered with scales, feathers, and fur walked over. Its head resembled both a crocodile's and a massive wolf's, and seven teeth protruded from between its lips. It approached An Zhe and sniffed him with its blood-red nose.

Unmoving, An Zhe quietly stayed next to a mushroom and breathed evenly until he had been sniffed all over.

The huge monster, seeming to have gained nothing, turned around and lumbered off.

An Zhe realized that nothing would notice him even if he was using a human form—perhaps because mushrooms could be found all over the place here, lacked nutritional value, weren't aggressive, and sometimes even contained toxins. So he and they seemed to be creatures from two different worlds, peacefully coexisting.

Perhaps An Ze had been correct. He *was* a tiny little mushroom.

2

"ARE YOU GOING BACK TO THE NORTHERN BASE?"

AN ZHE WALKED for a very long time.

Many nights and days later, the distance he had traversed on the map was merely the width of a human pinky nail, while the remaining distance to the Northern Base was the length of an entire finger. Since he had no human means of transportation, he didn't know exactly how much longer it would take for him to get there.

At last, he noticed the damp and gloomy smell fade away and felt the soil beneath his feet firm up.

That evening, the sun sank down behind the distant unbroken chain of black mountains like a crimson eye blinking. The sunlight gradually disappeared, and as the dusk sky and aurora rose together, An Zhe tried hard to make out the writing and symbols on the map.

The dried-up river he had just walked across marked a border of the "Abyss," and after this border was a place named "Flatland 2." Flatland 2 had a three-star danger level and two-star pollution level, and it was home to large arthropod-class monsters and rodent-class animals. The land, no longer filled with mushrooms, was dominated by common low shrubbery instead.

Indeed, the Abyss's uneven terrain, the commonly seen rifts, and the entangled shadows of towering trees that appeared late at night were all gone. One could take in the view of this place with a single glance—a flat and boundless twilight.

But An Zhe felt uneasy.

Flatland 2's dry air seemed unsuited for the survival of mushrooms and he could not find any soil from which he could absorb nutrients, so he could only recover his strength via human methods such as sleeping.

Thus, he walked for another very long time before finally finding a shallow depression in the ground where short green and yellow grasses were sparsely growing. He sat down with his arms wrapped around his knees and curled up in a suitable posture.

A mushroom usually spent the vast majority of its life sleeping, but this was the first time An Zhe fell asleep in a human posture.

A mushroom's sleep usually consisted of staying quietly in a single place and waiting for time to pass, but it seemed that human sleep was different. Not long after he closed his eyes, infinite darkness came flooding forth like the tide, and An Zhe's body became light.

Or to put it another way, it seemed like he was losing his body bit by bit.

At some point, the whistling wind entered his ears. It was the sound of the wind in the wilderness, which used to be his favorite thing.

But those sounds were now meaningless, for he had lost his spore when it was rolling around in a patch of wilderness it liked. There were some human voices amongst the wind. He couldn't remember those syllables very well, only recall a tiny portion of them. Even when turned into human language, they were fragmented phrases that he couldn't put together—

"Very... strange, very..."

"... How is it?"

"Take... samples... this place."

In the following moment, an indescribable pain radiated to every part of his body. The feeling was very light, but also very deep. A void appeared in his consciousness, unable to be filled for ever and ever, and he knew he had lost his most important thing from then on.

Fear spread throughout his body in that instant. From then on, fearing the sound of the wind, he lived in the cave.

His heart pounded, and a wave of fear suddenly washed over him—the same kind of fear as when he lost his spore.

An Zhe's eyes flew open, and he promptly realized that he was dreaming. Only humans could dream. In the following moment, he stopped breathing entirely.

He knew the source of that fear. A black creature stood in front of him.

Two blood-red compound eyes glowed faintly. An Zhe tensed up all over, and his gaze traveled down the huge creature. It had three pairs of slender and sharp sickle-like forelimbs, each as long as an adult human, that gleamed with a luster as cold as moonlight.

After realizing what it was, his body shuddered with a distant feeling that stemmed from the trembling of the first ancestor thousands of years back—the feeling that, as a mushroom, he would die from being bitten by termites.

Perhaps the predators in the "Abyss" would not spare a mushroom a single glance, but the arthropod-class monsters of Flatland 2 may view them as a rare delicacy.

Just as this thought occurred to An Zhe, he unconsciously rolled to one side!

With a dull sound that made even the earth tremble, the arthropod monster's sharp forelimb stabbed into the soil next to him—where he had just been lying.

An Zhe snatched up his backpack, turned over, and got to

his feet before sprinting to the nearby shrubbery as the arthropod monster's rapid footsteps resounded in his ears. When the sound grew somewhat softer, An Zhe looked back. Beneath the aurora, he clearly saw the thing in its entirety at last. It was a massive black monster resembling an ant that had been magnified a few thousand times.

Luckily, its body looked overly cumbersome. The speed at which humans could run was superior, so as long as he could run into the shrubbery up ahead—

He stumbled.

In that instant, the monster's shadow enveloped him. Amidst the keen whistling of the wind, its forelimb swung toward his arm.

An Zhe's shirt sleeve suddenly became empty, causing the fabric to droop and the monster to cut nothing at all.

It paused, seemingly surprised by that.

At the same time, hyphae stretched out and grew again inside An Zhe's sleeve to form a complete human arm once more.

He dropped to the ground and rolled, narrowly avoiding the monster's next attack, then pushed off the ground and threw himself into the low shrubbery where two hardy shrubs shielded his body.

But that wasn't enough for him to escape this monster's eyes. An Zhe took a few hurried breaths, and his body began to transform. The outlines of his arms, fingers, and all other extremities became undefined and something heaved below the surface, turning more hyphae-like as he prepared to escape via a more agile means.

Right at that moment—

"Bang!"

A streak of white light flew through the air and struck the joint connecting the monster's head and thorax like a shooting star.

After the dull sound of the impact rang out, the white light silently exploded with a flare of red mixed in.

An Zhe lay in the shrubbery and watched, eyes wide open, as the huge thing broke into two parts and crashed to the ground.

The impact sent leaves flying into the air, falling over An Zhe.

The monster's head landed not more than half a meter away from him, its blood-red compound eyes still looking in his direction.

In the past, An Zhe had seen creatures in the "Abyss" who could still move even after being cut into thirds. Just as he thought to get a little further away from it, he suddenly heard sounds nearby.

"That was the last uranium shell. After harvesting the carcass, we're going back to the base." The man's voice was rich.

"Arthropod-type carapaces aren't cheap. I didn't think we'd end up snagging some." Another male voice, reedier than the previous one.

After a short exchange, they stopped talking, and the sounds of their footsteps traveled over. It was the sound of thick-soled leather boots treading on the sand mixed with the rustling sound of friction.

Humans.

After An Ze's death, An Zhe had not seen any humans for a long time. He furtively raised his head from the shrubbery.

The shrubbery rustled. He heard the first speaker quietly urge, "On your guard!"

In the following second, three pitch-black gun muzzles were aimed in his direction.

An Zhe looked at the men.

His muddled recollection of the night he lost his spore inexorably came to mind, but An Ze's existence had shown him the kindness and goodwill of humans. He thought over his current predicament, then said, "He-... hello."

Beneath the aurora's illumination, the scene before him could be taken in at a glance: three humans clad in dark gray clothes, all male. Wrapped around their waists were wide brown belts with magazines for their guns tied to them. The man standing in the middle towered over the other, shorter two.

He had been the one speaking just now about uranium. His voice was very calm as he asked, "You human?"

An Zhe hesitated briefly. Thinking of the weapon that blew up the monster at its midsection, he said, "Yes."

"What're you called? What's your ID number? What about your teammates?"

"An Zhe. 3261170514. We got separated."

The man looked down at him with a frown. He had thick and dark eyebrows, clear black eyes, a high nose bridge, and thick lips. Unlike the wild beasts of the Abyss, the combination of these facial features didn't make An Zhe feel a sense of peril, so he pursed his lips and returned the gaze.

Three seconds later, one of the men at that man's side—a short and dark-skinned man—loaded the gun once more with a click, the action full of implied threat. He looked at An Zhe and said, his voice low and words fast, "Take off your clothes."

An Zhe stood up from the shrubbery and undid the first button on his gray shirt, then the second, revealing the skin at his neckline. His skin was a smooth, milky white that looked a bit like the color of his hyphae.

Then he heard the third man whistle. That man had pallid skin tinted with a red flush and blond hair as well as many wrinkles on his face, which were signs of human aging. The man's eyes, gray-blue and turned up at the corners, were looking straight at him.

An Zhe lowered his head, undid the rest of the buttons, and took off his shirt.

The blue-eyed man walked closer to him, whistled a second time, and began to examine him from top to bottom.

This man's gaze was very sticky, similar to the saliva of the animals in the Abyss. After examining An Zhe once, he looped around to An Zhe's side.

Then he seized An Zhe's wrist and swiped the skin there with his fingers. With his thumb rubbing against An Zhe's wrist bone, he asked in a slightly piercing voice, "What's this?"

An Zhe looked down at the back of his hand and wrist. There were some random and irregular red marks there, which were scratches he had gotten from the shrubbery when he was dodging the monster's attacks earlier. He turned his head, using his gaze to indicate the shrubbery behind himself. "Leaves."

A brief silence followed. After a while, that man clicked his tongue and said, "You taking off the rest yourself, or shall I take it off for you?"

An Zhe didn't move.

He knew more or less what they were doing, for there were similar scenes in An Ze's memories.

Genetic contamination would occur between monsters and monsters or between monsters and people. The method of tentatively verifying whether someone had been contaminated was to check for wounds.

However, the man behind him made him feel uncomfortable. When he was still a mushroom, the feeling he got when snakes slithered past his stem and cap was just like this.

He lifted his head and looked at the man in the middle. He had seen many ferocious beasts in the Abyss and was also able to roughly judge how much of a threat they posed. Right now, he intuited that this man was the least aggressive out of the three.

"Hosen." After a brief exchanged glance, that man spoke up again, his voice very grim. "Don't fall back into your old habits while we're out here."

Letting out a derisive laugh, Hosen examined An Zhe with an even more unrestrained gaze.

Three seconds later, that man said to An Zhe, "Come to the back with me."

An Zhe obediently followed him around the monster's head to the other side. Apart from the scratch marks left by the branches and leaves, he didn't have any other wounds.

The man asked, "How long have you been separated from your teammates for?"

An Zhe thought for a while, then replied, "One day."

"You're very lucky."

"It seems that there aren't many monsters here."

"But there's no shortage of bugs." While the man's speech was always very curt, he seemed dependable.

An Zhe buttoned up his clothes, looked at the man, and asked in a soft voice, "Are you going back to the Northern Base?"

The man replied, "Yeah."

"Then... can you take me along?" An Zhe asked. "I have my own food and water."

"It's not up to me," the man said.

Just as the man finished speaking, he stepped out and looked at the other two men. "No wounds. Shall we take him along?"

Hosen smiled, looked at An Zhe with his arms crossed, and whistled a third time. Then he said, "Why not? It won't matter if we do."

Then he looked at the last man. "What do you think, scum?"

An Zhe looked over as well and directly met the dark-skinned man's dour gaze.

3

"DARLING, DON'T VOMIT FROM DISGUST"

THE AURORA CAST down a pale green glow that shone upon the man's dark complexion, creating a strange deep green hue that made it seem reptilian.

At last, he spoke. "We aren't Judges, so we can't confirm that he's one hundred percent human."

"Although you say that," Hosen said in an exaggerated drawl, his arms crossed, "Flatland 2's pollution level is only two stars."

The dark-skinned man went silent for some time again. Then he said, "The average time taken for mutation to occur in Flatland 2 is four hours. I'll agree *after* four hours have passed."

"Fine," Hosen said. "If he still hasn't mutated by the time we finish gathering up the loot, we'll take him."

The dark-skinned man finally nodded. Then the three of them looked at each other, seeming to have reached an agreement.

"I'm Vance," the tall man in the middle said by way of self-introduction as he turned toward An Zhe.

"Hello," An Zhe said.

Hosen, who made him feel slightly repulsed, said, "Hosen."

The last man, the one who had been called "scum," was silent for a while before spitting out, "Anthony."

An Zhe greeted him as well, then added, "Thank you."

"No need for thanks," Vance said with a smile. "We're all fellow humans. Plus we just lost a teammate, so we're short-handed."

With those words, he walked on to the nearby monster head and directed the others. "We're leaving as soon as we finish harvesting the carcass. Move quickly."

As he spoke, Vance took out a pair of gloves and a long dagger from his backpack and tossed them to An Zhe. "You go remove the legs."

An Zhe caught the items, obediently responded, and walked ten or so paces forward before stopping next to the monster's halved body, where he put the gloves on and began to examine it.

The arthropod's body was enormous, and its carapace was mostly smooth save for some places where long spines or protruding bulges stuck out. He looked down at the monster's legs. There were six altogether—slender and long, divided into three segments, and densely covered with shiny black fuzz.

On the other side, Vance and Anthony were taking care of the monster's head. They removed the carapace, allowing the brain and other fluids to flow out, then scraped the interior clean. Hosen was standing guard at the periphery.

So An Zhe also pulled out his dagger and attentively dug at the monster's joints. After approximately five minutes, he broke one of the joints, separating one leg from the monster's thorax. It fell to the ground, and viscous white brain-like fluid slowly leaked out from the opening and seeped into the yellow sand.

He heard Hosen say in a mocking voice, "Darling, don't vomit from disgust."

An Zhe didn't react, choosing instead to quietly continue digging at the next joint.

Not only did he feel nothing regarding this monster, he even felt that it was much cleaner than those animals that lived in the "Abyss."

But Hosen seemed to have no plans of letting him off the hook. Footsteps sounded behind him as Hosen walked over and pressed down on An Zhe's shoulder with his right hand, fingers sliding over it. "How old are you, sweetheart?"

An Zhe heard a sort of greed in his tone—the greed of animals in the face of food. But based on his limited understanding, humans wouldn't eat their own kind.

He calmly replied, "Nineteen."

An Ze was nineteen this year. He had consumed An Ze's genes, so he was probably nineteen or so as well.

"But you look to be only seventeen," Hosen said in a sharp voice with a raspy undertone, his snickers muffled in his chest.

An Zhe frowned, unsure how to answer.

"Hosen." Right at that moment, Vance's voice came from nearby. "Focus on standing guard."

Hosen made a contemptuous noise, then squeezed his shoulder a bit more before leaving.

An Zhe once again realized that among humans, each individual may have different characteristics. For example, An Ze was different from the humans who dug out his spore, and Vance was different from Hosen. He felt very grateful to Vance for stepping in when he did.

He lowered his head and continued to dig at the joints, dividing each leg into three segments. After he finished, he neatly stacked them up. The thing's carapace had a metallic sheen and was hard as stone, so they made crisp clacking sounds when they were stacked together.

By the time he removed all six legs, Vance and Anthony had also finished taking apart the head and came over to his half of the body. Vance took a look at the neatly stacked legs on the ground and smiled. "You're pretty diligent."

Then he said to Hosen, "Drive the car over here."

Without saying anything, Hosen turned and walked away.

An Zhe stood to one side and watched Vance and Anthony get started on the monster's thorax.

He asked, "Do you need my help?"

Vance, holding a black pincer-like tool the length of a human's lower leg in his gloved hands, asked, "You haven't come out here much, have you?"

"… Mm-hm," An Zhe replied.

"Then you can just wait over on the side." Vance pried away the piece of armor at the junction between the monster's thorax and abdomen with the pliers. The edges of the armor were irregular, forming a sharp black spine where it met the other pieces of armor, flashing with a chilly gray luster. Vance said, "This thing has a lot of spines. It's easy to get pricked if you don't have any experience handling them. Flatland 2's pollution level isn't high, but it is still possible to get infected that way."

An Zhe obediently took a few steps back and watched them circle around the carcass and dismantle it at various points. They lifted away one piece of black carapace after another, and white viscera and organs spilled all over the ground.

As he watched, a dull roar started up. An Zhe looked to his right and saw a rectangular black armored car driving in their direction, looking like a huge crustacean-class monster—An Zhe was very familiar with the sight of it, for the team An Ze used to be a part of had five such armored cars.

The car drew near, and Hosen jumped down from it. Without even lifting his head, Vance said, "First help him carry the goods onto the car."

An Zhe made a sound of acknowledgment and picked up the armor pieces from the ground, then carefully tied them with rope and handed them to Hosen, who put them in the armored car's storage space.

The enormous monster shrank as they took it apart, and the number of armor pieces An Zhe picked up increased.

Just as he was tying up a stack of armor pieces with rope, he abruptly stopped moving.

On the spiny black armor piece beneath his hand, a few tiny droplets of liquid were congealing at the tip of a spine, dark and very difficult to discover if one did not look carefully.

He looked at the splashes of viscera on the ground and confirmed that all of the monster's internal fluids were white, yellow, or clear.

Then what were these dark droplets? He recalled the blood that flowed out of An Ze's body before he died.

An Zhe looked at Vance and Anthony. The two of them were thoroughly engrossed in dismantling the carcass, their expressions calm and everything seeming normal. As a result, An Zhe could only act as if nothing had happened. He bowed his head once more and tied up the armor pieces.

A long time later, they finally finished dismantling the carcass, and the three men seemed to also be convinced that An Zhe wouldn't suddenly turn into some deadly monster.

Vance said, "Get in the car, we're going back to the base. An Zhe, you come too."

A single armored car could hold seven or eight people, and there was also a space where people could rest. It was divided into three simple compartments, but each one was very cramped and had a low ceiling, so humans had to hunch over in order to walk around inside.

An Zhe was assigned the outermost space, the car door to his right, and he lay down with his head pillowed on his backpack. Anthony went up to the front to drive, Vance was next door to him, and Hosen occupied the innermost space.

The car door shut, and it went dark. There was only a faint light shining in from a small window on the side. After a jolt, the armored car slowly started up and drove forward, the ride mostly smooth but for the occasional small bump.

An Zhe looked into the darkness before him with eyes wide

open, feeling like he was floating in a black tide. The tide was carrying him along as it flowed toward the Northern Base, a place he knew nothing of.

Enveloped by a slight sense of helplessness and confusion, he waited quietly in the darkness.

When the light coming through the small window gradually became stronger, the surroundings slightly brightened as well. The car stopped, and An Zhe heard Hosen get up, take a few steps inward, open the door leading to the cabin, and walk in to take over from Anthony. Anthony returned to where Hosen used to be and lay down. His breathing was very heavy, and his movements were very large—even the floor of the rest area shook. Soon afterward, Vance asked what the matter was, and Anthony replied that he was a bit tired.

Another long span of time passed, and it was Vance's turn to take over from Hosen.

An Zhe instinctively curled up. He knew that with this, Hosen would be sleeping next door, and he felt ill at ease.

But no sounds of a human lying down came from next door.

An Zhe opened his eyes wide, waiting.

In the following moment, with the soft rustling of footsteps, a person directly threw himself upon An Zhe.

"Darling…" Hosen lowered his voice, sounding very hoarse. He forced his own legs between An Zhe's and wrapped an arm around An Zhe's shoulders. An Zhe struggled a little, almost on reflex, but he was pressed to the floor by a strength greater than his own. "That stupid Vance isn't here… I know what you do, I've been with more mercenary teams than he's laid eyes on."

The struggles just now took up no small amount of An Zhe's strength, and he panted for breath. "Please don't do this."

"Don't do what?" Hosen smiled. In the dark environment, his smile looked very malevolent.

An Zhe didn't reply. Hosen lifted the hand that he was pressing down on An Zhe's shoulder with and made to undo his belt. He could hold An Zhe down firmly with only one hand, which seemed to please him greatly. His smile grew, and his tone of voice was crude and mocking. "Darling, what can you do with such little strength? You don't know how to drive and can't use heavy weapons. When you run into a monster, all you can do is wait to die. What did your teammates bring you out here for? Just to watch?"

As he spoke, he grabbed An Zhe's neck and leaned in close. His stubble-covered cheek pressed against the side of An Zhe's neck, and the acrid smell of smoke drifted from him. "I've seen plenty of little whores like you… But it is the first time I've seen one so beautiful. Which mercenary team were you a part of before?"

As An Zhe violently gasped for breath, Hosen pressed him down tightly and ran a hot, wet tongue over An Zhe's skin. An Zhe turned his head, coughing from the smell of smoke, and continued groping around in the darkness with his right hand until he finally touched the dagger Vance had tossed to him earlier.

Right at that moment, two compartments away, a huge noise came from where Anthony was. It sounded like something had been knocked over onto the floor.

"Don't be impatient, scum." Hosen laughed out loud. "It'll be your turn soon enough."

But his words seemed to have no effect, because footsteps approached.

With a soft curse, Hosen pulled An Zhe up and pressed him against the wall of the car, then yanked at his shirt collar.

An Zhe no longer resisted. Clutching the dagger in his hand, he looked at the dark aisle in silence while his white hyphae quietly spread out on the floor beside him, seemingly preparing for something.

But in the following second, all of his movements stopped.

A monster with a human torso and three pairs of slender

legs protruding from its back slowly walked through the aisle, dragging furled soft wings behind itself, and the two blood-red compound eyes atop its head glowed faintly.

The thing's skin was black—the color of Anthony's skin. But the shape of his human face had already become distorted. The place where his eyes used to be was covered with densely packed brown scales, the nose extended down at a slant to form a massive cleft, and the mouth area protruded outward with a long and curled black tube extending from the middle.

He stopped walking, and the edges of his wings scraped against the walls of the car, making ear-piercing noises.

"What are you doing, Anthony?" Hosen asked, his voice full of dissatisfaction. "I'm not fond of being watched."

After saying that, he lowered his head again and settled on top of An Zhe, who felt a set of teeth bite down at the junction between his neck and shoulder. The teeth worried at his skin, suffusing it with a slight pain. But he was in no position to care about it. Tensed up all over, he faced the monster Anthony had transformed into.

One second, two seconds, three seconds.

The wings behind Anthony vibrated slightly, and his proboscis curled and uncurled in the air.

"Scared?" Hosen, who was lying on top of him, seemed to have felt him stiffen up, and he muttered an inarticulate curse. "What are you acting for?" Then he grabbed An Zhe's waist with an unyielding grip and bit down hard on his skin.

Right at that moment—

With the buzz of vibrating wings, Anthony placed his six thin long limbs on the floor, leaned forward, and gathered energy as he sank down into a crouch. Then, just like a sleek spider, he rushed toward them!

The wind whistled in the cramped space. An Zhe's eyes went unfocused in a split second, and his body instantly transformed into his soft and agile mushroom form. His hyphae fluttered about in the compartment, filling almost the entire space and momentarily blocking Anthony's line of sight.

Immediately afterward, An Zhe felt the human on top of him first stiffen for a moment and cough a few times, then begin to flail all of his limbs. "Fuck, what's th—?"

He looked down and saw that Hosen had snapped countless soft hyphae with a single bite, which had then choked his windpipe and esophagus. When he coughed, he looked panic-stricken and pained.

At the same time, countless more hyphae were cut apart by Anthony's forelimbs. They were soft and easy to break, lacking the slightest durability, so they could win no more than a five- or six-second-long window to make an escape.

An Zhe estimated the distance between himself and Anthony, then swiftly used his hyphae to roll up his clothes and flowed out from the chaotic space beneath Hosen, regaining his freedom.

His snow-white hyphae surged toward the door like a snow-white tide. Once there, he changed back into human shape and pressed the switch near it.

With a dull sound, the car door sprang open. An Zhe instantly retracted all of his hyphae, then reached out with one hand to forcefully drag Hosen's collar before rolling out. The two of them fell out of the car together and made a solid landing on the sand.

At least it was safer here than in the cramped space of the car.

However, mere moments later, Anthony stuck his head out from the doorway as well, and a harsh buzzing started up. He first flapped his wings to fly four or five meters up into the air, then abruptly dove toward them—

Right when he flew up, An Zhe had swiftly gotten to his feet and run away.

But he saw Hosen simply lie on the sand, his gaze unfocused, and Anthony's sharp forelimbs pierced his chest in an instant.

In the Abyss, An Zhe had seen the ways by which many monsters hunted and escaped, so he knew how he should escape and thought Hosen knew as well. But it wasn't until the moment when blood spurted out that Hosen seemed to come alive suddenly. Yelling, he grabbed Anthony's front legs with both hands and madly kicked at Anthony's body, which had become a long black pupa, with both feet in an attempt to retreat.

The ground rumbled. An Zhe spun around and saw the armored car, which had already driven quite far away, make a sharp turn and head back toward them—Vance had finally noticed something was wrong.

He took a few breaths, then began running toward the armored car.

Vance's worried expression was visible through the car window. Before the armored car reached An Zhe, its door had already sprung open. When the armored car passed him, a pair of strong arms wrenched him up from the ground, and he scrambled into the driver's cabin in tandem with Vance's movements. Vance swiftly tossed him to the other side of the cabin, then slammed the door shut.

An Zhe said, "They…"

"There's no saving them!" Vance once again yanked the steering wheel hard, and the armored car turned back to its original direction. With the accelerator pressed to the floor, it sped northward.

An Zhe leaned back against the front passenger seat, panting. After catching his breath a little, he looked in the rearview mirror. The mutated Anthony and the mortally wounded Hosen were tangled up together and rolling on the ground. Anthony lifted his forelimbs, then brought them plummeting down to pierce through Hosen's torso and nail his body to the ground.

Then it lifted its head and looked in their direction. Approximately five seconds later, it seemed to have given up on chasing the armored car. It lowered its head, and its long and slim proboscis pierced Hosen's head. After another fit of convulsions, Hosen's body went utterly slack.

The car drove very quickly. Before long, their figures had disappeared in the yellow sand and shrubs, never to be seen again.

Vance asked, "Anthony mutated?"

An Zhe turned his head to look at Vance and saw that the rims of his eyes were slightly red.

He bowed his head. "I'm sorry."

He was still alive, but Vance had lost two teammates.

"What are you sorry for?" Vance forced a smile. "When we come out here for work, people often die. I'm used to it. Maybe the next one to die will be me."

But An Zhe truly did feel guilty. Anthony had been infected. If An Zhe had told Vance about the drops of what he suspected to be human blood on the ant armor right after he discovered it, they may have been able to discover that Anthony had been infected in advance.

He lowered his head and told Vance about it.

Vance was silent for a while before he lowered his voice and said, "What Anthony changed into wasn't an ant. He may have been infected earlier. Before we ran into you, we encountered a swarm of mutated wild mosquitos."

"After that… was he also pricked by the armor?" An Zhe asked.

Vance looked out the car window and went silent for another long while before speaking again. "Flatland 2's pollution level is very low—two stars—so one might not be infected from getting pricked or slightly wounded. But if they speak up about it, they'll be abandoned by their team for sure, so many people won't do so until after they've been wounded."

His voice grew a bit softer. "... Because they want to go home."

"Then what about Hosen?" An Zhe asked.

If they had discovered that Anthony had been infected in advance, Hosen might not have died.

"Don't take it to heart. Hosen's death wasn't an unjust one." Vance lit a cigarette and took a deep drag. "He had done no small number of wicked things and had the blood of at least five people on his hands. This time, if it weren't for the fact that we were truly short of hands, Anthony and I wouldn't have worked with him. What was he doing at the time? Bullying you?"

An Zhe said nothing, and Vance turned his head to look at him.

In the twilight, the boy's contours seemed both quiet and peaceful, like a crystalline drop of water. For this sort of person to appear in the perilous wilds, perhaps he was dealing with unspeakable difficulties, but Vance didn't ask.

Likewise, An Zhe didn't know what to say to Vance. He was thinking of what happened prior to Hosen's death. At the very beginning, Hosen seemed to have briefly lost consciousness, only coming around once he had been stabbed.

What had Hosen done before that?

He had bitten a mouthful of hyphae.

An Zhe frowned. He actually didn't know whether his mushroom self was poisonous or not.

Now he suspected that he was a poisonous mushroom.

As they continued forward, the vegetation became scarcer. In the boundless desert, there were no animals whatsoever, only their armored car traveling alone.

At night, when the aurora appeared in the sky again, Vance intended to stop the car and rest. He stubbed out his cigarette on the steering wheel, then opened the door connecting the driver's cabin and the rest area and jumped down. In the pitch-black rest area, his voice rang out. "Sleep first. We'll arrive at the base after driving for another day and a half."

An Zhe came to the door as well. To have a broader field of vision, the driver's cabin was very high up, whereas to save space for the storage compartment, the rest area was toward the bottom of the car and very low. The height difference between it and the driver's cabin was more than one meter, so he had to jump down.

He stood there, slightly hesitant. Merely three short seconds later, Vance seemed to have noticed his hesitation and said, "Sit there first."

An Zhe followed those instructions and sat down on the edge, his legs dangling. Then Vance reached out to hold his upper body and helped him down.

An Zhe landed steadily on the ground and said in a small voice, "Thank you."

"No problem." Vance smiled, and a slow affection came through in his voice. "My younger brother was afraid of heights, so he'd often be like this too. He was about your age."

An Zhe, doing his best to grasp the rules of human communication, asked tentatively, "Does he also come out into the wilds with you?"

"Mm-hm," Vance said. "We used to always be together."

"But not this time?"

"He's dead," Vance said. "It's been two months since he was killed by a Judge at the entrance to the base."

Judge.

This was the third time An Zhe heard that word. The first time was from An Ze. He was trying to dissuade An Zhe from going to the human base, saying, "You can't escape the Judges' eyes."

The second time was from Anthony. He hadn't wanted An Zhe to join their team, saying, "We aren't Judges, so we can't confirm that he's one hundred percent human."

And in the memories he obtained from An Ze, it seemed to be a word that appeared very frequently.

So he repeated, "...Judge?"

"You don't know?" Vance's voice pitched up in surprise. "Where exactly did you pop up from?"

An Zhe said in a small voice, "I haven't interacted with others before."

"I can see that." Vance twisted a knob on the car's wall, and a faint white light lit up at the top of the walls, barely illuminating the cramped space. He took out field rations from a cubbyhole in the wall, and An Zhe took out food and water from his own backpack as well before sitting across from Vance.

He heard Vance say, "The base has a system called the 'Arbiter's Code,' after which came an organization under the jurisdiction of the military. It has a very high rank, and it's called the Trial Court. The members of the Trial Court are Judges. They usually take shifts at the base's gates, and every one of them is licensed to kill, so it won't count as breaking the law when they kill people."

After listening to this sentence, An Zhe dimly recalled that he had found something related in the memories he obtained from An Ze.

He said, "... They determine whether the people entering the base are human or Infected Ones?"

"Mm-hm," Vance replied. "In addition to the kind of Infected Ones that can be distinguished on sight, there are also some that can't. The mutation process hasn't yet started, or the mutation level is too high, so there are no differences from humans on the surface. The base calls those kinds of people xenogenics."

An Zhe opened his eyes wide.

If that was the case, then he was a xenogenic.

Vance undid his jacket and put it aside, then twisted open the water flask's cap and continued speaking. "The base is too densely populated. After xenogenics enter the base, they will go on a killing spree, and following that will be large-scale infection. The Trial Court's responsibility is to determine if every single person entering the city is human or xenogenic, and the determining process is called the 'Trial.'"

"Then... what happens after they discover a xenogenic?" An Zhe asked.

"What else?" Vance raised his eyebrows. "They're shot on the spot."

Without saying anything, An Zhe bowed his head and took a bite of hardtack. He had just learned how to eat by human methods, but to him, human food was somewhat coarse. When he swallowed, his mouth and throat would get scratched. He ate very slowly, but his heart beat very quickly.

After a while, he asked, "Can they really identify all the xenogenics?"

Vance took a big gulp of water, leaned against the car wall, and closed his eyes. His voice carried a trace of despondency. "Who knows? The dead can't prove anything. Nobody knows whether the people killed were really xenogenics or not. That was the case with my younger brother."

An Zhe said nothing. Vance seemed to have answered a question he hadn't asked, but he still listened quietly.

"That time... he came with me to Flatland 1, where the pollution level was lower than even Flatland 2's. I kept an eye on him the entire time, and I could confirm that he hadn't been wounded." Vance smiled, but his voice was raspy. "When we returned to the entrance of the base, the one on duty wasn't any ordinary Judge, but their boss. Everyone calls him 'the Arbiter.' Other Judges will give their justifications for killing someone, but he doesn't have to. He doesn't need justification to kill anyone, nor does he accept any pleas. Even if it's the base's top brass, if he killed them, then that's that. It was like that on that day. He so much as glanced at my brother before opening fire on him."

"I didn't believe it, but there was nothing I could do. This sort of thing happens often. He's killed many people, so there are many people in the base who despise him, myself included. For all I know, someday he'll kill me too."

With those words, Vance looked at his own right hand in a daze for a while, then tossed the flask to one side. He lay down with his head pillowed upon his arm, but his eyes were still looking at the car ceiling. At last, he got back on track and answered the question An Zhe had asked at the very beginning. "They'd rather mistakenly kill someone than let them pass. If a xenogenic really made its way into the base, it would be discovered for sure. In the entirety of this year, there has been only one xenogenic attack."

An Zhe felt uneasy. To conceal this uneasiness, he closed his eyes and rubbed them with his left hand.

Vance said, "Go to sleep, kid."

An Zhe lay down next to him. No matter how tomorrow turned out, at least he was safe tonight. There were no monsters and there was no Hosen. There was only Vance, who treated him very well.

Before sleeping, he held the bullet shell in his hand and looked at the car door at the end of the aisle.

Supposing—supposing he secretly opened the car door right now, got out, and returned to the monster-infested wilds, he could still live. He would not face the Trial, and he would not be killed on the spot. He didn't know how long he could live, but it would definitely be for longer than tomorrow.

But was the spore something more important than his own life?

It was.

To the creatures in the Abyss, death was the most trivial thing. And in this short day outside of the Abyss, he had witnessed Anthony's mutation and Hosen's death. Human lives were by no means precious either.

An Zhe closed his eyes. He knew he had to go to the Northern Base.

––––––

Early the next morning, they continued driving toward the base. Because only Vance was driving and he lacked energy, their rest times became irregular. They stopped to rest that afternoon and continued driving north at midnight on the third day. When the aurora began to dim and the sky was suffused with white, Vance said, "We're almost there."

An Zhe looked forward. In the morning's gray fog, a round city gradually appeared from the horizon.

City—he knew this word. Humans clustered in cities the same way mushrooms clustered in the rainy season.

The armored car continued moving forward, and bit by bit as the early morning fog gradually dissipated, more of the city's details appeared. The round city was enclosed by gray steel walls, their height like that of the tallest mushrooms. Even if twenty people stood atop one another, with each person's feet on someone else's shoulders, it still may not have been enough to climb over the wall. Steel tusks and spines protruded from the walls as well, their hues sharp and icy cold like rocks and soil in winter.

The city boundary was filled with surveillance equipment and laser devices, so anyone who sneaked in would be immediately discovered. The two city gates were the only ways of getting in and out of the city, and one was entry only while the other was exit only. The one they were at right now was the one that only allowed entry.

Then An Zhe saw many small teams similar to Vance's drive back from all directions. Some of them were traveling light, while others were wearing heavy gear and carrying weapons. There were four or five people per team, and they drove similar armored cars to designated areas before getting out of them and walking through the city gate. The cars and people were inspected separately.

Vance got out first, and An Zhe jumped down from the car while grabbing onto his arm. Feeling that Vance's arm was somewhat tense, he thought that perhaps this city gate evoked Vance's bad memories of his younger brother.

They walked toward the city gate, where a long line had formed. There was a slight disturbance at the head of the line, but they couldn't clearly see the situation. People were still entering in order.

An Zhe trailed after Vance, walking toward the line and looking around as he walked.

Soldiers clothed in black uniforms stood at both sides of the city gate, two guns at their waists. One was a thermal weapon, while the other was a laser gun. Behind them were colossal heavy weapons that directly faced the city gates. One could imagine that as soon as a monster tried to break in, it would be blown to pieces by these heavy weapons.

After looking around, his gaze was drawn to a black figure. At an open space beneath the distant city walls, that person, also clad in a black uniform, appeared to be a sloppy and undisciplined soldier who had abandoned his post. He wasn't standing guard in an orderly fashion like his colleagues, but rather leaning against the city wall and slowly wiping a black gun with his head lowered.

However, the silver-trimmed black uniform he wore seemed more beautiful and imposing than the others, perhaps because his physique was tall, slim, and well proportioned.

Vance cast a glance in that direction and began walking much faster for some reason while pulling him straight forward. Just as they were about to join the end of the line—

An Zhe saw the man in the distance slowly raise his head.

A pair of ice-cold green eyes showed beneath the brim of the black uniform cap.

In an instant, An Zhe stopped dead in his tracks, feeling that the surroundings had turned as chilly as if they had frozen over.

Vance turned back and said, "What's the—"

His voice suddenly stopped.

A gunshot rang out.

Vance's tall body swayed on the spot, then toppled over with a thud. His eyes were wide open, his throat made gurgling noises, and blood gushed from his temple. After his body jerked a few times, there were no further movements.

But An Zhe could not even reach out to grab at the hem of his clothes, nor did he have any room whatsoever to think about what exactly had happened just then. He could only lift his head and meet the gaze of the uniformed soldier because, at that moment, the soldier was slowly turning the jet-black muzzle of the gun...

... toward him.

4

"LU FENG, I HOPE YOU DIE A MISERABLE DEATH—!"

VANCE'S BLOOD spread out in An Zhe's peripheral vision, forming a pool of crimson. When the people in line heard the sound, they turned around one after another to look, but after glimpsing this scene, they indifferently turned back again, as if nothing had happened at all.

But Vance was dead. A human had been killed at the human base's gates, and nobody raised any objection.

Thus, An Zhe suddenly realized that this person was the Arbiter, the person Vance had mentioned to him a day earlier.

He was the master of the Trial Court, determining whether each person entering the city was human or xenogenic. He could decide anyone's fate no matter who they were, needing no justification.

Now it was his own turn to stand trial.

An Zhe's heart thumped wildly at first. The instant that the barrel of the gun pointed at him, he realized that he was really going to die.

But as he looked at the Arbiter's icy green eyes, he gradually calmed down again.

Coming to the Northern Base was his unavoidable decision, so being judged was his fate, no matter the outcome.

He silently counted the seconds in his mind.

One, two, three.

A long time passed with no gunshot ringing out. The Arbiter, keeping the gun trained on him, slowly walked over.

The people in line, seeming to tacitly agree to speed up, spontaneously compressed forward. A moment later, this tiny area was deserted save for An Zhe alone.

Eleven, twelve, thirteen.

After An Zhe counted to the fourteenth second, the Arbiter stopped in front of him, ring finger resting on the gunstock, and lowered the muzzle. Then he put the weapon away.

"Come with me," An Zhe heard him say.

His voice was ice-cold and flat, just like his eyes.

An Zhe stood in place, waiting for him to go, but he didn't move even after three seconds had gone by.

He lifted his head up uncertainly, then heard the Arbiter's voice turn even colder. "Hold out your hand."

An Zhe obediently held out his hand.

"Click."

An ice-cold chill made him shiver.

One end of a silver handcuff was fastened around his wrist, while the other end was in the officer's hand.

It was in this manner in which An Zhe was led away.

The strange thing was, when Vance got shot, the people in line didn't react at all. Now that he was being taken away by the Arbiter, though, they put their heads together and whispered amongst themselves.

An Zhe only had time to look back at Vance's body lying flat on the ground before he was pulled through the city gate.

Once inside, he discovered that the interior space wasn't a cramped passageway, but rather a vast area divided into several spaces. Bright white lights shone everywhere, the bounce of their glow off the steel walls looking like winter snowfall's reflected shine cast upon light gray shale.

There were no fewer armed soldiers or heavy weapons compared to the outside. Within the tight encirclement of the heavy weapons and soldiers was a long snow-white table. Three officers in black uniforms just like the Arbiter's—An Zhe guessed they were the Judges—sat behind it, and a human sat across from them. One of the Judges was asking him, "How is the relationship between you and your wife? When you left the city this time, was she not with you?"

From An Ze's memories, An Zhe learned that besides changes to appearance, bearing, and habits, the intelligence and memories of infected humans would be affected as well, so interrogation was also a method of identifying xenogenics.

The person who brought him inside glanced in that direction and said, "Hurry up."

After the Judge in the middle replied with a "yes, sir," he looked at the person being tried. "You may go now."

As if he had survived a calamity, the man broke out into a smile, then got up and swiftly walked through the city gate's passageway.

Thus, An Zhe knew that this man who brought him here was indeed none other than the Arbiter, and his "hurry up" was not to hasten the Judges to speed up their interrogation, but rather to show that he had already determined in the span of a moment that the person being tried was human.

The next person to be tried walked from the line toward the long table. The distance between the line and the table was very long, with several door-shaped machines between them and a section that included turns as well as uphill and downhill slopes. An Zhe realized that this was to show the movement characteristics of the person being tried to the Judges to the fullest possible extent.

But he had no more time to see more because in the following second, he was led around a corner and into a long corridor.

That person took out a black communication device and said, "Trial Court, Lu Feng. Requesting genetic examination."

An Zhe guessed that the two words in the middle were his name.

A mechanical door promptly slid open in front of them and Lu Feng walked straight in, the force of his pull making An Zhe stumble before he caught up.

The room was silvery-white. Mysterious mechanical devices were arrayed from floor to ceiling, and six soldiers standing guard were scattered all about. Behind the workbench at one end of the room sat a young male human with short blonde hair and blue eyes clad in a white lab coat.

"What a surprise it is for Colonel Lu to come here." He pushed up the glasses on his nose, the tone of his voice lifting up at the end in provocation. "Don't you always solve all your problems with bullets?"

Lu Feng said coldly, "Please cooperate, Doctor."

The doctor glanced at Lu Feng, a shadow of a smile on his face. Then he got up and said to An Zhe, "Come with me."

After following him, An Zhe was made to lie on a silvery-white platform, and rings around his hands and feet fixed his limbs in place. The doctor said, "Don't move."

Immediately afterward, An Zhe felt a pain in his arm. He turned his head in that direction and saw the doctor slowly drawing a tube of bright red blood from his body.

The doctor said, "The color of your blood is very healthy."

"Thank you for the compliment," An Zhe replied.

The doctor was amused by his response.

"The blood will be sent for a genetic examination, which will take an hour. The full body enhanced scan is expected to take forty minutes. Don't move."

He finished speaking, and the silver platform began to glow with a blue light. The surroundings emitted a directionless low hum—the source of the sound was every single particle of air. The omnipresent noise made An Zhe recall those distant nights in the Abyss. The faraway ocean gave off the dull lapping sounds of waves, and in the darkest time of the night, the howls of unknown creatures came from that direction. Fluctuations that human language could not possibly describe swept away the entirety of the rain-drenched land.

The electric current was like countless ants crawling over and biting his body. To a mushroom, forty minutes was by no means a long time. But An Zhe thought that these may be the last forty minutes of his life. Cherishing them, he studied the mechanical lines on the ceiling.

He was unsure how much time had passed when he heard Lu Feng say outside, "Seraing told me that your examination methods have been upgraded."

"You're very well informed," the doctor said. "We've discovered that when the human body undergoes mutation, some special fragments of their DNA will be activated, and we've named them 'biological targets.' The biological targets of animal-type mutations and plant-type mutations are the two major categories. The improved gene detection has two processes that occur simultaneously. One is animal-type target detection while the other is plant-type target detection. The total time needed for both is an hour."

"Congratulations," Lu Feng said.

The doctor let out a laugh. "Colonel, if the time needed for genetic examinations is greatly shortened and the cost is reduced, won't your Trial Court be put out of work?"

"I look forward to it with relish."

"You're seriously boring."

Their conversation ceased.

Meanwhile, An Zhe looked up at the silvery-white ceiling and began to ponder what his own species was.

He was a mushroom.

The doctor had said that mutations were divided into animal-type mutations and plant-type mutations.

He thought that firstly, mushrooms weren't a kind of animal.

Secondly, mushrooms didn't seem to be plants either. He didn't have leaves.

An Zhe fell into a state of confusion. He strove to categorize himself as a plant, yet didn't find sufficient proof.

He spent too much time contemplating this question. Before he arrived at a conclusion, the blue light disappeared from his side like an ebbing tide.

"All right." The doctor's voice rang out, and the mechanical rings automatically released.

Then he heard the doctor continue talking. "Colonel, may I ask why you brought him here for a genetic examination?"

"No."

The doctor was clearly rendered speechless.

He helped An Zhe up and had him sit down in a swivel chair on one side, then patted his head. "Good boy. Rest here for a bit while I go look at the results of the blood test."

An Zhe sat in place.

That Colonel, the Arbiter, sat on the other side, still watching him with icy green eyes. His was a young face with clear contours, and at the brim of his hat, a few locks of black hair hung down over his forehead to rest against the ends of his sloped eyebrows. His expression, which the room painted with a thin layer of cold light, serrated An Zhe's eyes like a knife.

The stare from this pair of eyes made An Zhe feel very cold. Mushrooms were afraid of the cold. As a result, he rotated the swivel chair, turning his back to the Colonel.

He felt even colder.

A very long time later, the doctor's footsteps finally came, thawing the room. "There are no abnormalities in the genetic report. You two can go."

After a few seconds of silence, Lu Feng said, "You're one hundred percent sure he's human?"

The doctor replied, "Although it may disappoint you otherwise, we truly haven't found any biological targets. Other infected ones and xenogenics have at least ten or more."

After that, he said, "Look, this little friend of ours doesn't even want to acknowledge you."

Then An Zhe heard the Colonel say, "Turn back around."

An Zhe silently turned back around.

Facing Lu Feng's gaze, he was a bit avoidant because he truly wasn't human.

But even this tiny avoidance of his somehow irritated the Colonel; his voice was like ice water when he spoke again. "What are you afraid of?"

An Zhe didn't say a word. He knew that in front of this man, the more he spoke, the more mistakes he'd make, and perhaps his weakness would be discovered.

At last, Lu Feng raised his eyebrows. "You still aren't leaving?"

So An Zhe obediently jumped down from the chair and left with him again—but this time he was free, without being led in handcuffs.

In the deserted corridor, they reached the halfway point when Lu Feng suddenly spoke up. "At first glance, I instinctively felt that you weren't human."

An Zhe nearly had a heart attack.

A full three seconds passed before he asked, "Then... what about the second glance?"

"This is the first time I've requested a genetic examination." The Colonel held out the genetic examination report to him. "You'd best be one."

An Zhe could only silently accept the report stating that everything about him was normal. For a short while, there were only the monotonous sounds of their footsteps in the silvery-white corridor.

Near the exit, there was a corner where they ran into a party of people. In the lead was a Judge clad in a black uniform, and behind the Judge were two heavily armed soldiers restraining a man as they walked over. Next to them, there was also a tall woman with short hair and a distressed expression.

Spotting Lu Feng, the Judge said, "Colonel."

Lu Feng looked at the restrained man and received a look back. The man's throat spasmed a few times before exclaiming, "I haven't been infected!"

The Judge snapped to attention on the spot and said to Lu Feng, "Infection is strongly suspected, but there is no conclusive evidence. The next of kin are demanding a genetic examination."

Lu Feng made a soft sound of acknowledgement, and the soldiers continued forward with the man in their custody. Just as they passed Lu Feng—

"Bang!"

Lu Feng put away his gun and walked off without looking back. "There's no need."

The man's body instantly pitched forward, held up only by the soldiers. The woman following them shrieked and collapsed to the floor.

An Zhe turned to look at Lu Feng's expression. His gaze was so cold— the mushroom had never seen such a look before. He knew An Ze was always gentle, Vance was easygoing and generous, Hosen was filled with greed, and Anthony was completely on guard. But Lu Feng was different. There was nothing in his eyes at all.

An Zhe thought that to the Arbiter, killing others may have been more normal than breathing. He wouldn't experience any change in emotion because he had already gotten accustomed to the sight long ago.

They soon came to the exit.

Near the exit, two soldiers in simple attire were waiting for him with a body covered by white cloth.

An Zhe knew it was Vance.

His eyesight went blurry. He took a step forward, wishing to lift away the white cloth and look at Vance's face once more, but one of the soldiers stopped him.

The soldier held out a blue chip to him and said in a steady voice, "Mercenary team AR1147 has been confirmed to have no survivors, and the equipment and materials have been reclaimed by the base. The loot has been converted into currency and combined with the consolation payment for disbursement to the next of kin. Please claim the remains."

"Where are you taking him?" An Zhe asked.

The soldier replied, "The incinerator."

His body trembled slightly, and for a long time, he didn't accept the ID card.

Lu Feng's voice rang out. "Do you not want it?"

An Zhe said nothing. After a long while, he lifted his head to look at Lu Feng. "He really… wasn't wounded."

Within that pair of icy green eyes, he saw his own reflection —eyes slightly widened and a quiet grief.

Lu Feng was still expressionless, as if none of this had anything to do with him. However, just as An Zhe thought he would turn and leave, he took a step forward instead.

The black gunstock lifted up the edge of the white fabric, and the part revealed was Vance's right hand.

An Zhe got down on one knee and saw that on the tip of his ring finger was a tiny red dot. It seemed like the most trivial puncture, but at the edges of that red dot, a drop of ominous dark gray liquid was slowly oozing out.

He was stunned. In an instant, those images came to mind.

There was human blood on the ant armor—on that very day, Vance told him that some people would hide the fact that they'd been wounded because in places with a low degree of pollution, there was still a chance that they wouldn't be infected after getting wounded, and that person wanted to go home.

Therefore, therefore—the person pricked by the piece of ant armor wasn't Anthony, but *Vance*.

An Zhe found it difficult to breathe. With trembling fingers, he accepted Vance's ID card and put it into the bag at his side. Then he turned to look at Lu Feng, but the space next to him was empty.

He stood up and looked out to see a sharp black figure beneath the gray skies at the city gate traveling further away little by little.

A moment later, there was a commotion behind him, and he turned back to see the woman, whose companion had just been killed, stumbling forward before the soldiers restrained her.

"Lu Feng! Arbiter—!" She desperately struggled, throwing herself forward and flailing her arms in the air as she screeched, "I hope you die a miserable death—!"

The hoarse, shrill voice burst from her chest and echoed in the building, but she didn't even get so much as a backward glance from the Arbiter.

The surroundings gradually quieted, and the two corpses were taken away one at a time. In the spacious corridor, there were only the woman's broken sobs.

———

A long time passed before the woman by the wall stopped crying. With reddened eyes and disheveled hair, she leaned against the wall and looked at the distant sky, not saying a word. She was like a drop of water on a leaf, breaking with just a touch.

An Zhe carefully asked, "You aren't leaving?"

She shook her head, and her voice was raspy as she said, "The one who died, what relationship did he have with you?"

An Zhe spent a very long time finding the appropriate word from his memories. "My... friend. He saved me."

"My man also saved me before." After saying that, her head hung low, and her shoulders and back trembled as she occasionally let out one or two weepy sounds. She didn't speak again.

An Zhe held Vance's ID card in a tight grip. From his heart—that place belonging to the human heart—came a stifling feeling.

When he had been only and purely a mushroom, he had never experienced this sort of feeling before.

It was only after the feeling had finally dissipated a little that he found his strength. Following the direction of the distant stream of people, he walked toward the corridor exit.

At the end of the city gate passageway was a row of mechanical gates, and An Zhe selected the one the furthest to the left. When he walked over, a gentle robotic female voice said, "Please produce your ID card and look at the camera."

An Zhe put the card that had belonged to An Ze on the area of the platform to the right of the gate that glowed with white light, then lifted his gaze to look at the black camera in front.

"ID 3261170514. Name: An Ze. Home: Outer City, District 6. Time away from the city: twenty-seven days."

The camera made a slight noise, and the white light turned green.

"Facial recognition passed. Welcome home."

With a ding, the gate lifted, and An Zhe walked out.

The blinding morning sunlight made him squint, and he recovered only thirty seconds later. After the blurry world became clear again, a massive gray city appeared before his eyes.

Around him was a large open area, and the words "buffer zone" were written on the ground in blinding green paint. Up ahead, human creations sprang up from the ground. Tall concrete buildings were everywhere, even more massive than the tallest plants An Zhe had ever seen and seeming like they could topple over at any time. They stood upright, crowding together in overlapping arrangements, and blocked his line of sight. He looked up. Half of the orange sun was hidden behind the tallest building while the other half was exposed; it looked like a drop of diluted blood that was about to drip down the wall.

An Zhe turned back. The people who had come out from the city gate with him had been separated by the mechanical gates, but after passing through they spontaneously clustered together and traveled in the same direction. An Zhe moved forward with them, and after a few hundred steps he rounded a corner. On a sign were the words "Rail Transit," and a train was stopped on the rails. The body of the train read: Entrance - District 1 - Supply Depot 3 - District 5 - District 8 - City Affairs Office - Exit.

He followed the stream of people onto the train, then found a corner of the slightly empty coach to sit down in. In the seats before him were two strapping men who were conversing in low voices.

"Back from Basin 3? You guys sure gambled with your lives out there."

"We lost six."

"Not bad. You break even?"

"The military is still conducting their appraisal. I think I won't ever have to go out and risk my life in the wilderness again."

"Wow."

"We entered a school in Ghost City 441. It was full of mutated plants, so nobody dared to go in." The man laughed. "We went in and pried out three hard drives from the library's reference room. They're priceless treasures. We'll just have to see how valuable the things saved on them are."

An Zhe silently listened. Although he didn't quite understand, he knew that this man in front of him was very happy, so he felt a little happier as well.

He knew that happy people often didn't mind helping others, so he called out, "Sir."

Without even turning back, that man said, "What is it?"

"How do I get to District 6?"

"Transfer to Line 2 at the supply depot."

"Thank you."

Five minutes later, the train began to move, and a robotic voice announced the name of each platform. An Zhe was very unfamiliar with everything. After several setbacks and requests for directions, he finally got onto the Line 2 train at the supply depot, then got off correctly to arrive at District 6.

An Ze's ID number was 3261170514. This string of numbers was not only the proof of his human identity, it also represented his address, which was the outer city's District 6, Building 117, doorplate number 0514.

But not long after he got off the train, while he was attempting to find someone who he could ask for directions, a young boy suddenly grabbed him. "Hello, friend. Welcome. Would you mind getting to know us?"

Before An Zhe could say anything, a piece of white paper was stuffed into his hand. In large, blood-red words, it read: OPPOSE THE ARBITER'S TYRANNY.

He didn't understand the reason for it but didn't ask further either. He only said, "Excuse me, do you know how to get to Building 117?"

The boy said, "You don't mind coming along with us, right?"

"... I don't."

"Then we're comrades now." The boy lifted up the white paper in his own hands, which said in large, red words: ABOLISH THE "ARBITER'S CODE."

They weren't the only two carrying papers. Soon, An Zhe

was pulled into a crowd. There were around forty-odd people, all of whom had very young faces. Each person was either holding up a similar piece of white paper individually or working in tandem with a partner to hold up a long banner. The sentences on the papers and banners were roughly the same.

"We volunteer to bear the cost of genetic examinations."

"Judges are sinners against humanity."

"Dissolve the Trial Court and bring justice for the innocent."

At the same time, the crowd was slowly moving forward, so An Zhe too could only move with it.

The city's roads were very narrow. Sunlight shone down upon the buildings, and the buildings cast irregular shadows upon the ground. On the road, apart from them, there were also quite a few adults walking with their heads down. They occasionally lifted their heads and glanced in the crowd's direction, but then they very quickly looked away.

An Zhe asked, "What are we doing?"

"A silent demonstration," the boy said. "We'll march until the day that the Trial Court is dissolved."

"… Oh."

After walking for approximately half an hour, he once again asked the boy next to him, "Where's Building 117?"

"Up ahead, we're almost there."

Another half an hour passed, and An Zhe asked again, "Where's Building 117?"

"Sorry!" The boy scratched his head. "I forgot about you. We've walked past it, it's back there."

As he spoke, he turned and pointed. "Over there, it's not far away. The building number is written on the side. You can see it right there."

"Thank you," An Zhe said.

"You're welcome."

An Zhe handed the piece of paper to the boy. "I'll return this to you."

"No need!" The boy stuffed the paper back into his arms. "Remember to come back next week! We'll be gathering at Building 1!"

Thus, An Zhe could only put the bloody "OPPOSE THE ARBITER'S TYRANNY" paper together with the gene report the Arbiter himself had shoved at An Zhe. Holding them in his arms, he left this group of strange young humans and walked in the direction that had been pointed out to him.

While walking, he felt that the surrounding environment was gradually becoming familiar as the memories in his mind that had originally belonged to An Ze were awakened. He intuitively made a few turns and arrived at the building labeled "117" without any issues. It was a rectangular building, ten stories high but very wide. He entered Unit 0, and after climbing the quiet and steep stairs to the fifth floor, he entered a dim corridor and found No. 14.

A white seal was stuck to the door. An Zhe gently tore it off, revealing a sensor area underneath. When he put the ID card up to it, the lock sprang open, and he walked in.

It was a very small room. It was even smaller than the cave he used to live in, but it was much brighter and more spacious than the rest area in the armored car. Near the wall was a wooden desk, more than ten old books piled up on it, and sheets of loose-leaf paper and notebooks were stacked together on the other side. The desk faced a single-person bed. There was a nightstand at the head of the bed upon which a water cup, a mirror, and some odds and ends were placed, and a wardrobe slightly taller than the height of a human was shoved up against the foot of the bed.

The window was on the other side of the bed. Its gray curtains were half-open, sunlight shining in and lighting up the quilt that was the same color, and there was a dry fragrance that reminded him of An Ze's scent.

He walked over to the bed, then reached out and removed the palm-sized mirror. The mirror reflected his face.

He looked like An Ze, with soft black hair and eyes that were the same color. They were alike in many places, but there were also some details that weren't the same. In addition, he didn't have An Ze's gentle and calm expression.

Back then, An Ze had said to him, "It's like I've gained a younger brother. How about I give you a name, little mushroom?"

"Is there anything you have a very deep recollection of, little mushroom?"

Only two things were deeply etched into his limited memory: one was the loss of his spore, and the other was something that happened when he was very small—around when he was only about as long as a human's pinky finger.

In the rainy season when the mushrooms were growing, a raindrop falling at an angle had struck his slender stem, snapping him at the waist.

Then, just like any other injured creature, he strove to grow back, to live.

Then after that, he gradually gained some vague consciousness. He had healed.

From then on, he seemed to have become different from his own kind. He could control his own hyphae, move between the jungle and open fields, and perceive the sounds and movements outside. He was a free mushroom.

"Poor little thing." At that time, An Ze had ruffled his hair. "Did it hurt a lot when you snapped in half?"

"I've forgotten."

An Ze had said, "Then I'll call you An Zhe, written with the Chinese character for 'snap.'"

He had said, "Okay."

At this point in his recollection, An Zhe smiled at the mirror.

When the person in the mirror smiled, he seemed to see a shadow of An Ze again.

"Thank you," he said to the mirror.

After putting down the mirror, An Zhe sat down at the desk. What should he do next?

After some thinking, An Zhe held out his left hand and stared at his own fingertips beneath the light.

Snow-white hyphae quietly extended from his fingertips, then consolidated. He picked up the dagger and cut off a small, thin piece of it.

Then he picked it up with his right hand, put it up to his mouth, gently pushed it in, and bit down, for he had decided to investigate the matter of his toxicity.

A soft, sweet, and very tasty flavor—that was his first impression.

In the following second, the entire world began to sway before his eyes.

5

"YOU'RE NOT AN ZE."

THEN HE BECAME LIGHTER, bobbing up and down in the air. The sunlight shining in from the window turned into surging seawater, and the papers and notebooks on the table that were soaked in it became a mass of white.

An Zhe blinked. He didn't feel uncomfortable, only that all of his movements had become very, very slow and uncertain. He couldn't control his own body. It was like he had taken flight, yet also like he was on the verge of falling.

And after that—the world before his eyes gradually darkened, and he completely lost consciousness.

The cold woke him up. After awakening, he discovered that the unbroken backdrop of gray buildings outside the window was immersed in the red-gold glow of the setting sun. Since he had fallen asleep—or rather fainted—at least seven or eight hours had passed. It turned out that the poison in his hyphae made people lethargic.

Unlike the daytime, the temperature in the room was much lower in the evening. An Zhe lay back on the bed and wrapped himself in the quilt, only then recovering his warmth. But after the numbness brought on by the cold disappeared, he felt hungry.

An Zhe preferred to absorb nutrients the way mushrooms did, but on his way here, he didn't find even a single patch of damp soil in the entire base, so he could only eat food. Frowning, he thought that humans were a very troublesome sort of creature.

Fortunately, An Ze's residual memories told him where he should go to eat. The base was divided into eight districts, with Districts 6, 7, and 8 serving as the main residential districts. Here, every building was a community. The first floor was the main hall, where water and food would be provided every day at fixed times. Children sixteen years old and under received free allotments, while adults over sixteen years old needed to swipe their card to pay with the base's currency, the unit of which was the letter R.

The main hall didn't have too many people, perhaps fifty-some visible at a glance. There were only two windows for selling food. One was an edible paste made from the tuber of a certain plant, while the other was... a soup made from the same tuber. Searching his memories, he vaguely recalled that this plant was called "potato."

An Zhe swiped his card to pay.

Mashed potatoes—price 0.5R, balance 9.5R.

Potato soup—price 0.3R, balance 9.2R.

As he stared at the number representing the balance on the card, An Zhe realized that he would be on the edge of starvation in a few days. The feeling was like that of a mushroom taking root in a patch of dry soil, facing death at any given moment.

When he returned to the fifth floor after his meal and spent 0.1R to get water at the communal water room, the feeling became even clearer.

Thus, he now had one more thing to do: find a source of income.

After screwing shut the standard stainless steel bottle's cap, An Zhe held the bottle in his hand and was about to turn around when a voice suddenly rang out behind him.

"An Ze?"

The loud voice, trembling somewhat, echoed in the cramped space.

An Zhe turned around.

Standing in the corridor was a young man with a tall build and handsome face. He looked straight at An Zhe with eyes wide open and lips quivering; it was difficult to decide if his expression was actually joy or shock.

"An Ze?" he called out again. "You've... returned? Didn't you—?"

At those words, he abruptly lost his voice and his complexion turned blue. It was like he didn't know how to continue.

But An Zhe knew what he wanted to say because he knew this person. He was called Josh.

Josh was An Ze's neighbor and friend, and they had grown up together. Sometimes Josh would take care of An Ze, but more often, An Ze would take care of him—those spotty residual memories appeared before An Zhe's eyes.

But his knowledge of Josh didn't all come from An Ze's recollections. When he was a mushroom, he had seen this person before. The combination of what he had seen and An Ze's memories supplied the entire real cause of An Ze's death.

An Ze had been someone who lived off of writing. His work was to write novels, essays, and poems for the people's entertainment and submit them to the *Base Monthly* periodical, and the base would regularly publish these pamphlets. But just three months prior, to conserve the increasingly stretched manpower and resources, the base abolished that department.

Back then—

"An Ze, what are you reading?" Josh asked.

"I want to prepare for the base supply depot's selection exam." An Ze doodled circles on the book with his pen. "I think I'll like the work there, and the pay is good."

But Josh frowned.

"You want to stop being a civilian?" he asked. "The exam is very difficult."

An Ze said, "That's fine."

But Josh's voice became harsher. "An Ze, you've clearly known all this time that I want to be able to go out into the wilderness with you."

An Ze smiled. The tone of his voice was very soft, both like he was indulging this headstrong friend and also like a resigned sigh. "I'm not suited to going outside."

"I'll protect you." Josh held him by the shoulder, and the tone of his voice softened. "I can't leave you. Come with me into the wilderness. We won't go anywhere dangerous."

The fragments in his memories were more or less all like this. At last, in the face of Josh's relentless badgering, An Ze had agreed to go adventuring in the wilderness together with him. Josh was a member of a large mercenary team. Having previously performed some meritorious deeds, he very easily introduced An Ze to the team, where the latter was responsible for the allocation and record-keeping of their materials.

But anything could happen in the wilderness. That day, the team had gotten lost and driven into the fringes of the Abyss. By the time they noticed the unusual abundance of mushrooms there, it was already too late. The monsters of the Abyss wouldn't let slip any food that came to their mouths.

To humans, even the outermost fringes of the Abyss were mortally terrifying. Three of the five armored cars were damaged, and the people of those three cars transferred over to the intact armored cars in a panic. When they were fleeing, An Ze had pushed Josh, allowing him to narrowly escape the attacks from airborne winged monsters, but An Ze conse-quently tripped over the vines on the ground.

Josh had frozen up on the spot for a second. After that second passed, his survival instinct surpassed everything else. Between pulling An Ze up and fleeing with his own life, he chose the latter, gritting his teeth and sprinting forward before the captain pulled him into the armored car—whereas An Ze was watching their figures, having been stabbed through the chest by a monster's bony spur.

The mercenary team promptly began fighting with the monsters using their heaviest firepower, retreating as they fought. The sounds of their activity were so loud that they woke up An Zhe—he had come out to look for his spore, but he had always gone home empty-handed. This time was an exception. Taking advantage of the fierce fighting, he quietly brought An Ze back with him to the depths of the cave.

So now that he was facing Josh, An Zhe had nothing to say. When facing death, the first reaction of any living being was to flee. Josh didn't do anything wrong, but An Zhe didn't like him.

"You... kinda don't seem like yourself." Josh's Adam's apple bobbed hard. "Your wound healed? You escaped from the Abyss?"

An Zhe only looked calmly at him.

"No, you're not An Ze. You aren't human." Josh took an abrupt step backward, his face chalk white. "You're a xenogenic."

"My apologies." An Zhe walked out, brushing past him. "I accidentally ate a poisonous mushroom, so I don't remember who you are."

In a way, he hadn't lied.

With those words, An Zhe ceased paying attention to him and walked straight forward.

For a long time, there were no footsteps behind him. It was only when he swiped his ID card to open the door that Josh hurried over and grabbed his shoulder. "You're really An Ze? But you—"

An Zhe casually picked up the genetic examination report lying on the table and held it out to Josh.

Josh said, "This is…"

An Zhe looked down and discovered that the topmost page read "OPPOSE THE ARBITER'S TYRANNY."

He slowly pulled the paper away. Josh looked at the report.

"You…" He skimmed over it, then looked up at An Zhe. "You really escaped from the Abyss?"

"I was saved," An Zhe said. "I've forgotten the rest."

Josh's hand that was holding the gene report trembled. Then the corners of his mouth tugged upward, revealing a smile as he looked at An Zhe. "I… I was too agitated. I didn't think that you could come back."

He put the gene report on the table and leaned toward An Zhe with a slightly excited expression. Even the muscles at the ends of his eyebrows were twitching. "How much… have you forgotten?"

An Zhe took a step back.

"I've forgotten everything," he said. "Please don't bother me."

"You don't remember who I am either?" Josh lowered his voice a bit. "We grew up together."

"Thank you," An Zhe said. "Can you please get out now?"

"I—" Josh, obviously not expecting that An Zhe would treat him with this kind of attitude, was stunned. He said, "You weren't like this before."

But a moment later, his attitude softened again. "I won't bother you. Have a good rest, and I'll come to see you tomorrow. I'm overjoyed. An Ze, we're the people closest to each other in the world."

An Zhe remained silent up until when Josh turned around and left, softly shutting the door for him.

For Josh to let him off this easily and leave the room, An Zhe thought it was unrealistic, but it was also possible that Josh had fled due to his excessive sense of guilt.

Silence returned to the room. An Zhe slowly leaned against the bed and hugged the pillow, feeling a sadness that was like wispy smoke. This sadness wasn't for himself, but for An Ze.

The promises between humans were more or less this fragile; Josh would no longer be the person closest to An Ze. Once he found his spore, he would return to the Abyss, find that quiet cave, take root next to An Ze's snow-white bones, and spend the rest of his life as a mushroom.

… His spore.

Outside the window, the night was dark, and the aurora fluctuated in the pitch-black skies as usual. An Zhe sat at the table and turned on the desk lamp.

First of all, he had to find a job so he wouldn't starve to death. At the same time, he had to search for information related to his spore, and his only lead was that brass bullet shell.

At that thought, An Zhe anxiously touched his pocket. He was in constant fear of losing it—good, it was still there. He could hide it within his body as a mushroom, but not as a human. It was so small that it seemed able to slip out from his pocket at any given moment.

In the end, An Zhe found a black leather cord from one of the drawers in the room and hung the bullet shell around his neck.

There was a small black device in the drawer as well. He examined its exterior details with great effort, then found some information from his memories at last. This was a communicator, and every person's ID number was their communicator number. Humans used them for long-distance communication, but it was limited to within the base only—because there was no signal outside.

He charged the communicator. Although he didn't need it, this "having power" thing seemed to be able to make humans feel great joy.

After doing so, he finally calmed down and began to examine the desk.

In the notebooks on the table were things An Ze had written. The handwriting was very beautiful. On the side next to the wall stood twenty-odd books, most likely all of which An Ze used to enjoy reading. An Zhe glanced over the titles on the book spines, then reached out and picked up a crudely bound book with a gray cover named *Base Handbook*.

He flipped it open. There was only one sentence on the title page.

Humankind's interests take precedence over all else.

An Zhe unconsciously pursed his lips and continued flipping through it. The second page was the table of contents. The entire handbook was divided into four sections: the base's laws, the base's lifestyle regulations, summaries of the areas' functions, and maps.

An Zhe skipped over the laws section. He knew that he was a law-abiding mushroom, and a law-abiding mushroom would not violate the laws of any species. The lifestyle regulations section explained the work and rest times of the residential areas in detail. Power, water, and food were supplied for an hour starting from 6 a.m. and noon every day. Dinner was supplied at 6 p.m., and power was supplied for a little longer, not getting cut off until 9 p.m. Every residential area was equipped with tall alarm towers, and the alarms were divided into three types: "assembly," "evacuation," and "take shelter." The assembly alarm was a brief high-pitched sound, the evacuation alarm was a wave-like signal, and the take shelter alarm was a shrill wail. The base's residents had to abide by the lifestyle regulations and alarm tower instructions, but they could manage the other aspects of their lives by themselves.

At that point, An Zhe felt slightly confused. He thought that under such regulations, every person only had to lie in their room and come out at fixed times to eat and drink—but he very quickly realized the base's intentions.

Although every person could live how they liked, paying the costs of living in the base was mandatory. To obtain the currency that circulated throughout the base, people had to either find a job or become mercenaries and hand over valuable materials they collected in the wilderness to the base in exchange for payment.

But... in that case, everyone could simply go to the places with the lowest danger levels, grab something at random, and have enough for food and water.

An Zhe kept flipping the pages. The next section was the summaries of the areas' functions.

The first area in this section was called "Supply Depots," and they were numbered 1, 2, and 3. The first two belonged to the military, were constructed at the entrance and exit of the base, and were responsible for the appraisal and exchange of currency and combat preparation materials. Whenever a mercenary team came back from the wilderness, the supply depot workers would calculate the money to be disbursed based on the materials they gathered, and the remaining lethal weaponry and armored cars would be taken into their custody, barred from entering the city. Only when the mercenary team set out again would they be able to apply for their usage once more. The mercenary teams exchanged the currency for the guns, bullets, armor, fuel, and other necessities for exploring the wilderness, and they could even buy different types of armored cars.

Unlike the other two supply depots, Supply Depot 3 was located within the city. It was responsible for the exchange of civilian materials and used the base's currency. There, one could exchange for many goods such as daily necessities, food and ingredients, hard liquor, and electronics, or even carry out housing transactions.

Across from Supply Depot 3 was the "free market." Sometimes, what the mercenary teams obtained from human ruins were not materials the military needed, so they could then bring the goods confirmed to be safe into the city and trade them freely.

At that moment, An Zhe saw a small annotation below.

Note: The free market is not an authorized facility of the base. All actions are taken at your own risk.

Note: Employment and contractual relationships established through the free market are not subject to legal protection by the base. Proceed at your own risk.

There wasn't much else. An Zhe focused on the lone word "employment."

In other words, the free market was also a place where jobs could be provided.

Even further down were the summaries of each residential area. The crowded residential areas were Area 6 and Area 7. The other areas had vacant buildings and very few humans. Area 8 was a centralized shelter with perfect safety facilities.

Past even that was the summary of the Trial Court.

An Zhe recalled the Colonel with the cold green eyes, and his reading speed slowed down greatly as he began to read every single word.

The responsibilities of the Trial Court did not only include identifying xenogenics at the city gate. They also conducted daily patrols in the crowded parts of the city to carry out secondary screenings and eliminate hidden threats. The main patrol points were the areas around the supply depots, but they would also check the residential buildings on occasion—especially the ones with humans exhibiting abnormal behavior or who had been reported.

Strangely, An Zhe once again recalled the words "you'd best be."

If he could, An Zhe hoped that Lu Feng would stay at the city gate forever and that the Arbiter would not need to stoop to coming to the residential buildings.

He continued flipping the pages. The other areas weren't of much relevance to him—such as the City Affairs Office, the City Defense Agency, the main city, and so on. The handbook stated that the base was composed of the outer city, otherwise called the Fortress, and the main city. The main city was where the base's important scientific research and arms facilities were located as well as its energy and political center. Entry was prohibited to all unless one held a special pass or residence permit.

Finally, after glancing over the map of the base, An Zhe closed the book. He realized once more that humans were a different sort of living thing from mushrooms.

The second book he opened was called *Supply Depot Assessment Guidebook*. As soon as he saw its cover, the relevant memories surged to the forefront of his mind, much clearer than his other memories. An Zhe thought that perhaps this meant that going to the supply depot was something very important to An Ze.

Since that was the case, why did he agree to go out into the wilderness with Josh?

He pondered it for a long time. In the end, he thought that An Ze was just that kind of human.

An Ze had missed the exam. This year's supply depot recruitment exam was held fifteen days ago. At that time, he was already a set of white bones.

But it was all right, An Zhe thought. A year from now, when the supply depot recruited people again, he would go give it a try if he was still living in the human base at that time. This way, after returning to the cave, he could tell An Ze what it was like there.

Reading for a long time used up much of his energy. After trying to read two pages of the *Assessment Guidebook*, An Zhe started getting drowsy. In the end, he got into bed and slept. The next morning, in order to avoid running into Josh, he left his room at 4 a.m., then went downstairs to the transportation stop and got onto the train heading toward the supply depot— he wanted to go to the free market across from it to find a job.

It was 7 a.m. when he got off the train, and wisps of white mist still suffused the air. The free market was a large round building with four entrances, and he entered through the closest one.

The smell of liquor invaded his nose.

Set up near the entrance were four long tables where people dressed as mercenaries were playing drinking games and talking loudly. Cups of alcohol sat in front of them, and every so often, someone would ask for a top-up. When that happened, the waiter would pour out a refill, then take out a small device and stick it onto the ID cards the guests held out to charge them.

A burly, dark-skinned mercenary was drinking alone. Upon seeing An Zhe, the mercenary wiggled his eyebrows, grinned, and waved the cup in his hand. "Whatcha looking at, kid? Wanna come over and learn how to drink?"

A short-haired woman next to him promptly elbowed him in the chest. Her voice was husky but brimming with good cheer. "Article 32, minors are not allowed to drink alcohol."

The man said, "If he drinks, then so be it. Or would he be taken away by the Arbiter?"

The woman laughed openly. "Children not yet of age don't know the power of the Arbiter."

"He'll know soon enough."

An Zhe stood nearby, wishing to tell them "I'm not a minor," but while he thought about how to word it, the two of them embraced each other, lips pressed against lips as they became entangled. He realized that nobody genuinely cared about him.

Thus, he shifted his gaze away from that spot and looked somewhere else.

The aroma of potato soup drifted over from the right side of the entrance, but it was much stronger compared to that of the potato soup provided at the main hall on the residential building's first floor and mixed with a pleasant meaty scent. A mercenary had his head in a white plastic soup bowl as he ate his breakfast.

This smell made An Zhe feel a little hungry, for he hadn't eaten breakfast.

Further inside were similar scenes, and a boisterous atmosphere permeated the hall. Apart from the long tables selling food and alcohol, there were also many booths selling clothes, backpacks, and gloves. Even further inside, the stalls selling regular goods decreased in number; a single stall would have many strange odds and ends that An Zhe couldn't recognize.

"Newly unearthed smartphone from Ghost City 511—you can turn it on once it has power." As An Zhe walked, a youth clothed in black and carrying a backpack jumped out in front of him like a monkey. He was short and scrawny, with narrow-set eyes that constantly darted about. The moment he stopped An Zhe, he whipped out a black, rectangular object from his bag and waved it in front of An Zhe. "Wanna take a look? I'll give you a ten percent discount and throw in a free charging cable. You can play games on it."

An Zhe said, "Thank you, but no."

The youth then whipped out a white one from his bag. "How about a different version? The color suits you. It's a new model, you know, the final Apple model from before the Era of

Calamity. They sold for 10,000R back then, but now just 100R is enough."

An Zhe said, "Thank you, but I don't need it."

But that person continued by taking out something else. "You don't need it? You have a cell phone, huh? Do you need a portable charger? When power is out at the base, you can use this to charge. I've sold out of the large capacity ones. This one can only be charged twice, so I'll give you a discount, only 30R."

As An Zhe looked at him, he said honestly, "I don't have money."

The black-clad youth's expression froze. In an instant, he put everything back into his backpack, turned around, and got ready to leave, muttering, "What'd you come to the black market for if you don't have money?"

"Wait," An Zhe called out, stopping him.

He turned his head, but his attitude was extremely negative. "What?"

"I… want to get a job," An Zhe said. "Do you know where I have to go?"

The youth frowned, turned back around, and examined him carefully from head to toe. "… So you came to find work."

An Zhe truthfully replied, "Yes."

"Your natural assets are quite good," the youth said. "Once you have money, remember to come and buy a cell phone from me. I'll be staying at the black market this entire month."

After a moment's silence, An Zhe asked, "Where do I go?"

"Oh, that way." The youth pointed toward one of the corners. "Go down. Third underground floor, ask for the lady boss."

Feeling very grateful, An Zhe smiled at him. "Thank you."

The youth said, "You're good-looking, so find someone reliable. Once you're rich, remember to come find me and buy a cell phone!"

"… Okay," An Zhe replied.

Third underground floor.

Humid—that was An Zhe's first impression of the place. Mushrooms ought to like this type of moisture-laden atmosphere, but the acrid odor that came with the humidity made him frown.

Looking around, An Zhe saw that beneath the dim lighting, it was a honeycomb-like space with a corridor that zigged and zagged. Countless narrow compartments were built into the walls with simple plastic boards. There was no air circulation, and the water vapor condensed into numerous droplets on the plastic boards. The entire space emitted a slight tide-like hum; upon listening carefully, An Zhe realized it was from the aggregation and reverberation of many people speaking softly, mixed with occasional shrieks of laughter.

An Zhe hesitated briefly, then took a few steps forward.

He looked at the small compartments on both sides. The one on the left was empty, but there was a long-haired woman with her head bowed in the one on the right. After hearing his footsteps, she lifted her head to take a look, then bowed it again.

An Zhe continued forward. He heard the sound of dialogue, with the first speaker being female.

"How was the weather in Basin 2?"

"Not bad." This time, it was a low and soft male voice, a bit sticky and drawn out at the end. An Zhe suspected that his nose was clogged. "The weather was very comfortable, but there were too many earthquakes. We experienced three earthquakes in a month. The worst time, they were all outside while I was alone in the car. I had almost assumed that they couldn't make it back."

The female voice laughed. "If they couldn't make it back, then drive the car away."

"That team from the time before last, the captain said he'd teach me to drive, but it was all just sweet talk. He said next time he'd still bring me along, but that was sweet talk too. I accompanied them for a month for only 300R altogether. Is that still costly?"

"Don't take the mercenaries' words seriously," a woman said. "You haven't gotten used to being tricked yet?"

An Zhe stopped walking.

—He recalled Hosen's face and greedy, covetous eyes and suddenly knew what was going on with the work on the third underground floor.

Along with the sentence in the *Base Handbook*: Employment and contractual relationships established through the free market are not subject to legal protection by the base. Proceed at your own risk.

He didn't want to bear these consequences.

An Zhe silently planned to leave, but just as he turned around, he unexpectedly collided into a soft body.

"Oh," a high-pitched female voice said. "Little darling, is this your first time here?"

The shadow that the words "little darling" cast over him was too dark. An Zhe reflexively took two steps back.

Before him was a tall woman with honey-colored skin, upturned blue eyes, and long brown hair that ended in ringlets. She was smiling at him.

"Are you buying someone? Or selling yourself?" the woman asked, smiling as she blew into his ear.

"Neither." An Zhe took another step back and bumped into plastic board. "I went the wrong way."

"Went the wrong way?" the woman asked. "The second floor is the gambling den. You wanted to go there?"

She was holding a cigarette between the fingers of her right hand. After putting it up to her red lips and taking a drag, she said with a smile, "Take care to not lose yourself."

An Zhe looked around, but the woman had forced him into a

corner, so he couldn't get away. This gorgeous-looking human was even more difficult to deal with than the monsters of the Abyss.

"Don't be scared." She blew out a mouthful of snow-white smoke. "I'm not going to eat you."

An Zhe asked, "Then can you please let me leave?"

The woman smiled again.

"Leave?" She raised her eyebrows. "Only people who are driven into a corner come to the third floor. If you leave, where else can you go?"

As she spoke, she took him by the shoulder and pulled him forward. "Are you scared of this place? You don't need to be here. I'll give you a large room."

"Thank you," An Zhe said with his head down. "But I really did go the wrong way."

"Hm?"

"I just want to find a regular job," he said. "Then someone told me to come to the third underground floor."

"Only the aboveground floor of the black market is presentable." After listening to his words, the woman blinked, the look in her eyes just like drifting smoke. "You don't even know that?"

An Zhe said, "I know now."

He also learned that the "free market" in the *Base Handbook* was known informally as the black market.

"The laws of the base don't protect the black market." The woman smoked as she leaned against the wall, no longer pressing An Zhe into the corner but rather leaving a space.

An Zhe assumed it was a signal that she was going to let him out, but just as he took a step forward, he saw two tall men dressed in black step out from behind her, one on the left and one on the right, sealing off all possible paths.

"Once they've come to the third floor, nobody can leave."

The woman's voice was no longer syrupy-sweet and charming, but suffused with frost. "But you're rather lucky."

An Zhe lifted his head to look at her.

"I'll give you one chance," she said. "Mr. Shaw's workshop is lacking manpower. If he wants you, you'll go with him. If he doesn't want you—"

Her words stopped mid-sentence, and she turned to walk in a certain direction. "Come."

An Zhe stood in place and thought for three seconds, then walked deeper inside with her.

The compartments were so densely packed together that it was like he was walking in a maze built from honeycomb, with the lighting getting dimmer and dimmer.

Finally, at the end of this space, a door appeared on the gray wall.

The woman knocked on the door. "Mr. Shaw, I have business to discuss with you."

With a creak, the door opened.

Inside was an old man with a head of snow-white hair and dressed in black from head to toe, a bow tie around his neck. He examined the woman with narrowed eyes. "Doussay, how rare of you to visit."

With a smile, the woman finished smoking her cigarette and stubbed it out on the wall. "I was looking for you for something."

"How big is the business?" The man called "Mr. Shaw" looked at her, then turned to look at An Zhe.

The woman—Doussay—rested her elbow on An Zhe's shoulder. "Not big, just difficult. I feared you wouldn't agree, so I specially brought you a greeting gift—I heard your apprentice drank himself to death and that you're looking for the next one. If female, you think they're ugly. If male, they're usually clumsy. Take a look at this kid of mine."

Mr. Shaw's gray-blue eyes rolled, landing on An Zhe. "Looks obedient."

"He actually is obedient." Doussay tossed her hair. "I thought you'd like him as soon as I laid eyes on him, Mr. Shaw."

Mr. Shaw smiled.

Then he said to An Zhe, "Hold out your hand, let me take a look."

An Zhe held out a hand. His fingers were slim and white with a dusting of pink.

"Doussay, where'd you get him from?" Mr. Shaw asked. "How could this type of kid be willing to come to the third floor?"

"I tricked him here," Doussay replied.

An Zhe was speechless.

Then he heard Mr. Shaw say to him, "Make a fist, but slowly."

An Zhe slowly curled his fingers.

"Once more, even slower."

An Zhe slowed down.

"Even slower."

In the end, An Zhe had slowed down so much that his movements were difficult to detect with the naked eye. Although he didn't know why Mr. Shaw wanted this, it was no challenge for him. When he was in mushroom form, he had to control thousands upon thousands of minute hyphae at the same time, whereas now he only had five human fingers.

At last, even Doussay was drawn in.

"Mr. Shaw, you've picked up a treasure," she said, lighting up another cigarette. "His hands are even more steady than your last apprentice's."

As Mr. Shaw watched his hand, he let out a laugh and said, "Let me borrow him for a few days. If he's useful, I'll keep him."

Doussay said, "You have to give the kid a wage."

"Deal," Mr. Shaw replied.

An Zhe frowned. He did need a wage, but upon hearing the word "useful," he felt that he was in a bit of danger.

"Don't be scared. Although Mr. Shaw truly isn't a good person"—Doussay, seeming to have seen through his worries, patted him on the shoulder—"his crafts are very expensive."

"I'm not a good person?" Mr. Shaw let out a scornful laugh. "I'm the greatest person in the base."

With those words, he turned toward An Zhe. "You go ahead and look around the shop. I have something to discuss with this madwoman."

An Zhe was the best at being obedient. He turned his head to look at the nearest shelf and saw some strangely shaped bottles, filled with liquids or solids, upon which naked human bodies were printed. Further inside were some books with similar-looking covers—these, he knew about. A large part of the reason why the department An Ze used to contribute to had collapsed was that nobody cared about the reading materials the base published, whereas the pornographic reading materials that circulated out of the black market were in high demand.

Below the shelf was a transparent glass window filled with cigarettes, and the other drawer right next to it contained many USB drives.

At that moment, the sound of conversation drifted over from where Mr. Shaw was.

"The kid's good. For you to have given me such a large gift when you've always been so stingy, the business you wish to discuss with me must be extraordinary." The sound of a lighter came from around Mr. Shaw, and the concentration of the smoke in the room doubled.

"The kid was just picked up at random." Doussay giggled. "The thing I wanted to request you to make, Mr. Shaw, is indeed not simple."

"Anything's fine," Mr. Shaw said in a careless tone. "As long as you have enough money."

"You might not dare to make it," Doussay drawled.

"If you put up more money, I'll dare to," Mr. Shaw replied.

With a scoff of laughter, Doussay spoke two words.

"The Arbiter," she said. "Do you dare to make him, Mr. Shaw?"

An Zhe was stunned. He didn't know how the words "the Arbiter" could be connected to these two people in the black market.

Mr. Shaw also went silent.

In the end, he said, "I only make dead people and not living ones lest I attract trouble, and you want to attract the biggest trouble to me."

"To tell you the truth, I have a friend who is crazy about the Colonel and has to have him," Doussay said. "You may also know that no living person dares to get within three meters of the Arbiter. There's no other choice besides buying a fake from you. It'll just be kept at home, so it definitely won't cause problems. As for the price, it's up to you."

Mr. Shaw smiled but didn't speak.

At the same time, An Zhe slowly moved deeper into the shop.

His feet came to a standstill, for he had kicked something.

He looked down and saw a white hand lying on the concrete floor all by itself. Based on its condition, it had just been severed, but the place where it had been severed was smooth and clean, with no blood in sight.

An Zhe crouched down and poked the hand's skin. It was very soft, like a human hand, but it wasn't actually one.

It was a fake hand.

He stopped exploring and stood up.

With that motion, he met the gaze of a person standing in the glass display window. In the dim lighting, a pair of black eyes stared straight at him. Half of the person's body was hidden in the darkness, which was a bit startling.

An Zhe looked at him for a while. Three minutes later, he still hadn't seen this person breathe at all.

Perhaps, just like that fake hand, this was a fake human, he thought.

"Startled?" Mr. Shaw's voice suddenly rang out from behind him.

"I'm okay," An Zhe said.

Mr. Shaw asked, "Does it look real?"

"It does," An Zhe said.

He heard Mr. Shaw laugh in that raspy voice of his before pressing a switch on one side. The lighting in the area became much brighter.

An Zhe finally saw the entirety of the man in the glass display window. He was dressed in black and had a tall and trim physique along with clean-cut and handsome facial features. The light shone upon his face, causing a thin layer of white shimmer to reflect off it and arbitrarily adding a slight chill.

"Have you heard of Hubbard, mercenary team AR137's leader?" Mr. Shaw asked.

An Zhe didn't speak. In the room, there was only the sound of Mr. Shaw's voice. "One of the most powerful mercenaries. When he brings his team to places with five-star danger levels, it's just like child's play. He has money, right?"

An Zhe made an affirmative sound in response.

He knew that the materials brought back from the outside could be exchanged for the base's currency at the military's supply depots, so those powerful mercenaries did not lack for money.

Mr. Shaw pointed to the person standing in the display window. "This is his vice-captain. They grew up together, then became mercenaries together after coming of age. For more than twenty years, they had a friendship where they'd give their lives for each other. Last time they went out into the wilderness, he died without leaving behind even a single body part. What a tragedy."

With those words, Mr. Shaw let out a snort of laughter. "Three months after this person died, Hubbard came to me. Even his spirit was gone. He spent more than half of his wealth to buy this person and asked me to not make a mistake with even a single hair on his head."

"As for me, I definitely don't dare to make mistakes. Apart from not being alive, everything else is the same." Mr. Shaw sighed. "After all, they'll have to live the rest of their lives while looking at this fake person."

"When I made these before, it was for people to use for pleasure, the inflatable kind. Later, everyone thought the ones I made looked like living people—the easier it is for people to die outside, the easier it is for people to go crazy, so my crafts became valuable." Mr. Shaw patted him on the shoulder. "Study hard under me, and in ten years, you'll have more money than any mercenary."

As An Zhe looked at Mr. Shaw, he recalled his previous conversation with Doussay and asked, "Then are you going to make the Arbiter?"

"Yes, why not?" Mr. Shaw smiled. "The mighty Arbiter is so busy killing people that he can't be bothered to care about this kind of crap."

6

"FEAR OF YOU."

"MR. HUBBARD, it's me, Scott Shaw."

When Mr. Shaw sent the message to Hubbard, An Zhe was holding a head and practicing how to implant eyebrows.

The heated needle pricked a tiny hole in the silicone rubber skin into which a fiber simulating human hair was then planted. Once the softened silicone rubber cooled again, the eyebrow hair would be securely rooted in the doll's skin. Mr. Shaw's eyes had gone bad, so it was very difficult for him to do this kind of work well again; An Zhe guessed that this was one of the reasons why he was anxious to find an apprentice.

After putting down the communicator, Scott Shaw took the mannequin out of the display and placed it on a chair in the middle of the room. All of the mannequin's joints could rotate easily. He crossed its legs, rested its hands on its elbows, and finally twisted its head so that it was slightly bowed. The light cast shadows as it passed through the eyelashes. It was a commanding, yet slightly melancholy posture.

An Zhe lifted his head to look in that direction. The dim lighting cast uneven shadows on the mannequin's face, neutralizing all the subtle differences between silicone rubber and human skin. It seemed entirely like a silent living person.

The excessive silence—the display window and containers—the things that may be considered obscene to humans also became strange in this atmosphere.

The sound of a door being pushed open broke the strange atmosphere. White light from outside shone in, lighting up half of the mannequin's body. Squinting, An Zhe looked at the man who appeared in the doorway.

Lit up from behind, he had a tall figure, shoulder-length curly black hair, brown eyes, and chilly facial features. An Zhe could imagine what he looked like walking around in the wilderness with a gun in his hand.

An Zhe waited for him to enter, but he only stood in the doorway. With his gaze resting on the mannequin in the middle of the room, he didn't move at all for a long time, as if he had become a mannequin himself.

It wasn't until Mr. Shaw coughed and said "please come in" that the man appeared to wake up from a dream and moved a bit. He strode into the room, but when he came close to the mannequin, he abruptly slowed down. An Zhe watched him move to touch the mannequin's face, but his fingers hung in the air without making contact for a long time. In the quiet room, there were only the sounds of this man's very soft, trembling breaths. Perhaps there was a butterfly perched on the mannequin's eyelashes that he was afraid to disturb.

In the end, he withdrew his right hand and said, while looking steadily at the doll, "Thank you."

"Don't thank me." Mr. Shaw walked over, looking at Hubbard with his gray-blue eyes. "I have to thank you, Mr. Hubbard, for giving me sufficient data."

Hubbard smiled, but his eyes were still downcast.

Mr. Shaw pointed to a human-sized case nearby. "Shall I?"

"I'll do it."

Hubbard's fingers finally landed on the mannequin's shoulder. He slowly leaned down, picked up the mannequin in his arms, and put it into the case.

Standing to one side, Mr. Shaw said, "I didn't know you were such a sentimental person, Captain Hubbard."

"There were some things I didn't get to say in time." As Hubbard knelt on one knee, he slowly closed the lid, and the knuckles of his fingers that were pressed against the lid turned white. A long time passed before he got back up.

Mr. Shaw crossed his arms. "The doll needs maintenance every two months. When the time comes, just deliver it here. If there are any new techniques, I'll use them."

Hubbard said, "You never run a losing business, Scott Shaw."

Mr. Shaw laughed happily.

"Captain Hubbard is infinitely resourceful. I'm no good," he said.

"What do you want?" Hubbard asked.

"I received a big order a few days ago. That person's data isn't easy to find, so I wanted to request your help."

"There's data that you can't get, Mr. Shaw?" Hubbard asked.

Mr. Shaw grinned, then lifted his arm and made a shooting gesture at Hubbard.

Hubbard's lips curled up in a smile, and he turned around and walked to the doorway while pulling the case's handle.

"Please wait," An Zhe blurted out.

Hubbard turned back.

An Zhe quickly walked over to him, undid the first button of his shirt, and took out the bullet case hanging from his neck.

"Mister," he said, "do you know where this is from?"

Without saying anything, Hubbard took the brass bullet shell, then turned it over to examine it beneath the light.

An Zhe's heart thumped hard.

"This model can't be found in the supply depots or the black market." A minute later, Hubbard let go, and the bullet shell dropped back down to An Zhe's chest. Hubbard turned and left, leaving only one sentence behind.

"It's the military's."

His figure receded into the distance. An Zhe put a hand to his chest and held the bullet shell, slightly lost in thought.

In the quiet room, Mr. Shaw let out a laugh.

"Since Hubbard said it's military issue, it definitely is." He closed the door, and his eyes narrowed into a squint as he smiled. "What, did you get into bed with someone from the military? The scope of Doussay's business is really broad."

An Zhe slowly shook his head.

If it was the military's, what should he do?

"Tsk," Mr. Shaw said. "Have you lost your spirit too?"

An Zhe said, "I want to find its owner."

"What, did this person not pay you?"

An Zhe felt that Mr. Shaw's way of thinking was very odd.

He explained, "That's not it."

"If it's the military's, people from the military will definitely be able to recognize its type. I'll teach you a way," Mr. Shaw said with sincerity.

"What way?" An Zhe asked.

Mr. Shaw said, "You can't reach them in the main city or the wilderness. Within the outer city, the City Defense Agency and the Trial Court are both military territories. Go wander around there in the middle of the night and seduce one. Although the military is very strict, it's inevitable that there will be members with corrupt morals."

An Zhe was speechless.

He thought for a while, then asked, "Which people from the military will go out into the wilderness?"

Mr. Shaw flicked him on the forehead without warning. "Who do you think drew the map of the wilderness?"

Having been hurt, An Zhe bit his lip.

"You're actually feeling wronged?" Mr. Shaw said. "Even the Arbiter is gone from the base for almost half a year every year. What do you think? All members of the military go out there."

With nothing left to say, An Zhe lowered his head and continued to implant eyebrows. He realized that he may have to stay at the base for a very long time.

A day of implanting eyebrows ended. Very satisfied, Mr. Shaw let An Zhe off work.

An Zhe wanted to drink the potato soup from the entrance of the black market's first floor. Today was his third day working for Mr. Shaw. Mr. Shaw paid him a month's worth of wages in advance, so his ID card now had 60R.

But right as he went to the aboveground floor, he suddenly felt that something was clearly amiss—the previous bustle was gone, everyone looked to be in a hurry, and there were few people near the exits.

He was a bit confused, but the temptation of the potato soup was even greater, so he still walked over.

Just as he got close to the potato soup, An Zhe's body suddenly froze up.

He stood motionless for a second, then turned around and retraced his steps.

"Get back here." A voice traveled over, as cold as the icy snow on a mountain peak.

Resigning himself to his misfortune, An Zhe turned around again, took a few steps forward, and met the Arbiter at the doorway.

The Arbiter did not come alone. Next to him were three young-looking Judges in simple clothes.

He had run right into the Trial Court's daily city patrol.

He heard Lu Feng say, "Stiffness in body movements, moving to evade. Mark one point."

The young Judges behind him were holding pens and paper.

Following his voice, they carefully looked at An Zhe, then lowered their heads and scribbled something down on their papers.

An Zhe looked in their direction but ran straight into Lu Feng's gaze, and he promptly averted his eyes.

"Avoidant gaze. Mark one point." Lu Feng's voice didn't change whatsoever, and the young Judges behind him continued to take notes.

An Zhe felt that this scene was a little similar. After some thought, he confirmed that the mighty Arbiter was not simply performing his patrol responsibilities. He was training newcomers, just like Mr. Shaw training his apprentice. But Lu Feng was obviously not as good at patient guidance as Mr. Shaw. With his brusque instructions, he did not count as a qualified supervisor.

He awaited the next point deduction.

But he discovered that although Lu Feng's instructions were very brusque, his attitude could not be considered half-hearted, for he began to quiz them. "The results?"

"Yes, Colonel," one of the young Judges said. "All biological signs indicate that the person being tried is human."

"The reason for the indications of abnormality?"

"Fear of you."

The corners of Lu Feng's lips curved up.

It was the first time An Zhe had seen Lu Feng smile, although they had only met once, and although the smile was nigh imperceptible.

But within this nigh imperceptible smile, An Zhe could still see that the Arbiter wanted something from him today.

After that tiny smile disappeared, Lu Feng went back to his expressionless self. Only his slender and cold white fingers played with the jet-black gun, the motions filled with danger.

An Zhe tentatively asked, "May I go now?"

Expressionless, Lu Feng asked, "What are you doing here?"

An Zhe replied honestly, "I work here."

"The first floor or second floor?"

"... The third floor."

"Oh."

Following that was another long silence until the scratching noises of the young Judges' note-taking stopped. Then he said, "There are no abnormalities in the verbal interrogation, proving the judgment that the person being tried is human."

An Zhe saw Lu Feng cast a flat look in the direction of that young Judge—but no matter how he looked at it, it didn't seem like an expression of approval.

He asked once again, "May—"

"You may go now."

"Thank you." An Zhe swiftly turned around and went deeper inside from the entrance to sit at the shop selling potato soup. He truly did want to drink it very much today.

The price of the potato soup the base supplied at the residential area was 0.3R, while the price here was 1R. The differences between the two were very clear. Here, the thickness of the soup was at least three times greater. Apart from the potatoes that had been nearly boiled until they fell apart, fine bits of ground pork had also been added into the soup, with perhaps a bit of milk as well. The fresh and sweet aroma of protein drifted through the air.

The spoon was white. An Zhe took it in hand, scooped up a mouthful of soup, blew away the white steam, then put it up to his mouth and swallowed.

Within the steam that wafted into his face, he squinted, feeling very satisfied—if the figure of the Arbiter was not in his peripheral vision, it would have been even better.

An Zhe ate very slowly but very earnestly and very quietly, making no noise at all. Approximately twenty minutes later, he finished eating and began to adjust his mentality, preparing to pass by the mighty Arbiter and leave this place.

At the moment he left his seat and turned toward the doorway, there came a harsh beeping sound—Lu Feng pressed down on his communicator.

When An Zhe passed by him, he only heard Lu Feng coldly say one word into the communicator.

"Trash."

An Zhe jumped out of fright, then increased his pace and left the black market.

It was currently evening. The sun had already set, the western sky was a boundless expanse of gray-blue, and the wind had begun turning cold. In two hours, the base would cut off the power. The supply depot across from the black market had also reached closing time and was spitting out a continuous stream of people.

The buildings of the supply depot, the black market, and the train station formed a triangle, and in the middle was a spacious public square. At this moment, people coming from all directions were swarming the public square like migrating ants and flowing toward the train station.

The trains ran from 6 a.m. to 8 p.m., one per hour and always on time.

When the time on the timetable approached, a slight roaring sound traveled from afar and gradually became louder. After a short and violent shudder, the train stopped on the rails like a silvery-white snake. On one side, a dozen or so coach doors slid open, and some of the people inside poured out. Among them were those who had come from other parts of the city back to their own residential areas and those who had just returned from the wilderness.

At that very moment, the sound of a lovely, robotic female voice was broadcast from the arrival area. "To all passengers, a mechanical failure has occurred. Please immediately deboard and wait. Passengers waiting for the train, please do not board for the time being. Please spread out and wait."

As the robotic instructions played on repeat, the people who heard them were initially puzzled and began moving at a pace neither fast nor slow. However, some people's expressions drastically changed, and they yanked at their peers to swiftly get up from their seats, squeeze their way off the coach, and sprint away. These movements affected the rest of them, and no more than three minutes had gone by before the frightened atmosphere spread throughout the entire train station and everyone started running toward the public square.

An Zhe, who had been waiting to get onto the train, was suddenly caught up in a tumultuous crowd. Although he didn't know what happened, he knew the rules of communal human life, and he turned around on the spot with the intent to spread out along with the rest of the crowd.

But the crowd pushed and shoved, causing him to stumble, and someone bumped into him from behind. The sound of high heels tapping on the ground rang out. An Zhe turned his head, smelling a familiar scent, and discovered that it was Doussay, the Madam D. of the third underground floor. It looked like she had just gotten off the train. Their eyes met, and Doussay recognized him as well. In a move that seemed unconscious, she promptly seized his wrist and pulled him along as they ran.

In the public square, the sounds of people falling and the screams they let out when they were trampled mixed together. On the other hand, Doussay took him through the crowd as if she had experienced this thousands of times before until they had come to the forefront with the people who had run the fastest to the edge of the public square—where they stopped.

Black light armored cars were parked in a neat line at the edge of the public square, one car every ten to twenty meters, and there were silver shield emblems on the car bodies. After reading the *Base Handbook*, An Zhe knew that this represented the City Defense Agency, the full name of which was the Base Outer City Defense Agency. Soldiers carrying loaded guns were getting out of the cars and sealing off all the exits.

An Zhe still didn't know what had happened. He was a bit out of breath from having run too fast. Nearby, Doussay bent over and violently gasped for breath, coughing a few times.

An Zhe patted her on the shoulder, and Doussay seemed to manage to recover only after approximately half a minute passed. The public square was still a scene of chaos, for people running like they were fleeing for their lives came to the edge of the public square and were stopped by the human wall consisting of the City Defense Agency's soldiers.

An Zhe helped Doussay over to a corner with slightly fewer people.

He asked, "What's the matter with them?"

"This sort of thing used to happen often." Doussay straightened up and looked at the crowd in the public square, saying, "A xenogenic sneaked in."

After taking a breath, she continued, "There must have been a xenogenic on the train. It'd take too much time to get onto the train and investigate. When the xenogenic attack starts, it'd be too late to kill it and several coaches of people will die. Spreading out makes investigation easier."

"This sort of thing hasn't happened in a long time," she said. "The Arbiter didn't recognize it?"

"He was on patrol today," An Zhe said.

Not only that, he heard Lu Feng receive a communication and coldly rebuke someone with the word "trash." Come to think of it, it must have been that he had received the news of a xenogenic sneaking into the base.

An Zhe felt the hand she was holding him with tremble slightly.

"He's here?" she asked.

He made an affirmative sound.

As if confirming his words, a dull "bang" sounded and a bright white streak of light lit up in the air. The streak of light had come shooting down from high above, resembling a bolt of blinding lightning as it instantly sliced through the evening sky and landed right on the shoulder of a person not far in front of An Zhe and Doussay.

An Zhe whipped his head around to look at the streak of light's origin point and saw that on top of the light gray main body of the black market building, looking down from the peak, was a tall and lean figure. It was Lu Feng, clad in a black uniform. At that moment, he was slowly putting down the black weapon in his right hand. In his left hand was a pair of binoculars, which he handed to one side, and the young Judge following him accepted it.

"Position has been marked by the magnesium light bullet!" In the following moment, a terse order came from the direction of the City Defense Agency's troops. "Ready!"

Just as the voice finished speaking, a sharp sound came from an armored vehicle that was extremely close by, and a harsh scream rang out in the public square. An incendiary shell trailing thick smoke had been fired at the spot marked earlier by the streak of light from the magnesium light bullet.

Everything happened in an instant.

The acrid smell of burning traveled over. Amidst the crowd, one person fell heavily to the ground, and smoke emanated from his body with a hissing sound. The sound of his shrill cries instantly resounded through the entire public square.

An Zhe suddenly felt Doussay's grip around his hand tighten.

"That person was sitting right behind me," she said.

"But he didn't attack anyone. I'm fine." She seemed to sigh in relief. "That was a white phosphorus shell... He should be completely dead."

She lifted her head to look at the top of the black market building.

Lu Feng's figure had already disappeared from the roof, but she still kept looking in that direction. An Zhe looked at her. In the twilight, Madam D.'s attractive, mature face suddenly showed an unusual tranquility.

A minute later, the screams near them gradually weakened. On the open space left from people spontaneously backing away, the blackened and twisted limbs had stopped convulsing and struggling, no longer moving at all. The other people in the public square seemed to all sigh in relief, but the City Defense Agency's blockade did not loosen up at all.

"Five years ago, the Colonel saved me once." An Zhe suddenly heard Doussay speak up. "At the city entrance. It was about the same as right now."

He didn't say anything, feeling the atmosphere gradually calm down. That day at the city gate, he understood why some people bitterly hated Lu Feng. Today, he also understood why some people didn't.

Three minutes later, the soldiers of the City Defense Agency forced open a path in the crowd, and Lu Feng swiftly walked over to the four bodies with his men in tow. Because of their location, An Zhe and Doussay were very close by.

He put on snow-white gloves, got down on one knee, pulled aside the human body in the very middle, and said curtly, "Knife."

The Judge next to him handed over a shining dagger.

Then he saw Lu Feng expressionlessly cut open the corpse's abdomen. The blackened body gave off an acrid smell. However, the interior revealed after the abdomen was opened didn't have the organs that humans ought to have, but rather small and plentiful yellowish and translucent things, thousands upon thousands of them tightly packed together.

Striving to look, An Zhe felt that they resembled insect

larvae—something akin to spiders, and they were still wriggling slightly.

He saw Lu Feng frown, and the knife in his hand neatly sliced upward to cut open the body's entire esophagus and throat.

Similar things continuously fell out.

"Parasitic species, high degree of proliferation possible." Lu Feng stood up, then took off his gloves and dropped them on the body. A Judge promptly handed him a fresh pair.

"All personnel, investigate," he said.

Doussay's entire body went soft, and she fell forward.

An Zhe abruptly recalled what she had said a few minutes ago.

She had said that that person was sitting right behind her.

He tried hard to prop Doussay up, but her motions were too big, and Lu Feng had already looked in their direction.

Lu Feng's eyes stopped on her face. Following his gaze, An Zhe looked there as well.

In the chaos earlier, he hadn't carefully looked at her face, but now that he was taking a closer look—on her forehead, there was a small blister-like thing emitting a crystalline light, and something inside of it was wriggling slightly.

"I..." As if she felt something, Doussay slowly reached up to touch that spot. Trembling, she stared at Lu Feng, and two streams of tears fell as she took a few steps toward him.

This was the first time An Zhe had seen such an expression in a human's eyes. He couldn't tell if Doussay's expression was one of love or hate. Perhaps the majority of it was despair.

A gunshot rang out.

She fell forward, and An Zhe wasn't able to grab onto her. After a dull sound, the human's body landed on the ground.

At that moment, An Zhe was only a short distance away from Lu Feng, and he met the other's gaze.

That pair of cold green eyes, the eyes that seemed like they had nothing—

Lu Feng suddenly reached out a hand toward him.

An Zhe shrank away.

But the Arbiter didn't move to pull the trigger. That wasn't the hand holding the gun. His fingers landed on the side of An Zhe's face and rested there for a moment. An Zhe recalled that when Doussay fell, some of her blood had splashed onto his face. It was warm at first, but it had very quickly turned cold.

The cold liquid was wiped away, leaving a smudge of red on the snow-white gloves, and the warm sensation of the touch lingered briefly on his cheek.

A slight shudder ran through An Zhe's body, and he closed his eyes.

Perhaps it was three seconds, or perhaps it was four. Lu Feng's fingers left his face, and that hint of warmth faded almost instantly in the evening wind before it swiftly disappeared altogether.

An Zhe opened his eyes again and saw his departing figure, which was identical to what he saw that day at the base's city gate.

At that moment, a bright white light suddenly came to life in the public square.

An Zhe squinted. In his field of vision, Lu Feng's figure was blurry. Once his vision cleared up again, that black figure had already been lost in the vast sea of people. Soldiers from the City Defense Agency came forward and carried away Doussay's body. A honey-like luster flowed along her long, brown hair beneath the lamplight. With her eyes closed, her expression looked very peaceful. What she had been thinking in her final moments, An Zhe didn't know. Perhaps he would never know.

Many people were looking in his direction. When the City Defense Agency soldiers had gone away, they began to whisper amongst themselves. An Zhe had good hearing, so he was able to catch a few snippets of conversation. Many people knew this mistress of the black market's third underground floor. Some of them mourned the departure of a beautiful woman, while a greater number of them feared being infected by monsters themselves.

Soon, the robotic female voice began giving instructions.

"Everyone, please spread out and wait in place. In thirty minutes, the Trial Court will begin inspecting people one at a time."

The voice was very lovely, but nobody was in the state of mind to appreciate it. The people first looked around at each other briefly, then quickly came to the realization that right now, nobody knew whether the people next to them were truly human. The crowd of people began squirming like a colony of ants. Every single person tried to separate from the people near them as best they could, no matter if they knew them or not. In the end, the chaotic crowd turned into a scattered grid. An Zhe stood at the very edge, next to the bloodstain Doussay had left behind. His gaze swept over the fearful, trembling expressions on the nearby humans' faces. Fundamentally, there were no differences between the human base and the Abyss.

A shrill voice suddenly rang out from somewhere in the distance. "There's something on his face!"

It was followed by the sound of movements. It seemed that some people had begun to fight, which was then followed by a noisy quarrel. Thirty seconds later, a gunshot ended it all.

A deathly silence. The deathly silent atmosphere shrouded the public square. Even the sound of breathing had quieted down. If someone had told An Zhe right now that where he was currently was actually a cemetery and that the surrounding humans were actually a multitude of gravestones, he would not have doubted the authenticity of the statement.

He looked around, wishing to know where Lu Feng was, but there were too many people, so he couldn't find him. In the end,

An Zhe retracted his gaze and looked at the marble floor, which appeared pale in the light.

Suddenly, his eyes stopped moving.

Around five meters in front of him, at a man's foot, there was a brassy glimmer.

His first thought was that the bullet shell hanging around his neck had fallen off, so he swiftly felt around his shirt collar. Through the layer of his shirt, the little cylindrical object pressed against his hand—he hadn't lost it.

Staring at the ground, he took a few steps forward—the man next to him let out a curse and pulled away.

"I'm sorry," An Zhe said. "I dropped something."

After passing by a few people and taking a few steps, he came to that place, crouched down, and picked up a brassy, cylindrical bullet shell.

The moment he held it, his hand trembled slightly.

Its weight, decorative pattern, and size were all very, very familiar. As he held the bullet shell, he was unable to discern any difference between it and the one hanging from his neck.

With his heart giving a few violent thumps, he tightened his grip around the bullet shell and stood up.

He thought back to five minutes ago, when Doussay touched the blister infected by bugs on her forehead and realized that she couldn't possibly live, that she was undoubtedly going to be executed by the Arbiter. But while she was afraid, she also seemed to want to get closer to the Arbiter, so she had taken a few steps in his direction. But before she could reach Lu Feng as she had wished, the bullet had already pierced through her body.

At that time, where had Lu Feng been standing?

An Zhe looked at the dark bloodstain on the ground nearby. At that time, Lu Feng had been standing where he was currently standing, or not far away, when he had opened fire.

What was a bullet shell? It was the jacket of a bullet, he

knew. There was similar knowledge in An Ze's memories. When the bullet leaves the chamber and is fired, the bullet shell will be ejected in the other direction and land on the ground.

There was no doubt that this bullet shell he picked up belonged to Lu Feng, and Lu Feng was the master of the Trial Court. Then what about the identical bullet shell he picked up in the wilderness where he had lost his spore? Was it also connected to the Trial Court?

An inexpressible sensation welled up in An Zhe's heart, and he felt a fear that could be precisely described. If his spore and the Trial Court were connected, then he could only imagine how difficult it would be to get back his spore. He couldn't directly ask, because asking about the spore was tantamount to admitting that he was a mushroom.

While he was in the midst of such fanciful thoughts, thirty minutes passed. The robotic female voice rang out again. "The buffer time has ended. Please line up in an orderly fashion and accept the infection inspection. After passing the inspection, please leave."

After the order was broadcast on repeat a few times, a large light lit up across from the public square, and people began to slowly move in that direction to be examined.

The people standing next to An Zhe seemed to be a father-and-son pair—they seemed to be father and son, because one of them was slightly older and growing a beard, while the other was a thirteen- or fourteen-year-old boy.

He heard the boy ask, "Why do we have to wait thirty minutes?"

"It's not like the Arbiter is a machine who can tell that you've been infected as soon as you've been bitten by a bug," his father said in a low voice. "The Trial Court says that they're able to pass judgment after thirty minutes have passed. You haven't gone to the city gate. At the gate, there is also a thirty-minute wait in line."

"Oh," the boy said.

But then he asked, "So how exactly do they tell?"

"Don't ask me," his father said. "How am I supposed to know that?"

"I heard that they kill whoever they—"

"Shut up." A trace of fear was present in the father's terse voice. "Do you want to get shot right now?"

As if to prove the father's words, the sound of a gunshot came from the direction of the public square.

They promptly stopped talking.

The Arbiter inspected people at a quick rate, and the intervals in between each gunshot made people tremble. For a while, it was very regular. Every ten minutes, there was at least one gunshot, and sometimes there were several in quick succession. After these gunshots, there were long spans of time in which the Arbiter did not shoot again. The father near An Zhe said, "They're pretty much done killing, I think."

Right as he finished speaking, the sounds of gunshots rang out again, and the boy with him shivered.

People judged to be infected were shot on the spot, while people judged to be safe left through the openings. As the number of people in the public square decreased, they spontaneously formed a haphazard line and slowly moved forward. An Zhe, standing at the very end of the line, counted the sound of each gunshot. By the time he got close to the exit himself, he had already counted to seventy-three. He saw a stone pillar near the exits and Lu Feng leaning against it, his contours slim beneath the light. Two Judges stood next to him. Further out along both sides were heavily armed City Defense Agency soldiers, and blood covered the ground in front of them.

No, not only blood. There were objects scattered on the ground in no discernible pattern, all brassy bullet shells.

The father-and-son pair up ahead passed through safely, and

it was then An Zhe's turn. He took a few steps forward and stopped in front of Lu Feng.

Lu Feng was taller than him, so he had to tilt his head back to meet Lu Feng's gaze—and then he felt Lu Feng examine him once from top to bottom.

"What's in your hand?"

An Zhe didn't think that even such a small object in his hand would be noticed. In the face of the Arbiter's commanding and aloof gaze, he could only lift his hand, uncurl his fingers, and reveal the bullet shell lying in his palm. Just like those bullet shells scattered on the ground, it represented a human the Arbiter had executed.

The silence between them was drawn out.

After a long time passed, An Zhe heard Lu Feng say, "Get going."

The late-night wind was so powerful that it even broke up the sound of Lu Feng's voice, so when it came to his ears, it was softer than usual.

An Zhe silently turned and walked into the deep night.

———

"At 7 p.m. on May 17th, a parasitic monster invasion occurred at the supply depot public square in the outer city via a new parasitization method. The Trial Court has implemented additional Trial conditions in response to the new parasitization method. At present, the danger within the base has been eliminated. Residents, please be at ease when moving about."

"To improve the accuracy of the Trials and ensure that the Arbiter is present throughout the entire process, the operation of the city gates will be reduced to the hours of 8 a.m. to 12 p.m. and 2 p.m. to 6 p.m. today. Please pay attention when you return to the city."

"According to the Lighthouse's observations, the breeding

season of arthropod-class and parasite-class monsters has begun early. To prevent airborne invasion, the operating strength of the base's ultrasonic dispersion device has been raised to level III. The danger levels of Flatland 2, Basin 6, and the Southwest Ravine have been updated to four stars. Please pay attention to personal safety in the wilderness and protect your entire body. The same information has been communicated to all teams out in the wilderness."

"At 7 p.m. on May 17th, a parasitic monster invasion occurred..."

The three announcements played on repeat. Mr. Shaw lifted a hand and switched it off, then lowered his head and continued polishing the mold.

An Zhe was still implanting eyebrows in the corner, but this time it wasn't ordinary eyebrow implantation, for Mr. Shaw had drawn the specific shape and direction on the mannequin's blank face with a gray pen. He was practicing implanting eyebrows for the Arbiter's mannequin.

Doussay was dead, but they still had to proceed with the order she had referred to them because Mr. Shaw already received half of the money—the delivery time they had previously agreed upon was one month later. They were to deliver the goods to a room in District 6's Building 13, and at that time, the commissioner was to hand over the other half of the payment.

The color of Lu Feng's eyebrows and hair was the same, both pure black. It was a very distinctive color. The long eyebrow slanted upward slightly, forming a sharply contoured peak, then gradually narrowed into a thin and sharp end. Mr. Shaw had spent an hour drawing just these eyebrows. After receiving the mannequin's head, An Zhe not only had to strictly follow the guidelines while implanting the eyebrows, he also had to lift his head from time to time to look at the profile-view photo of Lu Feng on the tablet computer propped up in front of him and check if there were any errors.

The phone-selling youth clad in black had delivered the tablet computer at seven o'clock this morning, saying that it was a gift from Hubbard to Mr. Shaw.

After delivering the gift, he glanced at An Zhe. "Whoa, you've found a nice gig. Do you have money to buy a cell phone from me now?"

An Zhe felt very apologetic. His wage was only enough to buy potato soup, so all he could say was "no." The youth sighed in disappointment and left.

Several close-up photos of Lu Feng were saved in the tablet computer he delivered. Most of them were from when he was patrolling the black market yesterday. The angles were very reasonable, and one of the photos even contained An Zhe. However, the focus of the photo was on Lu Feng, while everything else was very fuzzy. He was just a white smudge in one corner of the photo, and in front of him was a bowl of potato soup.

Mr. Shaw made a pleased sound, saying, "Hubbard has ways of getting what he wants out of the black market. It really isn't a trivial matter to get photos of the Arbiter. Although there's no exact data, the photos were taken well, so they'll suffice."

With those words, he swiped back and forth through the photos several times and said, "This face can really make women go crazy. Do you like him?"

According to the biological sexes of human bodies, An Zhe wasn't a woman, so he didn't go crazy. He only felt very uncomfortable. He felt a bit of visceral fear toward this Arbiter. In this human base, only Lu Feng suspected that he wasn't human. An Zhe thought that, supposing he died one day at the human base, it would definitely be at the end of the Arbiter's gun.

He said, "I don't like him."

"Then you're part of the opposition party," Mr. Shaw said. "I hate the opposition party the most. My last apprentice was one of them."

"How come?" An Zhe asked.

Mr. Shaw said, "He took the pay I gave him and actually had the cheek to ask for half a day off every week to participate in demonstrations."

"... I'm not part of the opposition party either," he said.

"I don't care if you're part of the opposition party or the supporting party," Mr. Shaw said with sincerity. "Just don't ask for time off."

"I... won't ask for time off," An Zhe said.

Facing the amicable smile on Mr. Shaw's face that appeared after he said those words, An Zhe tentatively asked, "Can I live here?"

Based on his observations from these past few days, Mr. Shaw's shop wasn't actually small. In a corner, there were some unused containers, and the space between the containers was enough for a person to live in.

Mr. Shaw asked, "What's the matter?"

An Zhe knew that the people of the base normally wouldn't move easily to a new home. They would all be assigned a residence at a very young age—of course, whether or not they lived there was another matter. The vast majority of mercenaries spent their lives in the wilderness, and the men and women of the third underground floor returned home very rarely as well.

But he truly did not wish to return to Building 117, for Josh's clinginess exhausted him.

"It's my neighbor," he explained to Mr. Shaw. "He always..."

Before he found the appropriate words, he saw Mr. Shaw wiggle his eyebrows understandingly. "He wants to bed you?"

An Zhe verified that there was only one thing in Scott Shaw's head.

"That's not it," he denied. "He just constantly wants to get close to me."

Mr. Shaw asked, "There's a difference between that and wanting to bed you?"

"There is." An Zhe earnestly thought back on Josh's actions. "We used to be very good friends."

There were some things that he couldn't say to Mr. Shaw, so he could only use "I" to substitute for "An Ze."

"I grew up together with him. We're neighbors. I submitted manuscripts to the City Affairs Office for small contribution fees, while he worked as a mercenary outside. Sometimes when I didn't have money, or when he didn't have money, we'd look after each other," An Zhe said.

"But afterward, I wanted to take the exam for the supply depot, and he didn't want me to. He said… that it was too difficult, that he wanted to go out into the wilderness with me and do a bit of light work."

At that point, Scott Shaw let out a scornful laugh.

An Zhe looked at Mr. Shaw, wishing to receive his assessment. He couldn't understand why Josh would be like that toward An Ze. "Why would he be like that?"

Mr. Shaw held a mannequin arm, polishing it with a small file as he said, "After you pass the test for the supply depot and leave the civilian population, you'll stand out from the rest. What could he do? He'll just be a common mercenary for his whole life. Would you still spend time with him?"

Having spoken up to this point, Mr. Shaw lifted his head up to cast a look at An Zhe. "In all likelihood, once you go, you'd be able to seduce one of the supply depot's higher-ups. He wouldn't be able to hold on to you then."

But An Ze wouldn't do that.

An Zhe said, "I wouldn't."

"Even if you wouldn't, he'd think that." Mr. Shaw finished polishing a fingernail, sprayed on a layer of varnish, and switched to the next fingernail. "Who can tell? People are just this ugly."

"So, as for you, you best not get mixed up with these kinds of good-for-nothings—"

An Zhe dropped his gaze, feeling that Mr. Shaw was indeed a good person. A good elder would provide life guidance to young humans. On occasion, some social monsters in the Abyss would exhibit similar behavior.

But then he heard Mr. Shaw say, "As for you, keep a sharp eye out on the third floor and find a big mercenary team's boss, someone on Hubbard's level, to ensure that he'll take the long way around when he sees you. If he still dares to come to you, shout for your man to give him a beating. It's also fine if they aren't a man. AR1104's female captain will definitely like you when she sees you, but she looks like a gorilla."

An Zhe said, "The Arbiter's fingers are longer than this."

Mr. Shaw jumped from shock, then began to rework it while spitting curses. He no longer had time to provide life guidance to An Zhe.

As he watched Mr. Shaw, who had his head buried in the repair work, An Zhe smiled.

In this manner, he moved into the third underground floor.

Without Josh, the world became much quieter. An Zhe bought a folding bed with an advance on his wages and lived between two empty shelves in a corner of the shop. At night, with the lights off, the mannequin limbs, eyeballs, and heads could all keep him company as he slept. Sometimes when he went out, mercenaries would stop him and ask his price, but Mr. Shaw had taught him a very useful phrase—"I have someone." These three words could deal with almost *all* the mercenaries. According to Mr. Shaw, the reason why this sentence could take care of them was not necessarily because these people possessed the virtue of knowing to respectfully back down.

At the time, Mr. Shaw had a cigarette dangling from his mouth as he said, "With your good looks, you seem like the type to have a very powerful man. Tsk, I better find one for you quickly."

An Zhe said nothing. In truth, all he had was a mannequin that hadn't yet taken shape. This mannequin was still being crafted day after day, and it resembled Lu Feng more and more.

7

"AD4117. MY COMMUNICATOR NUMBER."

"HOW COME you moved the Colonel to one side again?" Mr. Shaw asked loudly as soon as he entered the shop.

An Zhe had just sat up on the bed. Rubbing his eyes, he said in a small voice, "I can't sleep well with him next to me."

"You're so finicky." Mr. Shaw walked over and gave him a hard knock on his head. "Several days ago, you weren't even capable of sleeping while hugging a human head, right?"

An Zhe wordlessly buried his head beneath the quilt once more.

A human head was a human head, and Lu Feng was Lu Feng. As a xenogenic who the Arbiter had repeatedly nitpicked, he didn't need a reason to be afraid of that person.

"I'm deducting your wages."

Left with no other choice, An Zhe could only get back out from under the quilt and slowly put on his coat.

The tone of Mr. Shaw's voice turned facetious again. "I think you better not go out to seduce mercenaries. Just work hard with me instead."

"How come?" An Zhe asked.

Mr. Shaw wasn't saying that yesterday.

"With your small appearance, tsk, it's no good," Mr. Shaw said. "Those mercenary ruffians, they'll bully you."

"Why would they bully me?"

"For fun, probably."

Done talking, he knocked An Zhe on the head once more.

An Zhe frowned. He felt that Mr. Shaw was bullying him already with his actions just now.

However, he had no choice. He was currently just like a parasite, dependent on the pay from Mr. Shaw—so he could only obediently get out of bed and wash up, then throw himself into the day's work.

Today was the thirtieth day since he had started making mannequins. In other words, they had to completely finish the mannequin and then deliver the goods to the customer's doorstep by tonight at the very latest.

Mr. Shaw had finished the torso and limbs ten days ago—though it was mainly An Zhe who made them under his guidance. After doing those things, he picked out a prop gun from the ones being sold in the shop and put it together with the mannequin. Finally, through the black market, they obtained a near-identical black uniform and dressed the mannequin in it. Now the mannequin of the Arbiter had a perfect body and only needed a head.

At present, An Zhe was holding the mannequin head and checking to see whether the alignment of the hairs he had personally implanted were pleasing to the eye. In the meantime, Mr. Shaw had fired up a melting furnace nearby and was stirring transparent adhesive in a small white ceramic pot with one hand while adding green dye one drop at a time with the other hand. The dye initially formed a dark green blob in the pot, but after a short while, countless tiny tendrils stretched from it and dispersed outward. With the stirring, it was evenly distributed, and the adhesive became a light green that then gradually darkened. An Zhe had nothing to do after he finished examining the hair, so he stared at the color, recalling Lu Feng's eye color as he watched.

In the light, they were a green like that of leaves frosted over with ice. Often, when that pair of eyes looked at An Zhe, he would start feeling cold.

And in the dim lighting of the night, Lu Feng's eyes would appear to be a deep, dark green like a fathomless lake in the night that was hiding many unknown things.

As he was thinking, he paid attention to the substance's color. Once it matched the eyes in his memories, he said, "This is good."

With a smile, Mr. Shaw extinguished the melting furnace and said, "You have good eyes."

An Zhe handed the mold to Mr. Shaw without a word. The translucent material was poured into the spherical mold and allowed to cool and set. Then, once they were embedded into the eye whites, the eyes were completed.

Right away, these eyeballs were installed in the mannequin's eye sockets. The mannequin's eyelashes were also An Zhe's handiwork, implanted one by one. Now, the black eyelashes gently covered the green eyes, and even the most minute subtleties of the cold expression were visible. It was truly too similar to the real person. Feeling anxious, An Zhe picked up the black service cap and put it on the mannequin.

The next tasks were to tune the joints and polish the facial details. When they were completely finished, it was seven o'clock in the evening. An Zhe silently looked at the mannequin, and the mannequin silently looked back at him. He felt that it looked utterly like the Colonel himself.

They folded up the mannequin that looked utterly like the Colonel himself at the joints and placed it in a rolling suitcase. Mr. Shaw clapped his hands and said, "It can be delivered now. I'll get Jensen to deliver it. He's cheap."

Jensen was the black-clad youth who sold cell phones and handed over the Arbiter's data to Mr. Shaw.

But although Mr. Shaw dialed repeatedly on his communicator, nobody answered.

Mr. Shaw frowned. "What's going on?"

"Did he get discovered?" He dialed Hubbard's communicator instead, but a voice immediately came from the receiver. "The party you have dialed has left the base. Please leave a message."

Mr. Shaw turned to look at the tablet computer on the workbench, tapped on it, and deleted all of the photos with a few quick motions. He said to An Zhe, "Something's not quite right. Let's hurry up and get rid of the goods. There's nothing else to do tonight, so come deliver it with me."

Thus, An Zhe came to District 6, where he hadn't set foot for a month already.

Unit 4, Room 312 in District 6's Building 13 was their commissioner's location. The suitcase was very heavy, so An Zhe and Mr. Shaw took turns carrying it up the stairs to the third floor. Unlike Building 117, where An Zhe lived before, Building 13's residents were all women, and along the way, An Zhe ran into a good number of them. Most of them had short hair, tall statures, and distinctive and strong facial features. As he looked at them, An Zhe couldn't help but think of Doussay again.

Doussay was a very special woman. She was tall but slenderer than all the other women An Zhe had seen. At the same time, her bosom was fuller than other people's—because of this slender fullness, her body seemed strangely soft, and this softness was very rarely seen even on the third underground floor.

At the same time, he saw that Mr. Shaw was also casting unrestrained looks at the women passing by. In the end, Mr. Shaw said, "There's no second Doussay."

Without saying anything, An Zhe gently tapped on the door to No. 12. "Hello, we've come to make a delivery."

Nobody opened the door.

An Zhe's knocking became a little louder. "Hello, we're here to make a delivery."

Still nobody opened the door.

Mr. Shaw took a step forward and pounded the door a few times with his fist. "Is anyone there? It's a delivery from the third underground floor."

Silence.

Amidst the silence, footsteps came from behind them. An Zhe turned his head and saw a middle-aged woman dressed in gray. He said, "Hello, are you the resident of No. 12?"

The woman shook her head and looked at the door. "You two are looking for her?"

"Mm-hm," An Zhe said. "She ordered something, and we've come to deliver it."

There was no expression on the woman's face as her gaze shifted to the suitcase Mr. Shaw was pulling. "What goods?"

"Premium goods. Anything else, we can't say," Mr. Shaw said. "Is she not in? When will she return?"

The woman looked at him, the corners of her lips drawn taut. For a short while, she didn't say anything.

Unable to bear it any longer, Mr. Shaw said, "Is she—"

Just as the words left his mouth, the woman said, "She's dead. You guys didn't know?"

There was a brief silence.

"Dead?" After a brief pause, Mr. Shaw raised his voice. "Then who's going to give me the rest of my payment?"

The corners of the woman's mouth twitched. With an expression that held a shadow of a smile, she replied, "The Arbiter killed her. Go get him to pay."

Mr. Shaw, looking like a duck whose neck was being squeezed, said nothing for a while.

But An Zhe was suddenly stunned.

As he looked at the woman, he asked, "What was she called?"

As though the woman did not hear his words, she turned, lifted her hand, swiped open the room door on the opposite side with her ID card, and walked in. The moment before the door closed from the inside, two simple syllables came from within.

"Doussay."

An Zhe once again thought back to the expression Doussay showed to Lu Feng before she died and momentarily didn't know what he should say. Mr. Shaw was also silent. After a long time, he let out a sigh and said with a smile, "Do you know how much money this order was?"

"I don't," An Zhe said.

"Even more than Hubbard's order." Mr. Shaw looked at the rolling suitcase on the ground, his eyes half-closed, and said slowly, "She played with so many men, I didn't think that she'd also have genuine feelings."

An Zhe said, "Doussay said that the Arbiter saved her before."

"Fool." Mr. Shaw sighed and shook his head. "The kind of person that the Arbiter is... even if he did save her, it was because he wanted to kill xenogenics. She had scraped a living off of men since she was young. She wasn't a little girl anymore, so how could she not understand this? It's not worth it."

An Zhe didn't say anything.

He didn't understand why Doussay liked Lu Feng either. However—compared to other people, Lu Feng was indeed different. What those differences were, though, he couldn't say.

After a long time, Mr. Shaw said, "She's gone, so what should we do with the goods? It can't be tossed. If it's discovered, the Trial Court will definitely come looking for me."

An Zhe said, "Then bring it back to the shop?"

"Absolutely not." Mr. Shaw shook his head. "I can't get in touch with Jensen all of a sudden, so I'm afraid something's happened."

As he spoke, he looked at An Zhe and seemed to suddenly think of something. "I remember that your home is also in District 6?"

He jiggled the suitcase. "And you don't live over there, so there's no fear of being seen. Let's do this. For tonight, bring the goods back to your place. After a few days, if nobody checks, we'll find someone to buy it."

"What about you?" An Zhe asked.

Mr. Shaw looked down at his watch and frowned. "I have to go back first, it's the last train."

An Zhe thought for a while and felt that it was feasible. He didn't live at home, so it was fine to temporarily stash the mannequin up in there.

Mr. Shaw patted his shoulder. "You can do it."

Then he swiftly left to catch the train.

But it turned out that An Zhe couldn't do it.

District 6 was a circular area, so Building 13 and Building 117 weren't far apart. This was also the reason why Mr. Shaw felt at ease about having him take the goods home. But the mannequin was solid and really couldn't be considered light. With practically turtle-like speed, he dragged the massive suitcase along the road. By the time he reached the foot of Building 117, the sky had already darkened completely.

Indistinct black shadows were everywhere, and the outline of the building was visible only by way of the aurora's glow. As An Zhe stood in front of the unit and thought about how he still needed to climb up to the fifth floor with the suitcase, he felt despair, for it really was very heavy.

The despairing An Zhe turned around on the spot so that he no longer faced the pitch-black staircase entrance. He planned to stop and rest a while first.

The sound of burning breaths suddenly came from behind him, and he was wrapped up in an abrupt hug.

"An Ze!"

It was Josh's voice.

"I saw you from the window, so I immediately came down." Josh held him tightly. "Where have you been? How come you've only come back now? Why didn't you tell me? I've been looking for you all this time."

He took a breath, then continued. "You aren't allowed to leave again. Where have you been?"

Mr. Shaw's words were correct. Josh thought of An Ze as his personal belonging.

Thus, An Zhe calmly said, "Please let go."

Not only did Josh not let go, he tightened his grip instead.

"Are you angry at me?" Josh asked.

Before An Zhe said anything, he spoke up again in a low voice. "I was wrong, I'll apologize to you. Whatever way you want me to apologize is fine. An Ze, I love you."

An Zhe was speechless.

Mr. Shaw's words seemed to be correct again. He really did want to bed An Ze.

"Thank you," An Zhe said, "but I have someone."

"You're truly angry?" Josh smiled. "You always did like to deliberately make me mad when you were angry."

An Zhe really was very annoyed with this human. He struggled to free himself, but Josh forcibly turned him around. "Look at me, An Ze."

"Bang!"

A gunshot rang out.

Josh gave a start and reflexively let go of An Zhe, then looked around.

An Zhe also looked in the direction where the sound had come from and saw that beneath the shadow of the black building, a person was standing there. The person had just fired into the air and was putting the gun away while walking over. Slim and tall, it was a figure he was extremely familiar with.

Only military people could legally bear arms within the city.

And within the military's various branches, only one kind of person could fire at will.

An Zhe thought that he seemed to have stumbled into the path of the Arbiter's city patrol again—what a coincidence.

Before he could carefully think about it, he heard Lu Feng's familiar cold voice. "What is he to you?"

"A neighbor," An Zhe said.

Lu Feng walked up to him.

From such a small distance, anyone could recognize that this was the Arbiter.

An Zhe felt Josh abruptly stiffen next to him.

"AD4117. My communicator number." Lu Feng's voice sounded nonchalant. "Next time this kind of thing happens, if you are willing to contact me, he'll be arrested for indecency."

An Zhe lifted his head to look at Lu Feng, his reaction temporarily delayed somewhat. But since this man was the military's Colonel, it seemed that he really did have the duty of maintaining law and order within the city.

He said, "Okay."

He felt Josh, who was behind him, get even more stiff.

But An Zhe couldn't be bothered to care about Josh at all.

Because Lu Feng's hand was gently resting on the handle of the rolling suitcase.

He asked, "Shall I help you bring it up?"

An Zhe and Lu Feng looked at each other.

The expression in Lu Feng's eyes was one of slight indifference, his gaze calm. He was being serious.

An Zhe stuttered, not even able to speak clearly. "There's… there's no need."

If it had been something else in the suitcase and the Arbiter had suddenly wanted to help for some strange reason, although he didn't want to interact with this man more than necessary, he wouldn't have gone so far as to refuse.

However, what this box contained right now was nothing good.

An Zhe put his hand on the handle as well and tried to take it out of Lu Feng's grip. "I can do it myself."

"Can you?" As Lu Feng looked at him, his long brows slightly furrowed. "You live on the first floor?"

"... I live on the fifth floor. But I can still do it."

"Oh."

His hand pressed down on An Zhe's fingers, and then An Zhe's hand was somehow instantly removed from the handle.

With a click, the handle slid neatly back into the suitcase. Lu Feng grasped the handle on the suitcase's side, then effortlessly lifted the entire thing.

An Zhe gave a start.

He said, "There's really no need."

"The fifth floor?"

Fine.

An Zhe realized that he himself had given away the floor earlier.

But without waiting for An Zhe to react, Lu Feng already started walking to the unit's entrance, so he could only follow. Before entering the building, An Zhe even turned his head back to glance at Josh and saw that he was watching them, disconcerted, and hadn't moved a single step. Mr. Shaw had said that if An Zhe seduced a powerful mercenary, Josh would definitely take the long way around upon seeing him. By the looks of things now, that statement may have really been correct, even though the one at his side was the Arbiter rather than some mercenary and even though he actually had no relationship with Lu Feng whatsoever.

However, in the brief span of this distraction, An Zhe had already fallen several steps behind Lu Feng. The Colonel's legs were longer than his, so he could only increase his pace to catch up before entering the building together with Lu Feng.

To conserve power, only the corridor's tiny emergency lights were giving off a faint glow. The place was very dark and very cramped. In the silence, the sounds of the Colonel's combat boots treading on the floor was particularly distinct, every single sound seeming to knock on An Zhe's heart. Based on his understanding of Lu Feng, the man was about to ask, "What's in the box?"

But in a strange stroke of fortune, on the entire way to the fifth floor, Lu Feng didn't say anything at all.

An Zhe stood at the entrance to No. 14, took out his ID card, and swiped it to open the door. The room's curtains hadn't been drawn shut, so as soon as he opened the door, the aurora's glow came in through the window. The aurora's bright luster covered the greater part of the pitch-black sky. It was mainly green, with orange and purple at the edges. An Zhe entered and turned on the little light in the room. Based on the courtesy that the human community should have, he looked at the Colonel, who was standing next to the door, and said, "Please come in."

Lu Feng readily walked in and put the rolling suitcase next to the wall. Observing his expression, An Zhe felt that he was actually in a good mood and also seemed like he didn't want to leave.

He asked tentatively, "Are you going to continue patrolling?"

Lu Feng leaned against the wall with his arms crossed and said, "No need."

With those green eyes watching him, An Zhe felt that the Arbiter did not completely believe that he was human even now and that he was still fastidiously searching for any possible slip-up.

An Zhe asked in a small voice, "Then what will you be doing later?"

"Head back to the City Defense Agency to rest," Lu Feng said.

An Zhe strove to converse with him in the manner of humans. "You aren't going back to the Trial Court?"

"It's too far."

"… Oh."

He felt that under the current circumstances, he ought to invite the Colonel in to sit for a while, but he wanted very badly for the other man to leave because although there appeared to only be one Colonel in the room, there were actually two.

He asked, "When are you going?"

Lu Feng looked at him.

An Zhe cast his gaze down and pursed his lips.

"Go get me a glass of water," Lu Feng said.

The tone was completely unlike that of a discussion or suggestion. No matter what this person said, it sounded like he was issuing orders.

"Okay," An Zhe replied.

He picked up the water cup on the table and opened the door. From here, it was very far to the communal water room in the corridor on this floor. He walked over and, facing the red and blue buttons, guessed as to whether Lu Feng liked to drink warm water or cold water.

Very quickly, he pressed the blue button that represented cold water. There was no ice water here, otherwise he definitely would've gotten it for Lu Feng.

Afterward, as he held the water cup and thought about how he had to continue facing Lu Feng, he walked back to his room with a heavy heart.

The Arbiter helping him carry the suitcase upstairs late at night was just so he could come over and drink a glass of water. Could it have been that he was thirsty after being out on patrol all night?

Once he told Mr. Shaw about this experience tomorrow, based on the fact that Mr. Shaw's head only contained one thing, he would definitely say, "He wants to bed you."

Wrong.

An Zhe stopped dead in his tracks.

He suddenly recalled why Mr. Shaw had left the box with him.

Because Jensen had clearly always been selling cell phones in the black market without causing any trouble, but he suddenly couldn't be reached. Mr. Shaw felt that something was fishy, so they couldn't take the mannequin of the Arbiter back to the shop.

Frowning, he began to think back on Lu Feng's every action.

The Trial Court's patrols were all conducted in groups, just like that time at the entrance to the black market when Lu Feng had led three people. Why was he by himself now? And right downstairs from his home?

Furthermore, this Lu Feng person seemed to have the ability to read minds. Previously, whatever abnormalities he had were all discovered, so how come he didn't ask at all about the suitcase's contents this time?

An Zhe's hand, which had just landed on the door handle, froze.

He thought that the Arbiter, perhaps, had come to capture him.

He yanked his hand back, took out his communicator, and dialed AE77243, Mr. Shaw's number.

Four words appeared on the communicator's black-and-white electronic screen: "unable to accept call."

The alarm bells in An Zhe's heart went off.

But right at that moment, an authoritative and cold voice came from the other side of the closed door. "Come in."

An Zhe's heart thumped wildly. He took a deep breath, then opened the room door.

He saw Lu Feng standing in the same spot as before, head slightly bowed with the rolling suitcase upright at his side. An Zhe didn't know what he was thinking.

An Zhe took two steps and held out the cup. "Colonel, your water."

Lu Feng didn't move a muscle.

Something suddenly occurred to An Zhe.

He slowly, slowly turned his head to look at the other side of the room.

Then he met the gaze of the real Lu Feng.

Lu Feng was sitting at his desk with legs crossed, his sitting posture lofty. In his hand was a sheet of paper, and his head was tilted up to look at An Zhe.

An Zhe now knew true despair.

But at that very moment, all he could do was slowly take two steps forward and put the cup on the desk. "Your water."

Lu Feng picked up the water cup, put it to his mouth, and took a light sip, then frowned slightly. "Cold water?"

An Zhe didn't want to speak. He seemed to have done something wrong again.

He saw Lu Feng put the water cup onto the desk again, put the paper back on the table as well, and looked at him.

An Zhe swiftly admitted his mistake. "I was wrong."

Lu Feng didn't say anything. A full ten seconds went by before he asked, "What offense did you commit?"

"I didn't get warm water for you."

"Cold water is also fine."

An Zhe looked at the propaganda paper upon which "OPPOSE THE ARBITER'S TYRANNY" was written in bloody red, and his heart grew a bit colder again. He said, "I participated in an illegal demonstration."

"That's not it."

He was done for. There remained only one offense that he possibly could have committed.

What charge would cover the making of a mannequin of the Arbiter?

As An Zhe felt self-loathing for not carefully looking at the base's laws before, he strove to find the correct words. Mannequin, a mannequin used for *that* kind of bad purpose—

The words Lu Feng said to Josh when they were downstairs popped up in his mind. In despair, An Zhe said, "… Indecency?"

He saw a shadow of a smile appear in Lu Feng's eyes. "Have you looked at the base's laws before?"

"I haven't."

Lu Feng said, "Come here."

An Zhe took a step forward.

"Hold out your hand."

An Zhe obediently held out his hand.

Lu Feng's words were still clipped. In the same commanding tone, he said, "Put it up here."

"Where?"

"On me."

An Zhe hesitated for a moment, then slowly placed his hand on the left side of Lu Feng's chest. The uniform's silver buttons and the badge pinned to his chest were all cold and had lines decorating their surfaces. He didn't know why Lu Feng wanted him to do this.

"Click."

The icy silver handcuff was clipped onto An Zhe's wrist once more.

Lu Feng was expressionless. "For indecency."

An Zhe did not understand.

Immediately afterward, he saw Lu Feng lift up his communicator.

"Capture complete. One item of contraband seized," he said. "Come provide backup."

———

The City Defense Agency's corridor was even darker and colder than the one in the residential building.

An Zhe was taken to the first underground floor. In the dim

lighting, there were iron doors all around, and he realized that this may be the humans' prison.

He was locked up behind one of them.

"You'll be tried tomorrow," Lu Feng said as he locked the iron door. "You have ten hours to prepare a defense."

An Zhe said, "... I don't have a defense."

"That's what I thought," Lu Feng replied.

With those words, he turned around and departed without even looking back, leaving behind only one sentence. "Rest well."

Clutching at the iron door, An Zhe watched Lu Feng's figure disappear in the corridor.

Whispers came from the opposite side.

"Like I was saying, they won't skip over even one."

"If Hubbard hadn't gone out into the wilderness, he'd be eating prison meals too. He had me take the photographs in secret. You two really trapped me. After we get out, pay me."

"Go to Doussay. She placed the order, and the bill hasn't even been paid yet."

"Then take me with you."

Those were Mr. Shaw's and Jensen's voices.

An Zhe looked in the direction of the sound and strove to identify the two people who'd been locked up across from him in the dim lighting. "You two are also here?"

"Obviously," Jensen said. "I was happily selling cell phones when people from the Trial Court took me away."

Mr. Shaw sighed. "After I separated from you, I hadn't even entered the train station when I got caught."

Jensen asked, "What about you? How did you get caught?"

An Zhe didn't answer.

"Master," he said.

"What is it?"

"Do I really make people want to bully me a lot?"

"You only just realized?" Mr. Shaw said lazily. "Why do you ask?"

An Zhe didn't answer that either. He asked, "What offenses did you guys commit?"

"Does it still need to be said?" Mr. Shaw asked. "The crime of illegally stealing the Arbiter's information."

"Is that so?" An Zhe said.

"What?" Mr. Shaw asked. "Was that not the case for you?"

"It was," An Zhe said.

Mr. Shaw let out a long laugh. "Your tone has even changed. What, did someone bully you?"

An Zhe said indifferently, "No."

In the quiet space, Jensen yawned. "The prison beds are actually pretty soft."

An Zhe looked around his own space. In the cramped prison cell, there was a soft plastic board measuring one meter by two meters placed in a corner with a folded white blanket at its foot —this was probably the so-called bed.

He went over there and sat down cross-legged, then wrapped himself up in the thin blanket and leaned back against the wall.

Footsteps came from the end of the hall, and eye-watering light brightened the corridor. Three City Defense Agency soldiers were making the rounds with flashlights in hand. When the soldiers passed by them, the one on the left said, "There's three more now. Who brought them in?"

"The Arbiter, I guess. Colonel Lu's powerful. Let's be honest, the City Defense Agency is just the Trial Court's logistics team now."

"The Trial Court wants to completely take control of the City Defense Agency, but the director is still holding out."

The soldiers ran the flashlight beams over their faces and didn't say much else as they walked on. After examining them all one by one, they left through another corridor entrance.

After the sounds of their movements disappeared, the entire underground space became utterly silent except for the prisoners' breathing. An Zhe could sense that there were very few people. From the distance came the sound of water dripping onto plastic board, and Mr. Shaw muttered, "So this is how the City Defense Agency wastes water resources."

But the sound of the dripping water still continued, ceaseless and extremely consistent. Jensen said, "It's a watch."

Listening hard, An Zhe realized that the sound was coming from next door to him and sounding once every brief interval of time. It wasn't dripping water, but rather the sound of an old mechanical watch's movements.

In the dark, the second hand went around at a constant pace, and time stretched out endlessly.

At last, Jensen said, "Mr. Shaw, you have a lot of experience. How long will we be locked up for?"

"Not too long, probably," Mr. Shaw said. "For illegally stealing the Arbiter's information, it'll depend on its usage. It's fine so long as it doesn't bring harm to the Arbiter."

"I'm not sure that's right. You used it to make a profit," Jensen said. "Even if we aren't locked up for too long, we'll have to pay fines, won't we?"

"Then I'd rather be locked up for a few additional years," Mr. Shaw said.

Jensen said with a sigh, "The Arbiter is the Arbiter. Even taking pictures will get you detained. In the future, I'll just stick to quietly selling cell phones. I had just taken a photo when people from the Trial Court pulled me away. At the time, I even thought I'd become a xenogenic at some point without knowing and got scared to death."

Mr. Shaw didn't say anything. From An Zhe's neighboring cell, however, came the clear voice of a young man. "I've seen the crime of illegally stealing the Arbiter's information before."

Mr. Shaw asked, "How long were they locked up for?"

"The shortest was three days, the longest was three years, and one was executed. He wanted to assassinate the Arbiter."

Mr. Shaw tentatively asked, "… Did he succeed?"

"He didn't."

"And he was still executed?"

"That's just how the Arbiter's Code is." The voice's tone was calm. "Without the Arbiter's absolute safety, there would be no Arbiter's absolute authority."

Mr. Shaw said, "Then… we didn't have any intention to harm him, so how long will we be locked up for?"

"Depends on the Arbiter's mood, really," the voice replied.

An Zhe's fingers curled around the blanket. He felt that the Arbiter was in a good mood.

He heard Jensen ask curiously, "Buddy, what did you do?"

The voice said, "They brought me up on charges of incitement and spreading fear."

Jensen seemed perplexed. "Huh?"

"I wrote contributions for the Cultural Affairs Administration, and the City Defense Agency arrested me," the person next door said. "The Cultural Affairs Administration closed down afterward, yet I wasn't let out."

So he was An Ze's colleague, An Zhe thought.

Then he heard Jensen say, "How long have you been locked up for?"

"Lifetime imprisonment."

Jensen clearly went silent for a moment. "You're messing with me on this one."

The person let out a laugh but didn't reply.

An Zhe thought for a while. Based on An Ze's memories, the job he had performed was a very safe one.

He asked the neighbor, "What did you write?"

That person said, "Summaries of the base's history. My pen name is Poet. Have you read them before?"

"I haven't," An Zhe replied.

Poet said, "Then do you want to listen? Your voice sounds very nice."

"Your voice sounds very nice too." An Zhe felt that he seemed to really want to talk, so he said, "I want to listen."

"Stop." Mr. Shaw spoke up. "The crime you committed was incitement. Don't think about inciting our kid too."

"Just listening is fine, you don't need to be afraid of being arrested." There was a laugh in Poet's voice. "Since you guys have already been arrested, and all."

His words were very reasonable.

"Ever since I've been locked up here, I've had very few opportunities to talk about the things I spent a very long time sorting out," Poet said. "But you guys also roughly know those things."

An Zhe said, "I don't know them."

"Oh?" Poet said. "Then I'll go into a bit more detail."

"Let me think about where to start talking from…" His words gradually slowed. "I'll start from the Desert Era, I suppose."

"Before the Desert Era, was the 'Era of Great Prosperity.' The world had seven billion people altogether, and in flatland regions, you could drive for an hour and be able to come across a village or city. The cities were full of people. At the edges of the cities were croplands, livestock farms, and factories that provided manufacturing materials for the cities. There were wars during that period, but they were all wars between countries. Animals and plants were not the opponents of human weapons."

At that point, he paused, seemingly organizing his train of thought. A while passed before he said, "That was the year 2020. It's something from over a hundred years ago now."

"When I was a mercenary, I went to the ruins of a research institute in the nation's capital city. There, I dug out some information, which was a geomagnetism research report starting from 2020."

Nobody in the vicinity said anything. He continued, "Starting from that year, they detected that Earth's magnetic field was rapidly weakening—do you guys know about magnetic fields?"

Jensen said, "No need to ask me, buddy. I'm uneducated."

Mr. Shaw didn't say anything.

"The base doesn't teach these things," Poet said. "Anyhow, in 2030, the geomagnetic field disappeared."

Jensen bluntly asked, "So what exactly did the geomagnetic field do?"

"Earth was a massive magnet, with the South and North Poles as its positive and negative poles. The geomagnetic field was everything," Poet said. "After the geomagnetic field disappeared, compasses stopped working, biospheres all over the world were thrown into chaos, and human industries were all stopped, for there was no way to generate and use power. But those were the lightest consequences of the geomagnetic field's disappearance."

"The geomagnetic field... Its most important role was to protect Earth. Earth is suspended in the cosmos, and there's cosmic radiation in all directions along with solar winds, but after these things encountered the geomagnetic field, they were deflected in other directions and didn't harm organisms on Earth's surface. So in 2030, after the geomagnetic field disappeared, the entire planet directly faced the assault of solar storms and cosmic radiation. The external radiation was so strong that most of the land was directly blown away by the storms, the water disappeared, and the atmosphere thinned. Droughts, skin diseases, cancers... Half of the people on Earth died. That was the 'Desert Era.'"

"Shit," Jensen said.

"However, the Desert Era ended very quickly." Poet let out a laugh, then continued. "From when the geomagnetic field's changes were discovered in 2020, humans had already put forth countermeasures divided into Plan A and Plan B. I flipped through so much information in the city ruins before finding out."

Jensen's tone of voice had become respectful. "Do tell."

"Plan A was to construct massive magnetic field generators at two special locations on the continents of Asia and North America. One was called the 'East Pole' and the other was called the 'West Pole.' By replacing Earth's North and South Poles with the two magnetic field generators in the East and West and producing resonance with the charged particles in the solar winds, a new magnetic field would be produced and cover the entire world."

Jensen clapped his hands a few times. "Amazing."

"Plan B was to construct large underground cities and shift the heart of human existence from the planet's surface to the underground to be free from the assaults of radiation and solar winds."

Jensen continued clapping. "Nice."

"In 2040, Plan B succeeded, and the underground cities became available to live in."

"In 2043, Plan A succeeded, and a weak magnetic field covered the entire world. The atmosphere no longer deteriorated, and living organisms no longer died because of the cosmic radiation. Human technology began to recover, and this period of time between 2040 and 2043 was called the 'Dawn Age.'"

At this point, Poet sighed softly. "But humankind's most difficult times had only just begun."

An Zhe opened his eyes wide.

"I know," Jensen said from the opposite side. "The Era of Calamity came."

"Mm-hm," Poet said. "The cosmic radiation brought about

unknown genetic mutations, resulting in very frightening things."

"Initially it was superbacteria, fungi, and viruses. They propagated in the human cities, indiscriminately infecting all people and leaving corpses everywhere in the cities. Those who have been to the ruins in the wilderness all know about this."

An Zhe asked, "How did they survive?"

"Surviving was a matter of luck," Poet said. "Within your genes, if you had immunity to these germs, you'd be able to survive, but otherwise you'd die. The people remaining were all immune. In the end, of the three billion people on Earth who survived the Desert Era, only one hundred million or so remained. But this wasn't humankind's most difficult time either."

"And afterward?" An Zhe asked.

"What happened afterward, you all know. You could say that it was the unknown evolution brought about by cosmic radiation or some kind of virus we couldn't detect. Overall mutation of creatures occurred, and the entire world was occupied by these things. There must be something special on their bodies. As soon as humans come into contact, they'll be infected, gradually lose their human attributes, and be assimilated. They like to attack humans, and human genes are very tasty to them—and so the war began. This was the greatest war in human history."

After taking a soft breath, Poet continued. "The scattered humans had no way of withstanding the monsters' attacks, so humans began to combine their remaining resources and establish human bases. Our ID numbers begin with 3, which represents how this place is humankind's third base. The Underground City Base, Virginia Base, Northern Base, and Southeastern Base. The coalition of these four bases was the community of common destiny for mankind. After the bases were formed, humans could have a brief respite. Hence, you all can live like this now."

With this sentence, the atmosphere in the prison seemed to relax, but then with the next sentence, it dropped anew to the freezing point.

"Unfortunately, the bases weren't necessarily safe." Poet coughed a few times, and his voice gradually lowered.

"In 2061, there was an outbreak of rodent mutants, and the Southeastern Base fell."

"In 2073, marine xenogenics sneaked in, and the Virginia Base fell."

"Fuck." Jensen suddenly interrupted him. "Now I know why you'd commit crimes of incitement and maliciously spreading panic. The City Defense Agency ought to seal your mouth."

"But I didn't do anything wrong," Poet said with a smile. "I was only bumbling along in my boyfriend's mercenary team, collecting information everywhere from human ruins, and then organizing and publishing them when I was sentenced to life imprisonment."

Jensen said, "Your tongue ought to be cut out for good. You even had a boyfriend."

Poet laughed. "It's so boring inside the base. Why can't I have a boyfriend?"

No longer paying attention to Jensen, he said, "So now only the Northern Base and Underground City Base are still in operation. These two bases protect the magnetic field generators, so the auroras over the bases are brighter than in other places. The auroras are the flows of particles within the solar winds."

At that point, Poet sighed. "I don't know if there is still any communication between the two bases. There's the entire Pacific Ocean between them, after all. I said earlier that humankind's most difficult time wasn't the Desert Era, nor was it the Era of Calamity, because the most difficult time is right now. Who knows what will happen next?"

Just as he finished speaking, the earth shook violently

Dust fell from the prison's ceiling and landed on An Zhe's

head and body, making him cough, but then stronger vibrations started up.

Jensen sprang to his feet and called out, "Earthquake?"

"It's not an earthquake." An Zhe heard the sounds of Poet climbing to his feet next door, and the well-informed man rambled on about some things he couldn't understand. "Earthquakes have transverse and longitudinal waves. Right now, it's random vibrations with a very shallow hypocenter—"

"—There's something underground!"

An Zhe understood that sentence.

"Boom!"

In the span of a moment, a loud sound came from the depths of the corridor, accompanied by the clanging of iron doors falling onto the ground.

"Boom!" The sound came again.

A vibration a hundred times stronger than the previous one rippled through, and An Zhe clutched the bars of the iron door to steady himself.

He could tell what the sound was now.

There was something—a massive living creature—fiercely slamming into the floor from below.

8

"AN ZHE WAS SO ANGRY THAT HE EVEN WANTED TO EXTEND HIS HYPHAE."

"FUCK!" Jensen cried out. "It's right below me!"

He was right. Immediately following, An Zhe felt the ground beneath his own feet begin to shake. The feeling was very close and very real, like a heavy hammer was beating the floor across from him.

Loud crashing sounds came from the end of the corridor again, and the rattle of the iron doors was accompanied by the alarmed cries of the prisoners in that direction.

"It's over there too." Poet's words abruptly sped up. "Underground creatures—could it be rodents? They live in groups, and the Southeastern Base was—"

Before he finished speaking, he swiftly corrected himself. "That's not right, rodents don't have such strength. Underground…"

The jumbled sounds of hasty footsteps came as a group of black-clothed soldiers sped down from the corridor stairs while waving their flashlight beams, and the sound of the loudspeaker echoed in the corridor, its volume earsplitting. "Do not panic. The City Defense Agency's foundation is very sturdy, as it is filled with cement and special steel plates. We are currently ascertaining the cause. Do not panic."

If they hadn't been swiftly opening the cell doors to let the prisoners out while they shouted, their words would have seemed more credible.

At the same time, a shrill sound began playing outside. The sound of the alarm rose and fell like waves.

"The evacuation alarm is going off!" Jensen smacked the cell door hard. "Buddy! Hurry up and open it for me!"

A soldier hastily opened three prison doors in the distance, then quickly strode over. Mr. Shaw was toward the outside of the jail. After the soldier found the key corresponding to the cell door, he swiftly jammed it into the lock. With a click, the iron door opened. Mr. Shaw practically flung himself out, and the soldier swiftly said, "Turn right and go upstairs to find the exit!"

Mr. Shaw stumbled a little, then ran toward the right. Dust rained down from the ceiling, and a soldier wiped his face as he stood in front of Poet's door.

Just then, Jensen shouted, "He's been imprisoned for life! He's a dangerous element! Open mine first! I'm a good citizen!"

The soldier appeared to hesitate briefly. As the shaking of the ground intensified, he turned to open Jensen's cell door.

Jensen clutched at the iron door with both hands, his voice trembling violently. "Hey, buddy, hurry up."

An Zhe saw that the soldier's hand was trembling too. Only after making multiple attempts did he manage to stick the key into the lock.

Jensen said, "You're my savior—"

His voice was abruptly cut off.

The floor creaked, and he was lifted up without warning. A huge black thing, pushing against broken bits of floor and dust, had suddenly sprung up!

With a dull "pff," Jensen's body was squeezed between the monster and the ceiling, and his eyes bulged out. Something sharp sliced open his abdomen, and blood mixed with viscera fell in splatters. There came a shrill scream. An Zhe's pupils dilated and he slowly turned his head. The soldier who had opened the door had been stabbed in the thigh and the right side of his chest by the crushed and twisted iron door and was convulsing and rolling on the floor while holding his leg, coughing violently. Large globs of bloody foam continually gushed from his mouth, so perhaps his lung had been punctured.

With a bang, the black thing fell back down again heavily. It broke open a hole in the ground, and it was empty underneath. Jensen's body fell in, never to be seen again.

The other soldiers' shouts came from the depths of the corridor. "Pull out—!"

But in the following second, the tremendous roar of the ground cracking sounded over there as well. The iron doors clanged as they fell to the ground, and the ceiling splintered and fell. Two fearful yells rang out, then stopped abruptly.

An Zhe heard the sounds of chewing.

First was the sound of water, then the dull sound of friction —the sounds of bodies being squeezed—and lastly there was the sounds of bones creaking and then splintering.

The sounds came from the end of the corridor as well as from the underground cavity in front of An Zhe.

While the soldier twitched and rolled around, his flashlight landed on the ground and rolled a few times. Its pale white glow lit up the pitch-black fissure.

At the same time, a single hypha reached out from the crack of the iron door, and additional hyphae then followed. They convened and snagged the splayed keys on the ground, then dragged them slowly through the iron door. The keys scraped against the floor, making a harsh sound. An Zhe saw the soldier's fearful gaze that was aimed in his direction—but he was in no position to care, and he knew the soldier was in no position to care either, because the latter had already breathed his last.

An Zhe asked his neighbor, "What number is my door?"

Poet's voice was trembling. "17. Are you okay?"

"I'm okay," An Zhe said. He thought for a moment. His iron door was right next to Poet's iron door, so Poet's line of sight was limited and he could not see An Zhe taking the keys.

The hyphae retracted. He swiftly grabbed the keys, found the one for No. 17, and detached it from the rest.

The chewing sounds sped up.

Holding the key to No. 17, the hyphae once again extended out through the iron door. A portion of the hyphae stuck to the iron door, feeling for the keyhole's location, while the other portion of the hyphae inserted the key. The hyphae were very fragile and had limited strength. An increasing number of hyphae converged, and the key finally turned. With a click, the lock sprang open.

Clutching the remaining keys, An Zhe pushed the door open and came to the neighboring door. His hands trembled a little as he found the key to No. 18. Then, with the flashlight beam facing the keyhole, he shoved the key in and forcefully turned it to the left. At that moment, the chewing sounds stopped entirely.

"My God…" A young man broke through the door and stumbled out. Before An Zhe even had the time to get a good look at his face, he firmly pulled him over a soldier's body, and the two of them ran toward the right-hand corridor, the only safe direction. The floor was still shaking, as there were more than two things under the ground.

At that moment, the emergency lights up ahead flashed a few times before going out completely, and the area ahead went entirely dark.

An Zhe heard Poet gasp for breath next to him. "Don't look back."

But An Zhe still turned his head back, unable to help himself.

A bug.

It was a black worm that spanned more than half the width of the corridor.

Its body was snake-like, but it was also divided into distinct segments. At that moment, it was slithering out through the massive fissure in the ground, its head raised as it looked in An Zhe and Poet's direction—perhaps it could not be called a head, for it had no eyes, nor did it have any structures that a head ought to have. The front end of its body only had a round mouth containing densely packed teeth.

And behind it, another identical worm was slithering over. Two mouths in which densely packed teeth pressing against each other unanimously faced them with a rustling noise. They approached, their speed not slow at all, and they were less than twenty meters away. An Zhe smelled the stench from their bodies.

Poet gritted his teeth and said, "Go!"

But the ground abruptly shook again, and the great force flung An Zhe against the wall. A sharp pain shot up his left arm —it seemed that he had collided with a deformed iron door. He pushed himself back up with his arms, and Poet gave him a tug as well. In the pitch-black darkness, they once again sprinted toward what they recalled to be the direction of the corridor entrance. In the darkness, anything could happen. Perhaps a third worm would break through the earth in front of them the very next second, or perhaps they would run straight into the wall because they could not see.

He truly did run into the wall.

An Zhe bumped his head against something with the consistency of metal and felt pain again. His entire body had collided with something. Then something wrapped around his waist in an attempt to scoop him up and stand him upright once more.

This wall also had hands.

"Are there still living people behind you?" Lu Feng's voice

sounded from extremely close proximity, his words faster than usual.

An Zhe's heart practically stopped. He said, "No."

The people inside were all dead.

"Prepare the uranium shells, maximum equivalent," Lu Feng said. Just as he finished speaking, eye-watering white lights lit up from where they were and swiftly flew into the depths of the corridor.

Before An Zhe could react, Lu Feng once again pushed him down. They rolled on the ground, and An Zhe found himself pressed beneath the man.

In the following moment, the muffled sounds of explosions rang out, and the lightning-like white lights disappeared in an instant. Lu Feng's figure left a dazzling imprint on An Zhe's retinas. He closed his eyes and clutched at Lu Feng's sleeve cuff with his right hand, harshly gasping for breath—just now, he had run too quickly.

The ground was still violently shaking. Merely three seconds later, Lu Feng pulled him up from the ground again. There were other people nearby, and lights brightened the area where they were. Lu Feng said, "Go."

An Zhe followed as they turned and ascended the staircase. He didn't have much strength left, but miraculously, the hand Lu Feng was helping him with seemed to have some special skill. Whenever he couldn't keep up, the man pulled him along.

He didn't know how long he had been blindly following for when the ice-cold air from the outside finally poured into his windpipe. He practically leaned against Lu Feng, panting the entire time.

Lu Feng said, "It's fine now."

"Apprentice! Apprentice!" A figure nearby approached and latched onto his arm, taking him from Lu Feng. It was Mr. Shaw.

An Zhe finally recovered a bit, and his vision cleared as well. He said, "Poet..."

"I'm here." A voice came from behind him. An Zhe turned back and saw a young and good-looking person leaning against the wall with arms crossed, gasping hard from strenuous exertion as well. Once his breathing finally evened out, he said in a leisurely manner, "You're great at bumping into people."

An Zhe was at a loss for words.

However, without waiting for him to say anything, Lu Feng spoke up.

"Director Howard," Lu Feng said, "you're late."

An Zhe looked forward and saw a row of soldiers standing up ahead. Their leader was a tall man dressed in the City Defense Agency's uniform with iron gray hair, a magnificent hooked nose, and an emblem on his shoulder identical to Lu Feng's. He also held the rank of Colonel, and he looked to be the City Defense Agency's director.

Howard's voice was as steady and cold as his person. "We originally were prepared to bomb indiscriminately. Stepping outside the bounds of your authority and entering put me in a difficult position, Colonel Lu."

"My prisoners were still in there, after all." Lu Feng's voice was icy. "Do you also dare to indiscriminately bomb at the ultrasonic disperser's location?"

"There's no need for the Trial Court to be concerned with the City Defense Agency's facilities," Howard said. "You'd better see if the people who came out from underground have been infected or not."

Lu Feng said, "There's no need for you to be concerned with the Trial Court's work either."

But Howard's gaze landed heavily on An Zhe. An Zhe briefly met his eyes and realized that the man was looking at his left arm—it had gotten injured underground and bled.

Lu Feng's right hand clapped An Zhe on his shoulder. "I'll

take him away and keep him under watch during the buffer period."

Howard said, "Thank you for your hard work."

Immediately afterward, he turned to the soldiers of the City Defense Agency. "Prepare for bombardment."

Then Lu Feng took An Zhe away as Mr. Shaw watched.

Lu Feng's office in the City Defense Agency was in an annex of the main building. It was a room without any decoration whatsoever. Just as An Zhe entered, he locked the door.

This might have been a type of preventative measure, An Zhe thought. If he really had been infected and turned into a monster, he wouldn't leave this room.

He saw Lu Feng walk over to the gray office desk, open a drawer, and take out a white object that he tossed over. An Zhe unconsciously caught it, and saw that it was a roll of bandages. The Arbiter probably meant for him to wrap up his wound. He sat down at another desk and chair set near the window and began to fiddle with the bandages. He thought that although the Arbiter declared people guilty as he pleased, perhaps he could yet be regarded as a good person.

He was wounded on his left arm. It was small, only a scratch from the sheet iron. It didn't hurt much, but blood had oozed out. An Zhe tore off a length of bandage approximately half a meter long and began to wrap it around his left arm with his right hand—but he couldn't wrap it up.

With great difficulty, he loosely wrapped it using one hand, but he couldn't tie a knot. Human fingers were not as dexterous as hyphae in the first place, and moreover he only had one hand to use, and furthermore he was by no means particularly familiar with human limbs. But An Zhe felt that as someone who was human on the surface, it would be somewhat embarrassing if he couldn't even wrap a bandage, so he frowned and continued trying to tie a knot.

He felt a gaze land on him. Lu Feng was watching him.

He continued tying the knot. But as soon as he thought about how the Arbiter was watching his every move, his knot-tying technique worsened. After trying hard for three minutes, not only did he not tie the knot, with a shake of his hand, the bandages that had been wrapped around his arm came unraveled as well. The moment it unraveled, An Zhe was so angry that he even wanted to extend his hyphae.

A soft laugh came from the opposite side.

In fact, it couldn't count as a laugh. It was only the sound of a breath, very short, but An Zhe could tell—that sound was a derisive laugh, a mocking laugh.

An Zhe was speechless.

The Arbiter was mocking him.

Right at that moment, a hand appeared in front of his eyes. Long fingers and pale skin. An Zhe was far too familiar with this shape, for after Mr. Shaw finished making this hand, it was placed in the container at the head of his bed where he could see it every night before going to sleep. It was Lu Feng's hand.

That hand picked up one end of the bandage while the other hand picked up the other end and looped the bandage around his arm a few times before tightening it slightly.

Then An Zhe watched those ten fingers nimbly interlock to tie a neat knot in the bandage.

Lu Feng had helped him with wrapping the bandage, although the man had laughed mockingly at him a second ago.

He tugged down his shirt cuff and mumbled, "Thank you."

Lu Feng said nothing in return.

The sound of a loud explosion suddenly came from downstairs, but it was very muffled, as if it was coming from deep underground. An Zhe looked down. The City Defense Agency's layout consisted of four tall buildings surrounding a spacious atrium, and the building he was locked up in tonight was the shortest one. Right now, the interior of the building was in complete chaos—the people inside were evacuating, and heavily armed soldiers entered one unit at a time with their weaponry. The sound of explosions rang out continuously, and the building creaked. The vibrations made the glass shatter, and some rooms had already collapsed. The building that had been solid and magnificent just half an hour ago gradually turned into ruins. Like a white fog, dust and the smoke from the uranium shell explosions enveloped the area. The City Defense Agency's soldiers, armed to the teeth, set up a cordon around it and erected radiation signs.

The uranium shells used by the military were depleted uranium shells. They had strong penetrative power and relatively weak radiation, though long-term exposure would still harm people and required special handling.

Most of the people evacuated from the building were scattered outside the City Defense Agency, but Mr. Shaw, Poet, and the other prisoners were placed in a makeshift tent in the atrium with five gun-carrying soldiers guarding them. An Zhe could see them.

He saw Lu Feng stand up and walk to the window.

Large ribbons of dark green aurora spread across the sky outside the window, looking very dazzling. Lu Feng's figure as he stood in front of the window was transformed into a black silhouette, and he turned his head to look at the other side of the atrium.

An Zhe looked in the direction of his gaze and saw that on the other side of the atrium, there was a massive black device resembling a black round disk, and layer after layer of massive octagonal coils encircled it. The disk curved smoothly inward starting from the edges, and a stout conical object stood erect in the center. Very thin things—something akin to wires or utility lines—radiated outward, connecting the black cone and the coils. The entire device was even more colossal than two buildings put together. If one were to stand beneath the disk and look up, it would be impossible to see the sky no matter what direction they faced.

An Zhe looked at it with his chin resting in one hand. He always felt that human creations were colossal and strange.

Out of the corner of his eye, he saw Lu Feng take out his communicator and dial a number. His cold and quiet voice rang out, sounding like snow in the depths of wintertime.

"Trial Court, Lu Feng. Requesting transfer to the Lighthouse center."

The two of them were in close proximity. When the sound dispersed from the communicator's receiver, it reached An Zhe's ears as well.

The other side replied, "Transferring now, please wait."

After approximately twenty seconds, a male voice came from the other side. "What's going on with the City Defense Agency?"

Lu Feng said, "Underground invasion, large worm-class. Suspected to live in groups. The City Defense Agency is safe for now."

"Understood," the other party said. "The possibility of worms living in groups is extremely high. We will immediately dispatch the research team to the City Defense Agency. Pay attention to protecting the disperser."

"All right."

Just as he hung up, his communicator rang again on its own. This time, someone had dialed him.

"Howard?" Lu Feng asked.

"The ground underneath Building 3 can't be shelled anymore. Our men found crawl tracks and fought at close quarters with the monsters underground," Howard said. "Some men were wounded. The ones with heavy wounds have already been shot, and the ones with light wounds are currently being sent out. You have to keep watch."

Lu Feng looked downstairs. "I can see them."

After saying that, he added, "Worms are highly dangerous. Send them out immediately once they come into contact with mucus as well."

Howard uttered a curse, but Lu Feng's expression remained unchanged. He said, "Pay attention to the disperser."

"At present, no tracks heading toward the disperser have been discovered." Howard's tone of voice was a bit forceful. "The foundation beneath the disperser is stronger than that of the buildings. Just concentrate on your own job duties, Colonel Lu."

Lu Feng said flatly, "Thank you for your hard work."

The call ended. From the tone, it may not have been a pleasant call, but Lu Feng seemed to not care. He leaned against the window, his bearing slightly languid, but he was constantly watching the soldiers coming and going from the atrium. An Zhe knew he was monitoring the soldiers to see if they were safe or not.

With nothing to do, An Zhe continued examining the massive apparatus in the atrium.

From the conversations between Lu Feng and the others just now, he guessed that this was the aforesaid "ultrasonic disperser."

He was familiar with this term, for it was mentioned in the *Base Handbook*. The base's outer city had a total of ten ultrasonic dispersers, all of which were managed by the Dispersion Center located in District 1. Before, in Mr. Shaw's shop, he had also heard the base broadcast say that it was currently the breeding season for arthropod-class and parasitic-class monsters. To prevent aerial invasion, the base raised the operating strength of the ultrasonic dispersers to level III.

That was to say, the apparatus's function was to protect the entire base against invasion by airborne monsters such as arthropods and birds. An Zhe didn't know how it worked. He only felt it seemed very magical.

After examining every single one of the disperser's details, he turned his gaze back to the interior of the room. This office was by no means large and did not have anything except for two sets of desks and chairs, a gun rack, and a few filing cabinets. Many things were neatly stacked within the filing cabinets. There were papers with contents he couldn't see and file folders, a few copies of the *Base Handbook*, some apparatus operation guides, and a *Base Constitution* that was four finger widths thick—it turned out that the laws portion in the *Base Handbook* was an abridged version.

An Zhe continued looking around. Below the document organizers were some glass jars. Most of them were empty, but there was one on the side that seemed to contain a dozen or so plant seeds. To the side of that, there was also a bag of something akin to soil samples with a white "safe" label stuck to it.

An Zhe thought of his spore once again.

Seeds and spores were roughly similar. Would his spore, which the military had dug out, have also been placed in a glass jar or some other container? As soon as he imagined it, the instinctive discomfort surged up again; he seemed to have been placed in an airtight jar as well. His spore was the most important part of him, but he still didn't know where it was. Moreover, all of the leads were cut off by this Arbiter next to him.

If he wanted to find his spore, he had to ask Lu Feng for information.

But he was only a mushroom. He knew he wasn't like humans. He also knew that Lu Feng's power of observation was very fearsome. There was a very high probability that as soon as he spoke up, he would be suspected.

Or he could also do his best to observe Lu Feng for some time.

With that thought, he suddenly gave a start, then turned his head and met Lu Feng's eyes. In the lamplight, he didn't know how long those long and narrow deep green eyes had been watching him for, his expression indifferent.

An Zhe suspected that he was being suspected again, but he had to bluff his way through.

Facing the Colonel's gaze, he blinked.

The Colonel's expression didn't change at all as he said in a calm voice, "You may go."

The buffer period was over.

"Back down there?" An Zhe asked.

The prisoners were all living in the makeshift tents in the atrium.

"Mm."

An Zhe bit his lower lip. After a while, his yearning for his spore overcame his fear of the Colonel. He said, "It's cold there."

Eyeing him, Lu Feng said, "You're a prisoner."

"But I haven't committed any crimes of indecency."

Lu Feng looked at him. Two seconds later, he smiled.

"All right," Lu Feng said. "For the crime of illegally stealing the Arbiter's information, the penalty will be doubled."

"I didn't steal it." An Zhe tried hard to explain himself. "I only made something according to your information."

"Oh," Lu Feng said. "For the crime of using the Arbiter's information to make illegal profits, the penalty will be doubled twice."

An Zhe lowered his voice. "I didn't make a profit either."

Lu Feng looked at him with arms crossed. "Didn't make a profit? Did you take it for personal use?"

An Zhe was at a loss for words.

He couldn't outspeak him.

Lu Feng looked at him, frowning slightly. "How much profit?"

"I don't know," An Zhe said.

"What are your wages?"

"60R."

Lu Feng laughed again.

"How pitiful," he said. "Your boss cheated you. After you get out of prison, remember to ask him for a raise."

An Zhe felt that he was being mocked again. This was the third time tonight that this person angered him. He firmly believed that Lu Feng was the human who was the best at bullying others within the base.

Before he thought of what to say, he saw Lu Feng glance down at his watch.

"It's early morning now." His voice once again took on the commanding tone An Zhe was familiar with. "Go down and sleep."

At that very moment, the cold night wind blew in from the window directly onto An Zhe's face. The temperature difference between day and night at the base was very big.

He let out a very small sneeze, then saw Lu Feng across from him furrow his brow, seemingly disgusted.

Frowning, Lu Feng said coldly, "So delicate."

An Zhe confirmed that he was being viewed with disgust. But the wind was too cold. Unable to resist, he sneezed again.

He truly was very afraid of the cold, and he also truly wanted to look for clues at Lu Feng's side. But as he looked at the Colonel's facial expression, he realized that if he stayed any longer, he may be thrown out the window.

He had no choice but to bow his head and silently gather his shirt collar, stand up, and turn to leave.

Just as he reached the doorway, he heard Lu Feng's voice come from behind him. "Halt."

An Zhe halted and turned back.

Lu Feng was still leaning against the window with his arms crossed. His gaze shifted to the right side of the room and he said, "You can go over there."

Following his gaze, An Zhe saw another door on the right-hand wall. He walked over and opened it.

It was a nap room with a simple bed and desk. At the door

was an upright clothes stand upon which a black uniform coat hung.

An Zhe realized whose room this was.

He said, "You…"

"I can't sleep tonight," Lu Feng said. "You can choose to sleep here or outside."

After weighing the two options, An Zhe said resolutely, "Thank you."

Without a word, Lu Feng turned to face the window and continued observing the area below. The sounds outside had never stopped; it was still utter chaos.

An Zhe walked into the room, and after closing the door, he examined the place. The room was filled with a cheerless atmosphere. There weren't many traces of human habitation save for a few creases in the folded quilt at the foot of the bed.

On the wooden table were some detachable magazines and a blunt silver military knife next to them, but those were not what attracted An Zhe's gaze. In the middle of the table was an open book. On its pages was black handwriting.

6.16, normal.
6.15, normal.
6.14, normal.

An Zhe realized what it was. This was the Arbiter's work notebook—during that demonstration against the Trial Court, there was a poster written with the words "publicize the Arbiter's work notes."

But by the looks of it, based on how perfunctory Lu Feng's notebook was, even if it was publicized, there wasn't much worth seeing.

He flipped back to May.

Amidst a string of "normals," there was an additional line:

5.17, parasitic invasion, resolved, report to be submitted.

5.18, normal, 5.17 report submitted.

He continued upward.

5.11, normal, suspect ID3261170514 (extremely low
risk), passed genetic examination, permitted to enter city.

It seemed that on that day at the city gates, Lu Feng had not
only discovered his abnormality, but also how weak he was.

But he didn't stop there, for a kind of intuition drove him to
keep flipping backward through the pages.

Mr. Shaw said that all members of the military, even if they
belonged to the Trial Court, would go out on missions in the
wilderness.

And there was one of the Trial Court's bullet shells at the
place where he lost his spore.

An Zhe's heart pounded as he hastily flipped through a
dozen or so pages when one record different from the rest
stood out before his eyes.

2.20, returned to base, samples handed over to
Lighthouse.

An Zhe's gaze paused on this line before he continued to flip.
The records on this page suddenly became much more
compacted.

2.12, wilderness, Abyss, supplemented 4 map records,
collected 7 plant samples, 4 animal samples, 7 secretion
samples, 3 mixed polymorphic monster behavior information footages.

2.13, wilderness, Abyss, collected 13 plant samples, 3

animal samples, 3 secretion samples, 6 mixed polymorphic monster behavior information footage.

He had gone to the Abyss.
An Zhe's eyes flew wide open, and his gaze stopped on the
page's last record.

2.14, wilderness, return home, collected 1 abnormal
fungus sample (spore).

An Zhe's mind went blank for a moment, and his hand that
was holding the page trembled.

In his time as a mushroom, he didn't have much of a concept
of time. Sunrises and sunsets were only a type of change in the
course of nature. He didn't know how long he had lost his
spore for.

February 14th. According to human seasons, that was when
winter had not yet ended. It was indeed so, for the howling cold
winds of the night he lost his spore still echoed in his memories
and dreams.

There would be no other mushroom in the world who had
likewise lost its spore in the same winter. His meeting with Lu
Feng occurred far earlier than that time at the city gates. And
perhaps it was the Arbiter himself, separated from him by only
a wall, who had personally taken his spore.

He paused, then flipped forward through this work notebook. On the next page, February 20th, Lu Feng had returned to
the base and written down "samples handed over to
Lighthouse."

After his gaze lingered on that line for three seconds, he
flipped the journal back to June 17th and put the black ballpoint
pen back on the page, as if it had never been flipped through.

An Zhe looked away from the book and at the wall behind
the desk. The Arbiter held ultimate authority within the base.

He could open fire on any person and also order the cooperation of all organizations in the city. In emergency situations, he could mobilize the City Defense Agency's soldiers, just like that day at the supply depot's square. But despite his high position and authority, his quarters in the City Defense Agency were even more desolate and simple than An Zhe's own room. Even the walls had only received a thin layer of paint, faintly revealing the texture of the gray cement beneath.

And on this light gray wall, on a place slightly above the height of a person, seven words and a period were written with red paint.

"Humankind's interests take precedence over all else."

An Zhe shivered lightly. The underground prison was too cold, and he still hadn't yet recovered. He turned his gaze to the nearby bed. After hesitating for a few seconds, he got in.

His head sank down into the pillow, but he didn't dare to wrap the quilt around himself as usual. He only loosely draped it over himself and curled up. The quilt, pillow, and bedsheets were all the base's standard issue, with no differences whatsoever from the underground prison's prisoners' bedding. Even the scent of the synthetic material was identical. But An Zhe felt that it was very different—sleeping upon the Arbiter's bed, along with the sound of brief conversation between Lu Feng and some other person from the office on the other side of the wall, the feeling was difficult to describe. Very dangerous, yet also very safe.

Anyone would have trouble sleeping in this situation, let alone himself, a mushroom.

But he actually didn't have trouble sleeping for too long. Lost in fanciful thoughts, his body gradually warmed up due to the quilt, the world before his eyes gradually blurred, and in that manner, he tumbled into a dream.

Someone woke An Zhe up, and he was convinced that only a short time had passed since he fell asleep.

Just a moment ago, he was still experiencing the feeling of having his spore dug out for the umpteenth time in the wilderness, and then he felt a hand patting the pillow next to him.

An Zhe gave a start and opened his eyes, meeting a pair of cold green eyes. It was the murderer who dug out his spore.

Lu Feng lifted the quilt off of him and quickly said, "Evacuate."

There was no need for him to explain. The moment An Zhe woke up, he also realized the building beneath him was trembling slightly, just like the underground prison—had worms appeared beneath this building as well?

After pondering briefly, the wave-like alarm went off again. It was another evacuation signal.

Before he had time to think much, he leapt out of bed and put on his shoes. Lu Feng grabbed An Zhe's shoulder with his right hand and led him out of the room. A cold wind blew in from the open door, and An Zhe instinctively shivered, having suddenly come to this situation from the warm quilt. Right away, he felt the hand Lu Feng was holding him with pause.

A black shadow dropped onto him, and he felt its weight on his body. Lu Feng had grabbed the coat from the nearby clothes rack and tossed it onto him. An Zhe did not have time to say "thank you," only gathering the coat around himself. Lu Feng's movements didn't stop. He swiftly picked up the work notebook and ballpoint pen from the table, stuffed them into the pocket of the coat covering An Zhe, then grabbed his wrist and quickly walked toward the exit. Two Judges were already waiting at the doorway. Upon seeing Lu Feng, they promptly called out, "Colonel!"

Then the two of them simultaneously glanced at An Zhe.

Lu Feng didn't say anything, and the group went downstairs from the nearest emergency passage. The interior of the passage was pitch black, for the monsters' assault had affected the power systems. Only the green fluorescent guiding lights were still glowing. The stairs were both narrow and steep, so they could only just manage to accommodate two people side by side. But the other three moved too quickly. After Lu Feng dragged An Zhe down one floor, the latter had already stumbled a good number of times and realized that unless he changed into hyphae, he would not only be unable to keep pace with these people, but also slow down Lu Feng.

Just as he was about to say that there was no need for Lu Feng to pull on him and that he'd walk on his own, a force was suddenly applied to his shoulder as Lu Feng grabbed it and twisted him backward—the momentum of going down the stairs was still there, so An Zhe instantly ran into Lu Feng's back. He had bumped his head against the badge on Lu Feng's chest earlier, and now he bumped it against the epaulette. The stairs sloped downward and he was in a higher position than Lu Feng, so with this collision, he instinctively clutched at Lu Feng.

Then the man picked him up in a piggy-back carry.

With arms wrapped around the Arbiter's neck, An Zhe recalled the chaotic but also seemingly logical sequence of movements and felt very mystified.

The key point was that this person didn't seem to exert any effort while carrying him, instead easily leaping down the stairs and landing steadily on the ground. Then he made a run-up to the second-floor window, leapt out of it, and leveraged the platform outside the first-floor window. The wind howled in An Zhe's ears, and somehow Lu Feng landed on the lawn beneath the building.

Lu Feng clearly did not have the obvious bulky brawn of Vance or Howard, but through the layers of clothing, An Zhe still felt his terrifying explosive power the moment he tensed up. Human bodies were by no means the same as soft hyphae.

After Lu Feng landed, the sound of two other landings came in quick succession behind them. It was the other two Judges.

An Zhe felt that just holding on to Lu Feng used up a lot of his energy, but his was clearly also a human body.

He realized that the differences between people were greater still than the differences between people and mushrooms.

But three seconds later, he realized that all the people inside the atrium were looking at him. The sky had brightened earlier, and the light mist couldn't block others' gazes at all. Mr. Shaw stuck his head out from the nearest tent, glanced first at Lu Feng, then glanced at him, and promptly began to make suggestive faces at him.

Lu Feng put him down, and An Zhe also loosened his grip around Lu Feng's neck as he landed.

"Thank you," he said.

"You're welcome," Lu Feng said. "Go to the tents."

The tents were just a few steps away. An Zhe gave an affirmative response and turned, only to run right into the approaching Howard.

"What's the matter?" Lu Feng asked.

"The situation has changed. Many more have suddenly come. When the Lighthouse's people came and turned on the radar, it showed that there are bugs beneath all four buildings," Howard said. "It's not just one or two, but a group. There's a bug nest beneath the City Defense Agency. They broke through the earth to attack the people in the buildings."

"Full evacuation?" Lu Feng asked.

"Full evacuation. You as well," Howard said with finality.

Lu Feng said, "Let me see the radar imaging."

"No need to look, it's beyond saving."

"The disperser is here."

Howard's voice went cold as he dug in his heels. "The disperser can't be protected anymore. How many more times do you want me to say it? After evacuating, I'll immediately contact the Dispersion Center to increase the operating strength of the other nine dispersers."

An Zhe looked back and saw that Lu Feng's expression was icy and that his right hand had come to rest on the gun at his waist as he repeated, articulating each word clearly, "Show me the radar imaging."

"You—!" Howard, seeming furious yet afraid of the Arbiter's privilege of killing at any time and any place, waved his hand in a certain direction.

A man in a plain shirt walked over from the other side, holding a black instrument in a hand. Lu Feng took the instrument from him and scanned the screen.

An Zhe watched helplessly as the temperature on his face dropped from zero degrees Celsius to eighteen below zero, and his voice was so cold that it could make shards of ice form.

"The monsters' objective isn't the people in the buildings, it's the disperser." He lifted his gaze to look at Howard, his speech quick. "The atrium has the disperser and its foundation is reinforced and can't be broken, so they can only emerge from beneath the four buildings."

"The Lighthouse's report does not support your conclusion, Colonel Lu," Howard said.

"I spend half of every year in the Abyss." With fingers pressed down on the gunstock, Lu Feng narrowed his eyes slightly, and his icy intimidation made everyone freeze. "Howard, I've seen more monsters than you have people."

Howard was silent for three seconds, not saying anything. Then, as if he suddenly thought of something, his pupils dilated and his expression changed drastically. "Then the other dispersers—"

"Contact the Dispersion Center," Lu Feng said. "Immediately."

The Judge behind him took out a communicator, dialed a string of numbers, and pressed the speaker key.

"Beep—"

The monotonous hold tone played.

"Beep—"

"Beep—"

It was silent throughout the atrium.

After nine hold tones, a hurried busy tone came from the communicator, and three seconds later, the busy tone stopped, nobody answered, and the communicator automatically hung up.

Howard swiftly pulled out his communicator, and after punching in a few buttons, he said to the other side, "City Defense Agency Colonel Howard, transfer me to the Dispersion Center, any line is fine, at once."

"Please wait." The operator's voice came through.

After that sentence, there was a long silence. A full three minutes later, the operator's voice came again, a slight tremble at the end of his words.

"The Dispersion Center is unreachable."

9

"THOSE TEN DAYS WERE TRULY A BLOODBATH."

THE SECOND AFTER the operator finished speaking, Lu Feng's countenance changed.

He turned on his heel and left, and the Lighthouse researcher quickly followed. One of the Trial Court's cars was parked outside the City Defense Agency, and a young Judge came running over. "Colonel!"

"You all will stay and assist the City Defense Agency," Lu Feng said.

"Colonel, do we need to convene the Trial Court?"

Lu Feng's gaze swept over the thin streams of people on the road. "Close the city gates and gather in District 5."

"Yes sir," the Judge said. "Stay safe, Colonel."

Lu Feng didn't say anything as he slammed the car door shut and started the engine. He turned the steering wheel hard, and the black car made a swift U-turn before heading toward the Dispersion Center in District 1 like an arrow leaving its bowstring. Following closely in its wake were Howard's car and the City Defense Agency's heavily armored vehicles.

In the back seat, the researcher was holding a communicator and having a conversation as well. He was being questioned.

"We're currently heading to the Dispersion Center," the researcher said. "We must prepare for the worst-case scenario.

"For now, it's suspected that the special frequency used by the ultrasonic dispersers to drive off arthropods and birds is simultaneously attracting underground worms. But there is also no doubt that this was a premeditated attack.

"Yes, we are currently contacting the other disperser locations."

At the same time, in the middle of the city, the sound of the alarm tower abruptly rang out. Its constant shrill wail was deafening. After hearing it, the countenances of the people sparsely scattered on the early morning streets changed dramatically, and after looking at each other, they bolted toward the nearest buildings as the sustained sound meant "find emergency shelter."

At the same time, the street broadcast began to play and a pleasant robotic female voice said, "Alert. Due to a breakdown of the ultrasonic disperser, insects, birds, and worm-class monsters may appear in the city in the near future. Before repairs are confirmed, please immediately close all doors and windows and refrain from going out. Upon discovering a suspicious situation, please immediately dial the emergency line and contact the City Defense Agency. The base's military will do all it can to protect your safety."

"Alert. Due to a breakdown of the ultrasonic disperser, insects, birds, and worm-class monsters may appear in the city in the near future..."

The sounds of windows slamming shut came in an unbroken succession from the residential buildings all around, and the City Defense Agency's workers and prisoners were swiftly transferred to the nearest residential area. Steady streams of armored vehicles emerged from the City Defense Agency's various garrison points within the base and dispersed all over the roads.

An Zhe, Mr. Shaw, and Poet were in the same room. The City Defense Agency had its hands full with its own matters, and of the three of them, one had committed the crime of incitement, one had committed the crime of illegally stealing the Arbiter's information, and one had been charged with some strange accusations by the Arbiter—in short, they posed no lethal threat, so no soldiers kept watch on them and they were only locked in.

"The Dispersion Center remotely manages all the dispersers in the outer city." Poet looked out the window. "In the air of the wilderness, even a tiny flying bug may infect humans. Only by using special frequency ultrasound to disperse them can the base maintain the residents' absolute safety. Not even a fly can get into the base. If something really has happened to the Dispersion Center, then the entire city is exposed to the possibility of infection. To insects in the midst of breeding season, human flesh and blood make the best breeding grounds for their eggs."

An Zhe sat on the bare bed board, hugging his knees. He asked, "What will happen?"

Poet reached out and pinched the nape of An Zhe's neck. "Supposing that a little bug laid its eggs beneath your skin last night, the bug genes and your human genes will fuse. In another three days at most, you'll be a bag of skin wrapped around up to a hundred million insect eggs. The little bugs will fly out from your eyes and windpipe onto other people, and very soon—"

"Don't scare the kid," Mr. Shaw said, clearly disgruntled by this exchange.

Poet leisurely retracted his hand. "I'm speaking the truth."

The xenogenic whose stomach Lu Feng had cut open that day at the supply depot square suddenly appeared before An Zhe's eyes. His abdominal cavity and windpipe were full of small translucent bugs.

He asked, "Then what can we do?"

Poet shook his head.

"We can only pray that nothing major happened to the Dispersion Center or that the disperser can be quickly repaired soon after, otherwise..." He sighed softly. "Otherwise, either there will be a base-wide outbreak or... Judgment Day will repeat itself."

An Zhe frowned as he looked at the deserted streets through the window.

But he heard Mr. Shaw ask, "You know about Judgment Day?"

"I've heard a bit about it," Poet said.

Mr. Shaw sighed. "I thought that so long as I obediently stayed within the base, I could live until I died of old age."

"The base has been safe for too long." Poet was still looking into the distance. "I always forget that safety is what's temporary while danger is eternal. Life isn't something we're owed. Life is a gift."

An Zhe didn't really understand, nor did he know how to ask about it.

He only had one question. "What is Judgment Day?"

But Mr. Shaw glanced at him. "I forgot to ask you. What's the story behind your clothes?"

An Zhe was at a loss for words.

Lu Feng's coat was still draped over his shoulders, and in the coat's pocket were Lu Feng's work notebook and ballpoint pen.

Mr. Shaw narrowed his eyes.

"Last night, when Poet and I were in the tents, where were you?" he asked. "Did you sleep with him?"

"No." An Zhe always felt that Mr. Shaw was interrogating him. He replied in a small voice, "He didn't sleep."

Mr. Shaw let out a huff of laughter. "How did you know he didn't sleep? You did sleep with him. How was he? 'Fess up."

An Zhe knew that he couldn't outspeak anyone, so he

pretended to not hear his question. Instead, he repeated his own. "What is Judgment Day?"

"Then do you know how the Arbiter's Code was proposed?" Poet asked him.

"I don't," An Zhe said.

Poet looked at Mr. Shaw. "The elder must know."

Mr. Shaw said with a lift of his eyebrows, "I do."

Poet said, "How old are you?"

But Mr. Shaw didn't reply. He said, "When I was young, everyone greatly supported the bill."

Poet sat down on the corner of the bed right next to An Zhe. His gray prison uniform was worn out in some places, his black shoulder-length hair was tied at the back of his head in a simple manner, and his facial expression was very calm. When he spoke, it was with a contrived cadence that was perhaps the tone commonly used by those in Poet's line of work. "The Arbiter's Code has lasted for almost seventy years. I think the Northern Base is very grateful toward it. I don't know much about that thing in particular, because the base has too few old people."

Mr. Shaw's interest seemed to have finally shifted from the question of how An Zhe slept. As he played with small mannequin parts he had taken out from his pocket, he said, "I also heard it from others when I was young."

"Do tell," Poet said.

"After the Southeastern Base met its doom, everyone was very afraid. In those days, the xenogenics' degree of mutation was not yet as severe as it is now. When people returned to the base from the outside, they only needed to pass a full-body examination. Which was fine, as long as they didn't have wounds or other abnormalities. There were soldiers every-where within the base, and as soon as a mutant was discovered, it would be immediately killed," Mr. Shaw said. "The ultrasonic dispersers hadn't been invented yet either, so insects flew around within the base. The soldiers killed the big ones with obvious mutations, but the small ones couldn't be caught, so insect-catching lights were hung up everywhere within the base. Minors weren't permitted to leave the base, so they formed insect-catching teams and stamped out insects everywhere."

Poet said, "The Turmoil Age."

"Pretty much," Mr. Shaw said. "I was even an insect-catching team captain in my youth. It wasn't until more than ten years later that we had the ultrasonic dispersers and not even a single bug could fly into the base."

"At that time, the Arbiter's Code had already been enacted," Poet said.

"Correct," Mr. Shaw said. "But the enactment of the bill wasn't because of the bugs, but because of a surveillance recording. When a supervisor was making a routine inspection of the water tower footage, he saw that something had happened in one corner, but the spot was too dark and not clearly captured on video, so nobody discovered it at the time. The moment the supervisor saw the footage, he was scared out of his wits. You guys can't imagine the sight."

Mr. Shaw's story piqued An Zhe's interest, and he saw that Poet was also listening with rapt attention.

Then he heard Mr. Shaw continue. "He saw a person with a very strange posture walk to the edge of the circulating pool. Then that person sat down like they had no bones in their body. I heard from the people who recorded the footage that the person was like a human-shaped leech. After sitting down, he stuck his legs into the pool."

"He was a xenogenic and using his secretions to pollute the water source?" Poet asked.

Mr. Shaw smiled. "Hah, that wouldn't have caused that much fear."

Poet raised his eyebrows.

"Then that person's legs turned into something translucent and whitish. As if they had exploded, a large patch diffused into the water. There's no way to describe it." Mr. Shaw shook his head and continued. "And after that, the person's entire body also flowed into the pond, and the water level immediately rose by a lot. I heard people say that it was like it had been stuffed full of white minced pork. That water was a part of the base's water circulation system."

"And after that, it flowed away through the outlet along with the water, which was the base's drinking water," Mr. Shaw said. "What made it even worse was that it was a recording from more than twenty hours prior already."

Poet frowned slightly, seeming somewhat nauseated. Only after his Adam's apple had bobbed a few times did he say, "The whole city was exposed."

"Correct," Mr. Shaw said. "The Lighthouse gave out its investigation results. It was a soft-bodied aquatic xenogenic, and diffusing into the water may have been a reproduction method. In short, the entire base was at risk of infection, and nobody was safe. That bill was urgently enacted soon afterward."

"There's a saying," Poet said, "that the initial generations of Arbiters and the Trial Court did not belong to the military but were subordinate institutions of the Lighthouse instead."

"That's also correct. After the aquatic xenogenic invasion, amongst the Lighthouse's scientists, some studied humanoid xenogenics and understood quite a lot about their characteristics. They formed the Trial Court, and in ten days, they organized for everyone in the base to be examined one by one. Nobody was wounded, but anyone could have been infected. They also did not have any methods with which to perform inspections, so it was entirely dependent on observation by the naked eye and intuitive judgment. Although you've done nothing but drink a mouthful of water, if the Trial Court wanted you to die, you had to die." Mr. Shaw sighed. "Those ten days were truly a bloodbath. It's said that half of the entire base died."

"It's roughly the same as the information I collected before," Poet said. "Those ten days were the legendary Judgment Days."

"Only those of you who fiddle with your pens, all mysterious-like, say that those ten days are 'Judgment Day' and talk about God and whatnot—" Mr. Shaw said with a frown.

Poet smiled. "On doomsday, everyone on Earth will be judged before God and either ascend to Heaven or be cast down into Hell. That is Judgment Day."

"Who knows?" Mr. Shaw brushed the dust off his sleeve cuffs. "After the Virginia Base caught wind of it, they cursed out our base's strategic decision, dispatched a scientific research team over so that we could have devices that differentiate xenogenics on a scientific basis, and circulated opposition leaflets everywhere with drones, denouncing the Northern Base for its loss of humanity and violations of human rights. And the result?"

Poet said in a low voice, "Three years later, humanoid marine xenogenics invaded, and the Virginia Base was completely infected and declared fallen."

"With the idiots of the Virginia Base as an example, the Arbiter's Code was formally extended. Any Judge could shoot people. Those whom the Judges couldn't make decisions on were given over to the Arbiter to make a decision with their full powers, and they would bear no responsibility for manslaughter. The Arbiter is God." Mr. Shaw grinned. "Unfortunately, it's easy for God to go mad. After killing too many of their own people, they won't be able to stop. The Lighthouse's scientists who were responsible for the Trials were switched out batch after batch. In ten years, three went mad and two committed suicide. Nobody else was willing to do it, so the military took over."

"People in the military are stationed in the wilderness for

long periods of time, have seen many monsters, have a decent ability to distinguish xenogenics, and are psychologically strong. The speed at which Arbiters were replaced finally changed from one going mad every three years to one going mad every five years. Lu Feng wasn't even twenty years old when he became the Arbiter. I think he's too young, and I even bet with others that he wouldn't last past three years." Mr. Shaw shrugged. "I've lost no small amount of money. This year will be his seventh. Hubbard said that the number of people he's killed is several times the amount of the previous Arbiter. Moreover, in each of these past three years, the number kept doubling. Everyone knows that he's not far off from going mad."

"Between the Arbiter and the person being judged, it's hard to say whose psychological pressure is greater." Poet leaned against the wall. "But since Colonel Lu still has the frame of mind to sleep with our young friend, it looks like he's still far away from losing control."

"No, that's wrong." Just as he finished speaking, he frowned and corrected himself. "On the contrary, for a cold and heartless person like Colonel Lu, this is one of the omens of madness."

He sidled up to An Zhe, a look similar to Mr. Shaw's in his eyes. "How was he? Did he hurt you?"

An Zhe tightly wrapped himself in the coat and shrank into the corner, reluctant to talk to them.

"Thump."

The sound of an impact.

The atmosphere in the room instantly tensed, and all three of them looked at the source of the sound.

A colorful beetle had struck the window.

10

"WAIT THERE."

SOMEWHERE DOWNSTAIRS, a woman screamed. Perhaps she had also seen the bugs.

The beetle, approximately the size of a human palm, crawled slowly over the glass. On its eight slender legs were densely packed, small protrusions that adhered smoothly to the glass, and in the middle of each protrusion was a pinprick-sized white dot, which was a suction cup. The beetle dragged along a long, soft brown tentacle behind its drop-shaped tail, leaving a wet, dark brown ooze in its wake as it crawled—it seemed to want to come in.

Poet tested the seams between two of the windowpanes by running over them with his fingers. "It's fine. It's sealed, so it can't get in."

"Each generation is worse than the last," Mr. Shaw said. "They just keep getting uglier. Before, they still looked like bugs."

"The fusion of genes." Poet looked at the glass. "The more fusing there is, the more bizarre its appearance and the stronger its infectiousness. I know a scientist, and he said that throughout the past hundred years, none of humankind's research could explain the principle of infection."

"Hah," Mr. Shaw said.

He released a meaningless sound from his mouth but then shrank into a corner of the room, as far away from the window as possible, and said, "Can't you close the curtains?"

"I want to look at the city some more." As Poet spoke, he lowered one side of the curtains, shrouding the room in darkness. Within the gloom, a strange grief showed in his profile. "This... city that may not have much time left."

An Zhe looked outside. It was early morning, and beneath the dim skies, the gray city stretched outward, half of it concealed in the thin white mist. The sun had risen and the mist was burning off, revealing some colossal mechanical structures at the maximum range of his field of vision that towered and pierced straight up into the sky. Humans always had many strange devices that guaranteed the base's safety, but there were some times in which they couldn't do so, such as right now.

Poet turned toward him. "You don't seem the slightest bit afraid."

An Zhe pursed his lips, unsure how to respond.

Poet lowered the other side of the curtains and smiled at him. "You're truly very strange."

"Am I?" An Zhe asked.

"You're too quiet, like it doesn't matter regardless of what happens next," Poet said. "In our generation, there are very few people with your type of character."

An Zhe smiled. "Perhaps."

It was impossible for there to not be even the slightest difference between mushrooms and humans. In an attempt to make himself more human-like, he asked Poet, "Then what shall we do now?"

Poet thought for three seconds, then said, "Pray."

"Pray that the ultrasonic disperser hasn't been completely destroyed. Or pray that this is just a group of bugs that are brainless and live entirely on instinct."

"After that, pray that our glass is sufficiently solid and won't be easily smashed."

Right as he finished speaking, the sounds of things pelting the window came in a flurry. It was the sound of countless bugs flying into the glass.

Mr. Shaw shot a dark look at Poet. "I pray for you to be a mute."

Poet became flustered too. He lifted a corner of the curtain, then swiftly closed it again. "Don't look, you guys."

"Already saw it," Mr. Shaw said. "The bug swarms have come."

In the following moment, his countenance abruptly changed. "Hurry! Check the vents!"

Poet suddenly looked toward one corner of the room. "The vent is there!"

The direction they looked in was right over An Zhe's head. It was a hole leading outside that was protected by wire mesh, but because it hadn't been repaired for a long time, it had deteriorated and an opening had formed. Seeing it, Poet tore off half of his shirt sleeve and handed it to An Zhe. "Plug it up!"

The vent was not small. An Zhe accepted the fabric, then wadded it up in his right hand and stuffed it into the hole. "It's not enough."

Poet tore off another piece. An Zhe held the first piece in place with one hand and took the other piece with his other hand.

He felt a sudden sting of pain in the tip of his right index finger.

An Zhe paused, then calmly stuffed the other wad of fabric in as well, firmly stopping up the vent before sitting back down on the bed. While Mr. Shaw and Poet were checking the rest of the room for other holes, he lifted his index finger up to his eyes.

A red spot the size of a pinprick.

The texture of his skin shifted slightly, changing into snow-white hyphae. Taking advantage of how the other two were facing away from him, he tore off those hyphae with a fierce yank.

New hyphae extended from the breakage point and formed a human finger once more, a new one without any wound.

An Zhe didn't know if doing so would have any effect, nor could he see anything wrong with the hyphae he tore off, but he didn't really have any other options.

"There aren't any other holes," Poet said, turning back around.

"… Mm," An Zhe replied.

However, the sounds of insects colliding into the glass came faster and harder, and the glass rattled as if it was about to shatter. The broadcast in the corridor continued to issue instructions, but they were nothing more than some nonsensical "please close the doors and windows, and do not panic."

Poet sat down, his face slightly pale. "It's in God's hands now, I guess."

"Shut up right now." Mr. Shaw's gaze was grim. After yelling at Poet, he looked at An Zhe.

An Zhe didn't understand why. "What is it?"

"Hurry," Mr. Shaw said. "Call your man."

An Zhe was speechless.

———

District 1, Dispersion Center.

The huge, black ultrasonic disperser loomed half-hidden beneath the gray skies, its disk-shaped main body making it look like an enormous flower blooming in the city.

. . .

As the car sped along the road, the buildings continuously drew away and the shadow of the disperser up ahead swiftly grew.

"If the Dispersion Center is destroyed," Lu Feng said, interrupting him, "will the other dispersers still work normally?"

"They might stop working," the researcher said, then briefly fell silent. "The operation of the dispersers is excessively complicated. To ensure that the entirety of the Outer City is perfectly covered by the ultrasonic waves, the intensity and wave bands of all the dispersers are uniformly managed from afar by the Dispersion Center. If the emergency procedures were not promptly initiated when the center was destroyed, I'm afraid there will be very serious consequences."

"However, that's only the worst outcome, and the probability of it happening is very low," he said. "The Disperser 1 at the Dispersion Center is the biggest ultrasonic disperser in the entirety of the Outer City. Because its power is too strong, it has adverse effects on the human body, which is why District 1 doesn't have permanent residents and there aren't many workers or troops stationed at or near the Dispersion Center. In the event of insufficient manpower, temporary loss of communication may be because of other reasons, not necessarily—"

His voice abruptly cut off as he looked through the car window and straight at the ultrasonic disperser up ahead.

Over a hundred years ago, in the Peaceful Age's springtime, when flowers and leaves were developing, gardeners would spray insect repellent on the plants so that they would be free from insect bites.

And at the present moment, the ultrasonic disperser—this black flower—was covered with protrusions that were striped in gray, white, black, and yellow. Huge worms had crawled all over it.

No, it wasn't only worms.

His breathing became sharp pants, stuttering all of a sudden.

"No…" he said. "Colonel, do you see it?"

Lu Feng yanked the steering wheel around!

The car executed a hair-raising sharp turn on the narrow road and drove back in the direction it came from!

At first, the armored vehicles behind it angrily flashed their lights, but then they all made sharp U-turns as well—

At the end of the road, the black swarm of bugs exploded like fireworks, covering the sky as they flew up and came back down like a sudden downpour of rain. The arthropods' exoskeleton-covered bodies pelted against the glass, and it felt like the entire car was moving forward in the face of stray bullets.

Inside the car, the communicator's volume was set to maximum, and the operator's violently trembling voice came from it.

"Colonel, emergency communication from District 2. Full-scale outbreak of bug swarms. Requesting assistance."

"Emergency communication from District 3. Large numbers of insect monsters were discovered during the evacuation process. Requesting assistance."

"Emergency communication from the City Defense Agency."

"Emergency communication from the City Affairs Office."

"Emergency communication from District 8—"

"Connect to District 8," Lu Feng said quickly. "Can the underground shelter safely accept the entire city's emergency evacuees?"

"Colonel Lu!" The person on the other end spoke even more quickly. "Small flying mosquitoes have entered via the ventilation system, and more than ten infected ones have appeared here. Requesting the Trial Court's assistance!"

A three-second-long silence.

Lu Feng said, "Kill the infected ones. Everyone else take refuge and wait for assistance."

The communication line was cut off.

"Colonel." A young voice rang out. "The Trial Court has assembled, and at present, there have been no casualties."

"Disperse assistance to the various districts. Prioritize District 8."

"Yes sir."

The call ended.

"Colonel." In the car, the researcher spoke with a forced veneer of composure. "We're returning to the Main City."

Lu Feng's tone of voice was flat. "The Main City?"

"The Main City has an independent defense and dispersion system, so it can ensure absolute safety."

The car gradually slowed. Up ahead was a fork in the road.

Lu Feng said, "What about the Outer City?"

"The entire Outer City is exposed. The insect monsters can penetrate anywhere with their advantageous body sizes, so the danger level of the insect swarms is higher than when the Southeastern Base fell to the rodent swarms." Calm gradually returned to the researcher's voice. "You may be the Arbiter, but under these circumstances, you can't save anyone."

The abundant justifications allowed the researcher to regain his reason and composure, and he even smiled as he said, "It's meaningless to go anywhere now. There's no way to reduce the number of casualties. You know that what I'm saying is correct. You can't protect anything else, but you can keep us safe."

A voice came from the communicator again. Previously, the situation was critical, so Lu Feng set it to emergency mode, and the communication was automatically answered three seconds later as a result.

But what came through wasn't an operator's voice.

"Colonel," a clear voice spoke, slower than the speed Lu Feng was accustomed to and with a soft lightness to the words. "Your things are still here with me."

"Where are you?" Lu Feng asked.

"Next to the City Defense Agency," An Zhe said. "... Lots of bugs are crashing into the windows."

There was a tremble at the end of his words, as if he was afraid.

Lu Feng turned the steering wheel halfway around and drove onto one of the road's branches. The researcher looked at the abandoned branch with eyes wide open, his body seemingly about to bounce up from the seat yet secured in place by the seat belt. He blurted out, "You—"

Lu Feng seemed to have not heard him at all. He only replied to the communicator, "Wait there."

11

"GOD JUDGED THE COMMON PEOPLE, EVEN USING GOOD AND EVIL AS THE BASIS."

AN ZHE FOUND himself being led out with his head wrapped up in the uniform coat after Lu Feng kicked the door open.

Of course, Poet and Mr. Shaw came along as well—but they wrapped up their own heads.

Lu Feng had brought over a small ultrasonic jammer to the building entrance, temporarily clearing out a space with a ten-meter circumference. An Zhe was safely stuffed into the car, and Poet and Mr. Shaw climbed in as well, and the three of them squeezed into the back seats.

Lu Feng returned to the driver's seat and said, "We're over capacity."

An Zhe somehow felt that the Arbiter was targeting him again.

Mr. Shaw took the initiative, saying, "Reporting in, I'm not a person, so we aren't over capacity."

"Oh," Lu Feng said.

He made a call. "The rescue plan using ultrasonic jammers is feasible. Organizing large-scale transfers of residents is recommended."

Howard's voice came from the other side. "Transfer to the underground shelter?"

Lu Feng said, "I'm going to District 8's shelter first to confirm that it's safe."

"Thank you for your hard work."

Lu Feng started the engine, and their car drove around a bend and headed towards District 8.

Along the way, Lu Feng's communicator rang madly. Just as the City Affairs Office sent a distress signal, District 5 requested reinforcements, and just after District 5 received reinforcements, the Trial Court called to say that their manpower was insufficient.

By the end, Lu Feng's replies had become very robotic.

"Please transfer to the City Defense Agency."

"Please transfer to the City Defense Agency."

"Please transfer to the City Defense Agency."

"You've worked hard, please transfer to the City Defense Agency."

"Lu Feng, you fucking—"

This time, the other party was Howard.

Lu Feng hung up right away.

But after hanging up, he frowned slightly and asked the researcher next to him, "Have I received communications from District 6?"

"I don't think so," the researcher said.

Lu Feng dialed a number. "District 6?"

"Hello, this is District 6's City Affairs Office. May I ask..."

The operator's voice was so calm that even An Zhe was surprised.

Lu Feng frowned even more deeply. "Trial Court, Lu Feng. How are things at District 6?"

The other party paused. "Everything is normal in District 6. Do you have any—"

Lu Feng interrupted again. "Everything is normal?"

"Indeed."

Lu Feng neatly hung up and looked at the researcher.

The researcher was initially stunned, but then his voice couldn't hide his excitement. "There's only one explanation, that District 6's ultrasonic disperser emergency procedure has successfully started."

"Wow," Poet said.

Lu Feng continued dialing. "Trial Court, Lu Feng. Please confirm again that everything is normal in District 6. Please confirm that the disperser is working normally."

"Confirming that everything is normal." The operator's voice even contained a hint of uncertainty. "Colonel, has something happened?"

"Yes." Lu Feng's reply was short and direct. "Immediately raise the isolation walls, confirm the material supplies, and prepare to shelter others."

"Yes sir!"

"Howard. The situation has changed. Have the entire city take shelter in District 6."

"Okay," the other party said. "The City Defense Agency will be responsible for the rescue and transfer of personnel."

"Roger that," Lu Feng said. "The Trial Court will be responsible for the screening of personnel."

"Thank you for your hard work."

After that call ended, Lu Feng once again dialed a number, and An Zhe noticed that the string of numbers was unusually short.

"Main City, United Front Center. Hello, Colonel Lu."

"Trial Court, Lu Feng. Requesting jurisdiction to try the whole city."

"Please give expected mortality and duration of implementation."

Lu Feng was silent for three seconds before saying, "Sixty percent, five days."

"Please wait."

"Trying the whole city..." An Zhe heard Poet mutter next to

him, "Isn't this..."

Mr. Shaw looked straight ahead as he said, "Judgment Day."

Five minutes later, a voice came from the communicator.

"Permission granted to implement."

"Understood."

The car turned and drove towards District 6.

On the whole way there, An Zhe felt that Lu Feng was unusually silent.

When they got onto District 5's road, one of the City Defense Agency's huge armored vehicles was parked up ahead, An ugly ultrasonic device was temporary installed on top of it, and it was currently rescuing the residents inside the building. Lu Feng stopped at the bottom of the armored vehicle and opened the car door.

"I'm going to a meeting to prepare for Judgment Day," he said. "You all go with the City Defense Agency."

An Zhe could only blindly obey the Arbiter's order. It wasn't until the City Defense Agency's soldiers stuffed him into the armored vehicle that he suddenly recalled he had forgotten to return the coat to Lu Feng again, and unexpectedly, Lu Feng hadn't asked for it.

There was no time to go find Lu Feng again. With a dull sound, the armored vehicle's compartment closed and the light disappeared before it drove towards District 6. In the darkness, there were human bodies all around. Poet clutched An Zhe's hand, and An Zhe's other hand clutched Mr. Shaw's sleeve. The car compartment shook slightly, and within the warm and humid air, the sounds of crying came from somewhere.

"Did you hear that?" Poet murmured. "This Judgment Day, the expected mortality rate is sixty percent."

An Zhe made an affirmative sound.

"I'm a bit scared," Poet said. "But we'll live."

An Zhe didn't know. He was indeed a bit anxious, not because of Judgment Day, but rather because of that bug bite.

Seeming to feel his stiffness, Poet gently patted his back. "Don't be scared. Sleep for now."

An Zhe made a soft sound in reply and closed his eyes. The slight swaying of the compartment made it very easy for one to enter dreamland.

The world gradually darkened and turned heavier when a scene suddenly appeared before his eyes.

The earth, wind, blurry but expansive vision, strange fluctuations. This wasn't something humans could see.

He was flying, with the wind around him, and his body was very light.

Where was he flying to?

He saw it. A blurry gray city, warmth coming from it—

With a start, An Zhe jerked awake.

He blankly looked at the darkness before him. The scene from just now was too blurry, so he didn't know what it meant. But he had encountered similar scenes before in the Abyss's cave, when his hyphae absorbed An Ze's blood and took root in An Ze's organs and bones—human knowledge had appeared before his eyes in the same way.

An Zhe softly panted for breath. He lowered his head, uneasily rubbing the fingerpad of his thumb with the bitten finger. In the Abyss, no monster would think to attack mushrooms, but he occasionally bumped into bloody remnants of some creatures' body parts or experienced his hyphae being broken by the sharp thorns on the vines, but he hadn't been infected before. He didn't know if it was because of luck or some other reason.

So what would happen this time?

———

The unexpected arrival of the next calamity was also like the sudden arrival of these Trials.

Late at night, at the entrance to District 6, dim yellow lamp-light shone silently, and the black crowd formed a long, snaking line along the isolation wall that extended to the limits of one's line of sight. The sounds of insects' flapping wings came from all directions, and one could imagine how they covetously gazed upon this city, as though they were gazing upon a warm room that could produce future generations. At the same time, the rumbling sounds of rolling vehicle wheels, the sounds of caterpillar treads, and the vibration of the earth as heavy armored vehicles rolled over it came as well. The military was rescuing the residents of the various residential districts in a continuous stream, and the rail transit trains likewise bore the responsibility of transporting residents. Sometimes bugs sneaked into the trains, but they were in no position to care. After these residents reached the periphery of District 6, they lined up at the end of the line, awaiting Trial.

The queue was a black stream with an uncountable number of people. They moved forward slowly, and after passing their Trial, they could enter the safe District 6.

The robotic broadcast didn't stop for even a moment as it emphasized "everyone please observe the queue discipline", "everyone please wait patiently", and so on. Screams would occasionally come from amidst the line as a person mutated in full view of the public, after which the soldiers patrolling around the line would immediately open fire. After some gunshots, the crowd would change from their initial restless-ness to a deathly silence. The speed at which they advanced was very slow. Nobody was willing to move forward, but the soldiers were constantly herding them along.

However, the main source of the gunshots was not the middle of the queue, but the city gate at the isolation wall.

"It's been a hundred years," an old man said. "Judgment Day has come again."

The nine-year-old boy the old man was holding by the hand

lifted his head and fearfully looked at his elder but didn't receive any hint of comfort worth mentioning. The old man's eyes were completely empty as he merely tightened his grip on the boy's hand.

Outside, it was bugs that were killing people. They had been rescued from the bug swarms and arrived at District 6, where people were killing people.

At least when God judged the common people, good and evil were His basis for doing so. In front of the Trial Court, however, some people had done nothing at all but had to face death.

The night deepened, and the boundless sound of wind came from afar, resembling distant ocean tides.

With a gunshot, someone in front of An Zhe fell, and two soldiers dragged his corpse away. Each residential district had a massive garbage incinerator, and now it was used to incinerate corpses.

Another gunshot, and another person fell.

The line continually shrank, and the people who were killed were more numerous than the people who passed the Trial and entered the city.

As the line continued moving forward, An Zhe saw this Trial's structure.

First, there was a closely-guarded buffer zone. If the person had already exhibited mutation characteristics distinguishable with the naked eye, the soldiers would shoot them first. After passing the first check, there were four Judges distributed on the sides of the isolation door. Each one had the power of veto and could open fire at any time—so long as they believed this person wasn't human, no matter if their colleagues' judgments were the same or not.

The people they killed accounted for approximately one-fourth of all the dead. Being used as a host for spawn was different from being bitten. The process was very slow, and many people's infection characteristics were not clearly visible. More often, they locked eyes and let the person pass.

At that time, that person would walk to the place where the stench of blood was strongest and face the final checkpoint.

Lu Feng.

His posture was not one where he was sitting solemnly upright or standing straight with hands at his sides. As before, he leaned a bit languidly at the bottom of the gate, seeming as though he were carelessly playing with the gun in his hand—it was with that gun that he exercised the highest and final jurisdiction.

Another gunshot. He had executed a twelve-year-old child whose eyes were still fixed on him after falling.

A young Judge's complexion was pallid. His throat twitching, he bent over at the waist and tried to suppress his dry-heaving.

Lu Feng cast a flat glance in that direction. "Switch him out."

Soldiers carried the Judge away, and within the short span of time it took to switch, nobody was tried. Clad in white shirts, the workers of the City Affairs Office came forward and gave each Judge a bottle of ice water in which green mint leaves were being soaked. But Lu Feng didn't want one.

Less than a minute later, a new Judge took the old one's place, and the Trial process began anew.

Mr. Shaw and Poet pushed and pulled, neither willing to be the first to go forward. In the end, An Zhe was pushed to the front.

The soldiers looked at him and gestured to indicate that he passed, and An Zhe continued walking forward. The four Judges all locked eyes with him briefly and let him go as well.

An Zhe walked up to Lu Feng, and the Arbiter looked at him with those green eyes of his. Beneath the lamplight, they were slightly darkened and completely lacking in emotion, similar to the day they met for the first time.

An Zhe slightly lowered his gaze.

Coincidentally, it had only been a month since he came to the human base, but it was already his fourth time facing the Arbiter's Trial.

Just this morning, a bug had bitten him on the hand, but apart from some brief strange images flashing through his mind, nothing happened.

If not even Lu Feng could discern any problems—

Just as he had this thought, he saw Lu Feng lift his left hand, then lower it slightly—the gesture indicating that he passed.

He sighed in relief and walked in—Lu Feng's clothes and work notebook were still on him, but in this scenario, it was clearly inappropriate to return them to Lu Feng, who was in such a state.

He stopped at the passageway entrance.

Up ahead were the military's big trucks. If people were to squeeze together in the most space-saving way, a single vehicle could hold sixty or seventy of them. People who passed through the city gates could choose to get in, and after the vehicle filled, the military would take them to the shelters—some vacant residential buildings. If even the vacant residential buildings were filled, they would be assigned to the regular buildings, where they would share rooms with the original residents. All in all, there were still places to go.

And if the person coming was originally a resident of District 6 or had friends or relatives they were close to in District 6, they could move about on their own.

Before a minute had passed, Mr. Shaw and Poet came in one after another as well.

"Phew," Mr. Shaw said. "I lived."

"It was confirmed that we hadn't been infected when the Arbiter rescued us from the City Defense Agency, and along the way, we've been in the car the entire time," Poet said with a smile. "Passing is a given."

Mr. Shaw cast him a sidelong glance. "Then who was the one

scared to be tried first just now?"

Poet said, "I've forgotten."

Mr. Shaw patted An Zhe on the shoulder. "Where's your home? I gotta find a place to sleep. I haven't slept for two days."

An Zhe said, "I'm not going home."

Mr. Shaw frowned. "Then what will you do?"

An Zhe pointed to the clothes he was wearing. "I'm waiting for when he's free so I can return this to him."

"I forgot. I can't go to your home." Mr. Shaw patted his head. "Never mind," he said, "I'll go find my paramour too."

An Zhe watched his master depart, momentarily unable to understand why he used the word "too".

Then he heard Poet say, "Mr. Shaw has run his business in the third underground floor for so many years, at least ninety percent of the base's pornographic books and films originated from his shop. It's said that when he was young, he had countless lovers."

An Zhe discovered that it seemed his master was truly very famous. He asked, "You all know him?"

"The base is only so big," Poet said with a smile. "Who doesn't know what Mr. Shaw does?"

"However, after he got older, he wasn't so prolific anymore," Poet said. "Speaking of the third floor, I thought of Doussay again. You've seen her before, right? Doussay was the most beautiful woman in the Outer City."

An Zhe nodded.

Poet sighed. "I don't know where she is right now. If she's dead, I'd feel very sorry."

An Zhe said nothing.

Poet had been locked up in prison, so of course he didn't know that the mistress of the black market's third floor had already died in the breeding season's prelude.

But upon seeing Poet's slightly listless expression, An Zhe suddenly understood something.

A person would feel grief at the death of another person, and this was an emotion that humans alone had. Perhaps this was one of the reasons why humans were more afraid of death compared to other creatures.

"You're showing that expression again," Poet said.

An Zhe softly asked, "What?"

"Everything that happens here has nothing to do with you. You seem to only be watching." Poet rested an elbow on An Zhe's shoulder, and with facetiousness in his tone, he said gently, "You seem to be either observing us or taking pity on us. Earlier, there was a second in which I felt some sort of divinity from you."

An Zhe blinked, not quite understanding.

Perhaps he was indeed unlike humans. He was a xenogenic, after all.

"It's gone now." Poet blew into his ear. "Now you're like a little simpleton."

An Zhe was speechless.

Poet patted his shoulder. "I'm leaving too."

"Where are you going?" An Zhe asked.

"Wherever, I suppose," Poet said. "The City Defense Agency is too busy to control me, so I'm going to break out of prison."

He smiled at An Zhe. "Goodbye."

An Zhe watched his receding figure vanish into the boundless night.

Poet was a prisoner the City Defense Agency had locked up. Where he could go without a communicator or an ID card, An Zhe didn't know.

Perhaps he'll go find his boyfriend, An Zhe thought.

Or perhaps he'll go find other people to tell the story of the bases' establishment to, and then after no more than three days, the City Defense Agency will take him away again.

After Poet left, only An Zhe remained standing at the base of the wall alone. It was an open space, and he wasn't the only person staying there. There were still many people milling around and talking nearby, and some people had gathered in the distance as well, but he didn't know what they were doing.

The temporarily-erected isolation barrier was low and translucent, so he could see Lu Feng's back view from here.

The aurora twisted and fluctuated in the sky. Every night, the color of the sky was different from the previous night. Corpses were being continually dragged away from the city gates, but the people entering were few in number. Gunshots and death seemed to be the only things that were eternal. The turbulent night wind blew in the stench of blood. An Zhe couldn't see Lu Feng's expression. He only felt that such a back view was very good-looking and very... lonely.

A person would feel grief at another person's death, so would the Arbiter feel grief for the people he killed? Perhaps he had already gotten used to it.

Footsteps came from behind him.

"How come you're here?" It was a familiar voice.

An Zhe turned around and saw that it was the young Judge who was often at Lu Feng's side. He was holding a bottle of mint water, his complexion poor, but the expression on his face was still very gentle. "You aren't going back?"

An Zhe nodded.

"I wanted to return the Colonel's things to him." He took off the coat. "Can you pass this on for me?"

The Judge smiled slightly. "You won't wait for him?"

An Zhe thought that he had only worn the Colonel's coat once, yet everyone seemed to tacitly recognize that they had some sort of relationship.

"The Colonel and I... We aren't very well-acquainted."

"I know." The Judge's reply was outside his expectations. "It's just that I haven't seen the Colonel with other people before."

He held out his hands. "Give it to me."

After An Zhe confirmed that the work notebook and ballpoint pen were both there, he folded the coat in a simple manner and handed it over. The Judge accepted it with both hands, and his pretty eyelashes dropped slightly.

"The Colonel has been working for a very long time already," he murmured. "Are you really not going to wait for him?"

Right at that moment, the aurora up in the sky abruptly changed, lighting up the sky and earth like a flash of lightning.

An Zhe's heart thudded, and an irresistible intuition came over him. Unable to hold back, he looked at the city gates and Lu Feng's figure, that tall yet lonely figure in the night.

He suddenly realized that if he left now, he would not have any connection whatsoever with this person for the rest of his life.

He once again grabbed the coat.

The Judge looked at him.

"I... I'll wait for him," An Zhe said.

The Judge gently smiled at him, unfolded the coat, and draped it over him once more. "Thank you."

An Zhe looked back at Lu Feng's figure. In just the span of their conversation, Lu Feng had killed two more people.

He asked, "When will he rest?"

"I don't know," the Judge said. "Perhaps in another two or three hours."

"Thank you," An Zhe said.

But he heard the Judge ask, "How did you get to know the Colonel?"

An Zhe thought back.

"At the city gates, I suppose." He skipped over the matter of his spore. "He suspected I wasn't human, so he took me to have a genetic examination done, and I passed it."

The Judge raised his eyebrows.

An Zhe continued. "Afterwards, he arrested me."

The Judge's eyes curved as he smiled. "I know. To make that kind of thing, you guys are really daring."

An Zhe was speechless.

"Then it was at the City Defense Agency. I'm a bit afraid of the cold, so he lent me his room for a night." An Zhe continued counting on his fingers. "And then my friends and I were trapped in a room and didn't know what to do, so I called him, and now we're here."

After he finished, he asked, "In normal times, does the Colonel also frequently help others?"

If that was the case, then Lu Feng was indeed a good person.

"I don't know. There are no others at his side," the Judge said.

After a while, he spoke again. "Sometimes, I also want to protect some people. But I don't have the opportunity, for nobody seeks help from the Trial Court."

An Zhe pursed his lips and said, "You're very kind."

Then added, "You don't seem like a Judge."

This Judge's temperament, even amongst all the people he had seen, could be considered a very gentle one.

The Judge smiled. "Many people say so. Perhaps only people like the Colonel are qualified."

"It seems so," An Zhe said.

He thought that perhaps Lu Feng's cold temperament was precisely the reason why he was able to make the most accurate judgments.

"This year is the seventh year that the Colonel has worked for the Trial Court," the Judge said. "Having to judge the true species of those things who are no different from humans on the surface is truly the most difficult thing in the world to do. Sometimes there will be mistakes and sometimes there will be accidental killings. When a Judge passes judgment, the Arbiter can tell him whether or not he was correct, but as for the Arbiter himself, there is nobody who can tell him if he was right or wrong. What he has to fight against are unimaginable giant monsters, hidden xenogenics, others' doubts... along with himself.

"That's why I think that, other than his indifference, there are some other things that have supported the Arbiter in his past seven years at the Trial Court." the Judge said. "I hope you can understand him."

This Judge always turned the conversation topic towards Lu Feng. An Zhe saw right through him.

But then he saw the Judge frown slightly and look somewhere within the walls not far in front of them.

A lot of people were concentrated there, even more than earlier. An Zhe had assumed that it was residents from within the city walls who had come to gawk at the spectacle, but their expressions were all very solemn, like they had come to participate in a large-scale gathering.

They were talking, but their voices were very soft. An Zhe heard only a few faint words.

"Scale... frightening..."

"Four thousand people."

"... Begin."

He saw the Judge next to him frown and gesture to the distant guards.

A team of guards walked over, and right when they did, the people who had gathered at the base of the walls dispersed. There were hundreds of them, and their scale seemed even more massive after they had dispersed. Furthermore, newcomers continuously walked out from the city to join them.

Amidst the crowds, someone waved, and An Zhe confirmed that the wave was directed at him. He looked over. It was a familiar young face, the person who had brought him to Building 117 on the first day he came to the human base.

At that time, they were demonstrating.

An Zhe suddenly knew what these people had come to do, and he looked at them with wide eyes.

The first person took a folded piece of white paper out from his clothes and unfolded it.

On the white paper, the words "oppose the Arbiter's brutality" were written in big red letters.

Then someone next to him also unfolded their own paper that said "publicize the Trial regulations now".

"Please publish the Trial criteria."

"Refuse a repeat of Judgment Day."

"Give an explanation to the dead."

"Reject unjustified murder."

"Refuse maintaining the base's safety via indiscriminate killing."

"Requesting regular assessments of the Arbiter's mental state."

"To the Trial Court: please take responsibility for the base's population loss rate."

"The current Arbiter's kill rate far surpasses his predecessors. Please give the base an explanation."

Beneath the aurora, these white papers unfolded like flowers. They converged, resembling a silently flowing ocean with a pallid white as the ocean's main color and the blood red words as its billowing spray.

The people outside the walls started moving. They stretched out their necks, their gazes passing through the translucent isolation walls to clearly see the situation on the opposite side. The silent atmosphere was suddenly broken by this change, and they began to quietly talk amongst themselves.

But An Zhe looked towards the city gates.

At the city gates, Lu Feng's figure moved slightly, turning so that he was looking into the city.

It was just an ordinary look. As if he'd seen nothing at all, he turned around, loaded his gun, and pressed the trigger. Yet another person, a short-haired girl, fell in a pool of blood.

If An Zhe did not misremember, this was the eleventh person in a row that Lu Feng had killed.

It was the twelfth person's turn. A man with bronze-toned

skin, he looked back and forth between Lu Feng, the Judges, and the deep pool of blood on the ground with a frightened gaze and didn't step forward for a long time.

Gun-carrying soldiers came forward to herd him along. His facial muscles twitched as he stared at the crowd demonstrating in place across from him. Finally, he gritted his teeth, closed his eyes. and sat on the ground. "I'm not going!"

This movement greatly roused the demonstrating crowd within the walls, and they held their posters even higher.

Outside the walls, a second person sat down.

And a third.

Then a fourth.

As though a powerful current swept through, within five short minutes, they all sat down like toppled dominoes. Nobody spoke, and not a single person stepped into the Trial area. As the aurora fluctuated wildly in the sky, they silently looked at Lu Feng standing in the middle, expressing their resistance with their refusal to cooperate.

In front was the Trial, and behind were the insect swarms. Sitting here, it seemed like they could resist everything in front and behind and thus obtain eternal life—

But Lu Feng's expression didn't change at all. His eyelashes lowered slightly as he bowed his head and loaded a new magazine into his gun. This man's slightly slanted eyebrows and long eyes naturally possessed an upwards curve. In normal times, they were forceful, but when his gaze was lowered, those arcs seemed to take on a cold disdain and scorn.

With a soft click, the magazine was loaded.

He said, "Bring him forward."

The soldiers of the City Defense Agency hesitated briefly. Only after the scene was at a standstill for a full ten seconds did two soldiers step forward and roughly pick up the first man who sat down.

Lu Feng slowly lifted his gun.

Everyone's gazes landed on them. A woman's broken sobs came from amidst the crowd, and then the sobbing spread like a virus to form a vast ocean of mournful cries. No place was free of crying. It was as though what they were about to face was not a trial, but rather a massacre.

Perhaps the intrinsic nature of Judgment Day was a massacre. It was the same the first time a hundred years ago, and it was the same a hundred years after.

The sound of armored vehicles broke the tense atmosphere. Howard, who had brought a team of guards with him, got out of a vehicle and asked Lu Feng, "What's going on?"

Lu Feng's voice was expressionless. "The residents are refusing to cooperate."

Howard looked around, frowned deeply, and said with a slightly critical tone, "Lu Feng, aren't you killing too many?"

Lu Feng's intonation did not change, but his voice was slightly hoarse. "No."

"Today's situation is urgent." Howard's aide handed him a loudspeaker, and he said to the residents, "This is related to the safety of the base. Large-scale infection may occur at any time, so please cooperate with the Trial Court and City Defense Agency's work."

Nobody moved. Perhaps between the infection that may break out at any time and the muzzle of the Arbiter's gun in front of them, the latter was more frightening.

It was obvious that Howard had also noticed everyone's silence. After his gaze passed over the demonstration banners, he thought briefly and said, "Let's both take a step back. The Trial Court will make public the detailed regulations of the Trials, and the residents will once again enter the Trial process."

"Howard," Lu Feng started in a flat voice.

Screams suddenly burst out from the crowd!

Because the muzzle of Lu Feng's gun had slowly turned to point at Howard.

Initially stunned, Howard then furrowed his brows and said, "Colonel Lu, what are you doing?"

Howard's guards all took a step forward, loaded their guns, and aimed at Lu Feng!

A stalemate.

Howard let out a cold laugh. "Colonel Lu, I've been outside the entire day, but I swear that I haven't come into contact with a single bug."

"You've been infected," Lu Feng said.

"I understand that the Trial Court wishes to take control of the City Defense Agency and does not wish to make public the detailed regulations of the Trials." Howard's voice was grim. "But this is the juncture of whether the base survives or perishes, Colonel Lu. You may abuse your power, but there has to be a limit."

As soon as he spoke those words, the crowd promptly became restless.

Lu Feng put his finger on the trigger. He didn't say a single word, but his movements made clear what he wanted to do.

It was the same with the City Defense Agency guards. Their movements were bigger. Obviously, so long as Lu Feng opened fire on their Director Howard, they would also wildly shoot him down right away.

A death-like silence spread out and condensed like ice.

In the suffocating silence, someone within the walls shouted.

"Oppose the Arbiter's tyranny!"

His rallying cry received a multitude of responses. Everyone —those inside the walls, those outside of the walls, those who were already there, those who newly arrived—shouted this slogan as well.

"Oppose the Arbiter's tyranny!"

"Oppose the Arbiter's tyranny!"

"Oppose the Arbiter's tyranny!"

The voices came in waves that were each louder than the

last, but Lu Feng, in the middle of it all, did not move from beginning to end.

As An Zhe looked at Lu Feng's back view, he nearly forgot to breathe.

His understanding of Lu Feng was not deep, but based on just that shallow understanding, he knew that Lu Feng would really open fire.

He would die.

The young Judge next to him also murmured, "Don't..."

The aurora abruptly jittered, and the atmosphere was as cold as ice.

Right at that moment.

An ear-piercing whistle tore through the heavy night and covered up the people's shouts. A white light suddenly appeared on the distant road, continually flickering as it approached, and the crowd all avoided it. A white mechanical car with a red triangle painted on its body speedily approached with a roar, and when it came near, the door opened and a young man dressed in a white coat stuck his upper half out of the window. An Zhe recognized him. At the city gates one month prior, it was this doctor who had performed his genetic examination.

"I'm the head of the Lighthouse's Inspection Division." Holding a loudspeaker, he took a few hurried breaths. "The first-generation genetic coupling agent was successfully deployed an hour ago. It can achieve rapid imaging of target spots, and it only needs..."

Out of breath, he panted some more before saying, "... Only needs five minutes."

Nobody moved. He hopped out of the car and hastily ran over.

At the entrance, he twisted open a disposable syringe and walked forward. "Director Howard—if you would be so kind as to cooperate."

Howard calmly rolled up the sleeves of his all-encompassing

protective military uniform and allowed his blood to be drawn, then looked at Lu Feng with a frown.

Everyone else looked at Lu Feng as well. An Zhe knew they were waiting for one particular result: the result that Howard's genetic examination was normal, so as to prove the Arbiter indeed killed indiscriminately.

Amongst the demonstrators behind him, someone said, "We're about to change history."

An Zhe saw Lu Feng lower his gun and expressionlessly wipe down his gun while leaning against the wall, seeming to not care about anything.

What was he thinking about? An Zhe thought.

Three minutes later, having finished wiping down his gun, Lu Feng clipped it to his waist again and scanned the crowd with a dispassionate gaze.

An Zhe looked at him, and perhaps there was a moment in which their gazes met for a brief fraction of a second.

An Zhe promptly stood closer to the Judge to make his own position clear.

Lu Feng's lips seemed to curl up into a smile, but An Zhe didn't see clearly because the man turned back in the following second.

One minute left.

The demonstrating crowd became increasingly riotous, holding animated discussions amongst themselves.

Half a minute.

Ten seconds.

They began counting the seconds.

"Ten, nine, eight, seven, six, five, four, three, two, one—"

The red light atop the detection car was decisive.

The ominous alarm sound had extremely high penetrative power as it abruptly sounded. "Alert—"

The crowd was plunged into a deathly silence for several seconds.

"Bang!"

A gunshot ran out.

There was no need for Lu Feng to take action, for the guards of the city gates had opened fire.

A silence spread throughout, for nobody spoke. In the end, the doctor said, "Colonel—"

Without saying a word, Lu Feng turned and walked towards the interior of the city. He walked straight past everyone, including An Zhe.

The silent crowd seemed like frozen wooden puppets, only reacting once he had walked near them. They slowly parted to form a path.

The view of his figure in An Zhe's eyes overlapped with his figure when he had turned and left the city gates that day. An Zhe had only seen him turn and leave, but never walk towards anybody.

The Judge suddenly nudged An Zhe with an elbow.

An Zhe promptly came to a realization. Holding Lu Feng's work notebook, he chased after Lu Feng—the Arbiter was tall and had long legs, so he could only catch up by jogging.

"Colonel."

Lu Feng didn't reply.

"Colonel, please wait."

Lu Feng still didn't reply.

"Colonel..." An Zhe took a few breaths. He didn't have much strength in the first place, and now that he had run, his voice had been affected, becoming somewhat softer. He frowned as he said, "Slow down a bit, I can't keep up..."

The Colonel stopped and turned to look at him.

An Zhe still hadn't caught his breath when he lifted his head. "Colonel..."

"Speak properly," Lu Feng said coldly with a glance at him. "Don't whine."

An Zhe was at a loss for words.

12

"ALTHOUGH YOU AREN'T OF MUCH USE, YOU CAN GO AND TAKE CARE OF CHILDREN."

"I DIDN'T," An Zhe said in a small voice.

He handed the work notebook to Lu Feng, who frowned slightly and accepted it.

"And the clothes." He took off the coat and handed that to Lu Feng as well. "Thank you."

Lu Feng draped the garment over the crook of his elbow and lowered his head to look at An Zhe.

"There was no need to wait for me," he said. "You could have just left it at the city gate."

An Zhe didn't reply. He and Lu Feng locked eyes for a few seconds before he carefully asked, "Are... you okay?"

Lu Feng looked away. "I'm okay."

His voice was flat, as if nothing had happened earlier.

"... Oh," An Zhe said.

Then An Zhe continued by asking, "Where are you going?"

Lu Feng looked at him. That pair of incisive cold green eyes always made An Zhe think of chilly things. With the addition of the mighty cold wind of the city at night, he, who had just left the warm coat, curled up upon himself slightly.

Lu Feng dropped the coat back in An Zhe's arms.

"I don't know," he said. "I'll escort you back first."

Holding the garment, An Zhe once again draped it over himself. After he put it on, Lu Feng walked ahead, and he followed.

To either side of them was the road formed by the parted protesters. Their expressions were solemn, the corners of their mouths taut and downturned, and they still had not put down the posters and pamphlets in their hands. The papers flapped noisily as they were blown by the night wind.

Every single person stared at them silently, their stances tense. The green, purple, and orange aurora shone on their faces, mixing with their skin tones to form a strange metallic tint.

From those eyes, An Zhe saw distinct hatred and cautious vigilance—if it weren't for their misgivings regarding the gun Lu Feng carried at all times and his privilege of killing people at any time, they seemed like they would be able to do anything.

The same eyes landed on An Zhe as well, and it could even be said that most of them were looking at him. An Zhe involuntarily drew closer to Lu Feng—he knew why Lu Feng wanted to escort him back now. He had voluntarily approached the Arbiter, so the dissenters stared at him like a pack of wolves.

Fortunately, although the size of the crowd was not small, it could not be considered large when compared to the entire city. In less than five minutes, they passed through the demonstration area and stepped onto the residential district's road.

The aurora made the numerous buildings of the residential district cast heavy black shadows on the ground, and the light gray cement road was broken into black and gray stripes by the lights and shadows. Lu Feng's and An Zhe's shadows were also cast onto the ground, elongated, and overlapped with those irregular stripes.

An Zhe didn't know what he should say to Lu Feng, and Lu Feng didn't take the initiative to speak up either.

Although it was nighttime, this place was by no means quiet.

One of the military's big trucks roared past them before coming to a stop at the fork in the road. The vehicle door opened, and the residents who came in through the city gate to seek shelter were released and led into the building and settled in place by a team of soldiers and a staff member of the City Affairs Office clad in a white shirt and holding a notebook.

A man asked a soldier, "How long do we have to take shelter for?"

The soldier said, "It depends on the situation."

Another resident asked, "I heard only District 6 is okay. Can you ensure District 6 will always be safe?"

The soldier said, "There's no definite information. Wait for the Lighthouse's research report."

"Then..." Someone still wanted to ask something but was promptly interrupted by the soldier. "Everyone come with me, hurry."

Disorderly footsteps sounded as they entered the building.

An Zhe lifted his head to look at the number on the upper right part of the building. This was Building 55.

Lu Feng's footsteps didn't stop, so he didn't stop either. They walked another thirty meters and arrived at Building 56.

Number 56—

Something in An Zhe's heart was touched, and he lifted his head to look at the number, then looked at the pitch-black unit door in the middle of the building.

This area was very close to the isolation gate, and the military had already begun settling people in Building 55, so they would very soon turn to Building 56.

Lu Feng asked, "You wish to go?"

An Zhe shook his head.

Lu Feng's tone of voice was forthright. "Go if you want to."

An Zhe said nothing.

He suspected that the Arbiter and Judges had received mind reading training.

He said, "Let's go, then."

Lu Feng changed directions and walked toward Building 56. An Zhe walked next to him, and as he walked, he pulled out an ID card from his pocket. A string of numbers was printed on the card: 3260563209, representing Building 56, Unit 3, Floor 2, No. 09.

This wasn't An Zhe's room, and nor was this ID card his—it had belonged to Vance, the man who brought him to the Northern Base.

That day, after Vance's body had been carried away, the soldiers gave this ID card to An Zhe to serve as a memento, and he carried it on him at all times ever since then.

An Zhe swiped the ID card to open the room door—it was not yet invalid, which indicated that the base had not yet taken back the right to use this room. He walked in and turned on the light. It was a simple room, and the quilt was carelessly heaped on the bed as if its owner had just gotten up and left. Some daily necessities—a water cup, cigarette case, and lighter—were placed on the table. This was Vance's home.

It had already been a month since Vance died, but An Zhe would sometimes think of him. This entire time, he did not understand why, despite being fully aware that he may have been infected, Vance still chose to return to the base. But on this day, after witnessing the deaths and terror of so many people, when he passed Building 56 again, he felt that, he understood Vance in some sense.

He himself was dominated by instinct, dead set on risking death by going deep into the base to search for his spore. Perhaps it was impossible for humans to agree with his motivation. But unlike monsters, which were dominated by instinct, humans were a kind of creature often dominated by emotion. They did things that did not conform to common sense or need too many reasons, so as long as he understood this, he wouldn't doubt humans' baffling behavior.

As An Zhe thought this, he gently placed the ID card beneath the cigarette case—he remembered that Vance liked smoking.

After doing so, he turned to leave. Lu Feng leaned against the door frame, waiting for him.

His gaze was akin to a falling snowflake as it landed on An Zhe, seemingly different from before.

An Zhe asked, "What's the matter?"

"I subjectively believe you're human now." Lu Feng turned and walked out.

An Zhe silently caught up, not wishing to make any sound. As expected, the Arbiter had constantly, continually, always suspected he wasn't human.

When they got back onto the road, Lu Feng's communicator rang, and the doctor's voice came from within.

"The detector has been incorporated into the Trial process at the city gate, and the residents' emotions have been placated to a certain extent. The Lighthouse will transfer five more instruments tomorrow, but their speed is still somewhat unable to keep up. Colonel, you may still need to return."

"I know." Lu Feng's voice was cold. "I'll go back in the daytime."

"Thank you. Rest well tonight." The doctor paused. "Now that Director Howard is dead, what'll happen next? In the Outer City, you are the only colonel with executive power remaining. The City Defense Agency's colonel is a civilian, and the distribution of emergency supplies alone is enough to make him lose all his hair."

"The Trial Court will temporarily take control of the City Defense Agency, and all troops will be assigned to rescue work for the time being," Lu Feng said. "After Judgment Day ends, I hope the Lighthouse can assist us in formulating a plan to restart the various dispersers."

The doctor said, "Of course."

Lu Feng hung up, then dialed another number and made

work arrangements for the Trial Court. An Zhe quietly listened with his ears pricked up. The Arbiter's words were clear and concise as always, and his tone of voice was cold and methodical as always. Many things happened tonight, but Lu Feng still seemed to remain as that Lu Feng.

An Zhe turned to look at his profile. According to the doctor's words, this person still had to return to the city gate tomorrow, and the man himself also tacitly agreed to return. That young Judge had said that what the Colonel was fighting against were unimaginable giant monsters—perhaps Lu Feng was already used to it.

The only unusual thing he did this night was turn and leave that place.

Once the phone call ended, they arrived at Building 117. Lu Feng seemed to be even more familiar with the roads than him, and the two of them arrived at the door to No. 14 without issue. After turning on the light, everything inside was as usual save for one thing missing from next to the wall.

But even if An Zhe was given the bravery of ten men, he didn't dare to ask where the mannequin was now after being confiscated.

An Zhe asked Lu Feng, who was standing at the door, "Would you like to come in and sit down?"

"No need," Lu Feng said. "You go and rest."

An Zhe hesitated for a while before asking, "Then... where are you going?"

Lu Feng frowned slightly, seeming to contemplate the question.

After a brief period of contemplation, he said, "I don't know."

The communicator screen showed that it was already eleven o'clock at night. An Zhe counted the hours and came to the conclusion that the Colonel may not have rested for nearly forty hours already.

He knew that today's incident was urgent and that many things were Lu Feng's and Howard's temporary arrangements. They tried their best to settle the residents in District 6, but those such as the soldiers and the staff of the Trial Court and City Defense Agency may temporarily not have offices or residences, or perhaps there were only simple arrangements for them to rest and spend the night at the residential district near the city gate.

But he felt that the current Lu Feng may not necessarily wish to return to the city gate.

An Zhe felt very conflicted.

His fingers involuntarily clenched and he pursed his lips.

"What is it?" Lu Feng asked.

His voice was a bit soft, and the corridor light was very dim. Perhaps as an effect of the lighting, his contours were not as fierce and forceful as usual.

An Zhe steeled himself.

Even if it was for the sake of his spore, he had to establish a better relationship with the Colonel.

"If… if you don't have anywhere to go," An Zhe said, lifting his head to look at Lu Feng, "you can stay here at my place."

———

To humans, it was very difficult to take back words that they had spoken.

So this was how things turned out.

In the public bathroom on the fifth floor, next to a sink that was covered in brown water scale marks, in front of a faucet, An Zhe held a cup in one hand and a toothbrush in the other as he earnestly washed up. He understood the daily living habits of humans and earnestly imitated them every day, but today, his attitude was even more careful than normal because the Colonel was right next to him.

After finishing, he continued cautiously putting everything away and looked at Lu Feng.

Lu Feng had just washed his face with cold water, and a few crystal-clear drops of water hung from the tips of his damp hair just like beads of freshly melted snow.

An Zhe silently handed him the towel.

Lu Feng accepted it with a terse word of thanks.

"You're welcome," An Zhe said.

He believed that what he did conformed to human etiquette, for sharing things was something humans commonly did.

He held out his cup to Lu Feng.

"Do you want to use it?" he asked. "But there's only one."

The base was short on materials, so there were limits on the daily necessities allocated to each person. If there was an additional need, one would have to go to the black market and buy on their own. An Zhe only had one cup and one toothbrush. Furthermore, the black market no longer existed, so there was nowhere he could go to buy more.

Lu Feng's eyes were fixed on him, and only after looking for approximately five or six seconds did he move.

An Zhe lowered his head. The dim yellow light of the bathroom cast a pale golden hue on the rim of the cup, and Lu Feng grasped the china-white handle with his slim fingers, taking the cup from his hand. His right hand was the one that held his gun, so there was a slight callus on the pad of his finger. When An Zhe let go, his fingers gently came into contact.

Lu Feng didn't use his toothbrush. He only used the cup to hold water and then rinsed his mouth with a mixture of liquid and toothpaste. Afterward, he put away the cup, and the two of them walked out.

It was eleven o'clock at night. If it were normal times, the bathroom and corridor's water and electricity would have been cut off in accordance with the base's rules, but the entirety of District 6 had entered a state of emergency shelter today, so the water and electricity restrictions were all canceled. In a state of trepidation, quite a number of people hadn't slept. And because of this, although it was late at night, there were other people in the bathroom—those few people washed either themselves or their clothes while casting surreptitious glances at the two of them. An Zhe noticed, and he knew Lu Feng definitely noticed as well, but the Colonel didn't seem to care too much.

An Zhe walked in front. The bathroom floor was damp and had a few puddles, so he had to walk with his head down to avoid those spots.

When they walked to the doorway, a black figure unexpectedly came from the corner up ahead. An Zhe lifted his head.

"You—" It was Josh's voice.

An Zhe unconsciously took a step back and bumped into Lu Feng's chest. He saw Josh looking at him, wanting to say something—but with a shift of his gaze, he froze in place.

An Zhe had also become half-frozen. Josh just happened to block the door, and he was neither going in nor out.

At that moment, he felt a slight weight on his shoulder, for Lu Feng's fingers had come to rest there.

Josh's eyes were wide open, and An Zhe could practically see his pupils jitter. Then Josh ducked his head, took a step back, and turned sideways, giving way with a deferential posture.

Lu Feng exerted a little bit of effort with the hand on An Zhe's shoulder and steered An Zhe out the door before letting go.

All of it happened within the span of a moment. An Zhe's heart thumped wildly, and his whole body was tensed up, for fear that in front of the Arbiter, Josh would call out "An Ze" or say "he's not like An Ze" or some such.

However, even after they walked more than ten steps away, Josh hadn't said a word.

An Zhe turned back to look at Josh's profile. Josh's fingers, which hung at his sides, were clenched around the hem of his shirt, and the corners of his mouth were taut.

An Zhe suddenly realized something—in this place, what the Arbiter held was authority over every person's life and death. Therefore, the vast majority of people in the base, including Josh, were afraid to say even a word to the Arbiter.

They walked through the corridor and returned to the room. Lu Feng didn't ask him just who that was, nor exactly what entanglements were between him and Josh. Strictly speaking, apart from staying overnight in each other's quarters, he and Lu Feng could only be considered strangers after all.

After returning to the room, Lu Feng sat down at An Zhe's desk, opened his work notebook, and began to take notes. He wrote very quickly, and on the line for 6.19 he wrote:

Judgment Day, countless dead.

Standing to one side, An Zhe watched him and once again pondered a question—what exactly was the purpose of such a work notebook?

He said, "You write so little."

Lu Feng closed the notebook. "It's to satisfy inspection."

His tone of voice was very matter-of-fact.

"Oh," An Zhe said.

Then he said, "I'm going to change my clothes."

"Mm," Lu Feng replied.

An Zhe changed out of his daytime clothes. He had a very soft white cotton nightgown. After changing, he burrowed under the quilt and slept on the side of the bed closer to the wall. Although the base's rooms only had a standard single bed, the bed was by no means narrow—he could even roll over on it. An Zhe guessed that this may have been because the base had many hulking mercenaries who took up a lot of space.

Therefore, after he lay down, this bed had more than enough space to accommodate another person.

After he settled in, he looked at Lu Feng and said, "I'm good now."

He discovered that Lu Feng was looking at the supply depot exam guidebook on his desk.

Lu Feng said, "You wished to go to the supply depot?"

"Mm-hm," An Zhe said.

It was a pity that it seemed like he'd never be able to go—if the Outer City was going to constantly be occupied by bugs.

"Go to the City Affairs Office tomorrow afternoon," Lu Feng said. "In the past few years, there have been many newborns and not enough manpower in the Main City, so the City Defense Agency has been tasked with recruiting people from the Outer City."

As he spoke, he got up from the chair, then took off his coat and draped it on the chair back before walking toward An Zhe. An Zhe knew that those green eyes were examining him.

Then he heard Lu Feng continue. "Although you aren't of much use otherwise, you can go and take care of children."

An Zhe wanted to refute his statement, but he discovered that he actually had no way of doing so.

Feeling very embarrassed, he covered himself up with the quilt.

He heard Lu Feng let out a laugh, and then the side of the bed dipped down as Lu Feng got in.

The chilly scent was very close, and he could hear the sound of Lu Feng's breathing. The things that happened today were like a dream. As a xenogenic, he was about to spend a night with the Arbiter.

"So," An Zhe murmured as he peeked out from under the quilt, "do you still suspect that I'm objectively not a human?"

"You've passed the genetic examination and the thirty-day

observation period." Lu Feng's face was expressionless. "You're a human objectively as well now."

"What's the observation period?"

"After being infected, within thirty days, those who have been infected will definitely lose their human mind, and the probability is infinitely close to 1," Lu Feng said.

"Then... would there be xenogenics who don't lose their minds?" An Zhe asked tentatively. "Although they're xenogenics, they still have a human shape and thoughts. They just have an additional ability, being able to change into other living creatures."

He knew that he was a xenogenic, but he also knew that he was still quite lucid.

"Do you think humans' willpower is very strong?" Lu Feng said.

An Zhe didn't know how to reply, but it seemed that Lu Feng didn't need him to reply.

"It's actually not worth mentioning. The Lighthouse has performed many experiments," Lu Feng said. "Humans will not surmount xenogenics' survival instinct. In contrast, xenogenics gradually digest humans' thinking ability and use it for their own survival. Take today's bugs for example. The Lighthouse's investigation report has not come out yet, but I unilaterally believe they were premeditated attacks."

An Zhe slowly opened his eyes wide. This was the first time Lu Feng had spoken for so long, and the weight of his words was very heavy.

He said that the specific will that made humans human was not worth mentioning in the face of gene fusion and that humans were such a weak sort of creature.

"I think that's not right." After being thought of as human both subjectively and objectively by the Arbiter, An Zhe felt much more at ease. At the very least, he dared to talk with Lu Feng a little more. "If their willpower was very strong..."

"It doesn't depend on strength, there is no 'if.'"

An Zhe frowned and thought hard. "For example, if you were infected—"

Lu Feng promptly covered him up with the quilt.

"I would immediately commit suicide," Lu Feng said coldly. "Go to sleep."

An Zhe thought that the Arbiter may have become drowsy and was no longer willing to talk nonsense with him—in fact, he himself was sleepy as well. Altogether, Lu Feng hadn't rested for forty hours, and he himself had only slept two or three more hours early yesterday morning in Lu Feng's room. At virtually the moment he closed his eyes, he passed out.

When An Zhe woke up again, he was momentarily unsure what time it was. He sat up from the bed. The entire room was still like how it was last night, with only a faint ray of light coming through the gap between the curtains like weak sunlight penetrating through the Abyss's layered plant branches and leaves. After pulling open the curtains, the room was still very dim, for it was overcast outside.

He took out the communicator and looked at it. It was already 11 a.m.

Suddenly, An Zhe felt that he had forgotten something. With a start, he woke up completely, and he first looked at the bed— there was nothing at all, only him alone, and the same could be said for the room.

Then he discovered a piece of paper lying flat on the table, and next to the paper was a ballpoint pen.

An Zhe got out of bed and came to the table, then picked it up—it was that "oppose the Arbiter's brutality" leaflet. It had been flipped over, and a few words were written on the back of it in black.

I've left.

Call if anything comes up.

Lu

For some reason, An Zhe smiled. He thought that Lu Feng's note was just like the man's work notebook, concisely worded.

After putting down the note, he came to the wardrobe and began picking out clothes to wear to the City Affairs Office. He thought for a very long time, and in the end, he finally took out a gray sweater and changed into it.

Gray—An Zhe lifted his head and looked outside.

The sky and the light in the sky were both light gray and very low, hanging on the tops of the buildings. Thick gray clouds gathered in clumps and extended to the ends of the city and the horizon. It looked like it was about to rain heavily.

An Zhe felt very happy, for mushrooms liked rainy days. Moreover, Lu Feng told him that piece of information yesterday, so assuming he could pass the City Defense Agency's recruitment, he could go to the Main City—and that was where the Lighthouse was. He seemed to have gotten one step closer to getting his spore back.

He decided to not quibble over the matter of Lu Feng digging out his spore anymore.

13

"WHAT WOULD HAPPEN NEXT?"

AT THE TOP of the street's utility pole, the broadcasting equipment repeatedly played the robotic female voice's announcement.

"At present, District 6 has sufficient materials. Water and electricity will be supplied as usual. The City Defense Agency has implemented real-time omnidirectional protection of the ultrasonic disperser."

"According to the observatory, the weather will turn overcast, and there will be a high probability of rainfall. Residents, please shut your doors and windows and cut down on travel."

"The City Defense Agency's personnel screening of the entire base has begun. Residents who meet the requirements, please go to the City Affairs Office as quickly as possible. The following are the personnel selection requirements…"

This was the only sound on the entire street apart from that of An Zhe's footsteps. After the incident happened at the base, the city gates were sealed off with nobody allowed in or out, and the various districts were paralyzed. The atmosphere in District 6 was likewise tense. On the way to the City Affairs Office, it was deserted everywhere, with only the "oppose the Arbiter's Code" pamphlets that had been sparsely pasted on the building walls drifting around on the ground after being blown off by the wind. After walking a while longer, he noticed the military's armored vehicles passing by on the road from time to time, their speed extremely fast, all driving in the direction of the entrance.

The base was divided into eight districts altogether. The Dispersion Center, the City Defense Agency, and the Trial Court together ensured safety within the city, while the City Affairs Office and supply depots managed the city's general affairs. Just like how the Trial Court was located at the city gates, the City Defense Agency headquarters were located in District 5, and the Dispersion Center was located in District 1, the City Affairs Office's headquarters were established in District 6—it was fortunate that this was the case, for the City Affairs Office had no casualties. It maintained normal operations and even could recruit people.

The City Affairs Office was located in the center of District 6 with its back to the train station and the alarm tower next to it. The main building was seven stories high, with a spacious office hall in the middle. Right now, the sky was entirely overcast. Although it was clearly noontime, the atmosphere was as gloomy as five or six o'clock in the evening, and the dark clouds seemed like they were on the verge of drenching the City Affairs Office building.

It wasn't until after walking into the large hall that An Zhe finally felt the aura of living people. There were five or six hundred people divided into two long lines, all young faces.

Their recruitment requirements were constantly repeated over the broadcast, and An Zhe heard it as well—they had to be between eighteen and twenty-five years old, free of disease and disability, and have no criminal record or records of inappropriate political views. Regarding that point, he pondered for a long time. Although he had been imprisoned, he had only received a verbal guilty verdict from Lu Feng, so perhaps there had not been time for it to be entered into the system.

And after meeting the basic conditions, there were additional requirements: civilian candidates had to have completed at least three of the base's basic education courses, and noncivilian candidates had to have been awarded more than five thousand of the base's currency as a mercenary.

These two requirements alone could filter out the vast majority of the young people within the base, such as Josh. When he was in his teens, he didn't choose to study the base's basic courses, but rather trained with mercenary units instead. However, his performance as a mercenary could not be considered outstanding either. Even now, his feats have not earned him five thousand R.

An Zhe walked in and lined up at the end of the civilian queue. Perhaps he had arrived late or perhaps the weather was too poor, for there were no other people behind him.

The person who used to be at the end of the line heard his footsteps and turned back to look at him.

Their eyes met.

An Zhe felt a trace of awkwardness suffuse the air.

Then he shifted his gaze to the nearby wall, and the young man swiftly turned his head away as well.

The reason was none other than the fact that they could be considered acquaintances—this was the boy who pulled An Zhe along to demonstrate at the very beginning and called him "comrade." Just yesterday, outside the city gate, he had mingled in the crowd of demonstrators opposing the Arbiter and even waved at An Zhe.

However, right on the spot, An Zhe had left with the Arbiter while draped in the Arbiter's clothes.

He didn't wish to acknowledge An Zhe, and An Zhe didn't wish to acknowledge him either. In this manner, they silently stood in line.

The interviewer was a man who wore silver wire-rimmed glasses and had delicate and cold facial features. At a glance, he wasn't easy to interact with. But strangely, the speed at which the line shrank was very fast. Every person was asked only a few simple questions before being admitted to another corridor behind the hall. There were occasionally some who were asked to leave, but their numbers were extremely few.

In no more than an hour and a half, the line only had a few people left, and it came to the boy in front of An Zhe.

But the interviewer gestured to pause and picked up his communicator.

"Please let the Colonel know that he must come as quickly as possible. Five minutes at most," he said. "Sending these people to the Main City is already breaking the rules. The Main City's safety is the most important thing. There cannot be any mistakes, so the Arbiter must be present."

"The Main City?" the boy in front of An Zhe said in surprise. "We're going to the Main City? Wasn't the City Affairs Office recruiting?"

"The situation now is indeed what we didn't wish to see. The weather's violent changes weren't predicted, and the recovery of the Dispersion Center isn't something that can be completed in a short span of time. To ensure the Main City's safety, the Arbiter must evacuate with us. Humankind's interests take precedence over all else. Please remember this sentence."

With those words, he put down his communicator and glanced at the boy in front of An Zhe.

The boy put his ID card on the sensor, and his information popped up on the screen.

Name: Colin
Age: 21
ID: 3260070412

There was another screen in front of the interviewer, and An Zhe thought that it should have more detailed information.

Colin voluntarily said, "I've completed the basic courses for mathematics, physics, and biology."

The interviewer gave a slight nod, then handed the ID card back to him and said, "Turn right and go out."

It was An Zhe's turn next.

After he swiped his card, he answered based on An Ze's experience. "I've completed the courses for literature, language, and economics."

"Your grades are good," the interviewer said.

At that very moment, the loud sound of rain suddenly came from outside.

The interviewer stuffed the card back into his hand and quickly said, "Hurry up and go!"

An Zhe swiftly caught up to Colin and walked into the corridor on the right. After the corridor was a glass-covered bridge that had already been splattered with densely packed sprays from the huge and concentrated raindrops, so the situation outside wasn't visible at all. They rapidly walked forward, but they saw that this covered bridge was connected to the train station platform. Next to the platform was a black-clothed ground traffic controller.

"My dad doesn't know yet!" Colin said. "Are we going to the Main City right now?!"

The interviewer grabbed his arm and stuffed him into a coach, saying, "Don't waste your breath!"

An Zhe was promptly stuffed in as well. The train's seats were packed. Colin was frantically dialing his communicator, but he couldn't get through, and they came to the last coach—it was empty.

An Zhe sat down in the very farthest corner, and behind him was the train's rear window, through which it was possible to clearly see the scene behind. The tracks were flooded in the boundless misty rain. Colin sat down in the place farthest from him, continually dialing his communicator while talking to himself. "Something's wrong, there's definitely a problem, I have to go back—"

He practically jumped up from his seat, but what immediately followed was the sound of all the train's doors slamming shut at the same time.

Colin hammered on the coach door several times, but he couldn't get it to move at all. On the contrary, he drew the train staff's attention.

"Sit down properly!" The train conductor was a strong man. "We're about to go to the Main City. What are you kicking up a fuss for?"

"My dad doesn't know yet," Colin said. "I can't suddenly leave. Is there something you guys are hiding from us?"

The conductor was silent for three seconds before saying, "Your dad will be happy for you."

In his seat, Colin gasped for breath. "Something's wrong, something's wrong..."

But despite repeating himself for a while, he couldn't articulate any reason for it, so he could only continue fiddling with his communicator.

An Zhe quietly waited in the corner. Five minutes later, the sounds of coach doors and a few voices carried over from the distance, and approximately ten minutes later, the entire coach suddenly fell silent.

"The Arbiter has come to perform his inspections," a person in front of him said in a low voice.

Following that was the sound of two people's footsteps, having the unique sound of military boots. It was very easy to recognize.

When the footsteps came closer, he lifted his head.

Then he met Lu Feng's eyes.

"My God." The young Judge behind Lu Feng said, looking at him as well, "We thought you weren't here."

"I'm... here." As An Zhe looked into Lu Feng's eyes, he felt faintly uneasy. Softly, he asked, "Did something happen?"

This was his first time seeing that sort of thing in Lu Feng's expression, although the man's exterior looked no different from before.

It wasn't coldness, yet it was very... heavy.

Lu Feng said, "Nothing's wrong."

A voice came from his communicator. "How's the situation?"

"Confirmed safe," Lu Feng replied.

"Roger."

An Zhe's uneasiness gradually increased, and he lifted his head to look at Lu Feng. Lu Feng looked at him as well, but he didn't speak.

Right at that moment, Colin suddenly said, his voice trembling and raspy, "I get it... I get it."

He turned his head to look at the nearby conductor. "The disperser has failed in the end, hasn't it—hasn't it?"

"I've studied physics. Ultrasound—ultrasound is a soundwave, and the transmission of soundwaves requires a medium. It's raining heavily right now, so the air temperature, density, and pressure have all changed. The medium has changed, so the frequency parameter must be adjusted anew, but, but—" He threw himself forward, latching onto the conductor's arm, his eyes red and entire body trembling. "But the Dispersion Center is gone, so there's no way to adjust it, isn't that right? The original frequency has lost its effectiveness in the heavy rain, hasn't it?"

As his trembling voice trailed off, a scream suddenly came from the coach ahead.

"Bang!" The glass next to An Zhe was also struck hard.

Amidst the rain, a black winged insect had rammed into the train glass. An Zhe looked outside the window, and the insect's six blood-red compound eyes stared at him. He locked eyes with this insect that was only the size of a human head and as long as a human arm, then watched it fly up in the rain before knocking into a window on the other side.

The crisp sounds of the collisions came from outside the train in a continuous barrage. After a sharp whistle, An Zhe saw that outside the window, the ground traffic controller in his fluorescent uniform made an abrupt "forward" gesture.

The sounds of shaking and rumbling started up together, and after a few clanks, the train gradually began moving forward.

Colin let out a loud cry, then fainted while clutching his communicator.

That ground traffic controller was swarmed by countless insects both big and small, and in the sheets of rain, the bugs became blurred shadows as well. After only five or six seconds passed, his body crumpled to the ground while surrounded by the shadows, sending up a bloody spray of water.

The train gradually sped up, and after going around a bend, his figure disappeared completely.

An Zhe watched all of it with wide eyes. He stood up, facing the coach window in the back.

Black shadows.

Black shadows that blotted out the sky, round ones, long ones, irregular ones, massive worms wriggling on the ground, and insects with huge sickles that could swiftly move and jump. When did they arrive? Perhaps it was at the very second the downpour started.

The roof clanged and cracks appeared on the windows' outer glass, but the inner glass remained.

The train sped up, flying forward, and An Zhe lifted his head and looked at the entire city.

What came down from the sky was not necessarily rain. Those things that blotted out the sky—it was an amalgam of red and green raindrops mixed with blood, monsters, monster body parts, and human body parts. Although the coach windows blocked some sound, he could still hear continuous screaming and shouting along with the sounds of the other people within the coach dry-heaving or trembling. After the heavy rain began, he stayed in the coach for ten minutes, so he didn't know what kind of massacre was going on outside. Now, he could imagine it.

How many people lived, and how many people would die?

He couldn't imagine it. He couldn't see the entire city.

"The base made a plan for the worst-case scenario yesterday," the young Judge murmured. "Transferring young and useful personnel was an emergency measure. It's just that we didn't imagine that the unexpected would arrive so quickly."

His voice was a bit hoarse. "My apologies. If we were given a few more days, perhaps the military could have recovered the Dispersion Center, but..."

But now there was no more time, and nobody could predict what would happen next. An Zhe knew what he wanted to say, just like how in the Abyss, nobody knew what would happen next.

He put his hand on the coach glass. The glass was stained with a layer of red and mixed with bits of flesh. As he looked outside, his breathing was slightly hurried.

Just like that, the train swiftly departed District 6. The bloody water gradually diluted, and the coach glass was washed clean and became clear again.

In the Abyss, he had seen countless monsters' attacks, struggles, injuries, and deaths.

But he had never seen something like this—this kind of one-sided slaughter and instant destruction.

The voice of the person in front of him trembled as he continued speaking. "Just... like that, it's... gone?"

It was gone.

All it needed was a bout of rain.

An Zhe saw large numbers of black birds fly toward District 6 from the upper edge of his field of vision.

After another few seconds, he noticed that those birds' wings were flat and unmoving as they flew forward in straight lines. Those weren't birds, but rather human fighter planes—they had come from the direction of the Main City and headed toward District 6. In less than a minute, they came to a hovering stop right above District 6's alarm tower.

He thought that perhaps this was the Main City's assistance to the Fortress.

Thus, he asked, "Are they rescuing people?"

"Human genes cannot be acquired by the monsters," Lu Feng said.

Within Lu Feng's steady voice was a trace of icy cold. With a few footsteps, he came to the rear window as well and stood behind An Zhe. An Zhe could hear his breathing from very close up; if he just backed up slightly, his shoulder would touch Lu Feng's chest.

He heard Lu Feng say into the communicator, "Get ready."

Indeed, human genes could not be acquired by the monsters. Every time an additional person died, the world would gain an additional or perhaps many more additional xenogenics with high intelligence. Therefore, no matter if it was in the wilderness or the base, once infection occurred, the person had to be immediately killed and their body burned in the incinerator. So now the Main City had to send troops to rescue as many of the Outer City's people as they could in order to prevent more people from being infected by the bugs—that was what An Zhe thought.

"… Okay," he said.

Poet and Mr. Shaw were both there. He hoped they could be rescued.

The soft sound of rustling fabric suddenly came to his ears

as Lu Feng held out a hand. An Zhe, not knowing what he intended to do, just watched the scenery in front. The train left the building zone and entered the massive buffer zone between the Outer City and Main City. Districts 6, 7, and 8's abundant buildings became smaller and more distant in his field of vision, turning into a gray forest amidst the rain and fog.

A searing white light suddenly lit up from that direction!

An Zhe instinctively squinted, but the strong light still penetrated through his eyelids, and all he could see was bright red. Then suddenly it was dark—Lu Feng's hand completely covered his eyes.

In the silence and darkness, An Zhe's senses were boundlessly amplified. Three seconds later, the train's floor and the whole ground suddenly trembled a little.

The silvery-white train swiftly traveled forward along the fixed rails.

At the very moment its last coach left the Outer City area, a massive mushroom cloud rose from District 6.

BOOK TWO: ROSES

14

"THE SYSTEM OF HUMAN SCIENCES IS ALL BUT WORTHLESS."

AFTER TEN MINUTES of high-speed train travel, the city had been completely left behind. Once Lu Feng took back his right hand, An Zhe saw thick clouds in the direction they had come from. The fighter planes, returning to their base, passed over the train with a roar before disappearing from his field of vision.

He said nothing. After quietly watching for a short while, he returned to his original spot and sat down.

The moment he boarded, he was still thinking that once communication was restored, he'd use his communicator to tell Mr. Shaw where he was going, but now it seemed that it would no longer be necessary.

He looked outside with his chin resting on his hands, and in his peripheral vision, there was a black figure. Lu Feng had sat down one seat away from him, and the young Judge who always followed him sat down at his side.

"Colonel, a message from the Trial Court," he said. "Of the Trial Court, twenty-one people have evacuated, nine people died, and four people were infected and have already been exterminated."

Lu Feng said, "What about the City Defense Agency?"

"No data at present."

Then their voices ceased. An Zhe looked out the window the whole time—but in truth, there was nothing outside the window that was worth looking at. In the rain and fog, all that was visible was the vast and barren cement ground.

It was a buffer zone. From the city gates to the Outer City, and even between each one of the Outer City's districts, there were huge buffer zones where no buildings whatsoever had been built. This was so that as soon as a xenogenic invasion or large-scale warfare occurred, the buffer zone could buy valuable rapid response time for the military instead of allowing xenogenics to charge directly into densely populated residential areas.

Before long, there was movement in the coach as Colin regained consciousness after his brief fainting spell. He got up from the aisle, returned to his original spot, and sat down, his face pale. Head bowed, he took out a pair of black-rimmed glasses from his pocket and repeatedly polished them with the hem of his shirt without saying another word. At that moment, An Zhe felt that this boy was no longer the same person as when they first met.

He turned back and looked at Lu Feng.

At the exact same time, Lu Feng looked away from Colin and at him.

Their eyes met, and An Zhe uneasily grabbed the hem of his own shirt.

Lu Feng only gave him a flat glance before breaking eye contact. He felt the current Lu Feng was very unfamiliar—even though they had slept in the same bed last night.

After some thought, An Zhe still said, "What's next?"

Lu Feng said, "Based on the courses you studied before, you might go teach children how to read."

"Then what about you?"

Lu Feng said, "I'll obey the Main City's plans."

An Zhe mustered up his courage. "Will you go to the Lighthouse?"

He knew his spore was likely at the Lighthouse.

Lu Feng looked at him.

An Zhe felt that this seemed to be the look he would give to someone slow in the head.

"I'm part of the military," Lu Feng said. "My next task is to recover the Dispersion Center."

"... Oh."

Then An Zhe said in a small voice, "Good luck."

Lu Feng quietly looked at him for a few seconds. "Thank you."

After that, neither of them spoke further. Somehow, An Zhe felt that the Colonel may not have been in much of a mood for conversation.

After yet another dozen or so minutes, the train arrived at the station, and Lu Feng walked toward the front of the train.

At the same time, an announcement was broadcast within the train. "Passengers, to ensure the safety of the Main City, please form a line for a second inspection."

The people in the train began to line up, and An Zhe and Colin were at the very back. The second inspection was a genetic examination using machines, and the inspector was still that young blonde and blue-eyed doctor in the white coat. After An Zhe and Colin had their blood drawn, the doctor started the machine and said, "Wait five minutes."

An Zhe obediently pressed a cotton swab to the spot where his blood had been drawn as he stood to one side. The doctor smiled. "It's you again."

"Hello," An Zhe said.

"So the Arbiter would actually bring people over for genetic examinations," the doctor said with a click of his tongue. "Everyone in our examination office was surprised."

An Zhe said, "He believes that I'm human now."

"He may have just wanted to nitpick." The doctor shrugged. "People of the Trial Court, you know, there'll always be minor problems with their minds."

An Zhe says, "He's all right."

The doctor tossed an admiring gaze at him. "You're the first person I've met who will speak on behalf of Colonel Lu."

As the doctor spoke, his gaze moved to An Zhe's left arm. "You got hurt?"

An Zhe noticed that because his movements were rather large, his sleeve cuff had been pulled up, and some of the bandages wrapped around his left arm peeked out.

"Mm-hm," An Zhe said.

"You should change the dressing." The doctor picked up a nearby medical kit and pulled out a new roll of bandages. "I'll change it for you."

The doctor seemed to be an easygoing and kind person. An Zhe murmured, "Thank you."

As the doctor took off An Zhe's original bandage, he said offhandedly, "This knot was tied well."

An Zhe thought for a while but didn't say anything. He decided to not tell the doctor that Lu Feng had wrapped it for him for fear that the examination office would be surprised again—they seemed to believe that Lu Feng was an evil person with no uncrossable line.

Once this thought popped up, An Zhe suddenly frowned.

At that moment, he seemed to understand why Lu Feng seldom conversed with others. The position of Arbiter was destined to be like this.

Just as he had that thought, he heard Colin softly say from next to him, "Doctor."

The doctor finished wrapping the bandage for An Zhe and looked at him. "Hm?"

"Now that the Outer City has completely fallen, there's no

need for the Trial Court anymore either," Colin said. "Can we know the principles behind the Trial Court's judgments now?"

An Zhe thought that Colin was indeed a steadfast member of the opposition party.

"Why do you want to know?" The doctor leaned against the instrument-bearing vehicle with arms crossed, looking at him as he said, "Did you have family members or friends whom Lu Feng killed?"

"My mother," Colin said. "That time she went into the wilderness, she hadn't gone out of the armored vehicle the entire trip."

"Although there are few tiny monsters, they are by no means nonexistent."

"But there was nothing abnormal about her appearance or behavior."

"Uh-huh," the doctor said flatly. "So? If every single person's relatives demanded an explanation from the Trial Court and the examination office, we wouldn't have any time to ensure the safety of the city gates."

"But it's different now. You guys have time now." Colin raised his voice. "We only want to know the reasons."

While watching him, the doctor smiled.

"You're right, it is different now," the doctor said softly. "Now you are people of the Main City, so you'll gradually come to know a lot of information."

He nonchalantly said, "Do you guys think that after being infected—that human bodies will slowly be corroded?"

Colin said, "What else?"

"That's not it." The doctor lifted his head and looked up at the sky. "At the very moment infection occurs, your strands of DNA—all the DNA structures—will instantly change. Once infection occurs, a person's fate is sealed."

"Impossible," Colin said. "I've studied biology. Viruses need time to spread, and there will be incubation periods—"

But the doctor interrupted him straight away.

"Following that, the DNA strands' structure will affect the composition of RNA, and the changes in RNA will affect the manufacture of proteins, and humans' biological characteristics will begin to change. All of these things begin happening within a very short span of time. Your skin, appearance, expressions, how you move, how you think, language ability... All of them will change. All the training Judges receive before formally becoming Judges is to observe these differences with the naked eye." He smiled. "Once their differentiation accuracy reaches eighty percent, they can graduate and formally serve. Do you think your shallow observation of human behavior is comparable to their more than ten years of training?"

"Eighty percent." Colin abruptly lifted his gaze. "So the Trial Court cannot completely identify xenogenics either. They really do ensure that they won't erroneously let xenogenics pass via large-scale random killings, right?"

"I'm very sorry, but there's something I must tell you." The doctor looked at him. "Lu Feng's result that year was a hundred percent."

Colin dumbly stood in place for a few seconds before saying, "... Impossible."

"I hope you don't use ordinary standards to determine the upper limits of other people's abilities, especially after entering the Main City." The doctor's tone of voice was flat. He was speaking to Colin, but he was looking at An Zhe. "At the very least, under circumstances where it could be tested whether the judgment outcome was correct or not, he has not made a mistake even once. The examination office and the Trial Court have a very close relationship. I've seen his examination results. Back then, the Arbiter received full marks on all indicators. However, that may not be the reason why he can determine xenogenics with a hundred percent accuracy either."

"He seems to have an innate gift, a kind of intuition," the

doctor said. "Back then, after discovering his talent in this field, the examination office drew his blood every month, but unfortunately their research bore no fruit."

"No..." Colin frowned deeply. "This goes against science. Intuition can't be used as the basis for science, and what you said about infection methods at the very start also—"

There was a brief beep, and a green light lit up on the machine.

"Here's your new ID cards and communicators. Get on the shuttle. The Main City will allocate living quarters to you." The doctor handed them two blue chips and communicators. "Afterward, wait for information from the communicator."

Colin accepted the items. "But..."

"I know it goes against some principles of biological science, but the most fearsome part of this era is—" As the doctor looked at him, his azure eyes seemingly frosted over, he said one syllable at a time, "We've discovered that the systems of human sciences are all but worthless."

"Human science is like mountain climbing, but a hundred years ago, we lost our footing." The doctor smiled. "Just like how we weren't able to explain from then until now why the geomagnetic field would suddenly disappear for such a long time."

With that, he was no longer talkative. "Get going, then."

Colin bowed his head and walked toward the shuttle without another word. After An Zhe bid the doctor goodbye, he boarded the shuttle as well.

Lu Feng's location was a mystery, for An Zhe hadn't seen him. He was a very busy man, and it also seemed that he didn't want to interact with An Zhe much today, so he had probably already left.

After confirming the last two people had boarded, the shuttle bus left the train station along the track. It was the last bus, and it was packed tight with close to a hundred people standing inside. The place they set out from was inside the building, so the situation outside was not clearly visible. It wasn't until three minutes later, when the shuttle passed through a tunnel, that the sound of rain and the light from the outside world came in. Up ahead, it suddenly became clear, and from within the vehicle came the sound of faint gasps.

An Zhe's gaze passed through both the crowd inside the vehicle and the vehicle window—there was another buffer zone, but right after the buffer zone, countless large gray-blue buildings that shone with a glassy sheen rose up.

His eyes slowly opened wide.

One month ago, the first time he came to the human base, he felt the mysticality of human buildings. They were taller than the vast majority of giant mushrooms, unusually magnificent and lofty—but those were the magnificence and loftiness with regard to a mushroom who had never seen the world.

It was different now. As someone who had become accustomed to the building standards of the Outer City, he once again felt that those skyscrapers were looking down at him. The Outer City's residential buildings were mainly ten stories high, but the buildings here were different. After he counted to thirty, because it took too long, that building had already retreated and disappeared from his field of vision, while he had only counted a little over half of it.

At the same time, they were unusually concentrated together and intricate, intertwining dazzlingly in An Zhe's sight. The rain gradually lightened up, for summer storms always left very quickly. Golden sunlight penetrated through the clouds and shone off of the glass curtain walls at the tops of the buildings.

An Zhe once heard the entire story of how the base was established from Poet's mouth. At first it was the weakening and then disappearance of the geomagnetic field—to solve this problem, humans built two magnetic field generators, and the Northern Base's Main City protected one of them.

It wasn't until afterward, when the mutation of bacteria and plants and animals occurred, that humans began gathering together to save themselves, which led to the emergence of the entire Northern Base. Therefore, the Main City was established earlier than the Outer City, and many things had not yet happened at that time. The magnetic generator and the Main City were the pinnacles of human technology and construction respectively at the time.

And after that, it all went downhill.

The robotic guide's voice said, "Passengers, due to the scarcity of housing in the Main City, the residential areas affiliated with the Lighthouse and Garden of Eden are at full capacity, so you will be temporarily placed in the military residential area. Please find the corresponding address based on your ID card number and await further instruction."

An Zhe took out his new ID card. The card number had changed; now it was 3124043702.

3 represented the human base, 1 represented the Main City, and the remaining numbers delineated the exact residential location.

The people within the shuttle began to whisper amongst themselves, and they discovered that their addresses were all very scattered.

"I got it," someone said. "There's no danger to the people working in the Lighthouse and the Garden of Eden. They won't die, so the residential areas are at full capacity. But the military's numbers are often depleted, leaving many spaces, so they're perfect for us to be stuffed into."

The other people all agreed with this view. Before too long, the shuttle stopped and let them out. There were a few others living in Building 24's Unit 04 with An Zhe. They walked into the building and began learning how to use the elevators in a flurry—those were something the Outer City did not have.

Finally, Colin got off at the thirty-sixth floor, and An Zhe came alone to the thirty-seventh floor. There were no other buttons above thirty-seven, as it was the top floor. Two doors faced each other, both with white seals pasted on them. An Zhe tore off the seal on the door to No. 02, then swiped his card and entered.

The living spaces in the Main City were clearly larger than those of the Outer City. This was a suite with a bedroom and a living room, and it had a separate bathroom and kitchen. In the living room was a simple tea table and small gray sofa, and on the wall facing the small sofa hung a black rectangular object. The rectangle's structure and color reminded him of the tablet he had played with at Mr. Shaw's place. He went up to it and pressed the button at the bottom.

"... have safely been transferred into the Main City, and the Main City has entered a state of emergency defense. The United Front Center has expressed that the base will enter a five- to ten-year withdrawal period until the next generation matures. At the same time, the Lighthouse has surmised that the monsters outside have produced high-intelligence mutants and that the swarm's invasion is the collective action of insects in the midst of their breeding season. To avoid the potential danger of gene leakage, the Lighthouse recommends that the United Front Center carefully dispatch troops to the outside, no longer carry out high-risk operations, shift their work focus to the production of resources and combat readiness research and development, and search for ways to overcome the current predicament. Next, we'll turn to Lighthouse researcher Mr. Chen."

The interface changed from a suit-clad broadcaster to a middle-aged man with a serious expression clad in a white coat.

"As everyone knows, arthropod-class monsters do not necessarily have a survival advantage in high-risk areas, but during their breeding season, they need nutrient-rich and genetically advantageous animal blood and flesh to serve as the breeding grounds for their eggs. We surmise that this is why they have collectively attacked the human base. After all, reproduction is the first priority of species, so they can do anything. But how they produced an intelligent group consciousness is unknown. We fear it may be related to some of the individuals absorbing human genes."

The broadcaster asked, "Regarding this situation, what would you like to convey to everyone?"

"It is a misfortune that the entirety of the base's Outer City has been lost. But in the end, we have eliminated the possibility of further human gene leakage and left the monsters no opportunities to reproduce, which is also a form of victory," the researcher said. "What I want to tell everyone is, there is currently no need to worry about the safety of the Main City. The Main City is the crystallization of the pinnacle of human technology, and the degree of its security is such that it will not be invaded by the monsters of the outside world. At the same time, there's no need to be anxious over the future of the human species. I've received news that our reproduction technology has advanced and that the number of newborns in the Garden of Eden has sharply increased in recent years, so the base is about to enter a period of population expansion. Our future is bright..."

The researcher spoke at length, generally focusing on placating the people. After he finished, the broadcaster connected to someone from the military and asked him to introduce the most recent progress of the work out in the field to everyone.

An Zhe thought that the Main City's news broadcasts were much more detailed than the Outer City's monotonous broadcasts.

He felt that it was very interesting. Once the news finally finished broadcasting, the screen turned a dull gray and began playing meaningless music, and only then did he turn it off.

It was now evening. Outside the bedroom window, stars had begun to appear, and a black silhouette in the shape of a massive cylindrical tower stood in the distance. It was too big, occupying almost a quarter of An Zhe's field of vision, and taller than all the other buildings, resembling a huge monster hibernating in the middle of the city. A thin aurora swiftly fluctuated around it, and An Zhe thought that perhaps it was the legendary magnetic field generator.

He watched for a while longer, then opened the door with the intention of going out for dinner. The Main City was just like the Outer City, with communal dining rooms on certain floors.

He noticed that the seal of the neighbor across the hallway had been torn off.

An Zhe had no intention of investigating when his neighbor had come back, nor what kind of person they were. This day had a hair-raising beginning, and he didn't like it. He intended for it to come to a quiet conclusion.

Thus, he achieved his wish and quietly reached the next morning. A message had come from his communicator, requesting all civilian personnel transferred from the Outer City to gather at the entrance to the Garden of Eden.

Last night, An Zhe read the map of the Main City and the *Base Handbook*, so he knew the Main City had twenty thousand permanent adult residents, seventy percent of whom belonged to the military and the remaining thirty percent consisting of scientific research personnel and various kinds of civil servants. The periphery of the Main City was composed of the military areas, military bases, landing fields, train stations, and residential areas, while the interior was the core area, containing three of the base's important institutions.

The first one was the United Front Center—the military— and it was responsible for managing military personnel and materials. The second one was the Scientific Research Center, which had the same function as its name. Because its symbol was a simplified lighthouse, it was also simply called the "Lighthouse." The United Front Center and the Lighthouse each had its own large building, and the two of them were connected by corridor bridges. The buildings that they were composed of were called the "Twin Towers."

The third one's name was rather long. It was called "Reproduction, Nurturing, and Education Center," and it had two functions. One was to provide foodstuffs and nutrition for the base—An Zhe thought that this may be where humans planted potatoes. The other was to grow their younglings. Human babies grew up and received their initial education here. Because the name was too difficult to pronounce, it was also known as the "Garden of Eden."

An Zhe's future workplace was the Garden of Eden.

He looked at the distant Twin Towers, then looked at the Garden of Eden. In truth, he was looking forward to it a little because he hadn't seen human younglings before. His spore was a very soft and white little thing. He didn't know if human younglings would be the same.

But could taking care of human younglings allow him to accumulate experience for taking care of his own youngling?

It seemed that it couldn't.

15

"DO NOT GO GENTLE INTO THAT GOOD NIGHT."

"DO NOT GO gentle into that good night—"

An Zhe and Colin walked through a long and narrow white corridor. From next to them came the synchronized sound of recitation, an assemblage of very young voices creating faintly discernible echoes in the surroundings.

This was the sixth floor of the Garden of Eden, and the one who brought them in was a man around thirty years old named Lin Zuo. In his white shirt and gold wire-rimmed glasses, he looked gentle and cultured.

Lin Zuo brought the two of them to the office, where he said, "It's nice here, isn't it?"

Colin said, "It's very nice."

Lin Zuo said, "The Main City's conditions are somewhat better than those of the Outer City."

An Zhe noticed. At the very least, when he was in the Outer City, he never thought that the world would have a building as massive as the Garden of Eden.

In this corridor, apart from the office, there were ten rooms altogether. Five were classrooms, and the other five were children's dormitories. The dormitories were packed with small, low beds, and each room could accommodate a hundred people.

According to Lin Zuo, this floor of the Garden of Eden consisted of a total of ten such corridors, and the children on each floor were the same age. In other words, there were four thousand nearly-six-years-old human younglings here.

"After the children reach six years old, the vast majority of them originally would have been sent to the Outer City to await adoption. But now that the Outer City has fallen, the Main City has to bear the work of their education past six years old and there's not enough manpower. It's good that you all have come," Lin Zuo said. "We dare not hand over babies under the age of six to newcomers, so this group of children will be assigned to you after they turn six."

An Zhe said, "Okay."

"At present, the plans for the next step in their education isn't quite set just as of yet. You two, come with me and familiarize yourselves with the process first, okay?"

Colin replied with an affirmative sound.

Lin Zuo smiled faintly, then took some books from a bookshelf. "These are the textbooks and shift plans. Take a look at them first, then ask me if you have questions."

An Zhe accepted his portion.

There were two education courses here, with one course being language and literature and the other course being mathematics and logic. What he received was the language and literature textbook. The six-year-old children had already grasped basic pinyin and grammar, so the textbook contained some short fables and poems. An Ze had learned these things very well, so there were no syllables or words An Zhe didn't recognize either.

After flipping through the textbook once, it was time for class. An Zhe moved a desk and chair into a back corner of the classroom and sat down, holding a copy of the children's seating chart. The task Lin Zuo gave to him, other than listening to class, was to take notes on the children's behavior. If a child took the initiative to answer a question or ask a question, points would be added, and if a child whispered or did irrelevant things, points would be deducted.

When he sat in, the younglings all turned their heads to look at him. The younglings had very tender skin, and their gazes were also pure and clean. They all wore white shirts, black shorts, and similar short hairstyles, so there was momentarily no way of differentiating between male and female. They whispered a little, continuing to examine An Zhe, and An Zhe smiled at them in response.

Thus, a few of the younglings smiled back at him as well. Among them, one blinked, eyelashes fluttering a few times, and asked, "Are you the new teacher?"

An Zhe said, "I am."

"Wow," another youngling said in a small voice. "You're so pretty."

An Zhe said, "Thank you."

The youngling said, "You're welcome."

Yet another youngling asked, "What're you called?"

An Zhe gave his name.

Chattering, the younglings introduced themselves as well. "I'm called Bai Nan."

"I'm called Ji Sha."

"I'm called Du Cheng."

Of course, there were some indifferent younglings as well, such as the one in the corner who turned back after one look at An Zhe.

But the excitement around An Zhe didn't last too long because Lin Zuo had come in.

The younglings instantly dispersed from An Zhe's side and returned to their own seats. Lin Zuo looked around and, after confirming that nobody was absent, began the lecture.

What he lectured on was the poem An Zhe had heard in the corridor earlier, and it was also the last one in the textbook—it was somewhat more complicated than the other contents, and it just happened to be what he heard the children in a classroom reciting when he was walking in the corridor.

The younglings first read the poem out loud from beginning to end.

"Do not go gentle into that good night.
Old age should burn and rave at close of day;
Rage, rage against the dying of the light."

"Though wise men at their end know dark is right,
Because their words had forked no lightning they
Do not go gentle into that good night."

After they read it out loud once, Lin Zuo stood in front of the podium and asked, "Is there any part you don't understand?"

One youngling raised their hand, and An Zhe checked the seating chart. That was the youngling Bai Nan.

Bai Nan said, "I don't understand any part."

The other younglings all laughed.

"Narrow the scope of your question," Lin Zuo said.

"Then..." Bai Nan scratched the back of his head. His tone was hesitant as he asked, "Why can't we go gentle into the night?"

An Zhe added a point for Bai Nan on the chart, then looked at Lin Zuo, waiting for his answer.

He didn't know the answer to Bai Nan's question either. In the Abyss and in the human base, he had seen twilight gradually replace the daylight too many times. Every single night gently descended upon the ground in that manner, unable to be resisted.

Lin Zuo's gaze swept over them, and his lips pursed slightly to form a faintly solemn arc.

"This is the last text of your course this year," he said. "It has a meaning different from all the previous texts, although to you all, it may be a bit difficult."

He turned around, wrote down the line "Do not go gentle into that good night" on the whiteboard, then once again turned toward the younglings below.

"This is a poem composed of metaphors and symbols," Lin Zuo said. "Do not go gentle into that good night. Its implied meaning is: do not meekly accept destruction."

An Zhe slowly opened his eyes wide, and he wrote down this sentence in his notebook.

Then Lin Zuo began explaining from the first line, and An Zhe earnestly took notes.

After he finished explaining, the younglings once again read the poem out loud from beginning to end.

"There on the sad height,
Curse, bless, me now with your fierce tears, I pray.
Do not go gentle into that good night."

The tip of the pen An Zhe was using paused. He lifted his head to look at the bright scenery outside the window. Nearby, the Twin Towers were shining gloriously beneath the sunlight, and the city gently sprawled, its edges disappearing into the blue horizon. He knew that this city had not yet gone into that good night and was striving to not go into that good night.

After the day's classes ended, Lin Zuo was off work, so he handed over the children to An Zhe and Colin. They had to take the younglings together with the dormitory teacher to eat, then gather in the dormitories to watch the day's news. In order to improve his relationship with the younglings, An Zhe had to explain any confusion they had regarding the news at any time, and he could only get off work after the news was done playing.

The well-fed younglings were very lively. In the corridor, they quarreled and talked. An Zhe felt like there were ten thousand mosquitoes screaming in his ear, but he tolerated these human younglings. Even in the Abyss, monsters would treat their younglings gently—but only their own.

Once it was time for the news, the dormitory teacher took out a scoring sheet, and the younglings instantly quieted down when they saw the sheet and spontaneously formed a ring next to the large projection screen with An Zhe sitting in the middle.

As he watched the screen, he suddenly felt something touching his fingers. When he looked down, he saw that it was the youngling named Bai Nan sitting next to him and hooking his own fingers around An Zhe's.

An Zhe didn't have much physical contact with humans before, and the one incident he had a strong recollection of was when he bumped into Lu Feng and even hurt his head on the badge on Lu Feng's chest—but the youngling's body was different from Lu Feng's. It was soft.

Like his spore, the human younglings quietly stayed by him, just like how his spore quietly stayed inside his body. Through this fantasy, An Zhe obtained a false sense of peace, and he once again rubbed Bai Nan's head.

Thus, Bai Nan scooted even closer to lean firmly against him and hugged his arm. At the same time, another youngling named Ji Sha leaned over as well. This youngling looked vaguely like a girl. Immediately afterward, the group of younglings wriggled toward him. Colin, who was to one side, also received the affection of a few younglings. Getting close to adults seemed to be an instinct of all species' younglings.

But there was a solitary youngling still sitting cross-legged in place, remaining unmoved. An Zhe remembered that his name was Si Nan. Si Nan never asked questions in class either. He made eye contact with Si Nan and smiled at him, but Si Nan avoided his gaze, turning his eyes back to the big screen.

The news started.

"After the bombing of District 6, the number of monsters in

the Outer City has significantly decreased. The military's Second Air Formation took flight at 6 a.m. this morning and landed in District 1 to assist the Outer City. The Trial Court's Colonel Lu Feng will command the existing troops to carry out the Dispersion Center recovery mission..."

An Zhe suddenly heard a familiar name. Since he came to the Main City, he hadn't seen Lu Feng. It turned out that he had already gone to the Outer City.

Bai Nan suddenly murmured, "It's the Arbiter."

Ji Sha said, "I'm so scared."

An Zhe asked them, "What's the matter?"

Bai Nan said, "The news will often say how many people the Arbiter executed."

Ji Sha added, "He also often goes to the Abyss. The Abyss is so scary."

An Zhe rubbed her head. "There's no need to be afraid."

Ji Sha wrinkled her nose.

"You're human, so the Arbiter will protect you."

Ji Sha continued wrinkling her nose.

Bai Nan asked, "Teacher, have you seen the Arbiter before?"

At the same time, the news said, "Next, we'll connect with our war correspondent."

With a flash, the camera lens showed the reporter interviewing an officer clad in a black uniform. When that figure first appeared, An Zhe thought it was Lu Feng, but then he noticed that it wasn't. That person was the young Judge by Lu Feng's side. The news screen showed his name: Seraing.

He softly answered Bai Nan's question. "I have."

"Then how does he look? He hasn't shown his face on the news before," Bai Nan asked.

Ji Sha chimed in too. "Does he look very mean?"

The younglings all looked in their direction, seemingly very interested in this question.

"He..." An Zhe recalled Lu Feng's appearance and strove to

decide based on human aesthetics. "He's a little fierce, but very handsome."

"What does he look like?"

Each of the younglings' questions were more difficult than the previous. An Zhe didn't know what kind of comparison to make at all. Just as he was pondering deeply, he suddenly recalled the color of Lu Feng's eyes. That cold deep green—like where the aurora proliferated in the sky.

He said, "Like... the aurora, I suppose."

Doubts appeared in the younglings' eyes.

Right then, An Zhe saw the dormitory teacher give him a thumbs-up from the side.

"As expected of a language and literature teacher," the dormitory teacher said.

An Zhe didn't know if the dorm teacher was praising or criticizing him, so he could only give a close-lipped smile.

In this manner, he passed the days in the Main City one at a time, and without even noticing, he had lived here for nearly a month.

Life in the Garden of Eden was very peaceful, with nothing more than arguments and fights between the younglings. There were a few times when An Zhe walked to the base of the Twin Towers, but these two towers both required for a card to be swiped before entering, and he did not have the permissions to enter. If he wanted to see his spore, he first needed to know where exactly it was within the Lighthouse, and he also needed to be able to gain entry to the Lighthouse. Right now, both goals were both far off.

However, at the same time, the information that came from the news was increasingly heartening. Ten days ago, Colonel Lu had led a team into the core of the Dispersion Center and worked out a detailed plan of action—the news stressed that because of the Trial Court's periodical training in the Abyss, they had an extreme abundance of experience in dealing with monsters.

Five days ago, the troops officially recovered the Dispersion Center, cleaned out the remaining monsters inside, and carried out large-scale cleaning and disinfection. The team sent by the Lighthouse then entered and began the emergency repairs.

Today, An Zhe had originally planned to continue listening to the news, but on this day, Lin Zuo had to take the night shift, so he was forced to leave work ahead of time.

At six o'clock in the summer, the sky was still very bright, with only the western sky being slowly suffused with a thin layer of gray-blue. An Zhe swiped his card, and the "Garden of Eden" building's glass door slowly slid open. He walked out, and Colin, who had also gotten off work early, walked out as well.

It wasn't the conventional time to get off work, so there were few pedestrians on the road. He wandered about the streets and took a shortcut toward the shuttle bus stop. He and Colin were both tired of the other, so even though they had to walk the same path, they maintained a very large distance with one in front and one behind.

The world was originally very quiet, but just as he was about to cross this small street and set foot on the wide road, hurried footsteps suddenly came from behind him, followed by a white shape passing him in his peripheral vision—a short white figure, and An Zhe frowned as he looked—that was a little girl, he was convinced.

Of the children in his class, the ways the boys and girls dressed and looked were very similar, but they were all five or six years old. This child before his eyes was undoubtedly a girl. She had an exceptionally slim body and shoulder-length black hair that hung loose, and she wore a white gauze dress.

Up ahead was the road, and vehicles were driving over it. An Zhe said, "Be careful!"

Coincidentally, a car roared as it passed by, and the girl

stopped dead in her tracks as though startled by it. As she rapidly gasped for breath, she turned back to look at An Zhe, her gaze terrified yet seeming very apprehensive.

An Zhe asked, "Do you need my help? Are you from the Garden of Eden?"

Unexpectedly, just as he finished speaking, the girl's tension increased instead, and she whipped her head around before rushing straight toward the road!

An Zhe chased after her.

At that very moment, a black figure appeared at the street corner and, with crisp and tidy movements, blocked the girl's path. Right as the girl's footsteps paused, that person leaned down and picked her up, then took a few steps back. The girl struggled violently, but she couldn't get free at all.

An Zhe, who had only just arrived, was speechless.

Their eyes met.

"... Hello," An Zhe said.

"Hello," Lu Feng replied.

An Zhe wanted to ask him if the Dispersion Center had been recovered, but at that moment, he had something even more important to say, and it had already been fermenting for a month.

That day on the train, Lu Feng was in a bad mood—in truth, his mood had never been particularly good before, and An Zhe inferred the reason—in this world, very few people could look at the Colonel rationally.

Combined with the Colonel's action of sacrificing himself on the dangerous road to save the little girl just now, that statement was even more well founded.

"Colonel," he said.

Lu Feng seemed to lift his eyebrows slightly. "What is it?"

The girl was still struggling. With her gaze empty and hair disheveled, it looked like there was something wrong with her. Lu Feng carelessly patted her on the back, and although the technique was very unpracticed, at the very least his intentions were good.

Thus, that statement was proven right once more. An Zhe looked at the little girl, then once again looked back at Lu Feng before he said sincerely, "You're a good person."

This time, the Colonel really lifted his eyebrows, and there was a hint of a smile in the corners of his lips, but it wasn't a genuine smile. It was like he had heard An Zhe say some blatant falsehood instead.

In the following second, he subdued the girl with one hand and picked up his communicator with the other. "Intersection 7, target captured."

With those words, he gave An Zhe a flat look.

An Zhe did not understand.

16

"I DON'T HATE YOU BECAUSE OF THOSE THINGS"

AN ZHE STOOD IN PLACE.

The evening wind lifted up his hair.

He saw a silver car bearing a Garden of Eden logo make a screeching turn before stopping in front of them. From inside, a man in white overalls rushed out, and he took the girl from Lu Feng. "Thank you for your help."

The expression in Lu Feng's eyes was flat. "Be more careful in the future."

The man got back into the car. "This time was an accident."

Without any further words, the man pulled the door shut, and the car swiftly started up and sped toward the Garden of Eden.

Lu Feng turned back.

An Zhe felt a little angry.

Then he saw Lu Feng give him a flat look before saying evenly, "I'm a good person?"

An Zhe finally knew how he should describe his own mood.

He thought that Lu Feng had deceived his feelings, if mushrooms also had feelings.

He didn't want to acknowledge this man anymore, so he turned around and walked past him onto the road.

Before he had taken many steps, Lu Feng had pressed down on his shoulder.

"Lead the way," Lu Feng said. "I don't know how to get back to the residential area."

An Zhe was confused.

He asked, "Don't you know your way around?"

"I haven't come back in many years," Lu Feng replied.

An Zhe thought for a while. What he said made a bit of sense. If the Colonel was not in the Abyss, then he was at the city gates, so he may not have stayed in the Main City for at least seven years. Whereas he himself had already stayed in the Main City for a month, so he was familiar with the way back.

Thus, he asked, "Where do you live?"

Lu Feng seemed to think for a while before taking out a blue ID card from his chest pocket and handing it over.

An Zhe accepted it. Even the decorative pattern on the Colonel's card was different from his.

He looked down and saw that the back of the card had a string of numbers printed on it in gilt.

3124043701.

Recalling his own new ID number, An Zhe expressionlessly said, "I'll take you there."

The Colonel seemed to have noticed his expression. "You aren't willing to?"

"I'm willing."

Thus, with Lu Feng in tow, he sat down on the Main City's free shuttle. There were seats on both sides, and the seats were arranged in connected pairs. He sat down at a window seat, and Lu Feng sat down next to him. Lu Feng was a good-looking man, and coupled with the imposing and tidy Trial Court uniform, he was very conspicuous amongst the crowd. As a result, when they boarded, all the people inside looked at them.

An Zhe said, "Get off at the last stop."

"Thank you," Lu Feng said. "Where do you live?"

"I live near you."

"All right."

The original residential area for the Garden of Eden's workers was nearby, but An Zhe was a late addition, and the military residential area he had been assigned to was far away. The shuttle stopped and went, and almost forty minutes passed before it reached the last stop, where he had to get off.

The Garden of Eden's younglings looked very well behaved, but they actually were not, especially when they asked about this and that. At the end of the day, An Zhe would be lethargic for a while—such as right now.

In the past, he would choose to lean against the vehicle and nap for a while, but Lu Feng was beside him today, so he felt that it was better to stay awake.

Thus, An Zhe chose to rest his chin in his hand and look at the scenery outside, such as the Twin Towers, Garden of Eden, and other various buildings and structures. It had been two months since he'd started living in the human city, but he still felt like he was dreaming.

As he looked, An Zhe's eyelids gradually drooped.

And after that, he lost consciousness.

———

The gentle robotic announcement played. "We have arrived at the last stop. Passengers, please get off in an orderly manner, and we will see you next time."

Lu Feng looked at An Zhe, who was leaning on his shoulder.

The glow of the setting sun spilled in through the window, and a golden sheen suffused the ends of An Zhe's eyelashes. His sleeping appearance was very quiet, with the gentle rise and fall of his breathing the only movement. He looked like he had no aggressiveness whatsoever nor any vigilance or caution against everything outside, just like a child who had not grown up. Lu Feng thought that it wouldn't be bad if he kept sleeping like this.

But immediately, the shuttle slowed down and came to a gradual stop. The people on board stood up one after another, and their footsteps sounded in the aisle.

An Zhe opened his eyes.

He discovered that he had slept more comfortably than any other time before.

His gaze slowly, slowly traveled to the side, and he saw black fabric and a silver badge.

With a start, he straightened up and saw Lu Feng watching him with a gaze that was by no means cold; it seemed that he hadn't gotten angry because of what happened just now.

Lu Feng said, "Let's go."

An Zhe rubbed his eyes. He fell asleep quickly and woke up quickly as well. He followed Lu Feng off the shuttle, and the evening wind brought with it a slight chill. He pointed toward a building up ahead. "Building 24 is there."

Lu Feng uttered a short word of thanks, then walked in that direction.

An Zhe followed.

Halfway there, Lu Feng said, "It's enough to bring me to this point."

Saying nothing, An Zhe continued following him.

At Unit 04, Lu Feng pressed the button for the thirty-seventh floor, and so An Zhe went up to the thirty-seventh floor via the elevator as well. Naturally, the kind of simple choice between No. 01 and No. 02 did not need another's directions.

An Zhe looked at the remains of the seal that had just been torn off from the door of No. 01 last night, thinking that even now, this Colonel was still unaware that his abominable conduct had been seen through long ago.

The seal on the door of his neighbor across the hall, No. 01, had been torn off a month ago. He had personally witnessed it. It meant that Lu Feng had stayed here for a night back then, so there was no possibility that he didn't know the way.

And Lu Feng made the false claim that he didn't know the way at all and wanted him to lead the way. This meant—Lu Feng was completely making fun of him, making him expend worthless and unnecessary labor.

Unfortunately, when he saw Lu Feng's ID card, the man's lie collapsed.

At that very moment, he heard Lu Feng say, "You're very conscientious."

This man truly thought he was conscientiously doing his best to lead the way—with this thought, An Zhe's expression became more merciless. He looked at Lu Feng, and Lu Feng looked back at him.

Mimicking Lu Feng, An Zhe indifferently turned and came to the door of No. 02, then placed his blue ID card on the sensor.

The sensor let out a crisp "beep" and lit up with a green light. Then there was a "click" as the door lock automatically opened.

An Zhe turned back and looked at Lu Feng.

Lu Feng was briefly stunned before saying, "What a coincidence."

An Zhe's face was blank.

"What is it?" There seemed to be a slight questioning in Lu Feng's eyes, but merely one second later, he seemed to understand everything. The expression in his eyes changed completely into a smile, and the corners of his lips lifted as well.

"I didn't lie to you," he said. "I had a night-long prewar meeting in the Main City one month ago right before leaving for the Outer City."

"The seal," An Zhe said.

"The military knew I had returned to the Main City, so they sent people to come tidy up," Lu Feng said.

"Oh."

But An Zhe had no plans to believe this man again.

He turned around and returned home. Right at that moment, Lu Feng's door suddenly let out a piercing and hurried "beep—"

He turned back and saw Lu Feng swiping his card, but although the correct card was clearly placed against the sensor, it glowed red.

Lu Feng frowned.

An Zhe looked at him with suspicion.

Then he saw Lu Feng dial a number and briefly describe the current situation.

The sound of an explanation came from the transmitter on the other end.

After hanging up, Lu Feng looked at An Zhe and said, "Three years ago, the Main City's ID cards were upgraded, but mine wasn't upgraded in time."

An Zhe thought that he may truly have unjustly blamed Lu Feng.

But, but—

The Main City's roads were not complicated at all, and the buildings all had conspicuous numbers. Once on the shuttle, even a mushroom like him knew when to get off.

For a moment, he wavered. But in the end, for the sake of his spore, he still said, "Then would you... like to come to my home for now?"

Lu Feng readily accepted.

After inviting the Arbiter to sit down on the sofa and then turning on the TV for him, An Zhe went into the kitchen.

Before entering the kitchen, he asked, "Have you eaten?"

Lu Feng said that he had not.

An Zhe's original intention for saying this was to hint that he could go downstairs to the communal dining hall to eat, but

Lu Feng's reply had a hidden meaning—it meant that he had to cook for two today.

An Zhe chopped two additional potatoes. The Main City's communal dining hall provided both food and raw materials. In this month, he had gradually gotten accustomed to cooking his own soup—it would be thicker and more delicious than that of the dining hall.

After putting the potatoes and bits of smoked pork into the pot, pouring in water, and adding milk, he turned on the heat, covered the pot, and returned to the living room.

The news announced that the restoration work of the Dispersion Center was proceeding smoothly.

Lu Feng was on the sofa and looking at his textbook, seemingly in a good mood.

When this man was in a good mood, he would bully others. When he was in a bad mood, he would not acknowledge others, such as that time a month ago on the train when he seemed to be completely unwilling to talk to An Zhe.

After the impulsive emotion of being lied to subsided, An Zhe calmed down. While he was chopping potatoes in the kitchen, he earnestly contemplated the relationship between himself and Lu Feng.

The key to finding his spore lay in establishing a good relationship with Lu Feng.

The premise upon which establishing a good relationship with humans rested on understanding his preferences.

Thus, An Zhe sat next to Lu Feng, and he saw that Lu Feng was looking at a poem in the textbook that described autumn's scenery.

"You teach this?" Lu Feng asked.

"I'm still learning," An Zhe said.

Lu Feng's unprompted question made An Zhe even more convinced that the man was in a good mood.

Thus, he said, "Colonel."

Lu Feng put down the textbook and looked at him. "What is it?"

"Before, on the train..." An Zhe murmured, slowly dropping his gaze, "You seemed unwilling to acknowledge me. Did I do something wrong?"

Lu Feng looked at him with a deep gaze.

"No," he said. "It's my problem."

"So that's what it was."

"Were you very bothered?"

"... Mm."

After a short silence, Lu Feng reached out a hand.

His fingers lingered briefly on the skin at An Zhe's neck, then traveled down and pulled out the bullet shell hanging around his neck.

An Zhe lifted his head to look up at Lu Feng, slightly panicked. At what point Lu Feng discovered the existence of the bullet shell, he didn't know.

"I killed the black market's mistress. At that time, you were by her side. Did you work under her?"

An Zhe shook his head. "I only followed Mr. Shaw."

"3260563209, at the city gates." Lu Feng continued, "Was he your teammate or boyfriend?"

"My friend."

Holding the bullet shell at his neck, Lu Feng asked, "Who was this?"

An Zhe said nothing. He couldn't say it, but silence was also a form of answer.

After the silence, Lu Feng did not ask further and simply stuffed the bullet shell back beneath An Zhe's collar.

"I've killed many people. However, for the most recent mass killings, you've always been present," he said. "Under these circumstances, the fact that you're still able to say I'm a good person surprises me greatly."

An Zhe thought back and discovered that things were indeed so.

The first time they met, Lu Feng killed Vance. The second time they met, it was Doussay. That night, xenogenics had invaded the city, and he had also killed seventy-three other people.

One month later, An Zhe stood within the isolation wall and witnessed Judgment Day being carried out with countless gunshots.

Finally, on the train leaving the Outer City, at his side, Lu Feng issued the order to bomb District 6.

Lu Feng had killed many people he had connections to.

However, this by no means impeded him from thinking that Lu Feng was a good person. Firstly, he knew Lu Feng was very accurate in distinguishing xenogenics. Secondly, even if he was recognized as a xenogenic by Lu Feng and killed, or when District 6 was bombed, he was one of them, and it seemed there was nothing to say. When in Rome, do as the Romans do. He had come to the human base, so he had to accept human rules.

But Lu Feng was the person who carried out the death sentences.

"Are you... sad because of this?" An Zhe asked.

"No." Lu Feng said while looking at him. "I know what I'm doing."

"Then..." An Zhe only managed to say that one word.

Was that because of some sort of emotional fluctuation?

But Lu Feng seemed to see what he was thinking.

"I haven't violated the principles," he said, "but nobody will come to determine whether I'm right or wrong."

An Zhe remembered what the young Judge Seraing said to him. He asked, "You aren't certain whether you've killed people correctly or not?"

"No, I am certain." Lu Feng looked out the window. His green eyes were like icebound lakes, containing an empty and distant stillness. "I'll just sometimes think about... the choices I made. Just what am I judging, and who will judge me in the end?"

An Zhe didn't fully understand his words. When humans have gone mad, perhaps they would say some nonsense that others did not understand.

But he also felt that he did understand.

As he looked at Lu Feng, he said, "I don't hate you because of those things."

After a pause, he added, "You haven't done wrong."

Lu Feng looked at him, and there was a long silence. It was so long that An Zhe felt an illusion—within that pair of eyes were not icebound lakes, but rather gentle cold water.

Twilight slowly descended upon the room. Lu Feng reached out with his right hand and ruffled An Zhe's hair.

An Zhe lowered his eyes slightly. The feeling of being patted on the head by the Arbiter was very wondrous. He felt that Lu Feng was now very soft.

If it was because his previous words comforted this man, he would feel rather happy.

Thus, he smiled at Lu Feng.

Then he saw Lu Feng's gaze turn malicious, and the fingers that had been patting his head moved downward and pinched his face.

An Zhe felt that it was better when this man was in a worse mood, because at least then he wouldn't randomly bully others.

He escaped from Lu Feng. "I need to go check on the pot."

"Uh-huh."

An Zhe returned to the kitchen and discovered that, as expected, the water had already started boiling, with the foam surging up and almost bursting through the pot lid. These days, he had grasped a sufficient number of cooking techniques. He lifted the transparent pot lid, and the white steam evaporated and the bubbles swiftly vanished. The smoked pork had been soaked through by the boiling water, and the edges of the small pieces of potato had also become rounded. The small amount of milk made the soup slightly white, and in the fresh and salty scent that wafted up, there was a subtle hint of a tender and lingering sweet fragrance. It was a smell An Zhe liked very much.

He picked up a nearby ladle and used the bottom of it to mash the softened pieces of potato. As they were stirred and mashed, the small pieces gradually dissolved into the soup, and the pot of potato soup became visibly thicker.

Lu Feng had also come into the kitchen at some point. Leaning against the doorframe, he asked, "Do you want me to help?"

An Zhe naturally didn't count on the mighty Colonel to be familiar with kitchen work, so he said, "No."

But Lu Feng didn't leave. He only stayed there and watched An Zhe. Then his gaze shifted to the kitchen, looking around the small space.

Finally, his gaze stopped on the silver faucet over the sink. "Does it leak?"

"Mm-hm," An Zhe said.

Since the first day he moved in, the kitchen faucet leaked. No matter how tightly he turned it, water would drip. In the daytime, the sound was not obvious, but in the profound quiet of the night, when even the lights of the distant Twin Towers were extinguished, the repeated sound of dripping water echoed throughout the rooms and would sometimes disturb his sleep—though disturbing his sleep came second. More importantly, with day after day of this, he was afraid he would have to pay a bigger water bill.

But then he saw Lu Feng take off and put aside his coat, roll up his uniform shirt sleeves, and lift his hand to close the black valve up on the water pipe—that was a place someone of An Zhe's height could not reach.

Then he unscrewed the faucet.

An Zhe silently watched his movements. He felt that Lu Feng's activity had only two possibilities: one was wanting to utterly destroy his faucet, and the other was wanting to help him repair it.

Rationally, he felt it was the former, but emotionally, he was more willing to believe the latter.

At that exact moment, someone knocked on the door.

Lu Feng was taking apart the faucet. Without even lifting his head, he said, "Go."

His manner of speaking was as self-assured as if he were the owner of these living quarters.

An Zhe, the true owner, put down the ladle, walked over to the entryway, and opened the door. It was a soldier clad in a military uniform.

The man looked around the living room and said, "Colonel Lu had me come here."

His voice was very loud.

Lu Feng's calm voice came from the direction of the kitchen. "Over here."

The soldier walked to the doorway, then clicked his heels and saluted. "Colonel Lu, I'm with the logistics service. Neglecting the issue with your ID card was the fault of our operating—"

His words suddenly cut off, and his gaze turned toward the faucet parts in Lu Feng's hand. With an expression like he'd seen a ghost, he then continued. "... For this, we sincerely apologize and—"

"Cut the chatter," Lu Feng said, coldly interrupting him.

The soldier said, "... I'm here to deliver your new ID card."

"Thank you." Lu Feng didn't even look at him as he put two parts back together with both hands. "You can put it down."

Potato peels lay piled up next to the sink, and next to them was the kitchen knife.

In the sink was water.

In the Colonel's hands were faucet parts.

The soldier held the ID card, momentarily unsure where he ought to put it.

An Zhe could only say in a small voice, "You can give it to me."

After taking the ID card, next was seeing the visitor off.

At the entrance, the soldier once again glanced at the Colonel in the kitchen, then looked at An Zhe. He deliberately lowered his voice, but because his voice was loud in the first place, it still wasn't quiet after he lowered it. "... What is the Colonel doing?"

"Fixing the faucet."

"The Colonel knows how to fix faucets?" The soldier looked at him with suspicion. "Then you and he are..."

"Right now, we're neighbors."

"What about before?"

"Before..." An Zhe recalled how they had slept in each other's beds. "Friends, I suppose."

The corners of the soldier's mouth twitched unnaturally. "... Ahaha."

He seemed to not believe An Zhe.

Perhaps it was that Lu Feng very rarely took apart other people's faucets. An Zhe calmly sent the soldier away.

As soon as he returned to the kitchen, he saw that the faucet had been reinstalled in its original place.

Lu Feng twisted open the valve.

The faucet did not leak at all.

"Wow," An Zhe said.

While looking at the faucet, he felt that the Colonel did not necessarily stay aloof at all times, refusing to acknowledge others, and also felt that this man seemed to know how to do everything.

He said, "You're really amazing."

His voice was still soft and very delicate. The aroma of the potato soup had already completely wafted out to fill the room with the dense steam. Without any hint of emotion, Lu Feng said, "You're not bad yourself."

After the potato soup was completely cooked, An Zhe divided it into two bowls and matched it with two packets of hardtack to serve as the staple food. Lu Feng looked to be in a very cheerful mood, but An Zhe had no appetite. He racked his brains, wanting to get some information related to the Lighthouse from Lu Feng, so he asked Lu Feng no small number of questions.

"What will you do next?"

"Wait for plans."

"Will you work in the Twin Towers?"

"Maybe."

"Does the Lighthouse and military often interact?"

"No."

"The doctor works at the Lighthouse... Do you know him very well?"

"No." Lu Feng was expressionless.

The blatant coldness made An Zhe give up the thought of continuing his questioning, but to stop there seemed more suspicious, so he continued. "That little girl today..."

In the following second, Lu Feng looked at him.

"Don't ask questions you shouldn't be asking," he said, "and don't talk while you eat."

An Zhe disappointedly shut up.

By the time dinner ended, he hadn't gotten anything related to his spore at all, but the Arbiter's attitude toward him seemed to have improved a lot.

An Zhe opened the door to see Lu Feng out.

Lu Feng said, "Goodbye."

An Zhe also said, "Goodbye."

He saw Lu Feng put the new ID card up to the sensor. The green light lit up, and the lock successfully opened.

Lu Feng pushed the door open.

Then he suddenly stopped moving, his entire person seeming to have come to a standstill.

For the Colonel, this kind of behavior was very seldom seen, so An Zhe surreptitiously stuck out his head and looked inside the room.

With that look, he froze as well.

The room was not empty.

Next to the sofa that directly faced the entrance was a huge open suitcase, and on the sofa was an officer in a black uniform sitting upright. This officer had black hair and green eyes and was coldly looking at the doorway.

The Lu Feng standing in the doorway turned and looked at An Zhe with an identical gaze.

"... It wasn't me," An Zhe said.

It truly wasn't him.

Since his arrest, he had never seen the Arbiter's mannequin again, and he even assumed that the evil thing had been blown to bits along with District 6. Why would it appear in Lu Feng's home?

At that exact moment, Lu Feng's communicator rang. The other person's voice was very loud, for it was that soldier from the logistics department who had come earlier to deliver the card. "Colonel, have you returned to your living quarters? Can the new ID card be used normally?"

"It can, thank you," Lu Feng said. "But I wish to know, what is going on with the mannequin in my living room?"

"The mannequin?" The soldier on the other end was first a little uncertain, but then he suddenly had an epiphany. "Before, during the Trial Court's emergency evacuation, they were saving important documents and goods, and the soldiers responsible saw this and believed it may be an important military tool, so they brought it over. We didn't know how to deal with it, so we put it in your living quarters."

Lu Feng repeated a sentence. "Important military tool?"

"Indeed. Although we're in the Main City, we also know the Outer City has some reactionary groups opposing the Trial Court. We judged the replica mannequin to perhaps be one of the Trial Court's tools to bait the enemy. Moreover, its manufacturing cost looks to be very…" The man talked endlessly.

Lu Feng didn't say a word.

The other person finally noticed that something was amiss. "Colonel, did I say something wrong?"

"You haven't. Thank you." Lu Feng hung up.

After hanging up, he said to An Zhe, "Come here."

An Zhe felt deep despair. He had not been convicted in his previous case, and it was only because of a sudden worm attack that he was able to get out of prison. Now that the dirty goods reappeared, would the Arbiter bring up the past again and convict him?

He walked over.

Lu Feng carelessly picked up the mannequin from the sofa, put it back in the suitcase, then pushed the suitcase toward An Zhe. Uncomprehending, An Zhe pressed down on the suitcase handle.

"For you," Lu Feng said, leaving An Zhe at a loss for words.

17

"IT'S LIKE A BEEHIVE."

GRASPING THE HANDLE, An Zhe asked, stupefied, "I haven't committed a crime of indecency now?"

"No." Lu Feng turned to go back to the bedroom. "Whether the crime of indecency is established or not depends on the wishes of the victim."

This man had the gall to call himself a victim.

An Zhe had already seen through him. After pulling the suitcase home, he put it in the most inconspicuous corner of the room. He wouldn't allow the Lu Feng inside to see the sun again.

The news broadcast on the TV had just finished and transitioned into the next day's weather forecast. In a sweet voice, the anchor said that the flatland where the base was located would be welcoming a rare windy day and asked everyone to please close their doors and windows.

At the start, when An Zhe was a mushroom, he feared strong winds because they would destroy mushrooms. It wasn't until later, after he snapped and his body changed, that he slowly stopped being afraid of the wind. On the contrary, he liked the feeling of the wind blowing against him.

Once he washed up and returned to his bedroom, he looked

at his textbook for a while. After the night gradually deepened, An Zhe planned to sleep.

Right at that moment, a strange low noise sounded in his ear.

Long and undulating, it resembled the sound of the wind echoing in the narrowest of canyons. Sometimes it was a very low whine, and sometimes it would abruptly turn shrill. It was like the sound of the wind outside, yet also like it was coming from the inside of the whole room, but he couldn't find the sound's source.

This was by no means the first time he heard this sound. On many previous nights in this room, the low and distant noise was accompanied by the plip-plop of dripping water, forming a strange harmony. The combination of these two sounds often gave him the illusion that he was still in the Abyss—outside the cave, wind blowing in from the depths of the dense jungle, and the mucus and saliva secreted by animals or plants dripping on the moss-covered rocks. Sometimes the wind and the structure of the cave produced a strange resonance, causing a low noise to sound from all directions, resembling the sleep-talk of some creature.

But tonight, the sound was louder than any other time before, and An Zhe was finally able to confirm that the origin of the sound was in his own room.

He frowned, then closed his eyes and carefully perceived his surroundings. Apart from the sound of the wind outside the window, that kind of sound, the sound near himself—

His eyes flew open, and he got out of bed. Standing barefoot on the floor, he picked up the flashlight on the table and turned it on, then got down on one knee, lifted the bedsheets, and shone the flashlight beam beneath the bed.

A pitch-black round hole appeared before him—it was on the wall the bed was up against, around where the wall connected to the floor.

The hole was the size of a human head and resembled a man-made pipe mouth. Its interior was completely dark, with nothing inside and nothing visible. He felt a wind blowing out from it. The sound that had disturbed him for a month was the sound of the wind in the pipe.

After examining the hole for half a minute, An Zhe put down the bedsheets and climbed back up onto the bed. Human rooms always had some odd structures. He had to sleep early tonight, for tomorrow was a very important day.

———

"Your bodies
still struggle
to return."

"And yet the nameless wildflowers
have bloomed amply upon your heads."

An Zhe watched Bai Nan write down a poem from memory onto the exam paper. Today was the graduation exam for this group of younglings, and he was responsible for patrolling the examination room to prevent cheating.

The low noise from last night also echoed in the classroom, but everyone seemed used to it. In an inconspicuous part of one of the classroom's corners, An Zhe discovered a similar hole. It seemed that this was a commonly seen thing in human buildings. He hadn't noticed it before because it was too noisy during the day, causing this sound to be covered up, but today, the strong wind outside made the wind inside the hole stronger as well.

Passing Bai Nan, he walked forward. Ji Sha's exam paper was a mess, full of marks from scribbles and corrections. She had only filled in a scattered few neat and tidy words in the English questions, but when An Zhe took a look, it seemed that she hadn't gotten many correct.

Most of the younglings were in a similar situation as Ji Sha. Some of the other ones hadn't even put forth the effort to make corrections, the exam papers in front of them practically blank. Of course, there were an exceedingly few seven or eight younglings whose exam sheets had been filled out well.

An Zhe looked as he walked, and he came to a corner of the classroom, next to the cold youngling named Si Nan.

Si Nan's exam paper had already been completely filled out although only half an hour had passed since the exam started. He was faster than everyone else.

At the moment, he wasn't checking his answers nor daydreaming, but rather drawing in the blank space of the exam sheet with a black pen.

In truth, it was not appropriate to call it drawing. Those were some irregular black lines, and they messily tangled together, resembling the vines in the Abyss and possessing a madness that broke out of the surface of the paper. By the time the one-and-a-half-hour exam ended, the deranged lines had already filled the entire exam sheet, and only in the answer areas could his writing still be seen.

After the papers were collected, the dormitory teacher took the younglings back to the dormitory. An Zhe took the papers back to the office, where Lin Zuo and Colin were both inside. Lin Zuo had just finished correcting the mathematics and logic exam papers. Upon seeing An Zhe enter, he took the papers and said, "Record the scores with Colin."

An Zhe obediently agreed and came to Colin's side. Colin read out loud the younglings' names and grades, and An Zhe entered the grades into the chart on the computer.

"Si Nan," Colin read out loud. "One hundred."

An Zhe recorded his grade and said softly, "He's so amazing."

He had looked over the mathematics and logics exam sheet.

Addition, subtraction, multiplication, and division were already the simplest of its contents, and An Zhe believed he himself might not be able to solve the geometry and logic questions.

Just then, Lin Zuo, who was correcting the language and literature exam papers, said, "Si Nan is a very rarely seen genius."

"Mm," An Zhe said.

"But I don't plan on having him enter Class A," Lin Zuo said.

After working with them for the past month, An Zhe now knew the rules governing the younglings' school promotions.

The dormitory teacher had a chart for adding and deducting points, and there was one during class as well. These records of added or deducted points were added to the grades for the typical major and minor exams, and with the scores from the final exam added in the end, they formed the younglings' final grades. The handful of younglings with the best grades in this class would get promoted into Class A and continue receiving the Main City's education, and after they grew up, they would enter the Main City's various organizations based on their own strengths. The other younglings would enter the military base for training and assessments, and after a month, the military would select a dozen or so Class B younglings based on the situation and continue developing them. After those younglings grew up, they would become the military's soldiers. The remaining younglings would be classified as Class C and sent to the Outer City to await adoption by the Outer City's residents. If nobody adopted them, they would continue living a communal life in the district assigned by the Outer City and become Outer City residents from then on.

But Lin Zuo said that he did not plan to allow Si Nan to enter Class A.

An Zhe asked, "Why not?"

"There are problems with his character," Lin Zuo said. "He is also unsuited for joining the military. He lacks emotions and simultaneously harbors resentment against the base, so he cannot serve the Main City. The Garden of Eden also agrees with my assessment of him. He'll be assigned to Class C. I'll be counting on you two in the future."

"… All right," An Zhe said.

"He is a very strange child," Lin Zuo said. "The dormitory teacher told me that he often wakes up at night and will sometimes tremble, but no cause can be found. I heard from the nanny who took care of him before he turned three years old that he had once lost a friend, which may have left a psychological scar."

The morning passed, and the calculations of the final grades were completed. Five of the younglings, including Bai Nan, were selected and sent together with the outstanding younglings of the other classes to the Garden of Eden's seventh floor to be educated. Lin Zuo was transferred to the third floor and began taking care of the new first-years. An Zhe and Colin officially became the teachers in charge of the remaining younglings. Their duty was to take the younglings to the military base and watch them take the military's training and assessments.

The Main City was very efficient. That very afternoon, they took a shuttle to the military training ground on one side of the city, and with them were the younglings from other classes.

The wind at the training ground was strong and brought with it fine grit, but the younglings were in high spirits, running and jumping about in the spacious grounds—the military's personnel who were in charge of screening the younglings were about to come over to take over them, so An Zhe and Colin became idle. All they needed to do was watch from the side.

As they sat side by side on the iron bench, Colin suddenly spoke—in this past month, neither he nor An Zhe made conversation with the other.

"I'm willing to let go of a little of my hatred for the Arbiter now," he said.

An Zhe looked at Colin and noticed his gaze pass through the buildings as he looked at a gray corner of the distant Garden of Eden that stuck out. It was a very cold gaze.

"Because the entire Main City is just as cold and heartless as the Arbiter," Colin said while looking over there.

"How come?" An Zhe asked.

"Have you seen the Garden of Eden?" Colin asked. "It's like a beehive."

The Garden of Eden was a massive hexagonal building, and it did have some similarities to a beehive. An Zhe said nothing, and Colin continued talking to himself.

"The Garden of Eden is the queen bee, producing up to ten thousand children every year. Starting from when they're three years old, they're made to take difficult assessments so as to cherry-pick the small portion with the highest IQ and have them stay in the Main City to do scientific research or whatnot in the future. To the Main City, these children are useful—are drones—so they can receive the Main City's superior living conditions," he said. "The others are all worker bees, and they're allocated to the Outer City, where conditions are poor. The base controls the supply of food and water, and the worker bees can only become mercenaries. Only by going out to struggle in the wilderness and bringing back materials can they survive. And those materials are used by the base to benefit the Main City."

He let out a cold laugh. "This is how the entire base operates. Only people with value to the Main City are people. They wouldn't feel the slightest bit of distress at blowing up District 6 because the people of the Outer City were things they had abandoned in the first place."

An Zhe said, "But the Main City is sufficient for only a very few people to live in."

Colin turned toward him. "Do you think what they're doing

is right?"

After briefly hesitating, An Zhe nodded.

"You think what they're doing is right because you survived. You're standing here, taking the Main City's position." Colin became agitated, and his chest heaved.

"Humankind's interests take precedence over all else, so whatever they do is right," he said. "But the people who died—the people they blew up, your family and friends—what did they do wrong? Were they not human?"

An Zhe said nothing. He was by no means perplexed because of Colin's question, for the Abyss also had social creatures. Through his long-term observations, for a solitary creature, living was the most important thing, but for a group of social creatures, the continuation of the entire group was more important. He didn't think that Colin was wrong, it was simply that this person may have been more suited to living in the Virginia Base.

Colin looked into his eyes, and at last, he said, "I get it. You don't have feelings at all."

Their conversation stopped there.

An Zhe turned his gaze back to the younglings once again. The younglings were much cuter than Colin.

But at that moment, the younglings were in total chaos, for a fight was going on.

An Zhe stood up and walked into the group of younglings, and Colin came over as well.

The ones fighting were Si Nan and a sturdy-looking boy. Si Nan's eyes were a little red as he pressed the other boy securely to the ground.

"Let go of him," Colin said. "Si Nan, I'm deducting points."

Si Nan still didn't let go of the boy, so Colin had no choice but to come forward and separate them by force. Adults had much greater strength than children, after all.

Si Nan stood to one side, a cold expression on his face. An

Zhe looked down at him and asked, "What's the matter with you two?"

Si Nan said nothing, but the other boy said loudly, "You were sleep-talking at night! You shouted out Lily's name! Lily's been taken away and locked up ages ago, and in any case, you can't find her!"

An Zhe saw Si Nan clench his fists.

Lily. It sounded like a girl's name.

He asked, "Who is Lily?"

This time, Si Nan finally answered him. "My friend."

"Where is she?"

"The Garden of Eden," Si Nan said icily.

An Zhe recalled Lin Zuo saying "he had once lost a friend" and guessed that the reason for this dispute was because that boy had mentioned Si Nan's sore spot.

"Don't be angry anymore." He got down on one knee to get to Si Nan's eye level and gently patted his shoulder. "I won't allow him to mention this in the future."

Si Nan's expression didn't change. He was clearly a youngling, but he had a coldness that was different from all the other younglings.

An Zhe could only pat Si Nan's hair and then stand up. At the training ground, the younglings were in total chaos. Colin, who was next to him, was educating another youngling, and his education was much more successful than An Zhe's. So long as he said the two words "deduct points," the youngling would immediately obey him.

Inspired, An Zhe said to Si Nan, "You aren't allowed to fight in the future, otherwise your points will be deducted."

The corners of Si Nan's mouth curled up, and he said, "You guys don't want to let me stay in the Main City anyway."

At times when the other younglings stumbled over their own words, this youngling knew everything.

An Zhe felt helpless, but nobody could help him.

Right at that moment, in his peripheral vision, a black car stopped and three people emerged from it.

An Zhe looked over and met the eyes of the person in the middle.

He blinked.

Lu Feng had seen him as well. With a slight raise of his eyebrows, Lu Feng walked toward them.

"You were here too?" An Zhe asked.

"For a meeting," Lu Feng said. "What happened to you?"

In An Zhe's voice was a hint of helplessness along with a request for help. "Two of the children were fighting."

"Just give each one a beating," Lu Feng said.

His words made An Zhe laugh involuntarily. Then An Zhe leaned down and said to Si Nan, "Next time you fight, I'll beat you."

Lu Feng looked at him.

"You're so good-natured," he said coolly, "that not only will they continue to fight, they'll beat you too."

An Zhe was speechless.

He adjusted his expression, striving to make himself look a bit fiercer. If he had even one-tenth of Lu Feng's fierceness, everything would go smoothly when he taught the younglings.

As Lu Feng looked at him, the corners of his lips curled up, and then he turned his gaze to Si Nan.

His gaze froze in place.

"Get away from him," Lu Feng said coldly.

Uncomprehending, An Zhe obeyed Lu Feng almost on reflex and backed two steps away.

Lu Feng took two steps forward, placing himself between An Zhe and Si Nan. He put on gloves, grabbed Si Nan's jaw, and forced the child to look at the sun.

The sunlight was glaring, and Si Nan's pupils contracted.

"There's something wrong with him." Lu Feng effortlessly held Si Nan in place. "Contact the Lighthouse."

18

"DR. JI, YOU'RE WAVERING."

"PRELIMINARY INFECTION, infection progress twenty units, thirteen animal-type targets, which points to arthropod mutation." The doctor walked over while carrying a thick report, then put them in front of Lu Feng. "How is it that wherever you go, there will be xenogenics?"

Lu Feng picked up the report.

The doctor crossed his arms and said, "I'm surprised you didn't shoot him on the spot."

"I'm not familiar with the infection characteristics in children," Lu Feng said.

"Then don't kill him. Leave him for me to use as a sample."

"As you like."

"With arthropod mutations, there's not much to say." The doctor looked at the report in his hands. "Why don't you go ahead and prepare for the meeting now? Since an infection has occurred in the Main City, and a child of Eden at that, I've already reported it. It's no small matter."

"Arthropod," Lu Feng said. "Does it have any connection to what happened before in the Outer City?"

"The final investigation results of the Outer City's insect swarm just came out today. It was determined to have been a one-time collective action of mutant insects under the pressure of the breeding season." The doctor's voice was very soft, and his expression was solemn. "But we don't know exactly what method they used to become connected, nor if there was a commander role."

"But... The Main City is impregnable from top to bottom, so things from the outside can't get in." He took a deep breath, then thought with his eyes closed as he said, "Even if an accident did occur in the Main City, it should have been the escape of one of the Lighthouse's xenogenic samples. Why was it a child from the Garden of Eden?"

Lu Feng looked over the report once, then looked at An Zhe.

As Si Nan's teacher, An Zhe bore the responsibility of going to the Lighthouse with them.

"What places has he been to?" Lu Feng asked.

"He's been with the other children the entire time," An Zhe said. "When I got off work yesterday evening, they were either watching the news or sleeping. This morning, they were taking an exam in the classroom, and in the afternoon, they were at the base."

Lu Feng said, "Contact his teacher and dormitory teacher."

An Zhe gave an affirmative reply.

After calling Lin Zuo and explaining the situation, he thought for a while, then said, "I can go ask him... He's very smart."

Lu Feng hummed in response.

Thus, An Zhe walked up to the sealed glass door—as one of the infected, Si Nan was isolated from other people, and his current location was a silvery-white laboratory.

Within the laboratory was a very small figure. Si Nan sat alone on a silvery-white dissection table, his head slightly bowed. He still had that same expression on his face, as if everything that happened outside had nothing to do with him.

A sound came from behind An Zhe. Lu Feng's communicator was ringing frantically, showing the seriousness of the situation. In merely these two or three minutes, already three groups of people had come here to find him. Lu Feng said something to the doctor, then got up and walked out into the corridor.

There were audio devices inside and outside of the door. An Zhe picked up the handset. "Si Nan."

Si Nan looked at him.

"Are you aware of what happened to you?" An Zhe asked.

Si Nan nodded.

"Then do you know the reason for it?" An Zhe asked. "In the Garden of Eden, did you come across anything strange?"

Si Nan looked straight at An Zhe with his jet-black eyes, that gaze seemingly wanting to pierce through him.

In that instant, An Zhe suddenly understood why xenogenics and humans had differences that could be distinguished with the naked eye—that kind of gaze was like a... a... something that was different from humans. If a pair of eyes like this existed on a monster of the Abyss, he would not feel the slightest bit of incongruity.

After a minute of silence, Si Nan said, "No."

"Think a little harder." An Zhe strove to guide this youngling. "What did you do yesterday? Were you with your classmates the entire time?"

Si Nan only looked at him with that dark gaze. No matter what An Zhe asked, he said nothing more.

Just as they entered a stalemate, the doctor's communicator rang as well, and An Zhe looked over.

The doctor pressed the hands-free mode button, and Lin Zuo's voice came out. His tone of voice was very steady, but he spoke quickly. An Zhe knew this was the behavior of humans when they were forcing themselves to keep calm.

"We've retrieved all the footage from the past three days, and he's always been with others. He'd leave the scope of surveillance when using the restroom and during the occasional free time, but that is normal. The longest duration he was away was no more than three minutes, and he could only move about in the corridor on our floor," Lin Zuo said. "There are no abnormalities in the Garden of Eden whatsoever. Could he have been infected on the way to the training base or at the training base itself? I heard that the speed of a child's infection outbreak is much faster than that of an adult."

"I'm very sorry, Mr. Lin. Although children are infected more quickly than adults, based on the degree of morphological change in his tissue cells, he was infected at least fifteen to twenty hours ago."

Lin Zuo was silent for a while before he said, "If that's the case, then he was indeed infected in the Garden of Eden—but the Garden of Eden's other children and teachers are all very normal, with no signs whatsoever of infection."

"Please do not panic," the doctor said. "We're currently awaiting further orders from the higher-ups. At three o'clock at the latest, the Lighthouse will ally with the Trial Court to screen for infection amongst the children who were moving about on the sixth floor during that period of time. Please get ready to cooperate."

Lin Zuo said, "Okay."

"Thank you for understanding. If there's nothing else..." the doctor said.

"Wait," Lin Zuo said.

"Do you have other clues?" the doctor asked.

"It's not a clue, but I hope it may be helpful to you," Lin Zuo said. "Si Nan has always been a very strange child... His IQ is very high, but his state of mind has always been very... dissociative. I watched him grow up, and I'm sure that there are differences in either his way of thinking or his senses compared to the other children."

"Thank you for informing me. I will look into it," the doctor said. "The Arbiter has returned. We're about to set out, so let's discuss in greater detail after meeting up."

Lin Zuo said, "All right."

Lu Feng walked back into the room.

"How is it?" the doctor asked.

"The Garden of Eden and training base have already been placed under martial law," Lu Feng said. "We're currently counting the number of people and will set out in ten minutes."

"Okay," the doctor said.

Lu Feng looked up at Si Nan, who was in the laboratory. "How are things on your end?"

The doctor shrugged.

Lu Feng walked forward and stood next to An Zhe.

Si Nan's eyes slowly turned toward Lu Feng, and at that very moment, An Zhe noticed that his black eyes, which originally had clear borders, were slowly diffusing outward radially, resembling threads of spiderweb extending outward.

Lu Feng said, "Ten hours."

An Zhe was stunned. He knew what Lu Feng meant—within ten hours, Si Nan would completely change from a human youngling into an irrational monster.

He called out Si Nan's name again in an attempt to produce a bit of communication.

But he saw Si Nan's gaze fixed unmovingly on Lu Feng, and Lu Feng returned the look.

Si Nan opened his mouth.

The child's voice was youthful, but he spat out five words in an ice-cold tone.

"All of you will die."

Lu Feng smiled.

He took the handset from An Zhe.

"There's no person who will not die," he said. "Humankind will survive."

With that, he hung the handset back up, then turned and left.

An Zhe compared them. In terms of ice-cold expression and tone of voice, the Colonel was still superior.

A few researchers took control of Si Nan, and the partition door rose. The doctor said, "This child is very strange."

"I'll transfer people over for questioning," Lu Feng said.

"Thank you for your hard work," the doctor replied.

Right at that moment, the windy noise sounded in An Zhe's ears again. He looked around and saw a similarly hidden round hole at the junction between ceiling and wall.

"Lu Feng," An Zhe said as he gently tugged on Lu Feng's sleeve, "what's that?"

Lu Feng followed his gaze and looked up at the ceiling, then said, "It's a vent."

An Zhe blinked.

"You haven't seen one before?" the doctor asked. "The Outer City doesn't have them because it was constructed later."

The doctor was always willing to explain knowledge to others, so An Zhe continued asking questions. "What does it do?"

"It supplies air." The doctor's reply was very simple. Then he explained, "When the Main City was constructed, the magnetic field had not yet disappeared entirely, and humankind's industrial capabilities were still at their peak. To construct a base that was capable of resisting cosmic radiation and solar wind to the maximum extent, the walls of all buildings were four to five times thicker than those of ordinary buildings, and the materials are special. They're completely closed off and rely on the ventilation systems to provide clean air."

"For the Main City to have been able to survive, the ventilation system can receive at least a First-Class Merit award." He smiled. "After the artificial magnetic poles were built, various mutations began. Before the disperser was invented, there were insects everywhere, so the Main City added three-layer filtering and strangulation systems at the air inlets and outlets of the ventilation system to ensure that not even a single bug could fly in."

"In other words, no matter what, as long as we control the ins and outs at the city gates, the Main City will be absolutely safe." As he typed out an email on his computer, he talked almost to himself. "Why exactly would an infection incident happen? This doesn't make any sense. Moreover, the Garden of Eden's other children are all fine."

At that point, his movements stopped, and then he looked at Lu Feng. "I heard that a girl escaped from the Garden of Eden yesterday."

"I've asked," Lu Feng said. "That girl is completely normal."

The doctor frowned even more deeply, and he typed out some information on the keyboard.

Lu Feng looked at the computer screen. "Are you contacting the Underground City Base?"

"Because of the series of events that have happened recently, I'm a little... afraid." The doctor took a deep breath. "I want to know to what extent the monsters in North America have evolved. However, the emergency channel between our bases has always been subject to the vagaries of fate, and it's almost certain that we won't be able to get a result."

With those words, he clicked send, and An Zhe saw him send an identical email to another recipient labeled "Research Institute" at the same time.

"All right." The doctor closed the interface. "I'm going to go calibrate the instrument."

"I'll go to the Garden of Eden first," Lu Feng said.

The Lighthouse's corridor was long and white, lit by a cold light. There was a break room in the corridor, and when they pushed the door open and exited, two researchers in white coats were kissing in the break room. After hearing the sound of footsteps outside, one of the researchers grabbed the other and turned, and their figures disappeared into the depths of the break room.

This spectacle seemed to pique Lu Feng's distaste, for he frowned slightly. "What happened to your discipline?"

"It can't be helped," the doctor said. "The more we research, the more we despair. Right now, the Lighthouse is suffused from top to bottom with an air of carpe diem. You can't ask for the military's discipline from us. I myself also feel hopeless sometimes."

Lu Feng didn't say anything. At the corner, he took An Zhe in a different direction from the doctor.

That afternoon, An Zhe blindly followed Lu Feng. The reason was because he didn't know where he ought to go—he could only be considered a temporary worker in the Garden of Eden, so he hadn't received any other orders or instructions. However, despite being followed, Lu Feng didn't seem to feel displeased. When this man examined the Garden of Eden's children one by one, he even had An Zhe go to the main hall to rest for a while.

Thus, An Zhe read a book while on the sofa in the main hall, and upon the wall in front of him was the blood-red "humankind's interests take precedence over all else" slogan again. At 4 p.m., the doctor brought others to the Garden of Eden. He was a bit dispirited as he led several subordinates in starting up the detection instrument in the hall.

Seraing had been sent by Lu Feng to cooperate with the doctor's work.

The young Judge saw the instrument in the center of the hall and frowned slightly. "There's only one of them?"

"What else?" the doctor said. "The other one was left at the entrance to the Main City, receiving the returning mercenaries who were originally from the Outer City."

"In other words, the entire base currently has only two instruments?" Seraing asked.

"Darling, aren't you misunderstanding something about our current industrial production capacity?" the doctor said. "For high-precision large instruments such as these detectors, two units is already the limit."

"My apologies," Seraing said.

"It's fine," the doctor said. "You all go over things once first, and we'll use the instrument to screen slowly."

Seraing said earnestly, "The Trial Court has not conducted special training focusing on children."

The doctor said, "I believe in the Arbiter's eyesight. He'll definitely be able to ferret out other infected bodies."

While they were talking, the sound of Lu Feng's footsteps came over.

"The investigation of the fifth, sixth, and seventh floors is complete," Lu Feng said into his communicator. "No suspected infected ones have been found."

An Zhe saw the doctor's hand trembling as he adjusted the instrument's control stick.

Lu Feng walked past him. "This side will be left to you all."

The doctor's face was a little pale for some reason as he said, "All right."

After that, he also said, "The Lighthouse has many xenogenic samples. Since infection has occurred in the Garden of Eden, I'm afraid of an accident happening in the Lighthouse as well. Could you apply for a temporary stationing of the Trial Court with the United Front Center?"

Lu Feng asked, "What's my level of authority?"

The doctor said, "The same as mine."

"All right."

He walked to the elevator entrance.

An Zhe silently watched him go.

And then he saw the man turn back and look at him.

In that gaze was written a command.

Come here.

An Zhe put down the book in his hands and obediently followed him.

Right at that moment—

"Lu Feng," the doctor suddenly said.

Lu Feng didn't turn back. "What is it?"

An Zhe turned slightly and saw the doctor looking in their direction. There was a lost look in his azure eyes, and their rims were slightly red.

"A hundred years ago, after people were wounded, there was only a thirty percent infection rate, and slight scratches or pricks wouldn't result in mutations at all. But these past few years, the situation has been constantly deteriorating. Especially this year, the infection rate has skyrocketed. You know as well that even a wound the size of a needle's eye can result in infection. I've always been thinking whether or not there would be a day like this when we do nothing at all and our genes will become disordered regardless, turning us *all* into xenogenics."

Lu Feng neither moved nor spoke. With a ding announcing the elevator's arrival, the silver doors smoothly opened.

The doctor's voice was slightly tremulous. "The Garden of Eden doesn't have monsters or xenogenics. This child's infection happened without any rhyme or reason, and we still don't know what causes infection or how it spreads. The Lighthouse cannot capture that virus and does not know how to defend against it. If those things have already crawled their way to our insides like an epidemic... The weakest children will be infected first because of their individual constitutions."

He gasped for breath. "Then what exactly are we to do?"

"Dr. Ji." Lu Feng's voice was cold. "You're wavering."

With that, he rested his right hand on An Zhe's shoulder and steered him toward the elevator without even a backward look.

———

After reaching the residential building and getting out of Lu Feng's car, An Zhe said, "Thank you."

"No problem," Lu Feng said. "What are your meal plans?"

"I'll cook," An Zhe said.

"Potato soup?"

"Mm-hm."

"You like it?"

An Zhe earnestly pondered for a while.

"I do," he said. "But I also don't have money to buy anything else."

"I can see that," Lu Feng said. "Tonight, I'll treat you to something else."

"How come?" An Zhe asked.

Lu Feng said, "To thank you for helping me discover a xenogenic."

These words sounded correct. It was only because of him that Lu Feng noticed Si Nan.

Thus, An Zhe received the opportunity to pick and choose from the ingredients area. Referencing the menu given by the base, in the end, he bought tomatoes, potatoes, and frozen beef. The price of the beef was very high, and it was specially marked with a label next to it indicating that its production was about to stop. He was undecided for a while on whether to buy it or not, but while he was undecided, Lu Feng had already swiped his card. The balance displayed on the card machine made An Zhe feel the differences between people.

Next to the ingredients were simple usage instructions. An Zhe didn't know anything else, so he still made soup.

As the soup cooked, An Zhe discovered something.

He stood in place, silently watching the slightly turbulent surface of the water in the pot.

The soup had become very thick, and the potatoes had completely softened as well. The soft sweet-sour aroma of the tomatoes and fragrance of the beef mixed together, forming a smell different from that of potato soup. It was very delicious.

However...

Lu Feng looked at him. "What is it?"

"I..." An Zhe lifted his head to look at Lu Feng.

But Lu Feng returned the gaze with his green eyes, and through a layer of white steam, they didn't seem very fierce.

"I..." An Zhe said. "I seem to have made too much."

"Too much?" Lu Feng walked over to him, leaned over slightly, and looked into the pot.

It truly was too much, An Zhe knew.

He had added too many ingredients and too much water.

When he made potato soup, in order to make the potatoes a bit softer and the soup a bit thicker, he liked to add a lot of water and then slowly reduce the large quantity of water into a very small amount of soup.

However, the principles of this soup seemed different from those of potato soup—if he continued to reduce it, the ingredients would fall apart, and then it would become a pot of mysterious things mixed together.

He estimated that even if this soup was divided into portions for three, it would be more than enough.

Lu Feng said, "It is too much."

An Zhe thought hard and finally arrived at a corrective measure. "I can invite Colin up to eat."

Lu Feng turned and gave him a flat look.

From that flat look, An Zhe astutely picked up on a hint of Lu Feng's feelings. It seemed that making too much soup had become a severe mistake.

Lu Feng said, "Seraing lives in No. 3202. Go give him a portion."

After ringing No. 3202's doorbell, Seraing opened the door very quickly from inside.

"It's you?" He seemed slightly surprised.

An Zhe handed the thermos to him. "I made soup. Here's a portion for you."

"Wow," Seraing said. "Thank you. I was just about to go out for dinner."

An Zhe gave him the soup and said, "You're welcome."

Seraing spoke up again. "Why… Did you give this to me? Perhaps the Colonel will like it."

An Zhe was momentarily unsure how to respond.

In the end, he said, "The Colonel has some too."

Seraing smiled. "That's what I guessed. So it was the Colonel who told you that I live here?"

An Zhe nodded.

Seraing brought An Zhe inside and, after putting the thermos on the living room table, took out something wrapped in pink from a drawer—by the looks of it, it seemed to be a human snack.

He stuffed it into An Zhe's hand, saying, "I'll treat you to some candy."

An Zhe said, "Thank you."

Seraing said, "Have you gotten used to living in the Main City? Which floor do you live on?"

An Zhe said, "I'm in No. 3702."

"My God." Seraing smiled. "What a coincidence."

Wild gales blew outside, and the wailing sound of the wind in the pipe was coming from Seraing's room as well.

An Zhe looked in the direction of the sound's origin.

"The ventilation pipes were originally closed, but in the summer when the wind is strong, they will be entirely opened for a period of time to prevent the insides of the pipes from getting too damp. During this time, it'll always make noise. When the sound is too loud, sometimes even those who have lived in the Main City since they were young will be unable to sleep because of it, but there's no need to be afraid." Seraing's tone of voice was very gentle. Once he was done talking, he gave another smile. "But the Colonel has probably reassured you already."

An Zhe felt confused.

Firstly, he didn't feel afraid, so he didn't need to be reassured, and secondly, Lu Feng had never reassured him before at all.

He said, "He hasn't."

"… Maybe he forgot."

An Zhe felt that Seraing thought of Lu Feng as too kind of a person and the relationship between the two of them to be too good.

He returned to No. 3702, where the Colonel had unexpectedly deigned to set the table himself—but unfortunately, even though a portion of it had been given away, there was still quite a lot of soup remaining.

A certain Colonel's ice-cold green eyes looked at him. "You can do it."

"I can't."

"You can't waste the base's resources."

An Zhe scooped up a small piece of beef with his spoon and strove to swallow it. After he had finished eating his own portion, he had been forced by Lu Feng to face the remainder in the pot, and now half of it was gone.

Lu Feng's tone of voice was flat. "Keep going."

An Zhe ate another piece of potato and a spoonful of soup.

He felt like he had reached his limit.

Humans' appetites had limits, even if this soup was very delicious.

He'd break.

He lifted his head and looked at Lu Feng.

But he saw this man looking at him, eyebrows slightly lifted and a hint of quiet joy in his expression.

An Zhe was speechless.

He should've already known. Lu Feng's objective wasn't to

conserve the base's resources at all. The Colonel's happiness was built upon bullying him.

He frowned, slightly angry. This time, with a resolute attitude, as he said, "I'm not eating any more."

Lu Feng said, "Crime of wasting provisions."

An Zhe retorted, "Then you've committed it too."

Lu Feng looked at him with crossed arms, and after seeming to examine him once from top to bottom, he said, "You've gotten smart."

An Zhe understood what he meant.

He vowed that the next time this man came to eat, he would cut off a piece of his own hyphae and put it in to poison him. Planning to no longer acknowledge this man, he dropped his spoon.

But on the contrary, Lu Feng smiled. He reached out and put the remaining soup in front of himself. It looked like the Arbiter was going to exonerate himself. An Zhe observed his actions for a while, then decided to reduce it from one piece to half a piece.

After dinner, he saw Lu Feng out. The Colonel still had telephone conferences to attend at night.

At the doorway, Lu Feng seemed to suddenly recall something.

He took a small, translucent box from the front pocket of his uniform and tossed it to An Zhe.

"If you can't sleep, you can use that," he said.

After returning to his own room, An Zhe took apart the box. It was a pair of white umbrella-shaped rubber noise prevention earplugs.

He contemplated over and over, still wavering between whether Lu Feng was really a good or bad person, and in the end, he temporarily defined the man as a changeable person.

The wind outside continued picking up, and the sound inside the hole turned faintly shrill to a degree where it indeed made it difficult for humans to fall asleep—but he had no intention of putting in those earplugs, at least not for now.

An Zhe stood in front of his bed. This entire afternoon, he had been thinking of one thing.

If he couldn't move about freely within the Lighthouse, then when exactly would he be able to find his spore?

Once he felt that this was an insurmountable problem, but now he had a path he could walk. All of this city's buildings were linked together by the ventilation pipes.

He turned his head and looked at the window.

The window was very small, only about the size of two textbooks put together, and at its sides were two sliding metal shutters. He walked over to the window and forcefully pushed the sliding doors together. With a click, the shutters fit together perfectly. Like this, nobody could see into the room from the outside.

Hyphae.

Hyphae extended outward from An Zhe's body. His clothes and the bullet shell necklace around his neck fell to the ground together, making a soft noise. At the same time, a ball of snow-white hyphae made its way out from the shirt collar and rolled under the bed, quietly facing the pitch-black hole.

When his body changed into a mushroom, An Zhe had a vague perception of the outside world. His senses of sight and hearing combined while his senses of smell and touch could not be distinguished from each other. They were no longer sights or sounds, but rather a peculiar feeling; there was no way to describe this kind of change with human language.

The hole had fine wire mesh—three layers of it—which was enough to block all insects big or small.

But it couldn't block a soft mushroom.

19

"HE WAS BY NO MEANS AN IMPATIENT MUSHROOM."

A SINGLE SNOW-WHITE hypha reached out and gently rested on the surface of the wire mesh. Then it made its way inside through a tiny chink in the metal lattice.

It was safe, at least at this point. There were no lethal weapons, only the barrier of the lattice.

After the first hypha went through the three layers of the lattice barrier to the other side, the remaining hyphae moved forward as well. They gathered together, and because they were so soft and flexible, they appeared to be almost liquid. The snow-white tide was pervasive as it penetrated the three layers of wire mesh and then recombined behind them. A pipe leading forward appeared in An Zhe's perception. The pipe was smooth overall, but spots of rust were beginning to appear in some places. The smell of rust spread, resembling the smell of blood. Wind was blowing in from the end of the pipe.

An Zhe proceeded forward. His hyphae stuck to the pipe walls like tentacles as he smoothly flowed ahead. This pipe was straight, and after turning at a right angle, it was still a straight path. He continued, and a four-way intersection appeared up ahead. A horizontal and slightly wider pipe was connected to the pipe he was currently in.

The wind got stronger, and the direction of the airflow was also very complex, indicating that this massive pipe system was like a winding maze.

An Zhe briefly hesitated on the spot. Then he extended one long hypha, leaving it in the pipe before he continued moving forward—although Lu Feng thought he wasn't smart, An Zhe felt that he couldn't be considered stupid either. He decided to mark his path with this hypha. That way, no matter where he went, he could make his way back via the same path by following this hypha.

After making this decision, An Zhe felt much more at ease. He went straight through the four-way intersection, proceeding in the same direction as before. After another right-angle turn, there was a faint light up ahead.

An Zhe came to the light's source—another vent. The familiar news broadcaster's voice was playing. Predictably, he had come to the vent in someone else's home.

"Over the course of a month, the Main City has recalled a total of twelve thousand mercenaries from the outside and formally entered a recovery period. In the expected ten-year recovery period, the Main City's research power will be entirely invested in the investigation of the source of infections..."

"Tap tap tap." There came the even sounds of knocks on the door.

An Zhe had entered by mistake in the first place. He didn't intend to pry into other humans' secrets, so he planned to leave, but then he temporarily gave up on the idea.

There was the sound of a door opening.

"Colonel Lu." A female voice rang out, its tone very crisp.

Colonel Lu.

This was Lu Feng's room.

An Zhe surreptitiously emerged from the vent and moved outward a bit so that he could hear more clearly, for he was indeed somewhat curious about Lu Feng's life.

Then he heard a familiar cold voice. "Hello."

"Hello, Colonel Lu. I am a staff member of the Garden of Eden's twenty-first floor."

The Garden of Eden.

An Zhe pricked up his ears—or he would have if his current form had such things.

"What do you want?" Lu Feng asked.

"It's like this." The woman smiled. "Firstly, congratulations on your return from the Outer City, Colonel. Secondly, I'm asking on behalf of my superiors if you have any desire to donate sperm to the Garden of Eden at present."

Lu Feng's reply was very succinct and heartless. "No."

"That is truly regrettable. If you are interested in the future, please contact us. Your genes are extremely outstanding, so if they cannot be put to effective use, it is a loss for the entire base."

"Thank you." Lu Feng's tone was not softened by her praise. He said, "Is there anything else?"

"The flowers Madam Lu planted have bloomed," the woman said. "She requested that I deliver you a bunch along the way. The Main City's work is very busy, and the Madam urges you to make sure to rest and take good care of yourself."

After a short silence, Lu Feng asked, "Is she still in good health?"

"Everything is normal."

"Thank you." Lu Feng's voice dropped somewhat. "Give her my regards."

Their conversation ended there, and after the door closed again, there was no other activity within the room.

The weather forecast stated that the gales would continue and the temperature would drop.

The sound suddenly stopped, presumably because Lu Feng turned off the TV. Then footsteps gradually approached as Lu Feng returned to the bedroom and then sat down at his desk.

After a few sounds of sheets of paper being flipped, a silence descended upon the room, and there was only the sound of Lu Feng's breathing.

An Zhe wanted very much to extend a few hyphae out from underneath the bed and see what the Colonel was doing, but he didn't dare to. At last, he slowly went back the way he came through the vent.

At the four-way intersection, he chose the direction that the wind was blowing from, and with the slender hypha he used to mark his path in his wake, he continued forward.

The wind, ice-cold and smelling like blood, blew at his hyphae. The pipe walls were connected to other pipe mouths, and each pipe mouth was connected to other complex pipe structures. At the same time, there was yet another intersection up ahead—a path merely this short was enough to make An Zhe realize the complexity of the entire system. He didn't have a road map, only knowledge of the Lighthouse's general direction, so he could imagine the difficulty of entering the Lighthouse via the pipes.

But he could keep searching, for he was by no means an impatient mushroom.

After several turns, An Zhe was completely unable to discern directions, nor did he have any way of being conscious of the passage of time. He only knew that when he was traveling in the direction the wind was blowing from, the pipe would get wider and the wind would get stronger as well. He guessed that this was because he had found the ventilation system's backbone. Sometimes, he worried that his hypha would break, but he could not reinforce it or leave another strand. To mushrooms, their hyphae were like blood to humans. Excessive blood loss would lead to death, so he couldn't use it all up.

Sometimes, there would be wire mesh or some sharp turbines that seemed capable of slicing up all flesh and joints up ahead. At these times, he would carefully slide past the cutting edges to avoid his hypha getting severed.

An Zhe didn't know how long he had traveled for. Only the sound of the wind and the minute rustling of his hyphae moving over the rusted pipe walls accompanied him.

In front of him was an infinitely long black pipe, and behind him was the same. This feeling made him return to the span of time when he lost his spore—mindlessly wandering here and there in the Abyss, perhaps he'd find it tomorrow, perhaps he'd never be able to find it.

When the pipe's diameter was as wide as the height of two men, An Zhe felt a blurry red glow light up ahead. He moved forward, carefully passing a large turbine—then unexpectedly fell out of the pipe mouth.

He landed on the hard and rough metal ground and was illuminated by the dim red light. An Zhe looked around—this place was no longer the inside of a pipe, but rather an open and roomy cylindrical space. It was as big as the Garden of Eden's main hall, and both wind and the red light poured in from above. It was too high up, so An Zhe couldn't feel it.

His snow-white mass elongated on the ground, and the hyphae gathered together to become a human body and skin. It was very cold, so the hyphae spread over his body, creating a closely woven loose white robe that blocked the biting chill outside.

An Zhe stepped barefoot upon the metal floor and lifted his head to look upward.

A massive turbine was placed at a slant at the very top of the entire space, and it occupied his entire field of vision. A dim red curtain of laser light shone around the turbine, similar to the city walls of the Outer City. He knew that this was one kind of the humans' defense weapons. As soon as a creature attempts to pass it by force, it would immediately trigger an alarm.

Looking past the turbine's iron teeth, An Zhe saw the sky

outside, where the aurora was still shining. This place was connected to the outside world. He realized that this was the air inlet of the ventilation system, and after the turbine started up, the air from the world outside would continuously be taken in and then supplied to the pipes in all directions.

He retracted his gaze and looked forward. In the center of this cylindrical space, there was a rectangular metal workbench —it may have been the console for the entire system. He walked over, but he discovered that it was not the case.

Upon this metal platform, three small rectangular boxes were welded. Using the light, An Zhe could see that next to the boxes were mottled writings that seemed to have been plated on.

An Zhe leaned down slightly and wiped away the dust and rust to clearly see those cramped writings.

It was a letter.

To those who come after:

I am Kang Jinlan, the person in charge of constructing the Northern Base's underground ventilation project. The ventilation system took one year to design and nine years to build, with a construction cost of 110 million yuan per kilometer.

Opponents have suggested delaying the construction period due to the difficulty of the base construction and the enormous amount of manpower and resources consumed. But through discussion, we believe that once the weakened geomagnetic field continues deteriorating, within ten years, the human economy will inevitably collapse, and within fifty years, the surviving humans will inevitably lose the entirety of heavy industry's research and development along with production capacity. The means of production and focus of scientific research are all biased toward the medical field. We no longer have time.

Fortunately, the construction of both the underground ventilation system and the aboveground base have been completed without any issues this year, and my fellow humans can live under the strict protection of the base from now on. This is the only thing I feel relieved about. Thanks to cosmic radiation, despite being under strict protection, I'm still suffering from various cancers and autoimmune diseases. I have requested that the base inter my ashes in the ventilation system's core. That way, when each generation of engineers enters it for maintenance, I can know that the base is still safe and that the great species of humankind still exists.

May you have a bright future.

Best regards

June 2030.

These were ashes.

This box contained what was once a human body. It was a tomb, and these writings left behind were a message this human left for later generations.

Perhaps it was more appropriate to call it an epitaph.

An Zhe looked to the right. On its right side was a box that was almost identical in shape and welded to the table surface at the bottom. There were plated words next to it as well, a letter with an identical tone.

To Mr. Kang Jinlan, and those who come after:

I am Liao Ping'an, the person in charge of the Northern Base's underground ventilation system project maintenance. The ventilation system is serviced every half a year and undergoes overall maintenance every two years. At present, it is operating in perfect condition.

As Mr. Kang expected, not only did the situation with the weakening geomagnetic field not improve, it completely disappeared in December of the year 2030 instead. Fortunately, the artificial magnetic pole project succeeded not long afterward, and the world once again came under the protection of a magnetic field. Humans no longer suffer from illnesses because of radiation exposure. Unfortunately, cosmic radiation gave rise to the infection and mutation of bacteria, fungi, and viruses, and humankind has met an unprecedented catastrophe. As one who experienced this catastrophe, I've witnessed the shrinkage of the territory in which humans live, the collapse of the economic system, and the gradual loss of industrial capacity. The base has invested all of humankind's remaining production capacity into military production, the construction of military bases, and the expansion of the base, producing a steady stream of guns, ammunition, nuclear weapons, aircraft, armor, and tanks. I do not know where the purpose of this base lies, nor do I know if these actions have accelerated the depletion of humankind's resources. I can only hope that the base has a deeper purpose.

In the midst of this catastrophe, I have unfortunately been infected with deadly bacteria. As my life is coming to a close, I am still feeling endless panic regarding the base's future, so I chose to be interred here with Mr. Kang and wait for the next generation of engineers to report that it is safe.

May you have a bright future.

Best regards

November 2052.

Next was a third box of ashes and epitaph.

To Mr. Kang Jinlan, Ms. Liao Ping'an, and those who come after:

I am Yang Ye, the person in charge of the Northern Base's underground ventilation system project maintenance. The ventilation system is serviced every half a year and undergoes overall maintenance every two years. At present, it is operating in perfect condition.

I must inform the two predecessors that in this era, the ventilation system is no longer one of the base's countless infrastructures, but rather has played a peerlessly brilliant role in protecting humankind's safety. In the year 2053, the start of global biological mutations, the human bases have committed themselves to the vast defensive war with the military as their primary forces and the civilian mercenaries as auxiliary forces. With the deficiencies in resources and industrial construction capacity, the strong military bases and powerful military weapons left to us by the previous generation have played an unimaginable role, ensuring the safety of the remaining humans. And after being transformed, the ventilation system has become one of the defenses of the base's Main City, protecting people from the invasion of insect monsters.

At present, the Northern Base is still safe. The military and mercenary teams are continuously bringing back monster samples from the outer world and recovering scientific research equipment, cultural documents, and other needed materials from abandoned cities. The base's scientific research strength is centered on the research of infection theory and human reproduction. At present, no direction has been found for the former, whereas initial steps have been taken for the latter. A large number of new lives have come, and the human population has begun to rise. Although the environment is still hostile, I believe that everything will take a turn for the better.

Under the protection of the base, I die happily of geriatric illness.

May you have a bright future.

Best regards

January 2104.

An Zhe carefully finished reading, then looked to the side. It was empty, with no more boxes. 2104 was already a very distant age. Perhaps the next generation of engineers would soon lie here too, with epitaphs telling stories of what occurred recently, such as the fall of the Outer City or something else.

Just then, great mournful sounds came from all around. The mighty night wind blew in from the air inlet, and An Zhe shivered. The strong wind was like an unstoppable flood current, rendering him almost unable to open his eyes—he put his elbow up to his eyes to resist the blowing of the gale and bowed his head slightly.

At that very moment, he suddenly felt pain.

In the wind, a length of snow-white hypha fluttered up in his peripheral vision. The white shape flickered, then disappeared in an instant.

An Zhe whipped around. Only a short length of the white hypha he had previously left to mark his path dragged along on the ground, trembling in the wind. The fierce wind had broken his hypha, and he didn't know where the wind had carried the broken portion off to.

His pupils contracted sharply, and when he looked in the direction he had come from, six pitch-black holes were lined up, all identical to each other.

20

"THIS BASTARD LU FENG."

IN THE DIM RED LIGHT, the six round and pitch-black holes looked at him as if they were the compound eyes of insects.

An Zhe unconsciously took a step back and bumped into the metal table. In that instant, he lost his balance, and his hand landed on the epitaph with its engraved words that were uneven to the touch. For some reason, this ice-cold metal table that stood alone in the empty hall and held the ashes of the deceased made him feel safe instead.

He let out a soft sigh, then tentatively walked forward until he reached the row of holes.

He climbed into each one of the six pipes in succession, but he still could not find the slightest trace of his hypha. It was too thin and would have contracted after snapping, and lastly, after it was blown up by the wind, he didn't know what corner it would have gotten stuck in. It was also too dark in this place.

An Zhe blankly looked around. In this cylindrical space, all sides—in front of him, behind him, to his left, and to his right— had six pipe mouths each for a total of twenty-four that led in different directions. This was the source of the entire city's ventilation system.

He knew he had two choices: hurry to find his way back to his living quarters before sunrise and then continue searching tomorrow evening or… or simply just not go back.

He could give up his human identity from this moment onward, allowing the person named An Zhe to disappear from the city. As a mushroom, An Zhe could wander in the underground pipes for a long time, without regard to day or night. So long as he roamed long enough before he withered, he would be able to sneak into the Lighthouse.

The wind grew stronger, and he gently shivered. He knew that the decision he was about to make would affect his entire destiny hereafter.

But even if he decided to go back, could he really do it?

An Zhe didn't know.

As he looked at the six holes in the direction he came from, he clenched his teeth and crawled into the middle right one—he was unsure whether this was the original path.

He could only let fate decide.

It actually would have been more convenient to crawl into the hole in his hyphae form, but three of humankind's predecessors were here, and he did not wish for them to see a xenogenic come in. Thus, it wasn't until An Zhe had completely entered the pipe that he once again changed into a ball of hyphae.

The hyphae sped up, moving along the direction of the wind, and the wind was also pushing him from behind. An Zhe made a few turns and passed many intersections. Now, he only wanted to wander to a pipe mouth that was connected to a human's room as quickly as possible—it would be even better if the room had a window, because he could sneak out of the window, find the nearest shuttle stop under cover of night, and surreptitiously stick to the bottom of the shuttle. The nighttime shuttle would take him to the final stop near Building 24, and then he could slip back to his own corridor. So long as the night was dark enough, nobody would discover him.

He traveled in this haphazard manner for a long time. When the pipe became narrower and narrower, a dim light finally appeared in front of him. He had arrived at a pipe mouth.

This was a ventilation pipe located on a ceiling.

An Zhe looked down from the pipe mouth. What appeared in the center of his field of vision was a transparent cylindrical container containing a slightly cloudy liquid, and inside the liquid, a flesh-colored object was floating. It was very small, about the size of two human fists. One end of a transparent tube was connected to this flesh-colored thing, and the other end was connected to a complicated-looking device.

A peculiar feeling arose in this device. An Zhe couldn't describe exactly what he was feeling; he only knew that the container held a living thing.

Suddenly, he was stunned.

He knew.

This was a youngling.

No. It was an embryo, the embryo of a human youngling.

Further to the side, there was an identical device. Not only that, the entire spacious room was densely packed with such things. His field of vision was limited, so he couldn't tell exactly how big of a room it was, but he knew that the base could produce five to ten thousand younglings per year.

This was no other place—to his surprise, he had accidentally come to the Garden of Eden.

An Zhe let out a sigh of relief. The Garden of Eden was a place he was familiar with, but at the same time, he felt even more troubled, for he knew how much humans cherished their younglings. Practically all areas in the Garden of Eden were covered by video cameras as well as constantly guarded by staff. Nobody could harm the younglings.

At this thought, he became angry again.

If the world of mushrooms had video cameras, how could his youngling have been dug out by Lu Feng?

But merely three seconds later, he discovered the mistake in his logic. Even if there were video cameras, they would not be able to stop Lu Feng from digging out his spore. The crux of this matter rested not in the video cameras, but rather the existence of this bastard Lu Feng.

… Wrong.

The crux of the matter was how he was to get out now.

21

"THEN YOU DON'T KNOW THE 'ROSE MANIFESTO' EITHER."

"BEEP—"

"Beep—"

"Beep—"

The instrument's monotonous sounds came from somewhere. But there was another kind of sound throughout the entire room as well.

"Ba-thump."

"Ba-thump."

"Ba-thump."

This sound was extremely similar to a human heartbeat, but it wasn't real, because it permeated the entire room. It seemed like there were sound-playing devices in the four corners of the room.

Right at that moment, footsteps came from the end of the room. It was two humans who were conversing as they walked, seeming to be taking notes on something.

After a while, the sounds of a simple conversation drifted over.

"Area 4 is normal."

"Area 6 is normal."

"Number 113's development has stopped."

"Continue observing."

"Number 334's cell growth is abnormal. It must be destroyed."

"Number 334 was transplanted too early."

"There was no choice, the last report wasn't approved. The higher-ups are determined to counter the high abnormality rate with a high birth rate."

"The abnormality rate of the embryos has been constantly increasing in these past two years. This isn't a wise decision at all. Only by staying in the mother's body for at least another month can the embryo's smooth development be ensured."

"The mothers' flowering periods are too short. If that time is too prolonged, the birth rate will be insufficient."

"Why is it this difficult?"

"Look on the bright side, the overall number of children is increasing."

The footsteps drew away, and all that remained were the heartbeats that still pervaded the room. The light in the room was dim and soft. It was a safe nest, or a massive hollow organ. That powerful heartbeat was like a form of proof of the existence of life.

An Zhe slowly backed out of the pipe. He felt a bit of discomfort in his own body—in this place, there seemed to be some strange waves affecting his body. But fortunately, after seeing the arrangement of the human rooms, he finally regained his sense of spatial orientation. He had to go toward the outside of the building.

After circling in the pipes many more times, he found many vents, and these vents all led to one small square room after another. It seemed that it was still the time for people to be sleeping, for one person slept in each room. He had no way of getting out from under the beds to see, but he could hear weak breathing sounds, the breathing sounds of younglings. The windows were sealed shut, and the red light of video cameras shone high up in the rooms. He had no way of getting out of this kind of room.

It wasn't until after another very long time that An Zhe successfully found a vent placed in a corridor ceiling at last.

He carefully emerged, and his body spread out on the ceiling before he moved through the corridor along the ceiling—the cameras were angled downward, so they couldn't capture the visuals of the ceiling.

Every floor in the Garden of Eden had a similar layout. He recognized that this ought to be a corridor used for taking care of chores, for the storehouses that held indoor cleaning tools, household goods, foodstuffs, and junk were here.

He became slightly excited. Based on the pattern, at three-quarters of the way down the corridor, there would be a door leading to a mid-sized balcony—occasionally it would be used for drying things, and staff members would sometimes smoke there.

Very soon, An Zhe found the door. Striving to stretch out his hyphae, he flowed in through the crack of the door.

The sky was bright outside—unexpectedly, it was already daytime.

But before An Zhe had time to think carefully, his attention was completely diverted.

On the spacious balcony, a very small white figure stood upon the concrete railing. It was a girl in a white dress. She had her back turned toward An Zhe as she faced the outside. She was slowly spreading her arms, and her body leaned forward—she was about to fall.

His human form materialized, and he took a few steps forward, grabbed the girl's shoulder, carried her down from the railing, and put her onto the floor. "You…"

The girl turned around.

An Zhe was stunned.

He had seen her before, just two days ago. She had run from

the Garden of Eden to the road outside, been stopped by Lu Feng, and finally taken away by the staff members of the Garden of Eden. He wouldn't mistake her for anyone else.

She looked at An Zhe. It was a look almost devoid of spirit, without the brightness of the children in An Zhe's class. For a moment, An Zhe felt that this girl was a lifeless doll. He knew that his current appearance was not ordinary, draped in a robe woven from hyphae. Perhaps he looked like a human who had come outside draped in a bedsheet—but normal humans wouldn't come outside draped in a bedsheet.

But the girl acted like she hadn't seen anything at all. She seemed to not think that there was anything peculiar about An Zhe's attire or that there was anything abrupt about An Zhe's appearance. She also seemed to not recognize him. Perhaps she didn't remember his existence at all. Three seconds later, she once again slowly turned to look forward.

It was currently early morning. The aurora had just disappeared, and thick white mist overflowed within the dark gray city, surging toward the gray-blue skies like rolling waves. From this angle, half of one's field of vision was blocked by the nearby cylindrical magnetic field generator. Bigger and taller than all other buildings, it was like a mountain, an island in the sea of mist, or a spiral staircase connecting the sky and the earth. The streetlights and the dawn stars flickered together, but in front of such a massive form, they were eclipsed.

The girl lifted her head and looked at the limitless sky above.

"I don't want to jump." Her voice was very young, but her words were very clear. "I want to fly."

An Zhe said, "You'll fall."

She said, "I know."

Her tone of voice was calm, not befitting a child her age. The morning wind blew, lifting her white dress and black hair. That was an unusual delicacy and softness. The women and girls outside didn't have this kind of thing—Doussay had this quality as well, but it was even more obvious in this girl.

An Zhe stood behind her. He had just protected a human youngling, and at the same time, he had paid a price. At least, his existence had been exposed to this girl's eyes, and now he stood in the midst of extreme danger, unable to reveal any weaknesses.

He said, "Why are you here?"

"Sometimes, the surveillance will be messed up for a while. They haven't discovered it yet," the girl said. "I come out to look at the sky."

"You can look at the sky during free activity time too," An Zhe said. "What floor and class are you in?"

He earnestly carried out the responsibility of a teacher. He couldn't allow a youngling to stay in such a dangerous place.

She said, "I'm in the Garden of Eden."

"Which floor and which class of the Garden of Eden are you in?"

"I'm not in any floor or class," she said. "Only boys are there."

An Zhe patiently explained, "The classes have girls too."

There were many girls in his class alone, such as Ji Sha—although their appearances were about the same as the boys, not wearing dresses or letting their hair grow to shoulder-length like the girl in front of him.

"Those girls aren't girls." She turned her head to look at him. "Only the ones on the twentieth floor and above are real girls."

"How come?" he asked.

"You don't even know that?" she said.

"I don't know," An Zhe said.

It was the truth. He indeed knew very little about this human base.

An expression other than indifference appeared on the girl's face for the first time. The corners of her lips lifted, carrying a faint pride. "Then you don't know the 'Rose Manifesto' either."

"What is it?" he asked.

The girl turned around and draped herself on the railing. The sun rose faintly in the sky.

"Then you wouldn't also be unaware of bacterial infection, right?" she said.

"I know about it," An Zhe said. He did indeed know about the calamity that led to the death of ninety percent of this planet's humans, once upon a time.

"Only people with outstanding genes could survive," she said.

"Mm-hm," An Zhe said.

Against strong mutated bacteria, human treatment methods had no effect, so they could only escape infection by relying on innate immunity. If a human's genes destined him to resist this disease, he would be able to survive.

"Then, after those people survived, they discovered that very few live children were being born in the world." She reached up to comb her hair and paused for a while, as if she was sorting out her words. Only then did she say, "After being infected, the surviving girls all had defects in their ability to give birth. Only a very few of them had relatively small defects that would allow them to safely do so."

An Zhe didn't say anything. She wrinkled her nose and continued. "Scientists would give them genetic examinations. The rubric said that if they had beneath sixty points, they lost the ability to do so entirely. Above sixty points, there was a chance they could have normal children. Then there was the 'Rose Manifesto.' You're a boy, so the Manifesto has nothing to do with you."

An Zhe asked, "What is the Rose Manifesto?"

"We just memorized it," she said. "Would you like to hear it?"

"Okay," An Zhe said.

In a calm voice, she recited, "The 23,371 women of the four human bases with a fertility score of 60 and above passed the following manifesto with zero rejection votes: I'm willing to devote myself to the destiny of humankind, accepting genetic experiments and all forms of assisted reproduction, to strive for an entire lifetime for the continuation of the human race."

"That's how it is," she said. "That's why I'm on the twentieth floor, and you guys are down below. Now you know."

"Thank you," he said. "But you still need to take care to not come to such a dangerous place."

"I won't jump down," she said. "I come every week. Haven't you come as well?"

She looked at An Zhe again and repeated, "I want to look at the sky, so I come here. Why are you here?"

"I can't find my way back," An Zhe said.

"I know the way," she said. "I have a secret passage."

He thought for a while. "I also don't have clothes to wear."

"I also know where the laundry room is," she said.

An Zhe asked her, "Could you tell me where it is?"

But she didn't give a direct reply. Instead, she asked, "Are you a student from the lower floors?"

"I'm a teacher," An Zhe said.

"Promise me one thing." Her eyes seemed to gain a bit of spirit as she said to An Zhe, "Promise me one thing, and I'll go find clothes for you, then take you outside through the secret passage."

An Zhe asked, "What thing?"

"Find a boy on the sixth floor called Si Nan and tell him that I've been injected with a tracking agent, so I can't go out to play with him anymore," she said. "At this time next week, come back here and tell me what he said."

He was silent.

The girl looked at him and asked, "Are you unable to do that?"

"I…" An Zhe met her eyes. She blinked, and only at this time did she seem like a normal child.

In the end, he said, "I may not be able to."

She said, "You can find him. He's just on the sixth floor."

An Zhe didn't say anything.

But she seemed to become a bit anxious. As she pushed open the balcony door, she said, "I'll go find some clothes for you."

Before An Zhe could stop her, her white dress disappeared behind the door.

If the Si Nan she spoke of was the Si Nan who An Zhe knew, then he was already no longer in the Garden of Eden, but rather the Lighthouse. But he didn't know how she would react if he really told her this information. He knew that human emotions would bring her pain.

So even after the girl left and came back, pulled him along through the quiet and deserted empty corridor, and finally stopped at a half-open small door in a pile of odds and ends, he still hadn't figured out how to respond.

"If you can get in, you can go down to the first floor." She pointed to the door.

That door was half-open. Strictly speaking, because it had been long neglected, it was no longer perfectly shut, but rather loosened. But the rusty door bolt still hung on one side of the door, one side of it embedded in the wall, making it so that the door could only open far enough to allow a child to slip through sideways.

An Zhe said, "I'll try."

He walked up to the door and leaned over slightly.

It was impossible for an adult human to pass through here, but he was still a mushroom after all. Under the cover of his clothing, his body briefly changed into hyphae. After losing the limitations of a human skeleton, he very easily got through the door.

"Your body is so soft," the girl said.

"I have something as well," An Zhe said. "Can you not tell others that I came here today?"

The girl said, "If you come here again next week—"

Her voice cut off.

"Lily?" A female voice sounded.

"You came here again." The voice carried an undertone of reproach.

An Zhe dodged to the side, and he heard Lily say, "I'm sorry, Madam."

"This time it was I who found you." The voice of the woman referred to as "Madam" was gentle. "If it was them, you'd be locked up again."

Lily said, "I won't do it again."

Following that conversation was the sound of footsteps as they seemed to walk away. An Zhe looked in that direction through the crack and saw that a madam in a long white dress was holding Lily's hand as their figures gradually receded in the dimly lit corridor.

Lily hadn't finished speaking, but he knew what she wanted to say. He seemed to have reached an agreement with Lily. Next week, he had to come here again and tell her Si Nan's reply.

Preoccupied, he looked around—it was dark all around, and the aroma of dampness wafted toward him. He dimly saw that the walls were mottled and flaking and covered with grayish-green spots of mold and that the ground was covered with fallen light gray powdery debris—this was a narrow and steep staircase. Furthermore, it was obvious that it hadn't been used in who knew how many years.

An Zhe found the stair handrail and walked down along it bit by bit. There were no windows, and it was even darker than the night. This place wasn't much better than the pipes.

Every floor had twenty steps. As An Zhe walked, he counted the floors. When he got to the sixth floor, there was a gap in the staircase's small door approximately the same size as the one on the twentieth floor. He exited from there and reached the sixth floor's utility room.

The bright light shone upon him. The clothes Lily gave him

were the standard uniform of the Garden of Eden's staff members, a snow-white shirt—no different from his previous dress. He walked out and took a look at the time on the wall clock in the corridor. It was seven o'clock. If he went to work at the training base from the Garden of Eden—he was already late.

Thus, An Zhe went downstairs, speeding up as he walked toward the doorway. The bright red "Humankind's interests take precedence over all else" slogan was particularly eye-catching on the snow-white wall. The staff clad in white uniforms walked about on the bright ground, and children's voices traveled over from afar. Everything was different from the interior of the quiet and circuitous pipes.

He felt that he had been reborn.

The main hall's glass door opened, and he ran headfirst into someone.

An Zhe was at a loss for words.

Lu Feng.

Behind and slightly to one side of Lu Feng was Seraing.

He saw Lu Feng's eyes narrow, and from this movement, he felt an aura of danger.

As expected, Lu Feng said grimly, "Why are you here?"

Facing this person, An Zhe's hyphae were on the verge of standing on end.

He shouldn't be in the Garden of Eden right now; he should be at the training base with Colin.

"I..." He lifted his head to look at Lu Feng.

Those ice-cold green eyes observed him, seemingly saying: you can start telling your tall tales now.

An Zhe said, "... I went the wrong way."

He really did go the wrong way, having gotten utterly lost under the entire city. If he hadn't come to the Garden of Eden by coincidence, or if he hadn't found that balcony in time, he may have continued to be trapped in that place, then lose his identity as a human and never again be able to come out.

And...

And this bastard Lu Feng would never have anything to do with him from then on.

He slightly dropped his gaze. For some reason, he unexpectedly felt that the current Colonel wasn't as hateful as before.

Then he heard Seraing gently say, "You're supposed to go to the training base for work today. Did you not realize that the location has changed?"

An Zhe said nothing. The sun rose from behind the distant artificial magnetic pole, and its golden light shone on the silver buttons of Lu Feng's uniform.

His voice was a bit hoarse. "Moreover, you'll be late."

Lu Feng didn't say anything, but he also didn't deliberately make things difficult for An Zhe. He felt that, based on Lu Feng's understanding of his IQ, Seraing's reason was sufficiently convincing. He moved to one side, trying to bypass Lu Feng and leave.

Suddenly Lu Feng's voice came from next to him. "I'll take you there."

Lu Feng drove very steadily and quickly, his speed at least twice that of the shuttle. When he stopped at the entrance to the training base, the display inside the car showed that the time was just 7:25 a.m., five minutes before it was time to go to work. He wasn't late.

It was just that when he got out of Lu Feng's car, An Zhe felt that those other people who had also come to the training base for work all cast a look at him.

In any case, it wasn't his first time being looked at. An Zhe came to the card-reading turnstile at the entrance. People came over one after another, swiped their cards to open the turnstile, and walked in.

An Zhe froze—he realized something.

Footsteps came from behind him. He turned around and saw

Lu Feng standing very close behind, looking at him with eyebrows raised.

"… I forgot my card, too," An Zhe said.

He heard Lu Feng softly click his tongue.

Two slender fingers clasped the blue ID card and put it up to the sensor. With a "beep," the turnstile opened.

Lu Feng used his own ID card to open the gate for him.

At the same time, the Colonel's voice, tinged with a faint disdain, sounded in his ear.

"So stupid."

22

"COME WITH ME TO THE LIGHTHOUSE."

EVEN A MUSHROOM like him knew that these were not good words.

But An Zhe had no way to refute them.

He walked through that door, and the doormen at the sentry box observed the proceedings, looking angry but afraid to speak up.

He understood them.

This position of Arbiter, although it was not the greatest military rank, had the highest authority when it came to killing people. Nobody was willing to cross Lu Feng.

An Zhe himself wasn't, either.

He said, "Thank you, Colonel."

"No problem," Lu Feng said. "In the afternoon, request time off."

"… Huh?"

Lu Feng seemed to nonchalantly lift his eyelids as he said, "Come with me to the Lighthouse."

"What for?" An Zhe asked.

"Dr. Ji wants you for something," Lu Feng said.

An Zhe was a little suspicious of this sentence's authenticity. Why would the doctor want him?

For a moment, he suspected that this was Lu Feng's excuse to arrest him and bring him into the Lighthouse, but he felt that his own performance this morning was flawless. Even Seraing took the initiative to speak for him.

Then he suddenly realized that in Seraing's eyes as well, he didn't seem very smart.

But even if he wasn't a smart human, he was a rational mushroom, and going to the Lighthouse was actually just what he desired.

He said, "Okay."

Lu Feng gave a vague hum in reply, then turned and left.

———

While the children were being trained by the drillmaster, An Zhe sat on a bench nearby. When the instructor needed assistance—such as for scoring and timing and such—he would be called over.

There was nothing else to do, nor were there any reading materials in the office he was interested in, so he could only take an introductory manual on the operation of various weapons.

Colin didn't sit with him, but rather on another bench nearby. He had made a new friend, the language and literature teacher of the class next door, a boy around twenty years old.

The book page he was reading had described in detail a large fighter plane with the model name "PL1109." A masterpiece of human science and technology from the period when the magnetic field was in disorder, it had a top-tier exterior that shielded against radiation, top-tier engine and motors, and an independent cruise system that was unmatched throughout the entire base, capable of accurately determining its course in the absence of a magnetic field.

It sounded very amazing, but An Zhe really had no interest

in it whatsoever, and because he hadn't slept all night, he even began to doze off slightly.

To his right, Colin and the language teacher's greetings to each other had ended. They exchanged names, then began to converse, and the wind blew the contents of their conversation to An Zhe's ear.

"Do you like the Main City?" Colin asked.

An Zhe was astutely aware that Colin was about to start preaching again.

"Why wouldn't I like it?" the boy said. "The Main City gives us stable lives."

He seemed to also be a talkative person. Just as he finished this sentence, he continued with the next. "It must have been a month since we came to the Main City. How do you feel?"

"Liking it is out of the question," Colin said.

"How come?" the boy said. "You don't need to be a mercenary and go out to throw your life away, something that we previously wouldn't have even dared to think about. Every day I thank my mother for forcing me to finish three educational courses, although she mainly wanted me to finish studying language and economics to test into the supply depot in the future so that I wouldn't need to make a living out in the wilderness."

Colin was silent for a while before asking, "What about your mother?"

"Died in the wilderness," he said. "The two of them hadn't raised me for many years before my father failed to return, and then she failed to return as well."

"My apologies," Colin said.

"It's fine." The boy smiled. "I'm used to it. What about you?"

"My mother was killed by the Arbiter, and my father... When we went to the Main City, he was left behind in District 6."

"My apologies," the boy said as well.

But the exchange of their experiences seemed to swiftly bring the two of them closer together. After a short silence, the boy looked at the children on the training ground, put his arms behind his head, and sighed. "Having been in the Outer City for a long time, I've forgotten that we came from the Main City too when we were little."

"I remember quite clearly," Colin said. "When I was five or six years old, I wanted to be a biologist, and my grades were good as well, yet I still wasn't able to remain in the Main City."

"When I was young, I wanted to be a military officer," the boy said. "In the end, I fell during the final assessment, and the military didn't want me."

Colin said, "Fate is fickle."

"Look on the bright side. Our intelligence was insufficient, so even if we remained, it would be painful for us," the boy said with a sigh. "One might not be able to be happy even if they remain in the Main City. I heard that someone wanted to sort and study humankind's archives, but because of his outstanding talent in mathematics, he could only stay in the Lighthouse for his entire life and calculate ballistics trajectories. Think about it. You wanted to be a biologist, but the base thought you were more suited to be a linguist and made you translate documents. How painful that would be. If it were me, I would suddenly die."

"This is the reason why I don't like the base," Colin said. "It's a cold-blooded and ruthless machine."

"You have to think of yourself as a little part. A cog in a greater wheel. Your genes are your model number, determining which sector you work in."

Colin gave a rare smile. "You're very amusing."

The boy said, "Those of us who studied language are rather good at coming up with analogies."

"But people aren't parts. Under the banner of doing every-thing for the sake of serving humankind's interests, the base has been constantly losing its human characteristics instead."

"What alternative is there? We can't just mooch off of the base, we have to produce some value." The boy stood up and looked at the children before them.

"I truly like children," he said with a sudden and very happy smile. "I really like this job. Maybe someday, amongst the children I teach, there will be an unmatched genius who can save the whole world."

Then he spoke to himself. "In that case, I should prepare lessons in earnest."

With chin resting in hand, An Zhe looked at him curiously before looking at Colin again.

Colin didn't say anything else. An Zhe thought that this time, he wasn't able to succeed in finding a comrade.

When they were in the Outer City, Colin had held up a poster that read "oppose the Arbiter." If they were in the Main City, what would he hold up? He felt that it may be something like "oppose human classification" or "we want freedom."

His train of thought became more chaotic as he got sleepier. Trying to focus on the military's illustrated handbook, he cursorily flipped through the fighter plane section, then looked at the weapons section. Conventional bombs, nuclear bombs, and hydrogen bombs of varying equivalents could easily blow a mushroom to bits. But he was by no means afraid. Humans were unlike the things inside the Abyss. They were a rule-abiding existence, so as long as he complied with the rules, he would be able to live.

He spent the morning in this manner. At noon, the children finished training. A few of the younglings had received bumps, and some other younglings thought that the training was too difficult. They didn't go to eat, instead surrounding him at the bench and whimpering.

As An Zhe gently stuck a bandage on a youngling, he comforted a short-haired girl next to him who thought that training was too difficult. "Hang in there. After you pass the training, you can be an officer."

The girl said, "I can't just be eliminated?"

"No, you can't," he said.

He thought that even if she couldn't stay in the Main City, she ought to train hard. Otherwise, once they grew up—if the Outer City resumed operations by then—nobody would adopt children with poor physical fitness, no mercenary team would want them, and they wouldn't be able to pass the test and get into the civilian posts of the City Affairs Office or the supply depot. They'd only be able to go to the third underground floor, regardless of their gender.

Having stayed there for a month, he knew that the people there did not live well.

Thus, he said, "You all have to train hard."

The girl hugged his arm and said, "But even after becoming officers, we need to train every day."

An Zhe patted her hair and thought for a while. "But they have good-looking uniforms."

A boy looked at the soldiers at the training ground and said, "They're super ugly."

"Their military ranks aren't high enough," An Zhe said sincerely to him. "The uniforms get better once you reach... Once you reach Colonel, or so."

"Really?" a youngling asked.

"Will it be as good-looking as the one that person wears?" another youngling asked.

"Which person?" An Zhe asked.

The youngling pointed behind him.

An Zhe turned around.

Against a utility pole two or three meters behind him and to one side leaned a certain Colonel clad in a black uniform. At such a close distance, the younglings were unexpectedly unafraid of him.

Perhaps it was because this Colonel was currently looking straight at An Zhe, his slightly lifted eyebrows carrying a hint of joy.

An Zhe was at a loss for words.

What he said just now had probably been overheard.

———

In Lu Feng's car, An Zhe had fallen asleep.

The moment he woke up was when he instinctively sensed danger. As soon as he opened his eyes, he discovered that the car had stopped at the entrance to the Lighthouse, and the Colonel had opened the car door on his side and was examining him from above.

"Did you not sleep last night?" The Colonel's voice was cold enough to turn water into ice.

An Zhe's brain was still in a non-functioning state. He rubbed his eyes to wake himself up, then got out of the car.

But because he was sleepy to the point of toppling over, his unsteady footing made him pitch forward into Lu Feng.

A pair of powerful arms held him steady, and An Zhe finally stood firm. He didn't fall, but he did become quite a lot more awake.

The Lighthouse was quiet and bustling with activity as always. When they were walking through the corridor on the first floor, four soldiers carrying two bodies covered in white cloth passed by. Seraing was by their side, his face slightly pale. Upon seeing Lu Feng, he explained succinctly, "Experimental malfunction. They were exposed."

Lu Feng gave a slight nod, then took An Zhe to the elevator to go up to the tenth floor.

Dr. Ji was standing in the middle of the corridor on the tenth floor. "You're here."

Lu Feng said, "What's the matter?"

"I'm going to borrow your little cutie here for something." To An Zhe, the doctor said, "Come with me."

An Zhe didn't think he had become Lu Feng's property, but he still followed.

The doctor took him to the familiar laboratory where Si Nan had been locked up.

Through the transparent airtight glass wall, he spotted Si Nan.

But it also wasn't Si Nan.

He walked up to the glass wall.

Inside was a black—a black insect.

It was bigger than Si Nan's original form, about half the size of an adult.

There were two black compound eyes at the top of his head, glowing with a dark silver luster beneath the lamplight. Between the two compound eyes, on top of its head, a pair of thin, long antennae extended. Long translucent wings hung from its back, its abdomen was slender and long and covered with some dark gray fuzz, and the same fuzz also covered its mouthparts.

It looked like a bee.

Right now, it was wildly flying around and crashing into this transparent cage, its body continuously ramming into the glass wall as though it wanted to escape, but its torso and limbs were trembling non-stop, as if it was suffering extreme pain.

"Its situation is abnormal. There are great discrepancies between its brain waves and previous records in the database. I suspect that it still retains a portion of human consciousness and that it's resisting the xenogenic instincts," the doctor said. "But none of us have any way of effectively communicating with it, so we wanted to invite you here to try."

So An Zhe stood in front of the communicator once again.

"Si Nan," he said.

Si Nan's wing covers opened and closed, making rustling sounds as they rubbed together. He seemed to not hear anything, still flying wildly in the whole space as before.

But An Zhe was convinced that there was a moment in which that head with its compound eyes had looked in his direction.

"Si Nan," he said. "Do you remember Lily?"

The rustling sounds stopped for a moment, but then the gray bee rammed the glass wall even more fiercely.

As he watched Si Nan, he asked softly, "Do you have something you want to say to her?"

Si Nan's wings trembled madly, but he had already lost his human vocal organs, so all he presented to the doctor were irregular peaks and troughs on the EEG.

Dr. Ji said, "There are changes in the electric waves. He understands you. Who is Lily?"

An Zhe's gaze was slightly blank.

The conversation between himself and Lily was a secret nobody knew about, but now there was no other option.

An hour later, someone gently tapped on the laboratory door.

An Zhe turned around.

The first thing that caught his eye was a snow-white skirt.

"Madam Lu?" There was a note of slight surprise in Dr. Ji's voice. "Why are you here?"

An Zhe lifted his head. The woman who entered was a lady with an elegant, gentle bearing.

She had long black hair that was loosely twisted into a bun at the back of her head and was wearing a light blue mask, so An Zhe could only see a pair of kind black eyes. Her body was slightly plump, which served to make her disposition even more kindly.

The girl whose hand she was holding in her own right hand

was none other than Lily, and on each side of them was a Garden of Eden staff member.

"In the last three months, the Garden of Eden's aberration rate has risen. I must personally deliver my report to the Lighthouse and request them to decide again," she said. "I just happened to receive an application from the Lighthouse requesting Lily's assistance with a certain task, so I brought her here along the way."

Dr. Ji said, "Sorry to trouble you."

"This outing is an exception." Madam Lu handed Lily over to Dr. Ji. "Please treat her well."

"Please rest assured."

After completing the handover, Madam Lu slowly turned her head.

Lu Feng was in one corner of the room, eyes tracking her since she'd entered the lab.

"You're here too," she said.

Lu Feng dropped his gaze slightly and said, "Mother."

"It appears to be very important research." Madam Lu looked at him.

At that moment, one of them was at the room entrance while the other was at the corner of the room diagonally opposite, their gazes meeting. Madam Lu's expression was soft while Lu Feng's gaze was calm.

When An Zhe witnessed this, a type of intuition told him that there was some unknown undercurrent surging in their eye contact, but he couldn't understand it.

Approximately ten seconds later, Madam Lu said, "I should go."

One of the two staff members helped her turn around, and the two of them protected her completely.

The footsteps receded, and Dr. Ji closed the door.

"This is the thirty-fifth year Madam Lu has worked for the

Garden of Eden." His gaze seemed careworn. "She truly is a great woman. Why don't you talk to her a little more?"

Lu Feng looked at the tightly shut silver door. "We haven't met in a very long time."

"Then all the more reason to talk with her some more. Could it be that your work these years at the Trial Court has already made you cold-blooded and indifferent to this point?" Dr. Ji said. "Remember when I was younger, I even helped you mess up the surveillance on the twentieth floor, allowing you to often run out to see her—the candy Madam gave me was very tasty."

"Dr. Ji," Lu Feng said, "there's no harm in speaking less."

Dr. Ji shrugged.

Three seconds later, he suddenly said, "I really did a flawless job back then. Tell me, after all these years, has the surveillance been fixed?"

Lu Feng looked at Lily, then looked at An Zhe who was looking at Lily, and said, "Looks like it hasn't."

Lily had already pressed herself against the glass wall.

She looked at the bee-shaped xenogenic behind the glass, and an unprecedented delight at seeing something new appeared in her soulless eyes. "Is this a bee?"

The gray bee lay prone against the glass wall, locking eyes with her. Its movements finally stopped for a brief spell, but then it fell into painful convulsions again.

"It looks like it's in a lot of pain." Lily looked at An Zhe, obviously recognizing him, and asked, "Was it you who wanted me to come over and look at the bee?"

He murmured, "That's Si Nan."

Lily was stunned. Just as An Zhe thought she was about to show a sorrowful expression, she broke out into a sudden smile instead.

"Si Nan," she said to the gray bee through the glass wall. "You can fly now."

There was neither fear nor unfamiliarity in her eyes. She had never seen monsters kill people, nor had she ever been warned to stay away from xenogenics. In the eyes of children, there weren't many differences between bees and humans.

She wasn't even surprised by the fact that Si Nan had suddenly turned into a bee—probably because, in the eyes of younglings, the world was just this full of unpredictable changes.

"It's jumbled again." The doctor looked at the instrument. "But for three seconds just now, its electric waves were very close to those of humans."

Dr. Ji patted Lily's shoulder. "Lily, come help us with something."

"What thing?" Lily asked.

"Si Nan's consciousness is fighting against the bee's consciousness. Perhaps you can help him wake up. Can you keep talking to him?"

"I can," Lily said. "Can you change me into a bee too?"

"If you also changed into a bee, the Garden of Eden would execute me," Dr. Ji said. "If you can communicate with him, it would be even better. We have to know how exactly he was infected. The source of infection is in the Garden of Eden, but it has not been found so far. Only by finding it as quickly as possible can we ensure the Main City's safety."

"Okay." Lily put her hand on the glass wall. "Then can you give me a reward?"

Dr. Ji said warmly, "What would you like?"

"I don't want to stay on the twentieth floor." Lily pressed her cheek to the glass. "Can you rescue me from there?"

"My apologies," Dr. Ji said. "This exceeds the scope of my capabilities."

"It's okay. I guessed as much." Lily once again looked at the gray bee. "I'll try my best."

She truly did try her best for an entire afternoon, but Si Nan's condition swung between good and bad. There were only a few times in which he gave normal feedback, but according to Dr. Ji, his situation was much improved from before, and so he decided to invite Lily again the next day.

The doctor was busy with other research duties, and Lily didn't like interacting with others, so in the following few days, An Zhe also had to accompany Lily at the Lighthouse and communicate with Si Nan.

By 7 p.m., Lily had exhausted her young strength and energy. She was delivered back to the Garden of Eden, and An Zhe could also get off work.

At noon, he had fallen asleep in the car and received Lu Feng's ire. Having learned his lesson, he stayed awake the entire trip, got out of the car awake, and took the same elevator with Lu Feng up to the thirty-seventh floor while awake.

Similarly, he faced his own room door while awake.

The tightly shut room door.

One second, two seconds, three seconds.

Lu Feng's voice, carrying an undertone of a smile, rang out behind him. "How come you aren't going inside?"

An Zhe took a deep breath.

Rashly making his way into the pipes last night was one of the two biggest mistaken decisions he had made in his life. The other one was deciding to go roll around in that windy wilderness on the night of February 14th.

He was deeply regretful.

Of course the Colonel understood the dilemma An Zhe was facing. He said, "The Main City's City Affairs Office can reissue ID cards. For the next three days, find someplace to live."

With those words, he unhurriedly opened his own room door, walked in, and made to close the door.

On the other side, An Zhe turned around to look at him, brows slightly furrowed and gently biting his lower lip, the very image of someone struggling. He seemed to be pondering something.

But Lu Feng said nothing, only looking at him flatly.

Time passed quietly.

Unexpectedly, An Zhe turned around and pressed the elevator's down button.

"Then I'll go find Seraing."

23

"IS IT BECAUSE YOU CANNOT WAVER?"

THE COLONEL'S living quarters seemed like quarters nobody lived in.

It was just like his nap room in the Outer City's City Defense Agency.

As for why An Zhe knew how the Colonel's room looked, it was because at the very moment the elevator door opened, he felt that the surroundings were overly chilly.

After turning around again, he met Lu Feng's gaze.

The Colonel leaned against the door frame with his arms crossed. "Get back here."

An Zhe pressed his lips together into a flat line.

In truth, he was by no means close with Seraing. When he pressed the elevator's down button, he even thought that if Seraing was not at home or showed reluctance at his request, he would only be able to awkwardly request Colin's help instead.

He looked back at Lu Feng and was suddenly a bit distressed —he felt slightly wronged. This man clearly knew he didn't have any friends at the base.

Lu Feng also saw that something was amiss with him. "What is it?"

An Zhe lowered his eyes but didn't know what to say. He

actually wanted to speak up and stay in Lu Feng's room, but he feared the Colonel's rejection.

He heard Lu Feng let out a soft laugh.

"I was just teasing you." Lu Feng walked over and pulled him into the elevator. "Let's go eat first. At night, you'll sleep with me."

They ate dinner at the communal dining hall. This dinner was by no means tasty, and what's more, Lu Feng's order was a portion of mushroom soup.

But if he were to sleep with Lu Feng... Of course it would be a bit better than sleeping with Seraing, and it would be much, much better than sleeping with Colin. An Zhe attributed this to the fact that he was only familiar with Lu Feng after all, and moreover, they had stayed overnight at each other's quarters twice before.

After bathing in the Colonel's bathroom, he wiped himself dry, then quickly got into bed while wrapped in a big, snow-white towel. Holding the quilt in his arms, he sat on the inner-most side of the bed—he didn't have pajamas.

In the Colonel's room, all the appliances seemed to be more perfect than the ones in his room, which may have been special treatment the military gave to him.

However, no matter how special the treatment, there would be no extra quilt, nor would there be an extra pillow either. He voluntarily moved the pillow from the middle of the bed to the outer side.

At that moment, a bouquet of red at the head of the bed caught his eye.

There was a simple glass bottle there, and within the bottle were three bright red flowers with thorny stems and dark green leaves. Two of them were already in full bloom, while the last one was still a plump bud.

This was the first time An Zhe had seen plants inside the

human base. This city made of iron and steel seemed to prohibit the existence of any living thing besides humans.

The flowers' fragrance drifted through the air. Just then, Lu Feng, who had been listening to his subordinates report the state of work affairs, ended the call and returned to the bedroom.

At that very moment, Lu Feng noticed he was looking at the bouquet.

"My mother's," he said.

"Madam Lu?" An Zhe asked.

"Mm-hm," Lu Feng said.

His gaze also lingered on those three flowers. After a very long time, he looked outside.

The night sky outside the window was very dark, with shadows flickering, and the hexagonal Garden of Eden stood tall next to the artificial magnetic pole.

Following his gaze, An Zhe looked down as well. In this manner, the Garden of Eden really did look like a beehive. A thought suddenly occurred to him, and he looked back at the three bright red flowers at the head of the bed. He was a little familiar with this kind of color and shape, for it came from An Ze's memory of a picture album from a long time ago. It was a commonly seen plant from when human civilization was still flourishing.

"Roses..." he murmured.

"They are roses," Lu Feng said.

When the children in his class had free time, they would play games of house and pretend flower planting, using colored paper of various hues as flowers. However, it looked like the Garden of Eden had real roses.

"Does the Garden of Eden plant roses?" he said.

Lu Feng's reply was very concise. "No."

Just as An Zhe thought his response would stop there, Lu Feng spoke again.

"She likes plants, but the base doesn't have any." His voice was very calm. "When I was sixteen, I was training out in the wilderness and collected some seeds. After the Lighthouse confirmed that they were safe, I gave them to her."

"Then the Madam planted them?" An Zhe said.

Lu Feng said, "Mm-hm."

An Zhe suddenly recalled the sealed plant seeds he saw in Lu Feng's office cabinet a month ago. He thought that Lu Feng must greatly value his mother. At the Lighthouse today, Madam Lu had gone to submit some reports. She looked like she was a scientific researcher. So he asked, "Is Madam Lu a scientist?"

Only after some time had passed did Lu Feng reply to him. "More or less."

At that moment, Lu Feng suddenly said, "You knew the girl from the Garden of Eden."

An Zhe nodded. Lu Feng had already seen Lily, so he didn't have anything to hide.

"How much do you know?"

He guessed that the Colonel was asking him about his degree of understanding of the Garden of Eden. Recalling Lily's words, he said, "I know the 'Rose Manifesto.'"

He saw Lu Feng look out the window, seemingly recalling the past.

Lu Feng said, "Allegedly when she was twelve years old, because of her intellectual gifts... the base believed that compared to giving birth, she would bring greater contributions to humankind by throwing herself into scientific research, so she was sent to the Lighthouse to study."

"That's so amazing," An Zhe said.

He was invariably curious about humans with superior intellect.

"But afterward, she voluntarily applied to be transferred back to the Garden of Eden and bear the responsibility of birthing children while studying how to improve the technology of in vitro embryo culturing."

"And after that?" An Zhe asked.

"There is no after that," Lu Feng said. "It still holds true now."

An Zhe recalled Madam Lu's appearance. Even though she wore a mask today, showing merely a pair of eyes, the impression she left upon him was very deep. He said, "She's very beautiful."

Lu Feng said, "Thank you."

Upon recalling the situation from the daytime, An Zhe asked, "Do you have a bad relationship with her?"

"Yes."

An Zhe blinked. "Why is that?"

He felt that Lu Feng clearly cared about his mother very much.

"She had always thought I was at the United Front Center, but in fact, I chose to go to the Trial Court in the end." Lu Feng's tone was calm. "Perhaps I've killed too many."

"She can't accept it?"

"It was I who wasn't willing to maintain my relationship with her." Lu Feng picked up the pillow and tossed it to An Zhe's side.

An Zhe caught the pillow and looked at Lu Feng. Strangely, he understood what Lu Feng was saying.

In order to always be correct, always be clearheaded, and always be impassive, the Arbiter had to utterly exile himself—the word 'exile' abruptly appeared in An Zhe's mind.

"The Garden of Eden and the Trial Court are doing opposing things," he said. "Is it because you cannot waver?"

"Shut up." Lu Feng leaned over and yanked the pillow from An Zhe's arms, then lifted him up and put the pillow beneath his head. "You can't even keep your eyes open anymore."

Sinking into the soft pillow, An Zhe felt his consciousness

gradually blur. He really was sleepy, and this night, he had been forcibly trying to stay alert the entire time.

Before completely falling asleep, he saw Lu Feng pick up a silvery-white case, which was something a staff member had given to Lu Feng when they left the Lighthouse. An Zhe didn't know what it was, and he thought that he didn't need to know either. The Colonel always had his reasons for doing things.

———

An Zhe's folded clothes had been set to one side, some light gray dust on the shirt collar area. Neither the training grounds nor the Lighthouse had this sort of thing, but Lu Feng also knew that there was a small-scale disturbance in Garden of Eden's surveillance during that period of time, so there was no way of tracing An Zhe's whereabouts.

Lu Feng looked away from it, and his finger pressed the button on the suitcase. The silver suitcase opened, and wisps of white cold air escaped from within. Inside the refrigerated layer was a long and slender syringe, its contents an aquamarine hue.

Next to the suitcase was his gun.

After his gaze lingered briefly on the two items, he turned to look at An Zhe, his fingers resting on the gunstock.

Right at that moment—

An Zhe rolled over and gently leaned against him.

He was asleep.

Like a small animal curled up inside the snow-white quilt, he revealed a smooth and milk-white neck and shoulder, relaxed eyebrows, and slightly curled eyelashes, his breaths rising and falling in an even and calm rhythm.

Part of his fingers showed from beneath the quilt, gently curled, but it was also a very relaxed demeanor. Not a single nerve was tensed up. As he slept here, without the slightest alertness or vigilance, it was like he was sleeping in a... place he wholeheartedly trusted to be safe. He believed that in this place, nobody would harm him.

Lu Feng suddenly recalled that day from two months earlier.

That day was the first time they met. An Zhe looked into his eyes and said to him, "He hadn't gotten wounded."

He had long ago gotten accustomed to the sight of disputes and denials, and interrogations and rage were things he had to encounter countless times every single day.

But that was his first time seeing a pair of eyes like that. He did not ask questions, nor did he fail to understand. There was only grief. Yet within the grief was an innocent calm, as if, so long as Lu Feng gave a reason, he would accept anything and forgive anything.

He had never paid attention to anyone's pleas before, but that one time, he lifted the white cloth covering the corpse to reveal that person's wound.

A person's wavering starts from the first time their heart softens.

24

"WHAT DID YOU DO TO IT?"

AN ZHE HAD A DREAM.

He seemed to be standing above an abyss of flowing black water, and in front of him was a boundless empty world. The feeling of danger gripped him like a hand. There must have been something in the faraway darkness observing him; he couldn't catch his breath.

Feeling that it was dangerous, he unconsciously looked around and took two steps back. Within the dangerous gaze, he wanted to find someone or get close to someone to obtain a sense of safety.

Thus, his hand uneasily moved, gently grabbing the corner of Lu Feng's sleeve.

His breathing sped up slightly, as if he was afraid.

Lu Feng shut the silver refrigerated box, threw the emptied disposable syringe into the trash bin at the head of the bed, and put the gun back at the head of the bed within easy reach.

After doing all that, An Zhe's somewhat sped-up breathing calmed down, but his beautiful eyebrows were still slightly furrowed.

A tiny bead of bright red blood welled up on one side of his neck, but no more than three minutes later, that bead of blood coagulated into a red spot. It was a pinhole, but the substance that was injected would not do any harm to his body besides this spot of blood.

He was like a small animal with soft fur, having a sort of fragile comfort that seemed very easy to utterly destroy yet also seemed very easy to protect completely.

Lu Feng expressionlessly looked at him. After a long while, he reached out a hand and rested his fingertips on the skin at the center of An Zhe's eyebrows like a dragonfly resting on the water's surface—that pair of furrowed eyebrows slowly relaxed, and no more than three minutes later, he had fallen asleep again as peacefully as he did at the start.

———

When An Zhe woke up, the entire room had brightened. It was the sort of brightness of eight or nine o'clock in the morning. The fear of being late made him wake up completely.

Then he discovered that the towel he had wrapped himself in last night had opened up and slid down no small amount, leaving his upper back bare.

And his hand was clenched around the hem of a certain human's clothes while he leaned his whole body against this human, his face pressed into the other party's shoulder.

If it had been Seraing, An Zhe would have apologized to him in accordance with human etiquette.

If it had been Colin, An Zhe would have immediately gotten away at top speed.

But it was a certain Colonel named Lu who often got mad at him.

An Zhe quietly loosened his grip, then lifted his head to look at him.

But to his surprise, Lu Feng didn't get mad at him this time.

He pulled up the quilt to cover An Zhe's exposed arms and shoulders back up, then said, "It's 8:30."

Today, An Zhe's workplace was still the Lighthouse, but the job tasks were terribly dry and boring. And this Lu Feng person also seemed to not have any proper work today, staying together with him the whole time. The scene within the laboratory could be summed up as Si Nan looking at Lily, Lily looking at Si Nan, him looking at Lily, and Lu Feng looking at him.

After half the day had gone by, Si Nan's condition unexpectedly made steady improvements. The amount of time his brain waves were stable increased from a brief one or two seconds to a sustained four seconds straight. During these brief periods of lucidity, he would knock on the glass wall in regular patterns, as if he were telling Lily that he was there. The doctor was very happy upon hearing the results but said that he couldn't leave for the time being, so he had them continue on their own.

During the periods when Si Nan completely lost his sanity, Lily would talk to An Zhe.

"I still want to fly out," she said. "The outside is so big."

"You all can't go out?" An Zhe asked.

"No, they say the outside is too dangerous," Lily said. "When I was little, I begged them to let me out for five minutes, but they didn't agree. I'm angry with them every day."

"So the Madam will tell me not to squabble with them. She said that all of the base itself is made up of the Garden of Eden's children. Children will sometimes be wayward and will sometimes hurt their mother, but it's all understandable. Moreover, the things we eat, the places we live, and the electricity we use are all the base's things." Lily sighed, but for a girl who was still at the age of a youngling to do this, it was rather incongruous.

An Zhe patted her head.

"Only Madam Lu can go outside. She's a scientist," Lily continued. "I want to be a scientist too."

"I heard them say that previously, embryos had to grow

within the body for at least five months before they could be removed, so it was very painful. But the Madam and the Lighthouse's research team have constantly been cutting down this time, so now it only needs one month."

An Zhe silently listened to her talk.

Just then, Lu Feng's communicator rang. He picked it up, and An Zhe faintly heard a few words like "sample," "growth," and "verify" from the other side.

After hanging up, Lu Feng said to him, "I'm going out for a bit."

"Okay," An Zhe replied.

When Lu Feng's footsteps had receded in the corridor, Lily suddenly came closer to An Zhe and said in a very mysterious tone, "Colonel Lu is the Madam's child, did you know?"

An Zhe looked at the girl. After two days of interacting, she had become much livelier.

He said, "You even know this?"

"Because I'm smart." Lily lifted her chin slightly. "They only know how to sleep, but I know *everything*."

Regarding the words she said before, An Zhe wasn't too interested, but upon her mention of Lu Feng, his curiosity was piqued again. He asked, "What do you know?"

"The Madam's communicator has always had pictures of the Colonel. I've seen them before." Lily swung her little legs on the chair. "They said that only the Colonel is the Madam's real child because he didn't use a machine to supplement his development."

An Zhe thought that Lu Feng and Madam Lu's relationship was indeed very special. The Garden of Eden's children didn't know exactly who their own parents were. The only thing that accompanied them since birth was their ID card number.

Lily continued. "It seems that there were two reasons. The first one is that the Colonel's condition at that time wasn't stable, and therefore was unsuited to in vitro culture. The other one, everyone is only guessing."

"What are they guessing about?" An Zhe asked.

"The Madam stayed outside the Garden of Eden before. Afterward, she also wanted to go to the Lighthouse to hold meetings and wanted to negotiate with the people outside so she could go out. I'm guessing the Madam had fallen in love with someone outside. I bet Colonel Lu is the child of the Madam and her lover."

Upon saying this, Lily looked at An Zhe, her chin resting in her hands. "Are you Colonel Lu's lover?"

An Zhe pondered the implication of this word for a while, then shook his head.

"Then have you ever contributed sperm? You seem to have already come of age," Lily said. "Although you don't have a lover, you probably already have children."

"I don't," An Zhe said with a frown. "But…"

"But what?"

An Zhe slowly shook his head and said nothing more.

He didn't have a child in the human sense, but he had his spore, his spore that he didn't know the location of.

If he rashly asked Lu Feng, he feared that he would expose his identity as a xenogenic.

Yet if he continued to enter the ventilation pipes to search, there was an ever-present risk of getting lost or being exposed.

The only thing he knew was that based on Lu Feng's notebook, his spore was most likely within the Lighthouse—and now he was in the Lighthouse, but in the face of those complicated access doors and secretive laboratories, he had no idea how he should go look for it.

Clearly, he may have already gotten very close to his spore.

During these two days in the Lighthouse, every time he had this thought, An Zhe felt distressed.

Lily said, "Are you unhappy?"

"Mm-hm," An Zhe said.

He wasn't a complete mushroom. An incomplete mushroom couldn't be happy no matter what.

Right at that moment, soft tapping noises sounded again. Si Nan had recovered his sanity—Lily promptly abandoned him and went up to Si Nan.

An Zhe became even more dejected.

The sound of footsteps came from the corridor. It was Lu Feng and the doctor returning together.

The doctor was talking to Lu Feng. "What did you do to it?"

"What could I have done to it?" Lu Feng said.

"It was always completely motionless as if it were dead until these two days that you frequented the Lighthouse, when it suddenly began to grow. I think it's not a coincidence."

"Furthermore, as it soaked in nutrient solution, it has always floated irregularly. Why is it that when you went next to the culture chamber, it would float over to get close to you?"

Lu Feng coldly replied, "Isn't that what you and your people are supposed to research?"

"You must first provide enough information to us. What special relationship do you have with it?"

"I took it, sealed it up, and sent it to the Lighthouse." Lu Feng's tone of voice gradually became colder, which was a sign that he did not wish to continue this conversation. "That's it."

"This is a key project. You have to cooperate with their research."

"As you like."

The voices drew closer as the two of them returned to the laboratory. The doctor walked back over to the instrument, and Lu Feng took the illustrated base armaments handbook from An Zhe's backpack and leafed through it to kill time.

Upon recalling their conversation just now, An Zhe gradually felt a trace of suspicion.

He slowly looked at Lu Feng.

Lu Feng, feeling the weight of his gaze, lifted his head from the book pages to meet An Zhe's eyes.

An Zhe looked at him. "What did you go to do?"

Lu Feng gave him a flat look but didn't directly answer his question. Instead, he responded, "Hm?"

An Zhe saw that he looked unwilling to answer, but when he thought about the clues he might get, he still plucked up his courage and said, "Something got close to you..."

Lu Feng raised his eyebrows. "Nothing got close to me."

"Just now, the doctor said—"

"I went to go look at a project." Lu Feng's tone of voice was nonchalant. "Nothing else happened."

An Zhe was going to die of anger thanks to this person. He wanted to ask Lu Feng what project he went to go look at, but this person was obliquely saying he didn't do anything.

"A laboratory called for him." The doctor returned to the instrument. "It was normal work, and he came back after cooperating. But he may need to make a few more trips."

With that, the doctor began to concentrate on studying the earlier footage of Si Nan.

Lu Feng's way of thinking was difficult to figure out. Since An Zhe failed to grasp the key point, he would have left it at that, but the doctor unexpectedly also gave a reply that didn't answer his question. Having received no information whatsoever, An Zhe sat next to Lily, his mood restless. He felt both dejection because he didn't get an answer and self-hatred because he couldn't ask too obviously lest he reveal his identity; he even had the thought of following Lu Feng the next time he went—

He heard Lu Feng say from next to him, "Focus on your work."

An Zhe was left speechless.

At 5 p.m., it was time for Lily to go back. After she went back, Si Nan no longer lucidly knocked on the wall and began to bump about wildly in his cell. An Zhe took some simple notes on the day's situation, and the doctor told him that he could go back.

An Zhe looked at Lu Feng.

Lu Feng said, "I'm staying here."

The doctor said, "He's on duty tonight."

"… Oh," An Zhe said.

Various experiments took place within the Lighthouse, a majority of them having to do with research on xenogenics. Sometimes when improper operation or accidents happened, staff members would be infected, and therefore the Trial Court also had permanent staff in the Lighthouse.

With that thought, he suddenly felt that things were some- what difficult to deal with.

He didn't have his ID card, so he couldn't go back to his home, and if Lu Feng didn't go home, there were even fewer places he could go.

With that thought, he saw Lu Feng take out his ID card from the chest pocket of his uniform and give it to him. "Go back by yourself."

An Zhe accepted it and said, "Thank you."

The doctor clicked his tongue.

An Zhe asked, "Are you eating dinner here?"

Lu Feng continued looking at the illustrated armaments handbook and said flatly, "Mm."

An Zhe asked, "What are you eating?"

"The compressed nutrient tablets that the neighboring labo- ratory and the Garden of Eden recently invented together," the doctor said as he tapped on the keyboard. "For the time being, it's only provided for use within the Lighthouse."

With those words, the force he tapped the keyboard with increased by a few degrees. "It's the nastiest thing I've eaten in my entire life."

An Zhe stood in place and thought for a moment.

He realized that the ventilation pipes were empty and that the Lighthouse was also empty. The only one who truly had any connection to finding his spore was Lu Feng.

He said to Lu Feng, "Would you like me to bring you food?"

Lu Feng lifted his head and looked at him. Within those cold eyes, his emotions couldn't be seen.

An Zhe saw that he had also happened to flip to the page with the "PL1109" fighter plane.

Lu Feng didn't reply. An Zhe said in a small voice, "Then I'll bring you something."

The doctor clicked his tongue again.

The doctor said, "I want some too."

Lu Feng said, "There's none for you."

The doctor turned to look at An Zhe. "I want to drink tomato soup."

"There might not be any," An Zhe said.

By no means did he lie. Apart from potatoes, the residential area's food supply was different every day—specifically, it depended on the Garden of Eden's production circumstances at the time.

However, there were indeed tomatoes among the ingredients today.

An Zhe stood in front of the container that held the tomatoes and hesitated for a while.

Then he turned around to face the icebox where the mushrooms were.

He remembered that yesterday when eating dinner with Lu Feng, Lu Feng had chosen mushroom soup from among the identically watery potato soup, tomato soup, and mushroom soup that the communal dining hall provided that night. His choice made An Zhe feel somewhat uncomfortable, but...

He internally debated with himself for two minutes, but in the end, he took two portions of mushrooms.

The kind of mushrooms the base cultivated were a grayish-white and had round stems and soft caps. He often came here to buy things, so the staff members of the ingredients area already recognized him. "Cooking mushrooms tonight?"

"Mm-hm," An Zhe said. "Do I need other ingredients?"

Under the guidance of the staff member, An Zhe took back fresh meat and a packet of seasoning. He swiped Lu Feng's card. Originally, he would have felt that the cost of these ingredients was huge, but compared to the balance, it seemed unexpectedly trivial.

An Zhe picked up the knife, took a deep breath, and began chopping the mushrooms, which were so soft that they split into halves with just a gentle cut. Mushroom soup also took much less time than other soups—after the small chunks of fresh chicken were cooked through in the boiling water, he put the packet of seasoning in, then added the mushrooms. Before long, a light and fragrant aroma wafted from the water. An Zhe closed the pressure cooker lid, and after setting the timer, he left the kitchen.

He didn't have anything to do, so he watered the roses in the Colonel's room, and after tidying up the room, he turned on the TV in the living room.

It was the exact time for the news broadcast. The image appeared, and An Zhe was surprised to see a familiar figure.

Hubbard, the mercenary team captain who had once ordered a mannequin from Mr. Shaw and also helped Mr. Shaw get Lu Feng's information.

At the time, if he hadn't taken his team out on a mission again, perhaps he would have been amongst the accused as well.

"At present, the work of recalling mercenaries is progressing smoothly. This morning, all members of mercenary team AR137 returned to the base. This is the only team who can perform six-star level missions apart from the base's military, and they have brought back precious samples and the latest information on the outside world. Our reporter has interviewed AR137's captain, Mr. Hubbard."

In the frame, Hubbard, dressed in field equipment, had just gotten out of an armored vehicle. A reporter was interviewing him.

"Welcome back, Mr. Hubbard."

"Thank you," Hubbard said.

At one side, a staff member who was guiding them to get their blood tested said, "The Main City welcomes you."

"Thank you," Hubbard said. "The base's situation surprised me greatly."

The reporter said, "Your recall date is somewhat later than that of other mercenary teams. Did you encounter difficulties along the way?"

"No." Hubbard's reply was very terse. "The signal was bad. I just received the recall message."

The reporter smiled. "May I ask which region you returned from?"

"The fringes of the Abyss."

"How is the situation there now?"

"The monsters' shapes are even more varied."

"The Abyss is indeed a very fearsome place. What did you bring back from there?"

"Samples."

"Thank you for your contributions to the base," the reporter said.

"You're welcome."

An Zhe felt that with regard to being terse, Hubbard might be able to compete with Lu Feng, but his eyes were not as good-looking as Lu Feng's.

The frame switched back to the news anchor. "As far as we know, the returning mercenary teams will be classified as part of the military establishment after their meritorious feats are accounted for, and they will continue serving the base."

After that news broadcast finished, up next were a few unimportant pieces of information. Of the things that happened every day in the Main City, there weren't many worth reporting on. Most of the time, the anchors reported on the new progress in the Lighthouse's scientific research, and there were many specialized words and jargon, which made An Zhe drowsy.

The pressure cooker in the kitchen let out a long whistle, rescuing An Zhe. After opening the lid, a rich fragrance wafted into his face. The soup had become very thick and showed a velvety texture, and snow-white mushrooms bobbed up and down within. He tasted a mouthful. Feeling satisfied, he happily put enough for three people into a thermos, planning to take it to the Lighthouse.

But right when he walked out the kitchen door, he was stunned.

On the news was a silver laboratory with complicated machinery all around, and in the center of the laboratory was a cylindrical glass tank, inside which was a clear, pale green liquid.

And inside this tank that was the height of a man, there was a tiny little white thing quietly floating in the very center.

An Zhe's eyes widened, and he strode to the TV screen—at that exact moment, the camera drew closer, giving a close-up of that little white thing.

White like snow, a soft mass, its main body was like a cloud floating in the water, its size just like the mushrooms An Zhe used in his cooking today.

Apart from that, the fine snow-white hyphae had also spread out, soaking in the water and gently swaying in the wake of its trajectory as it floated in the water.

An Zhe practically stopped breathing.

He definitely wouldn't mistake his own spore—although compared to when it left him, it seemed to have grown a bit bigger.

An Zhe lifted his hand. His fingers trembled a little as they laid against the TV's ice-cold screen, as if he were touching the surface of the tank and only a glass wall separated him from that snow-white thing. But then the newscaster's voice broke that illusion. "Four months ago, the anomalous fungus sample collected by the Trial Court was listed as a first-class observation subject, for it has never undergone any mutations from its fundamental shape. As a result, the Lighthouse believes this sample has a high research value. Perhaps by studying the sample, we can reveal the process and principles of biological infection and mutation."

An Zhe frowned deeply. As expected, his spore had been taken for research.

Then the news broadcaster said, "According to the researchers, in the past four months, the sample had maintained a half-dead state. However, in these last two days, it has unexpectedly resumed activity and increased in size. This is very exciting news…"

An Zhe's heart thumped hard.

He knew the spore recognized him too.

Why else would it only start growing bigger in exactly these two days that he had been staying in the Lighthouse? The spore sensed him. It definitely also wished to return to him.

The announcer continued talking. "The laboratory contacted the Trial Court and confirmed that the sample's growth direction is similar to the original main body."

At the same time, in the frame, the spore floated unsteadily in a certain direction. An Zhe thought that this must have been the direction he was in relative to the laboratory. The spore wanted to find him.

In the very next second, a human figure appeared next to the glass tank. The person's body was outside the frame, and there was only a vague reflection, so he didn't know who it was.

An Zhe wanted this person to get away from his spore.

The situation was the exact opposite. This person reached out with a hand to gently touch the surface of the tank with their fingertips, the fingers slender and knuckles very beautiful. An Zhe frowned, for he was very familiar with the shape of this hand.

He was also very familiar with this person's sleeve as well as the silver buttons.

An Zhe ground his teeth. He confirmed that this person trying to touch his spore was, beyond a doubt, that bastard Lu Feng.

However, right at that moment, the spore floated over to that bastard, and its fine snow-white hyphae stretched out and touched his fingers across the tank.

Why would it do that?

An Zhe was confused.

25

"A RESPLENDENT MILKY WAY."

AN ZHE helplessly watched his spore reach out its hyphae and touch Lu Feng through the glass. When Lu Feng's hand left, the hyphae even drooped, its appearance carrying a hint of loss.

Seeing his spore act this way, An Zhe felt a bit distressed as well, as if he had just personally experienced it. When Lu Feng lifted his hand, An Zhe didn't want him to get close to the spore, but when the man let go, An Zhe wanted him to stay a little longer.

In this brief second, the camera switched to a researcher in a white coat who said that the sample showed an unprecedented inertia against infection and mutation.

"After four months of analysis and research, the sample's extracts will not infect any organisms. Likewise, when we infected the sample with mutated organism extracts, we have not observed any changes whatsoever in its composition," the researcher said. "The Lighthouse believes this may be our breakthrough point to overcoming mutations."

An Zhe gripped the thermos handle. The human said that his spore was the breakthrough point to overcoming mutations, which meant that the spore would be under heavy protection.

Finally, the newscaster summarized the news in a very optimistic tone, said that the future of the base was bright, and thanked the researchers for their efforts.

After the news ended, the weather forecast followed. According to the Lighthouse's observations, within the next three days, the region where the base was located would welcome a substantial rise in temperature, and there was a reminder to all areas—especially the Lighthouse's laboratories and the Garden of Eden's crop husbandry base—to respond to it.

An Zhe was not in the mood to continue listening. He left home and got onto a shuttle. Along the way, he pondered how exactly he should get close to his spore—firstly, he had to know the exact location of that laboratory, then observe the researchers' work patterns. Under normal circumstances, researchers wouldn't stay in the laboratory for all hours of the day. If he could enter the laboratory through the ventilation pipes when nobody was there, then think of a way to take the spore back into himself—

Then he could think of a way to leave the human base and return to the Abyss.

If the experimental sample was stolen, the humans would chase it to the end. Apart from escaping, he seemed to have no other options.

At that thought, An Zhe blankly turned his head and looked at this city with its lights blazing in the night through the shuttle's glass. The aurora had already risen, its green light fluctuating in the night sky and swiftly changing, just like the flow of time.

The announcement sounded. He had reached the Twin Towers.

An Zhe got off, holding the thermos in his arms, then swiped Lu Feng's ID card to open the door, entered the hall, and went upstairs. In the silver corridor, every laboratory was brightly lit. Various instruments emitted sounds at various rates, the back-

and-forth rising and falling. He found the doctor's laboratory, but only Dr. Ji and his assistant were inside.

"You've come." The doctor lifted his head and looked at An Zhe. "Lu Feng will be back later."

"All right." An Zhe put the thermos on the workbench, unscrewed it open, and filled a bowl for the doctor. The insulation device's function was very good. The soup was boiling hot, and the rich fragrance wafted out along with the rising steam, filling the laboratory.

"My God." The doctor picked up the tableware An Zhe handed over. "You're wonderful."

An Zhe smiled.

"You aren't eating?" the doctor asked.

"I'll wait for him to come back," An Zhe replied.

The doctor clicked his tongue.

"I'm not waiting for him," the doctor said, then looked at the assistant. "Continue rolling the clip."

The assistant replied, "All right."

An Zhe looked at the computer interface in front of the doctor. The window in the very center was playing footage of Si Nan. Beneath this window was another window that was partially covered, but a mailing list was visible. The doctor had sent one email each to the recipients "Underground City" and "Research Institute."

His gaze turned back to the Si Nan in the footage, the gray bee. Lily was aimlessly chatting with him, and in the previous second, she was even saying, "Will you have honey?" which was promptly followed by "Is it more fun to be a person or a bee?"

He said, "It's gotten bigger."

Moreover, it was a very easily detectable increase in size.

The doctor ate a piece of chicken and narrowed his eyes as he looked at the screen. "Indeed."

The assistant chimed in, "An increase of ten kilograms."

"What has it eaten?" the doctor asked.

"It has taken no sustenance," the assistant replied.

The doctor said, "It's like this yet again."

"I shouldn't have considered this question while eating," he said. "I was very happy."

An Zhe asked him, "What's the matter?"

"The change and growth of xenogenics not only violates the existing definition of biology, but also has always challenged the law of conservation of energy." The doctor looked at Si Nan. "Organisms take in energy from the outside world and convert it into the self. But when humans change into xenogenics, their bodies may grow tenfold in size, and the muscle mass is also many times higher than that of humans. Where does that energy come from? As Petri dishes, human flesh can't provide that much. They're practically made out of thin air."

An Zhe said nothing. He didn't have this knowledge, but the creatures in the Abyss were indeed all very massive.

"Never mind," the doctor said with a sigh. "The complete failure of our knowledge framework isn't something recent."

He continued devouring the bowl of delicious mushroom soup, but his gaze was still fixed on the screen.

When he was almost done drinking, An Zhe asked, "Do you want more?"

The doctor didn't reply. An Zhe looked at his eyes and discovered that he was staring relentlessly at the screen.

"Replay it," he said.

The assistant replayed the video from one minute prior.

Lily, already worn out from talking, was leaning against the glass wall. "Don't bump into the wall anymore, it hurts so much."

Then she added, "Although it's very tiring to constantly talk, the Lighthouse is more fun than the Garden of Eden."

Right at that moment, Si Nan recovered his lucidity for a brief spell, and his fluff- and spine-covered mouthparts gently tapped on the glass.

"You're awake," Lily said.

The gently trembling mouthparts continued tapping a few more times.

The doctor frowned.

"Half speed, play it again."

The frame was enlarged and the speed was reduced, focusing on the bee's movements as it tapped the glass.

"The intervals of the first and second taps are the same, tapping again after a long pause, and then another long pause." The doctor took out a notebook and swiftly made marks with a ballpoint pen. "This time after the pause, there were three consecutive taps with the same interval."

As he spoke, he jotted down on the paper the numbers 2, 1, and 3.

After the segment of footage finished playing, the doctor said, "The next recorded segment of when he was lucid."

The assistant began adjusting the video timing. He looked like he was the doctor's student. "Are you suspecting that he's transmitting a message via the tapping frequency?"

The doctor said, "This is absolutely not normal... but he's just a six-year-old child."

He looked at An Zhe. "What do you cover in your mathematics and logic classes?"

An Zhe said, "Arithmetic, geometry, and reasoning."

"Will you tell them stories outside the classes?" the doctor asked. "Such as about radio code and such."

"That's not right," he then said. "He hasn't entered Class A, so he wouldn't have such a high IQ."

An Zhe said, "He got full scores on his tests. Not being able to enter Class A was because of psychological factors."

The doctor nodded to indicate that he understood and began watching the next video. In this segment of footage, the period Si Nan was lucid for was very short. He swiftly tapped twice, the interval different than before.

The doctor drew two very closely spaced dots on the paper. "Next segment."

In the next segment, within the same span of time, Si Nan tapped the wall seven times.

Then the next segment—in this recorded segment, he was lucid for a full five seconds. In the first half of the recording, his behavior was surprisingly consistent with the first segment of footage. Two taps, one tap, three taps. After completing the third set of taps, he paused for a long span of time, then swiftly tapped twice immediately afterward. This segment of footage was like an amalgam of the first and second segments.

The doctor took notes in his notebook, and the videos continued to play. In the fifth segment of footage, he once again evenly tapped seven times in a row. After that, in all the lucid fragments, his tapping maintained this repetition until five o'clock rolled around and Lily was taken back by the Garden of Eden's staff.

The doctor recorded a string of numbers in his notebook.

2, 1, 3, 1, 1, 7, 2, 1, 3, 1, 1, 7, 2......

The assistant said, "Do you want to get someone well versed in mathematics to come and decode it?"

"No need," the doctor said. "The message he wants to convey is very short, so it won't be difficult... Let me think."

An Zhe frowned as he looked at the string of numbers. Humans communicated through language, so he didn't know how numbers were to assume the function of transmitting messages, unless these numbers implied characters.

"2, 1, 3..." The doctor's deeply furrowed brows seemed to relax a bit.

An Zhe hesitated for a while before saying, "Is it B, A, C?"

"The alphabet." The doctor scribbled down the letters "bac" on a page. An Zhe looked at the recording from before. After 2,

1, and 3, Si Nan knocked twice in a row, so it should have been "bacaa." The sixth knock consisted of seven hits, and the number 7 corresponded to the letter "g."

In accordance with An Zhe's thinking, the doctor wrote down the six letters "bacaag" but then underlined the consecutive "a"s.

The assistant said, "The interval between these two knocks is very short. It's a different expression of language."

"Eleven," the doctor suddenly said. "Two short knocks don't represent two separate 1s but rather the double digit 11."

The letter corresponding to 11 was "k," so that string of letters became "backg."

The doctor asked, "How was his English?"

"Full marks as well," An Zhe said.

Foreign languages accounted for nearly half of the content in the language and literature courses. If these children were to enter the Lighthouse after growing up, consulting the documents of human civilization would require very high levels of linguistic competence.

"Back." The doctor uttered one word, then moved the letter "g" up to the very front and narrowed his eyes. "'Go back,' a very concise expression. In other languages, it wouldn't be so short. Furthermore..."

The assistant said, "Furthermore, it's within the scope of Lily's understanding. If she is able to notice, she will understand it."

The doctor nodded. "He wanted to make her go back. What does this mean?"

The videos continued to play. Lily said listlessly to Si Nan, who was throwing himself and flying around wildly, "The doctor said that it's very dangerous in the base now. You have to help us or everyone will change into monsters. It's very scary."

The assistant said, "If they are very good friends, that means the Garden of Eden is a safe place, and he knows or predicts that the outside world is very dangerous, so he wants her to go back."

"But it was in precisely the Garden of Eden that this boy was infected and turned into a xenogenic." The doctor thought for a while. "Could he be saying that the first xenogenic appeared in the Garden of Eden, and then the Trial Court's investigation center was transferred there, so it is a feint strategy instead?"

"Do you want to hold a meeting and discuss it?" the assistant asked.

The doctor glanced at the laboratory door. "How come Lu Feng still hasn't returned yet?"

He picked up the communicator and dialed, but a busy tone came from the other side. The assistant said, "Perhaps he entered the signal-jammed laboratory."

An Zhe astutely picked up on the opportunity and seized the opportunity to ask, "What did he go to do?"

"The same project from this afternoon," the doctor said. "They believe the Colonel can advance the growth of a sample, so they insisted that he go over there and babysit."

An Zhe said without hesitation, "I can go find him."

Smiling, the doctor looked at him. "You two have a really good relationship. That's fine too. Bring him back and have dinner while you're at it," the doctor said. "That laboratory's level is very high, as it's combined between the military and the Lighthouse. Take the elevator up to the thirteenth floor, cross the corridor bridge, and look for room D1344."

"All right," An Zhe replied.

He turned and left the laboratory—it was obvious that Lu Feng was with his spore again now, and probably this person was somewhere very close to the glass tank or once again holding out his hand to play games of touch with the spore. He didn't know why this sort of thing would happen, but he absolutely didn't believe the "Lu Feng advances the spore's growth" nonsense. When the spore was taken away, it hadn't yet reached the point of maturity where it could grow by itself. It would only grow when it was either within his body or next to him.

The elevator arrived, and inside were two people. They were researchers, and they were discussing the recent weather.

"A rise in temperature after high winds. The recent weather has been very extreme."

"Summer has come, so it counts as normal. Compared to a rise in temperature, the base is more afraid of drops in temperature."

"That's true."

"But I heard this is because of fluctuations in the magnetic field's strength."

"Is it a problem with the artificial magnetic pole?"

"The neighboring laboratory observed several abnormal fluctuations. Our East Pole has no problems, so everyone believes that the frequency of the West Pole is being manually adjusted."

"Wow." The researcher smiled. "Has there been new progress in the Underground City Base's technology?"

"I'm guessing so, otherwise nobody would dare to touch the magnetic pole. They've already contacted the United Front Center, applying to open strong frequency short-wave communication and communicate with the Underground City Base."

"Everything is changing for the better."

Everything was indeed changing for the better, for he was about to see his spore—the elevator door opened, and An Zhe walked out.

The corridor bridge connecting the buildings of the Lighthouse and the United Front Center was very wide, and both sides were transparent, being made from glass or some other material.

Laboratory D1344 was very easy to find. He knocked on the door.

A female voice said, "Please enter."

As soon as An Zhe entered, he saw the glass tank in the center. It was identical to the one on the news, and that small white mass—

Next to the little white mass was Lu Feng in his black uniform. He had put his fingers on the tank, and the spore was once again bobbing toward him—then this person withdrew his finger and put it at a different place much farther away.

Then the spore slowly changed direction, going to a new place.

When it almost caught up, Lu Feng changed places again, deliberately not allowing it to touch.

When An Zhe saw this, he was so angry he almost forgot to breathe—whereas Lu Feng's expression looked impassive when he was in fact completely joyful. He seemed to be finding pleasure in bullying and playing with the spore.

At that very moment, Lu Feng lifted his head and looked over at An Zhe, eyebrows raised.

An Zhe looked around. With sophisticated instruments and surveillance equipment as well as a dozen or so researchers, he could only look at his spore from afar.

No, he could do one other thing, which was to take away this person who bullied his spore.

He walked over to the tank, but hatefully, the spore didn't approach him, but rather continued to linger around Lu Feng.

Lu Feng's tone was very light. "What is it?"

An Zhe said in a very unkind tone, "You should go back and eat."

There seemed to be a trace of a smile in the gaze Lu Feng looked at him with. Unexpectedly, playing with the spore made the man this happy.

Lu Feng walked over to him, then said to a researcher, "I'm leaving."

The researcher replied, "Please be sure to come tomorrow as well."

An Zhe gritted his teeth as he took one last look at the little spore floating helplessly in the nutrient solution, and the laboratory door mercilessly shut right in front of him.

He and Lu Feng walked through the corridor.

He said, "Are you coming here tomorrow too?"

"Mm-hm."

"Were you playing with the sample?"

"I'm cooperating with a study."

An Zhe wouldn't believe his blatant lies. He didn't say anything, and they turned around a corner and arrived at the corridor bridge leading to the Lighthouse. On either side was the city's night sky and the aurora on the horizon.

But Lu Feng seemed to have sensed his mood. "You're unhappy?"

An Zhe said nothing.

Lu Feng stopped walking and looked at him.

An Zhe turned to look at the aurora outside, and the entire world seemed to go quiet for a second.

Right at that moment—

An Zhe's pupils sharply contracted!

A sharp pain traveled through his entire body. The light was too strong, so he unconsciously shut his eyes. Just a moment ago, the aurora that filled the sky released a burst of light that was as bright as day, cleaving the sky like a flash of green lightning.

Lu Feng grabbed his shoulder and yanked him down, pressing him to the ground, and then the two of them rolled over once. All of it happened within tenths of a second.

An Zhe wasn't hurt by the impact, for Lu Feng had protected him with his arms. He opened his eyes and discovered that he had been brought back into the corridor.

Lu Feng pulled him up.

The inside of An Zhe's head buzzed. He looked at the outside of the corridor bridge and was stupefied.

The aurora was disappearing—all of it.

After the short-lived burst just now, it was like an ebb tide disappearing in the night sky. The color faded within ten short seconds, then completely disappeared.

A resplendent Milky Way spanned the indigo night sky.

He had never seen such a sight before. Then his gaze lowered. The entire human city's lights were blinking wildly, complementing the Milky Way.

The corridor lights flickered madly, and chaotic sounds came from the laboratories as several researchers ran out.

Lu Feng pulled An Zhe back to a place where the outside wasn't visible, then asked grimly to a researcher hurrying past, "What happened to the magnetic field?"

26

"WHEN THE AURORA LIGHTS UP AGAIN, THE COLONEL WILL RETURN."

"THE EMERGENCY POWER HAS BEEN ACTIVATED."

"The emergency internal communications channel has been activated."

"The emergency defenses have been activated."

"The ventilation system has been activated."

"The radiation defense windows have descended."

"All departments, please stand by."

In the corridor, amidst the chaotic footsteps and shouting, the broadcast system was turned on. It was no longer a robotic voice, but rather a human female one.

In the wake of the voice, muffled "clunk-clunk" sounds came continually from all directions. An Zhe looked at the connecting corridor once again. Ice-cold steel curtains had dropped abruptly, blocking all windows. It looked very thick—he recalled how Poet had said that once the magnetic field disappeared, the radiation and solar wind from the cosmos would immediately attack the earth's surface.

Thus, he knew that when Lu Feng pulled him away from the corridor just now, it was to leave the possible scope of the cosmic radiation—and as the construction from the era in which human science and technology were at their peaks, the thickness and special materials of the Main City's walls were able to defend against the radiation's assault.

After the lights of the United Front Center's building flickered madly, they lit steadily again, but the glow was now much weaker than before, displaying a feeble paleness.

The sound of a researcher dialing a number on his communicator came from the closest laboratory. He was too anxious, so his voice was very loud; it could be heard throughout the entire corridor.

"D1342 requesting an increase in power supply! The instruments cannot stop!"

A voice came from another laboratory as well. "D1343 requesting emergency power, otherwise valuable samples will be inactivated."

Who would answer their requests and whether or not they would be fulfilled, An Zhe didn't know. He looked in the direction of D1344 and unconsciously grabbed the edge of Lu Feng's sleeve.

Lu Feng looked down at him and said, "It's fine."

An Zhe nodded.

The announcements continued broadcasting.

"Would the persons in charge of the Equipment Center, City Defense Agency, Emergency Response Department, and Logistics Division please proceed to Conference Room 1 on the seventeenth floor of the United Front. Please refrain from taking the elevators and use the passages to go upstairs and downstairs."

"Requesting the Lighthouse's Magnetic Field Observation Office to immediately contact the United Front Center."

"Requesting the Lighthouse's Magnetic Field Observation Office to immediately contact the United Front Center."

The announcement voice was turned up to the maximum volume, and the echoes reverberated in the corridor.

An Zhe looked at Lu Feng. "Are we going back to the Lighthouse?"

"I'll wait for orders." Lu Feng looked at the far end of the corridor, seeming to be contemplating something, then turned his gaze back to An Zhe. "Don't run around. Stick with me."

An Zhe said, "Okay."

Then the announcement said, "Would the persons in charge of the Command Post, Joint Staff Department, Trial Court, and Combat Center please proceed to the communication center on the fourteenth floor of the United Front. Please refrain from taking the elevators and use the passages to go upstairs and downstairs."

As An Zhe followed Lu Feng through the communication center's entrance, he heard voices inside.

"Northern Base to Underground City Base, please respond."

"Northern Base to Underground City Base, please respond."

"Northern Base to Underground City Base, please respond."

The dispatcher, wearing a pair of massive black headphones, was speaking. In front of him, more than a dozen display screens were spread out, upon which curves and parameters jumped.

But in this communication channel, only he was talking. From the other side came nothing but empty electrical noises.

At the center of the hall was a middle-aged man in a black military uniform. His facial features were cold and expression was dignified, and the symbol on his epaulettes indicated that he was a lieutenant general in the military.

Upon seeing Lu Feng enter, he gave a nod in their direction. "You've come."

There were some other soldiers who entered before and after Lu Feng. Though their military ranks and the departments they belonged to differed, their expressions were identically cold and solemn.

The communication hall had chairs, so they dispersed and sat down. An Zhe quietly sat next to Lu Feng.

The lieutenant general answered a communication, and after a short thirty seconds, he hung up and said to the officers in the hall, "That was a notice from the Lighthouse's Magnetic Field Observation Office. Five minutes ago, the strength of the global magnetic field dropped to zero, but there were no abnormalities in the East Pole we are protecting."

"It's very clear that there was a major failure of the West Pole on the other side."

An Zhe listened to the lieutenant general's words. He knew the meaning the magnetic poles had to humans.

The magnetic field protected everything on Earth. Once it was lost, cosmic radiation and solar winds would enter without resistance. In the short term, it would bring severe drought to the entire world, and exposed humans would receive radiation, contract various malignant diseases, and then die or mutate. And if there was a long-term lack of protection from the magnetic field, the entire planet's atmosphere would be dispersed by the solar winds, and then the world would turn into a desert of death.

And of the two magnetic poles humans made, one was in the Northern Base and the other was in the Underground City Base. The two of them jointly maintained a weak magnetic field that covered the whole world and were indivisible. As soon as something went wrong with one of them, the other one would lose its function as well.

There was no need for unnecessary communication between the two of them, either. Every night, the aurora appearing in the sky would tell the other, we still exist and are still safe.

Now the aurora was gone.

Just then, the worker troubleshooting the equipment nearby said, "Reporting. The artificial magnetic field has disappeared, so the ionosphere is in chaos and short-wave communication is not feasible."

The lieutenant general frowned deeply. After three seconds of silence, he said, "At all costs, open the long-wave communication."

"Yes sir!"

In the era in which humans lost satellites and telecommunication, long-distance communication had become incomparably difficult, and only by using radio—short-wave radio communication through the atmosphere's ionosphere—could signals be transmitted. But the artificial magnetic field was weaker than the original geomagnetic field, after all. Communication was already very unstable, and now that the magnetic field completely disappeared and the ionosphere had become completely disordered, communication was even more difficult.

Long-wave communication was different. It was ground-based, using the earth and sea water as its medium. It was stable and reliable, but the activation cost was high, and only the most ancient code could be used to transmit messages.

It was also unidirectional, which meant that unless the other party also happened to activate long-wave communication at the same time, there would be no way to communicate.

The message was transmitted layer by layer, and at last, the communication center received a feedback message that the long-wave communication device had been activated.

The operator picked up the device. Codes with varying spacing and lengths made monotonous "beeps" as they were entered into the system in order, then uploaded to the communication channel.

"Northern Base to Underground City Base, please respond."

A long silence.

"The Underground City Base has the most perfect construction amongst the four human bases, so it's very difficult to imagine that it would encounter a catastrophe," an officer said. "If only it were just an equipment failure."

Just as he finished speaking, a piercing electrical noise suddenly came from the receiver!

With rustling sounds and scratching sounds, it was as chaotic as though it was coming from the boundless universe, yet it also resembled the dying breaths of a huge monster.

Everyone in the room stopped breathing until twenty-odd seconds had passed.

"Beep."

"Beep beep."

"Beep, beep—"

The message sounded, and the operator's entire body trembled. He practically threw himself onto the workbench and swiftly took notes.

Five minutes later, the lieutenant general asked, "What did they say?"

The operator's face was pale and lips were trembling. He looked at the paper with the signal notes and said, "They said... The Underground City Base... suffered an invasion of united xenogenics and suffered heavy losses. They're currently... resisting, and currently repairing the magnetic pole."

"The ammunition reserves are at less than one-fifth... Their thermonuclear weapon reserves are exhausted, and they have a shortage of soldiers. Requesting..." He gritted his teeth. "Requesting support."

Silence.

Silence frequently meant facing a crucial choice.

To rescue, or not to rescue.

"Is it possible to still contact the Underground City?" A voice broke the silence.

"There are no more responses."

"The meeting in Conference Room 1 has ended. With

existing resources, if guaranteeing the entire city's survival, we can hold out for three to ten days."

"And if not guaranteeing the entire city's survival?"

"If only guaranteeing the Twin Towers' and Garden of Eden's resource supplies, we can hold out for fifteen to thirty days regardless of climate factors."

"Under extreme circumstances, if core personnel are transferred to the Garden of Eden's underground shelter, we can consider long-term survival."

"There's still a little hope."

Another beat of silence.

At last, someone said, "Do we save them or not?"

The lieutenant general looked around the room. After hearing the announcement to convene the meetings, An Zhe knew that the room was now filled with the highest-ranked officers from the Command Post, Staff Department, and Combat Center. Unlike the logistics and city defense personnel who were meeting in Conference Room 1, they all had to go to the frontlines.

It was just that even An Zhe knew how dangerous of a place the frontlines would be this time. What was it that could render the most perfectly equipped human base and even the artificial magnetic pole unable to hold fast?

Perhaps by the time reinforcements arrived, it would have already become a dead city. Perhaps before they even reached their destination, the troops would crash their planes in the storm and fall to the earth or into the Pacific Ocean. Or perhaps after the Northern Base used its own armament reserves to help the Underground City Base, the next time xenogenics united to attack this place, it would've lost its ability to resist.

In the long silence, An Zhe heard Lu Feng say from next to him, "I'll go."

The lieutenant general looked at him for a long time.

"You're the best candidate," he said.

An Zhe looked at Lu Feng. He knew why the lieutenant general said Lu Feng was the best candidate.

In different regions on a continent, there were great differences between monsters. The Northern Base and Underground City Base were separated by the entire Pacific Ocean, so the monsters' habits and methods of fighting them may be entirely unknown.

Who could adapt the best to this kind of unknown?

Someone who often went into the Abyss. The monsters of the Abyss were both chaotic and frenzied, with practically all kinds of mutation types present.

Then another officer said, "I'm good at directing large-scale joint operations. I apply to go."

"AR137's captain," Lu Feng said. "Dispatcher, please inquire if he will voluntarily go."

"Mr. Hubbard agreed to go."

The meeting adjourned, and upon leaving, the lieutenant general called Lu Feng back.

"Who will take on the Trial Court's work?"

"My adjutant."

"Is he capable?"

"Yes."

After exiting, Seraing walked over. The Trial Court's work area was in this exact building. He said in a low voice, "Colonel."

Lu Feng gave a flat response.

In the dim lighting, the rims of Seraing's eyes were slightly red. Lu Feng left, for he still had much to prepare.

Seraing had An Zhe stay in the Trial Court's office to rest. Midway there, An Zhe made an excuse to go out and climbed up to the thirteenth floor. The entrance to D1344 was still lit up, and inside were the sounds of researchers talking. They said there was no time left—precisely because there was no time left, they had to seize every moment in completing all their research. An Zhe lowered his head. His body as a mushroom was too fragile and soft, so he couldn't rashly charge in after all. He returned to the main hall on the first floor.

In the main hall, people came and went, and Seraing came to his side. Saying nothing, An Zhe quietly watched everything happen. The throngs of people that were busy and moving back and forth, the continually playing announcements, the flashing lights and intermittent electricity supply. All of this happened very quickly. The fate of humankind was as changeable as the aurora in the sky.

At 11 p.m., the Equipment Center reported that their tasks were completed.

At midnight, the Logistics Division reported that their tasks were completed.

At 1 a.m., the PL1109 maintenance was completed, and the fighter plane formation set out.

Muffled rumbling came from afar. The ground command needed a wide field of vision, so the isolation walls rose, and scorching radiation and gusts of wind burst forth. Everyone backed up to the safe area in the depths of the main hall. A row of lights lit up in the distance, and An Zhe strove to look in that direction. Wing and nose lights delineated the fighter planes' massive contours. Three PL1109 fighter planes, along with an entire flight formation, smoothly traveled over.

PL1109—An Zhe knew it. The masterpiece of human science and technology, it had a hull that blocked out all radiation and an independent navigation system that needed no guidance from the magnetic field. Humans had long ago predicted and prepared for the coming Era of Calamity, it was just that nobody knew exactly what the effects of these predictions and preparations would be.

And he also finally knew why the base's roads were all made to be so smooth, sturdy, and wide. The military base that was tightly linked to the city center, the massive buffer strips, the tarmacs and runways that were everywhere to be seen... The humans of a hundred years ago gave everything they had to build them. All of this was not because of beauty or regularity, but because everything about this human base's Main City was for responding to possible war.

Another gate opened, and a few officers in black combat uniforms walked out.

Amidst the handful of people, An Zhe saw Lu Feng with only a glance—this person's figure was imposing and upright, his figure neat and tidy. Unlike the lofty grace and coldness of the Trial Court's uniform, although the shape was similar, the combat uniform seemed more casual, which magnified his bastardly characteristic.

But tonight, An Zhe had no plans to call him a bastard. Lu Feng was a very good human.

Lu Feng walked over toward him, his original uniform coat draped over the crook of his arm, and Seraing accepted it.

"Follow Seraing. Don't run around," Lu Feng said as he looked at An Zhe.

Then he said to Seraing, "Keep an eye on him."

Clearly it was a very simple handful of words, but An Zhe felt that he heard a threat from them, as if once he ran around, he would suffer punishment.

Frowning, he looked up at this man.

Lu Feng reached out and tousled An Zhe's hair.

His gaze wasn't as cold or malicious as usual; An Zhe even thought that it was a bit gentle.

He'd made up his mind to go to the Underground City Base on the other side of the world. An Zhe felt that he ought to say something, such as telling him to stay safe or to take care of himself... Those sorts of things.

He opened his mouth, then felt that the Colonel was probably accustomed to this kind of life. He seemed able to take care of everything, so there was no need to tell him.

In the end, An Zhe only said, "... I made mushroom soup tonight."

No matter how good the thermos was, having left it until now, it wouldn't be as tasty as when it was piping hot.

There was a slight smile in Lu Feng's eyes.

"Thank you," he said. "Make it for me again when I return."

That pair of eyes—those eyes with the same color as firefly glow in the deepest parts of the jungle—looked at An Zhe.

He seemed to lean down slightly, and for a moment, An Zhe felt that Lu Feng wanted to get close to him, but that feeling was fleeting.

"I may not be able to return," Lu Feng said, his voice slightly hoarse. "Take care of yourself."

An Zhe responded with an affirmative sound. He watched Lu Feng turn around and leave without looking back, walking into the makeshift boarding bridge.

How many times had he now watched Lu Feng's figure depart? He couldn't remember. He didn't know why this person was always able to constantly move forward. He could shoot his compatriots without the slightest hesitation and also sacrifice his own life at any given moment.

Outside, a sandstorm arrived with the great winds, and the night covered them, making the flying dust and grit seem like a boundless night fog—in precisely this boundless darkness and moonlight, the engines buzzed to life, and the pitch-black PL1109 fighter plane smoothly took off.

Its spread wings were like a massive bird. In An Zhe's sight, the further and higher it got, the smaller it became, turning into a black speck that was difficult to see before finally disappearing into the resplendent Milky Way that spanned across the skies.

There was a distant roar, which was a sonic boom, as the fighter planes accelerated again.

An Zhe couldn't find it at all anymore.

Everyone looked up at the boundless night sky. Within the hall, there was a respectful silence, and only after a long while did the people disperse.

An Zhe still stood there, and soft footsteps came from behind him. It was Seraing.

"Sometimes I'll think, why did the Colonel choose me as his successor? What kind of characteristics and guidelines does he think an Arbiter should have?" Seraing said. "Now I think, contrary to what people believe, it's not coldness, but mercy."

"Humankind's interests take precedence over all else. It's not kindness to a single person, it's kindness to the fate of all of humankind. This is the source of unwavering conviction." Seraing's voice was very soft and slightly raspy. "I sincerely hope that the people a hundred years from now won't have to face everything we are currently facing, if humans still exist at that time."

An Zhe said nothing. He lifted his head to look at the star-studded night sky, a boundless resplendent sea.

Seraing draped the military coat over him.

"When the aurora lights up again, the Colonel will return."

27

"THE RELATIONSHIP BETWEEN YOU TWO IS VERY COMPLICATED."

"ALTHOUGH WRONG, IT IS STILL CORRECT."

On the walls of the corridor connecting the work hall of the Trial Court and the training area, one side had "Humankind's interests take precedence over all else" while the other side had this sentence written.

Beneath the sentence was a row of silver picture frames. The first picture frame was blank, but further along, the second picture frame held a black-and-white photo depicting an officer around thirty years old with handsome and symmetrical features. He was dressed in the Arbiter's uniform, and the dates of his birth and death were engraved upon the wall beneath the picture frame. He died seven years prior, at the age of thirty-six.

At the next picture frame, there was also a black-and-white photo with dates of birth and death. An Zhe walked forward, and the next photo and birth and death dates were similar. The years in which they lived gradually went back in time. Thus, An Zhe knew that these were photos taken to commemorate successive Arbiters, and the blank picture frame on the very end was undoubtedly left for Lu Feng.

With that thought, An Zhe's pace slowed slightly, and an indescribable weight pressed down upon his heart. If it was possible, he hoped that Lu Feng's photo wouldn't be hung up so soon—just like how tonight, the moment Lu Feng boarded the plane, he hoped that this person could remain here in a safe place.

But Lu Feng had his own choices to make.

Following Seraing, he continued walking forward, and at the end of the photo gallery, a strange spectacle appeared.

On the light gray wall, there was a rectangular area that was whiter, the same size as a picture frame. There were nail holes at the four corners of the white area. It looked like this place also had a picture frame once, but it had been taken down. And below it, the place that originally was engraved with the name and birth and death dates had also been scraped off, leaving behind only a few mottled marks. An Zhe tried to make it out, but he could only see that it was a string of letters beginning with a capital P.

Seeing that he had stopped here, Seraing explained, "It's said that this was the first Arbiter and the person who proposed the 'Arbiter's Code' and established the Trial system."

An Zhe asked, "Was his photo taken down?"

"Mm-hm," Seraing said. "In the end, he questioned the rationality of the Arbiter system and betrayed the base."

An Zhe nodded. Human minds were difficult to figure out. He didn't inquire more deeply.

Seraing got him settled in a break room. The geomagnetic field had disappeared, and everything had become chaotic. The Logistics Division and Emergency Response Department were presumably in great tumult, and the base's other residents were panicking, only able to sleep and wait for the military's upcoming shelter arrangements.

There were numerous footsteps upstairs. Next door, Seraing was contacting someone, seeming to be arranging the Trial Court's follow-up work.

In the pitch-black room, the outside wasn't visible. An Zhe

could only hear his own heartbeat. Strangely, as if having some odd feeling, he lifted his head and looked into the depths of the darkness. That feeling was strange to describe—he seemed to have felt some massive wave. He, Seraing, everyone, the entire human base, along with everything in this world were all trivial parts of that indescribable wave, trembling and changing in its wake and generating minute ripples. In the younglings' textbook, there was a saying called "the current of fate," and he thought it was very fitting. The only part that wasn't fitting was that the wave seemed to exist around the entire world and wasn't an empty metaphor or imagining.

Right at that moment, his communicator rang. It was a call from the doctor.

The doctor asked him, "Lu Feng has taken off. Where are you?"

An Zhe truthfully told him.

"As long as you're safe," the doctor said. "I just finished the Lighthouse's emergency meeting, so now I'll be heading back to the laboratory to rest for the night. You get some good rest as well."

"Okay," An Zhe replied.

The doctor seemed to be climbing a set of stairs. Only after a while had passed did he say, "I was thinking about Si Nan's behavior this morning. He warned Lily to go back to the Garden of Eden. Could it be that he predicted the disappearance of the magnetic field? Different species have different sensory organs, and some organisms are sensitive to magnetic fields."

An Zhe said, "Perhaps."

After some thought, he said, "But it's so far."

Of course he knew every single species was different. In the Abyss, some monsters had extremely keen hearing, and some could detect the scent of prey from thousands of kilometers away. But if they were to say Si Nan sensed the xenogenic invasion of the Underground City Base all the way on the other side of the globe from the Northern Base, it seemed a bit unreasonable, for xenogenics did not have long-wave communication technology.

The doctor did not respond to him. From the other side there only came uneven breaths, and An Zhe thought that perhaps he was walking.

But three minutes later, the doctor still did not respond. There was only the sound of his breaths speeding up. With this sound playing in the darkness, An Zhe felt an inexplicable uneasiness.

"Doctor?" An Zhe called out.

Still no response.

He frowned. Right at that moment, he heard the doctor quickly say from the other end, "Have Seraing pick up."

An Zhe swiftly walked out of the break room. Seraing accepted the communicator, and after calling out "Doctor," he frowned deeply and swiftly said, "I'll be right over."

Then he immediately picked up the gun on the table, called a few men, and strode out!

An Zhe took a look at the direction he went in and chose to follow. But their speed was too quick, and his own speed climbing the stairs was too slow, so he was a step behind.

By the time he arrived in the corridor where the doctor's laboratory was, he heard a gunshot from the depths, immediately followed by the sound of a body falling to the ground.

The doctor was standing in the middle of the corridor, and An Zhe walked over to him.

"I... I saw that his walking posture wasn't quite right from far off." The doctor gasped for breath, his pupils dilated and face pallid, the very picture of someone who was badly shaken. An Zhe looked forward and saw Seraing put away his gun. The person who fell to the ground was the doctor's assistant. Just this afternoon, he had been working with the doctor, helping him repeatedly check the footage of Si Nan.

Seraing said to the doctor, "Infection confirmed. Was it exposure to an experiment?"

Infection?

An Zhe promptly thought of this place's sole source of infection, Si Nan.

"Impossible," the doctor said. "He didn't have the authority to open the glass cover, so he couldn't come into contact with the xenogenic."

Seraing said, "I'll go inside and take a look."

"Don't." The doctor abruptly raised his voice. "Don't go over there."

Seraing stopped walking and looked at the doctor.

"Do you remember how I once said if there was a day where we wouldn't need to come into contact with xenogenics at all to be infected?" The doctor's voice shook. "It's too abnormal... We must prepare for the worst."

Seraing frowned. "How will you prove your view?"

"There's no way to prove it." The doctor shook his head. "However, you all also know that after injecting a monster's interstitial fluid into the test animal's tail, genetic changes can be observed in the animal's head at the same time. Those interstitial fluids haven't participated in body fluid circulation at all, yet the genes throughout the animal's body have already changed. Since even this kind of thing can happen, then why can't infection occur even without coming into contact with a monster?"

With those words, a shudder ran through his body.

"Seraing," he said, his voice completely hoarse, "do-downstairs are all live xenogenic samples, and there are at least a hundred staff members there."

Seraing's expression was heavy. "I'll go down right away."

"Protect yourself," the doctor said. "Within the effective

range, the further away you can stay from all the living things there, the better."

He didn't say xenogenics, nor did he say humans, but rather "living things."

Seraing nodded. With speedy movements, they dispersed downstairs.

In the silent corridor, only An Zhe and the doctor remained.

Seeming to have lost his strength, the doctor leaned against the ice-cold wall, and An Zhe supported him.

After a silence, the doctor suddenly spoke.

"You aren't afraid?"

He shook his head.

The doctor looked at him.

"On you, there seems to be a kind of... something that people of this era don't have," the doctor said.

Saying nothing, An Zhe quietly listened to him continue.

His gaze lingered for a long time on An Zhe, and then he took a soft breath, lips trembling slightly, as if he obtained some extraordinary inspiration. Then he said, "You're so innocent... that it's like you're a bystander."

He said, "Everyone lives in terror, but you're very calm, standing out from everyone else."

With those words, he seemed to smile. "I know why Lu Feng likes being with you."

An Zhe looked at the doctor. The doctor's youthful face showed a faint haggardness. He seemed to be a bit tired. An Zhe asked, "Is there something I can help you with?"

"Thank you." The doctor looked into his eyes, and there was a slight quiver at the end of his sentence. "Just... live safely, that's enough."

An Zhe thought for a while, then said, "I'll try my best."

He didn't say anything else. In the corridor, the doctor's words echoed as he talked to himself. "No physical contact, and no aerial transmission. Can such a thing truly happen?"

Nobody replied to him.

However, a clear gunshot came from downstairs.

Then there came a second sound.

A third sound.

The sounds didn't stop, reverberating for a long time in the building.

In the wake of one gunshot after another, the theoretical framework humans used to explain the world was declared to have utterly collapsed.

The doctor's hand clutched An Zhe's arm, and his fingers were trembling.

"… Why?"

———

The gunshots stopped, and a scattered few people walked upstairs, with Seraing bringing up the rear.

"These are the ones who haven't been infected?"

Seraing replied, "Yes."

An Zhe heard the doctor ask the survivors about their whereabouts today. There were no issues with eating, drinking, or breathing, for everything was uniformly supplied by the Lighthouse. Even the air was brought in by the ventilation system. If there was an issue with any one amongst these three things, the entire Lighthouse would fall. But they had one thing in common. During this period of time since the magnetic field disappeared, none of them had been in close contact with the experimental subjects. Some had been in the office sorting records the entire time, while some had gone to other floors to participate in meetings and just returned—such as Dr. Ji himself.

And the staff members who had been infected also had one thing in common. They were all people who had been in close contact with the xenogenics—though this kind of contact was not necessarily true contact, but rather spatial proximity with monsters or xenogenics. For example, one researcher's assistant had spent the entire afternoon in a small office immersed in writing code, adapting a certain data model, but he was still judged to have been genetically infected—the only suspicious thing was that two reptile monsters were being raised in the laboratory on the other side of the wall from him.

Seraing requested guidance from the military. Using the floor where the xenogenic research center was as the axis, closed-style checks had to be carried out on the three floors above and below, and all personnel were prohibited from entering.

"Water, food, and air may all be the sources of infection." In the Trial Court's break room, An Zhe and the doctor shared a room. The doctor said to himself while facing the white wall, "If only that was it, but it just isn't."

"Is it radiation?" he then said. "If every monster was a source of radiation, at the very beginning, the radiation was very weak, so only those who were heavily injured would get infected. Later, infection would happen with even minor wounds, and then the radiation strength gradually increased... So long as one stays near a monster, their genes will experience instantaneous change because of the radiation."

An Zhe thought that what he said made a lot of sense, but right away, he saw the doctor bury his face in his palm and take a deep breath, his bearing that of a man on the verge of a break-down. "But our instruments cannot detect it."

An Zhe thought that the doctor was about to go mad. Putting himself in the doctor's shoes, he understood the source of his madness.

Regarding the research—the research of monsters—what made researchers suffer wasn't how complicated it was, how many resources it needed, or how dangerous it was, but rather that even now, they didn't know exactly what they were facing.

Like a man walking in the dark, having lost even his last crutch, he knew that the cliff edge was not far away, but he didn't know exactly when he would lose his footing.

He saw the doctor slowly lift his head, his blue eyes slightly unfocused and the muscles in his face trembling. That was a kind of despairing dread and terror, as if he were facing some massive, frightening, and indescribable existence—in front of him was a blank white wall. The scariest thing in the world was the unknown.

An Zhe poured out a cup of water for him. The doctor drank it and forced a smile.

"Thank you," he said. "I don't know how many more days the base's water supply can last."

The doctor's words weren't wrong. From the night when the aurora disappeared, the entire base entered a state of emergency shelter. Outside was the solar wind and radiation, so nobody could leave the buildings, but the heat outside traveled in through the thick walls. The temperature indoors was at least 30 degrees Celsius, and there were no methods of temperature control. It was frighteningly dry, and electricity was only used to keep the basic equipment running. Every day at 8 a.m. and 8 p.m., the base would regularly distribute a piece of hardtack or a packet of nutrition tablets along with a bottle of drinking water.

Three days later, bottles of water were distributed only in the mornings.

And this was the Twin Towers, the place where the military command center and scientific researchers were. Sometimes, An Zhe would think, if the Twin Towers' resource supply had already been reduced to this point, what would it be like in the ordinary residential buildings outside?

"The 1109 fighter planes need twelve hours to fly from the Northern Base to the Underground City base, and the return trip likewise needs twelve hours. A hundred and twenty hours have passed, and we still haven't received any news whatsoever," the doctor said to him while calculating some complicated formulas with paper and pen. "Emotionally I believe in Lu Feng, but now we must prepare for the worst."

Five days later, the nutrition tablets were gone as well.

The elevators stopped. An Zhe quietly slipped out of the Trial Court, and when he climbed up the stairs, he encountered at least three couples kissing in various corners—perhaps they weren't lovers either, but at least they were difficult to tear apart now.

"Even though I walk through the valley of the shadow of death, I fear no evil.

For You are with me. Your rod and Your staff, they comfort me.

Certainly goodness and faithfulness will follow me all the days of my life.

And my dwelling will be in the house of the Lord forever."

On the thirteenth floor, he passed a meeting room inside which over a dozen white military officers and researchers had gathered and were reciting the Bible. Inside, at least half of them had tissues stuffed up their nostrils, for the high temperature and dryness made humans get nosebleeds very easily.

Actually, high temperatures and dryness were even more unsuitable for a mushroom's survival. These days, An Zhe hadn't ever slept well. Sometimes he would feel himself bobbing up and down in the current of fate, and sometimes he would feel like he was being laid out in the sun, about to be baked dry. It was difficult to wake up, and he would also feel very hungry.

But he could wait, for it didn't matter. Just this morning, the doctor had said to him, "Although the situation is becoming more and more dire, you seem to be becoming more and more calm."

An Zhe was indeed not terrified. He was a calm mushroom.

These past five days, he quietly stayed in the Twin Towers, going in and out with the doctor and Seraing, so many people got accustomed to the sight of him.

He observed the dim red light that indicated the operational status of the surveillance cameras and pricked up his ears to listen to each announcement.

Just yesterday, that light dimmed.

And just this morning, the doctor was informed that because of insufficient energy, all research activities were terminated.

An Zhe softly took a deep breath as he stood in front of the door to the laboratory D1344. It was silent on the other side of the door, with even the beeping sounds of the machines' operations having stopped. He had finally waited until those researchers had left.

The laboratory door was tightly shut, and the sensor at the entrance flashed with a weak light.

He took out Lu Feng's ID card.

———

The Underground City.

Upon the open ground, the upper half of the artificial magnetic pole stood. On a patch of sandy yellow soil, it resembled a grand tombstone.

This place's geographical location was excellent, for there were tall mountains on all sides that blocked windstorms and cold waves. In the middle was a flat plain, and the geological structure was stable and solid, sufficient to support the construction of unimaginable underground fortifications. The underground city's surface area and volume was comparable to the metropolises from the time when humankind was at its zenith.

In the beginning, when humankind's four bases were taking shape, some people predicted that if there came a day where humans could not hold out, then the Underground City Base would definitely be the last one to fall.

But right now, this open plain was covered with blood. Blood from monsters, from xenogenics, and from humans. On top of the bloodstains were dismembered limbs, cut-off hands, and the remains of heavy weaponry.

A black fighter plane flew over the ground, dropping several powerful bombs. Dull explosions sounded, and the monsters howled deafeningly, but they were soon drowned out in the billowing smoke.

The fighter plane increased its elevation and steadily circled in the air. Lu Feng, holding a walkie-talkie in his hand, said, "The monsters on the ground have been eliminated."

Next to him was Hubbard. This legendary mercenary team captain from the outer city looked at the nearby entry passageway to the Underground City and said, "The inside will be difficult to deal with."

Lu Feng looked over there as well. He didn't say anything, tacitly agreeing with Hubbard's viewpoint. Over these past few days, he and the captain had coordinated command of the aerial operations and established sufficient tacit understanding— moreover, they were originally the kind of people who went the deepest into the frontlines of the Abyss, so nobody understood better than they the habits and lethality of those things.

The Underground City was easy to defend and difficult to attack. It was a sufficiently safe and formidable bastion, and it naturally had the advantage of guarding against radiation. But its structure also destined it to one thing: once xenogenics breached it, the interior would inevitably be a field of chaos.

And now it had been breached.

"What they're most lacking in is firepower. Their birthrate can't keep up and so they are short of soldiers. Thus, they can only increase their expenditure of armaments. They overdrew in advance, so now they have no way of effectively defending."

Hubbard's hawk-like eyes narrowed slightly. "We've brought enough and arrived on time, so we have a decent chance to win."

Right at that moment, a voice came from the walkie-talkie.

"The Underground City thanks you for your generous support." The operator's voice was trembling. "However, out of the principle of humanitarianism, we must inform our compatriots from the Northern Base: at present, contactless infection has already been observed within the base, and unpredictable infection may occur at any time and place..."

"The Northern Base has received it," Lu Feng said, interrupting the operator. "Please prepare for ground support."

Hubbard frowned deeply.

Lu Feng said, "Have the flight formation hover for now. I'll lead some men down."

"I'll go," Hubbard said. "By the sound of what they're saying, the inside is more dangerous than we imagined, and there may be no coming back after going down."

"You don't have this obligation."

"But I don't really have any worries."

Lu Feng's tone was flat. "I don't either."

But Hubbard smiled and asked in return, "You don't?"

Lu Feng met his gaze. No emotion whatsoever could be seen from his cold green eyes, but this time, he said nothing.

"Sometimes you'll look out the porthole, and when you do, you look for a very long time," Hubbard said.

"I left behind a person at the base." Lu Feng leaned against the porthole, his arms crossed. "A bullet I killed someone with hangs around his neck."

"What person of his did you kill?"

Lu Feng didn't reply.

"Putting it like that, he bears enmity against you," Hubbard said, but he seemed to recall something. "I met a boy who had one of your bullet shells and asked me if I knew its origin."

The corners of Lu Feng's lips curved up.

Hubbard said, "Then the relationship between you two is very complicated."

"Perhaps." Lu Feng walked toward the exit. "My relationship with everyone is very complicated."

His voice was cold as he said to the pilot, "Prepare to taxi."

Hubbard didn't stop him this time. He looked at Lu Feng's back, deep in thought.

Under the massive and blood-red sunset on the western skies, the flight formation landed and the cabin doors opened. Lu Feng walked out of the PL1109 and toward the sprawling and blood-soaked city under the ground.

———

The Northern Base.

Right when An Zhe was about to put the ID card up to the sensor, he heard footsteps behind him, and he turned around. It was soldiers on routine patrol, led by a familiar-looking Judge.

That Judge looked at him and said, "How come you're here?"

He dropped his gaze slightly. "I'm getting something for the doctor."

"The doctor is still doing research?" the Judge said.

An Zhe made a soft affirmative noise and said nothing else. That Judge didn't ask further. Instead, he said, "Go back soon, the military has work to do today."

He said, "Thank you."

They walked past, and An Zhe took a deep breath and pressed the ID card to the sensor. Fortunately, the access control system had not yet been shut off. With a click, the door unlocked.

An Zhe entered. The door hinge squeaked because of friction, and after he walked in, he promptly closed the door. In the dim lighting, the dark shadows of the massive instruments flickered, and in the center of the room, the cylindrical tank stood quietly. A faint light beneath the tank illuminated it, and a cluster of small bubbles had just emerged from below and was floating to the top.

An Zhe held his breath. Before opening the door, he had prepared for the worst: getting caught, the spore having already been transferred, other people being present in the laboratory... Now, his heart just about stopped beating entirely.

Until his gaze passed through the glass tank and through the pale green culture solution, and he saw the small white mass suspended all alone in the middle.

His breath trembled, the corners of his lips curled up, and his heart thumped hard. He wanted to throw himself over there right away, but because of his excessive mood swing, he was practically unable to move.

Within the liquid beneath the dim lighting, that snow-white little thing seemed as if it were wandering about on the deep-sea floor. An Zhe looked at it without blinking.

At that very moment, he saw the spore, which had been quietly floating, pause. Then the hyphae abruptly stretched out, or perhaps using "exploded" to describe it would be more fitting.

Then—it floated toward him at a speed that definitely could not be considered slow before suddenly pausing at the glass wall, as if it had struck it.

An Zhe took large strides over to the glass tank, pressing his hands and then his whole body against it.

His spore was also firmly pressed against the glass wall, and the hyphae touched him uneasily through the layer of glass, the movement clearly showing that it wanted to get closer to him.

An Zhe couldn't resist smiling. When Lu Feng was near, it seemed just like this spore didn't see An Zhe, but now it recognized him. Reluctant to even blink, he watched the spore extend its slender and fragile hyphae toward him, yet due to the glass obstructing it, it could only try even harder to press itself in his direction, practically turning into a small white pancake on the inner side of the tank. Every single hypha was emphasizing how much it wanted to get close to An Zhe.

An Zhe leaned against it. A long-lost comfort surrounded him, but it was also separated by a layer of unbreakable film.

He had to rescue it from the tank. An Zhe tore himself away from the tank with difficulty and came to the side, where there was a console. Based on the common rules of human machines, he tried pressing the biggest round button. The console screen lit up as expected, and the indicator light of the card slot on one side lit up. He swiped Lu Feng's card again, and the indicator light turned green. Throughout the entire base, this man's authority was virtually unchecked.

But right away, facing the buttons that were identically shaped and only had some complex symbols on them, An Zhe fell into a daze.

How could he open the tank?

His fingers hovered over the console. At last, he steeled himself and pressed the button in the very center.

Three seconds later, the water in the tank began to surge, and the spore was helplessly swept here and there by the current before finally spinning in the middle of the tank. Looking at that helplessly spinning little mass, An Zhe felt his own head also tumbling around and around. He clutched at his heart and pressed the first button.

A red laser lit up at the very top of the tank. Even An Zhe, who was standing nearby, felt the heat. The spore's hyphae exploded, and then it feebly sank down, seeming as if it'd be dried out in the next second, and then it exploded again after a while.

He suspected that it was silently screaming. He frowned in distress—was this sort of torment what the spore underwent in the human laboratory every day? But he had no time to think about anything else, and he pressed another button.

The red glow changed into pulses of light, and the spore helplessly exploded again and again.

An Zhe swiftly pressed a button far away. This time, the red light disappeared, and he sighed in relief. But in the following moment, a buzzing noise sounded, and blue ion sparks flared to life in the tank. Then the surface of the water began to tremble slightly—and the spore also trembled in the water as if it had gone mad.

He was taken aback.

He had electrified the water.

Flustered, he pressed one button after another, and finally with a loud noise, the pale green culture solution slowly drained out of the container. An Zhe pressed a button next to it, and with a click, the lid on top of the tank opened.

The tank was too tall, so he moved a chair over and stood on it, then finally reached the top of the tank.

But more than half of the culture solution had drained out by then, and the spore had no way of floating to that height.

Then he saw the spore press against the glass wall and slowly crawl upward along it. It slipped down as it climbed, and after sliding down a bit, it continued climbing up.

The little thing was not yet fully mature, yet it had inherited his ability to move independently. An Zhe reached out, and his arm and fingers turned into fluttering snow-white hyphae that descended along the container's inner wall and came into contact with the spore.

At that exact moment, it was like an electric current ran through his body and he had been reborn. He had taken back a part of himself, so there must be a strange wave enveloping him.

Holding that mass, he carefully fished it out, and all of the spore's hyphae that were scattered outside were obediently tucked back in, and the spore rolled over amidst his hyphae.

An Zhe's eyes curved as he smiled at it. His hyphae connected to its hyphae, and he carefully fitted it into his own body. The spore's body also relaxed completely and melded with his body. A euphoric emotion was transmitted to An Zhe's mind, for it had finally returned to the place where it ought to be. The humans' culture liquid was useless; only with the nourishment of the adult would it continue to grow until maturity.

This time, there were no bastards to dig it out again, although he didn't know why the spore would get close to that guy of its own volition.

In truth, the spore not getting close to him that day was a good thing, for once it expressed an inclination to get close to him, it would be promptly observed by the researchers, and then his identity would inevitably come under suspicion. Thus, An Zhe was one-sidedly convinced that his spore had uncommon intelligence.

With the return of the spore, the hollow in his body was finally filled, and all uneasy things instantly settled like dust. That was a feeling that could not possibly be described, like being reborn. An Zhe walked over to the window and pressed the button, raising the metal plate.

Eye-watering light shone in, and he squinted.

Outside, at the end of the wind-blown sands, amidst the first golden rays of the dawn, a resplendent red sun burst forth.

An Zhe slowly turned his head to look back at the silvery-white laboratory. Machines were arranged side by side, individual electrical cables were distinct from each other, and test-tube stands on top of the goods cabinet were arranged in a particularly neat manner. From this laboratory, he could imagine what the entire base looked like.

This was the humans' base. Its past, present, and future all had nothing to do with him.

His hand curled around the windowsill, his knuckles turning white, and he pushed open the transparent three-layered glass window with a burst of strength.

A gap the size of a finger's width opened, and scorching hot winds carrying grit blew in, followed by a prickling pain in his fingers. Within the wind and atmosphere outside was ubiquitous intense radiation from the cosmos. That colossal wave contained countless tiny ripples. He seemed to hear the Abyss calling him back.

He could leave now, depart from this place, go outside, and return to the Abyss. The outside was likewise cruel. He didn't know if he would be able to survive, but he had gotten his spore back, so he wasn't afraid of anything anymore.

… He wasn't afraid of anything anymore.

An Zhe gently pressed his left hand to his abdomen, rested his forehead against the windowsill, and closed his eyes. A slight shudder ran through his entire body.

He took back his right hand that was curled around the windowsill and exerted his strength in the opposite direction. With a gentle "thunk," the window closed again, and then the radiation-proof metal layer closed immediately after. He took a few breaths, his forehead pressed against the metal sheet, and his fingers slowly curled up at his side, as if he had made a difficult choice.

As the radiation was blocked out, the prickling pain on his body also gradually receded, just like that night when Lu Feng held him and used his own body as a shield before rolling away from that area with the radiation. In truth, if it had been anyone else, Lu Feng would have done the same, but it was precisely because that was the case that he deeply remembered the image, as vivid as each memory of Lu Feng's departing figure.

He walked out through the laboratory door, and right as he did, two soldiers walked past in the corridor. The pair of patrolling soldiers from earlier had walked away, and now it was other people.

An Zhe met their gazes and gave a close-lipped smile in greeting, then turned and walked toward the staircase.

On the dim staircase, he could only hear his own heartbeat,

one thump after another, faster than usual. When humans felt fear, their hearts would beat faster, but what exactly he was fearful of, he didn't know either.

He couldn't keep it hidden for long, he knew. Once order was restored and research began anew, it would definitely be possible to figure out the sequence of events of the humans' important laboratory losing something. He had to leave—the earlier, the better.

But he couldn't keep himself from taking a sharp, cool object out of his shirt pocket. It was the badge that Lu Feng had pinned to his coat, which An Zhe had taken off.

He held it in his hand, thinking that once the aurora lit up and he heard the news of the PL1109 returning, he'd leave then —if such a day came.

There wasn't anything good in this city. Only potato soup was quite nice.

If it weren't—if it weren't for his spore always wanting to get close to Lu Feng, he would have left long ago.